Shyly, Chantel handed Gabe the bottle of wine she'd brought.

"You'll have to share it with me," he said.

"But . . ." She felt herself blushing. "I have an errand to run, and I . . ."

He reached her side in two long strides and took her hand in his. He bent to kiss her lips. "You're not going anywhere, Chantel . . . not now."

She felt the searing heat of his bare chest pressing against her sheer voile bodice. A wild desire blazed in his eyes, and her head was whirling with giddiness. Gabe's hand brushed the tousled hair from her face; then he pulled her closer still and captured her lips in another thrilling kiss. When he released her, he whispered in his deep, husky voice, "You're my girl, Chantel. I won't let anyone else have you. Tell me—tell me you're my girl. My Louisiana Lady."

She gave a soft laugh. "I'm your girl, Gabe O'Roarke," she whispered back, but there were no more words after that for he held her in love's ultimate embrace all afternoon long . . . and each kiss burned hotter than the last.

They never got around to opening the wine . . .

WANDA OWEN

LOUISIANA LOVESONG

ZEBRA BOOKS
KENSINGTON PUBLISHING CORP.

ZEBRA BOOKS are published by

Kensington Publishing Corp.
475 Park Avenue South
New York, NY 10016

First Printing: September, 1993

Printed in the United States of America

This book is dedicated to my lovely grand-daughter, Nicole, and my first great-grand-duughter, Savannah. Welcome to our family, Savannah!

Part One
La Maison

One

Nothing was more enthralling and captivating than a bayou moon, its silvery rays reflecting on the water. It was a thing of splendor! At least that's what Gabe O'Roarke thought as he guided his fishing boat, *Louisiana Lady* toward his father's wharf after a long day of working the lakes and bays.

He had a right to feel this way since he was the third generation of his Irish family, who'd made their living catching fish on Lake Pontchartrain and Lake Borgne.

His grandfather's fishing boat, *Bayou Queen,* had supported the family, and when the old man could no longer make the runs, he'd turned it over to his son, Scott, who had prospered and bought himself another fishing boat. When Gabe turned eighteen, his father placed the operation of the *Louisiana Lady* in his hands.

All the girls in the bayou vied for Gabe's attention, but Gabe wasn't ready to get serious.

He was tall and trim with a firm, muscled body bronzed by the sun. He had the jet black hair of Angelique, his French Creole mother, and the devilish flashing blue eyes of his Irish father. And like his father, his charming wit and glib tongue allowed him to have his way just about anything.

By the time he was sixteen, it was obvious to his mother that girls were going to be easy prey if Gabe sought to use them sorely and this she didn't wish him to do. So she always made a point of telling him, "You just remember, Gabe O'Roarke, that you have a sister and Delphine could be used shamefully. So don't you do that to any young lady."

But Gabe didn't exactly call it shameful if some young lady eagerly invited him to lie with her on the banks of the bayou or accompanied him aboard the *Louisiana Lady* to go to his cabin.

By eighteen, he had known a few ladies up and down the bayou as well as in the city of New Orleans.

His father, Scott, had a little more understanding of his son's escapades. He, too, was a handsome rascal, so it was to be expected that ladies were willing to submit to his persuasive tongue.

Gabe had been a pampered child from the day he was born, blessed with not only a doting mother but an adoring aunt as well. His Tante

10

Gabriella always claimed there was a special connection between them, for Angelique had named him Gabriel as a tribute to her.

Angelique loved her half-sister, and it had never mattered to her that Gabriella was a quadroon. Her wealthy French Creole father had sired both of them, but life had brought the two of them together and formed a bond of devotion that would last their lifetime.

When the secret Maurice Dupree had concealed for years finally came out, he left New Orleans and Angelique never saw him again.

Her husband admired her deep feeling for her half-sister but then her great capacity to give love was what made her so dear to him. It was hardly what Maurice Dupree had planned for his only daughter—that she be the wife of a lowly Irish fisherman struggling to survive in the bayou—but she had defied her father to marry him.

They had lived and loved many years now in their creek's edge cottage. Gabe was their first-born, followed by an equally precious daughter, Delphine.

Nothing could have made Scott happier than having his son follow in his footsteps. And Gabe, an excellent fisherman, had proved a worthy captain over the last five years. Happily, the fish were flourishing in the Louisiana lakes and the O'Roarkes had enjoyed good fortune making a good living.

It was, Scott thought, a matter of history repeating itself, a passing of the torch from generation to generation to generation. He also recalled that he was about Gabe's age when, looking up from the deck of his boat one day, he'd been mesmerized by the most beautiful creature he'd ever seen. In that perfect instant, he'd lost his heart to Angelique Dupree. As far as he knew, though, Gabe's heart was still very much intact. He was like a butterfly, flitting from one pretty girl to another.

A happy-go-lucky rooster, Gabe had no plans for marriage right now. He was in constant demand. There was never a gathering or celebration that Gabe wasn't invited to attend, for he was the best dancer around these parts and the life of any party.

When he wasn't occupied whirling the ladies around the plank dance floors, he provided entertainment with his guitar. Scott could never figure where he'd inherited that talent, for he played no instrument, nor did Angelique. Scott couldn't carry a tune when he tried to sing.

Something else his father didn't know was that Gabe *had* met a young lady and she had taken his breath away and made his heart pound crazily. But he had a good reason not to mention her to his parents. He'd met the fair-haired goddess at *La Maison* when he'd made his weekly delivery of fish to Madame Lemogne, one of his best customers.

Everyone in New Orleans knew of *La Maison,* a high-class house of prostitution owned by Lily Lemogne. Gave liked the attractive, middle-aged lady. He never had to wait for his money from her. She paid him promptly with each delivery—which was more than he could say for some people.

He knew that many of New Orleans' wealthiest gentlemen went to *La Maison* regularly, and he'd heard that Madame Lemogne's girls were the most beautiful in the city.

What few people knew, Gabe included, was that Lily had a sixteen-year-old daughter—Chantel—who had been raised by a maiden aunt back East since she was eleven and attended an elegant—and expensive—boarding school.

When the young Chantel had started asking questions, Lily had told her that her establishment in New Orleans was a fine restaurant. She had also disclosed that Chantel's father had died when she was just a baby. The truth, however, was that Lily had never been married, but the madame was such a convincing liar that her daughter never doubted the truth of her fictions.

Until two or three years ago. Suddenly, inquisitiveness sparked and flamed in Chantel. As desperately as she tried to shrug it aside, she couldn't, for a young girl of thirteen and fourteen is always curious about the world around

13

her. And Chantel Lemogne was no exception. She was full of questions. Why did she have to live with Aunt Laurie during the school holidays? Why could she not travel to New Orleans for the summer months? Lily had often described the beautiful living quarters above her establishment, and Chantel found herself yearning to see them.

Although she'd been young when she'd left New Orleans, she remembered the fabulous city with its colorful history and streets that teemed with people of so many races.

Surprisingly, she remembered the ornate buildings influenced in structure by the Spanish and French. She recalled that as a child she had sat for hours on a balcony lavishly adorned with wrought iron, tended by a mulatto while Lily worked. Together they had watched the parade of people in the streets below.

By the time she was fifteen, Chantel had decided that she would return to the place where she was born and had lived for the first eleven years of her life.

Since Lily saw her daughter only for brief periods, she didn't realize how very much her daughter had grown like her in temperament. Her headstrong nature taxed her Aunt Laurie's patience, and her boldness and daring invariably got her into trouble at boarding school.

She had been caught smoking a cheroot that a friend had brought back to school, purloined from the friend's brother's stash.

On another occasion, Chantel had slipped a bottle of her aunt's prized sherry into her valise when she returned to school sharing the wine with her roommate, she'd urged the girl into a joyous prance up and down the hall that earned them both a harsh reprimand from the head mistress.

But apart from her spirit, nothing about Chantel resembled her sultry, dark-haired mother. Lily was tall and voluptuous. Chantel stood only a few inches over five feet, her gardenia complexion flawless and fair. Her green eyes shone like brilliant emeralds, exquisitely framed by thick dark lashes, but her hair was the light golden color of corn. Thick and naturally wavy, Chantel's curls flowed around her shoulders and down her back.

She had already learned that her beauty could cause young men to stare, and she could not deny that this pleased her. In Boston, one young dandy had been so entranced that he walked into a lamp post, spurring Chantel into a gale of giggles and laughter.

There was no question about it that Lily Lemogne was going to meet a different daughter this spring than the one she'd encountered last autumn.

Lily Lemogne had a lot on her mind when she left Laurie's house that May to go back to New Orleans, for that blasé, worldly-wise air of hers had been pierced, bombarded by questions from her daughter. Sooner or later, Lily knew that she would no longer be able to conceal the profession that made the money that supported both of them in a fine style.

She had always been a shrewd, clever lady, but she now faced a delicate situation and she didn't know how to deal with it. Equally alarming was that Chantel was an undeniably sensuous sixteen-year-old, a temptress.

Lily saw the tantalizing ripeness of her young body: The wasplike waist offset by the full, round curves of her hips; her young breasts newly blossomed; and the tempting cleavage beneath the scooped neckline of her blouse.

What she beheld was enough to ignite a fire in any man. Lily was well aware of the furor the sight of her could stir if she were around *La Maison*.

For days after she returned to New Orleans, Lily searched in vain for an answer. What was she to do about Chantel?

Although Lily could find no neat solutions, Chantel had made her mind up: She would not go back to boarding school; she would go instead to New Orleans. She had more than enough money and she would leave a note for her aunt so she would not worry.

It was a sultry August day when Chantel arrived in New Orleans. Her journey from the East had been an exciting adventure and she'd loved every minute of it. When the carriage came to a halt at the front entrance of *La Maison,* she saw that her mother, had not exaggerated: It was a very nice restaurant.

A black man, Jonah, ushered her inside when Chantel announced, "I'm Madame Lemogne's daughter."

"You is, ma'am?" Jonah drawled politely. He hadn't known Madame Lemogne had a grown-up daughter, and this little miss was sure a pretty thing.

On the second-floor landing, a tiny octoroon stopped to listen, spellbound by the beauty of the girl below. But she saw nothing to confirm the child was mam'selle's daughter. Mimi, Madame Lemogne's maid for the last four years, had come to work at *La Maison* after Chantel had been sent back East. Nevertheless, Mimi had heard enough to rush to madame's living quarters to warn her that her daughter had arrived.

She dashed through the small parlor to the bedroom where her mistress was still sleeping. With a courage born of panic, she shook Lily awake. "Mam'selle—mam'selle, wake up! Your daughter she is downstairs!"

Lily's dark eyes stared at her in disbelief. "My daughter couldn't be here, Mimi. She's miles away." She propped herself up against the satin pillows.

"Well, there's a beautiful young girl downstairs and she told old Jonah her name was Chantel," Mimi declared. She reached for Lily's crème-colored silk wrapper.

"Oh, my God!" Lily exclaimed turning as pale as the dressing gown. "Did she come here alone?" At Mimi's nod, she motioned for her brush and the jeweled hair comb on her dressing table. How could Laurie have allowed this to happen?

But there was no more time for thought. A soft rap sent Mimi to the door to admit Chantel Lemogne.

"Is my mother asleep still?" the pretty young girl asked with a surprising display of confidence in madame's boudoir.

"No, mademoiselle. She is awake," Mimi told her as Lily entered the parlor.

"Chantel, darling! You have given your mother quite a shock," Lily professed as she gave her a warm embrace.

"I realized I would, but I'm glad I did it, Mother. Tell me you're not too angry with me." Lily's green-eyed daughter pleaded with her, a teasing grin lighting her face.

"We'll speak of that later. Come—let's sit down and, while Mimi gets us some coffee, you can fill me in on how this little escapade came about."

"I just got a deep yearning to come to you and New Orleans. I'm tired of Boston."

"And you did this on your own, Laurie didn't

18

know?" Lily asked her, feeling more kindly toward her sister.

"She would have had a fit if I'd even hinted that I wanted to come here, so I just didn't tell her." Chantel tossed her shoulders, then shot her a wistful glance of appeal.

Lily felt giddy. Chantel's arrival was going to create an enormous number of complications, but at least this wing was strictly her domain. She could put Chantel in the bedroom directly across the hall from her own quarters and curtail the child's explorations.

Mimi served the coffee and disappeared from the parlor as was appropriate for madam's personal maid. Mother and daughter lingered over their untouched cups for another hour, talking.

"Chantel, all your beautiful clothes—how did you ever manage that?"

"I didn't. I traveled light." The girl laughed.

"You imp," Lily accused, but her stern tone gave way as an adoring smile spread across her face. Somehow she'd work everything out. She'd always managed to figure out a way to survive in this crazy world.

The first thing Lily did, once she had Chantel settled in the bedroom across the hall, was to send a message to Adrienne, Jonah, and Raul—the cook.

"Madame's daughter has arrived unexpectedly," panted little Mimi as she delivered the missives. "We are to tell her this is a restaurant if she runs into Adrienne or any of the other girls." And, finally, she trotted to Andre Deverone's office with a handwritten note of apology from Lily begging off from the late dinner they had planned.

Disaster momentarily thwarted, Lily collapsed in an overstuffed chair and lit up one of the Turkish cigarettes Andre had brought back from Europe. Lily, usually a cool, calm lady in full charge, chafed at the unsettled atmosphere that followed in the wake of Chantel's arrival.

But how could she be angry with her beautiful, green-eyed daughter when she'd said that she just wanted to see Lily and get back to New Orleans? It was good to have Chantel home.

Lily sighed, she was too realistic not to realize that she could only delay the moment of truth. Sooner or later Chantel would discover her mother's deception and see *La Maison* for the bordello it was.

It was inevitable.

Two

Lily shared an early dinner with her daughter instead of enjoying her usual late night dinner with Andre at eleven. Lily's second-floor wing jutted over the back of the establishment so that the noise and music below were blocked out.

But Lily knew that some of her intimate private dining rooms were already occupied and that by now the young black man named Brandy would be playing the piano in the elegant parlor.

"I want to see everything," Chantel pronounced as she tasted the cold peach soup that Raul had prepared. "Jonah brought me directly upstairs and I didn't get to see much, but, Mother, it's so grand."

"Chantel," Lily took a deep breath and plunged in. "We'd better have an understanding about a few things right now, sweetie. During the day you can roam anywhere you wish, even raid the kitchen. Raul always has plenty prepared. But come evening, I can't allow you that freedom. I am the hostess at *La Maison*, and I can't have my beautiful, young daughter tempting our wealthy gentlemen patrons. That could prove awkward. You understand, don't you honey?" Chantel's face fell, but she nodded her assurance.

"You are only sixteen, sweetie. You are not ready for New Orleans' nightlife." Lily smiled and reached over to pat her hand. "I've got to go downstairs soon," she added after a moment, pleased that Chantel had raised no objections. "You get yourself a nice night of rest after that long trip from Boston, and in the morning we'll go shopping. You need everything."

Chantel yawned and nodded a sleepy agreement. "I think I will turn in early this evening," she murmured, her hand covering her mouth.

It was almost nine-thirty when Lily made her descent down the stairs dressed, the silk of her purple gown rustling on the stairs and teardrop amethyst earrings glinting in the brilliant light of the chandelier. Her black hair was piled high on her head, clusters of purple velvet flowers scattered among the waves and curls.

Lily always made a striking appearance as she swept down the staircase each night. It was Lily Lemogne who gave *La Maison* a touch of class. Wealthy gentlemen of the city frequented Lily's place because they found her to be a gracious, discreet lady.

Immediately, she encountered Adrienne, looking gorgeous in a scarlet gown. Like Lily, she had a dark sultry look about her, and the two women had always understood each other well. Lily relied on Adrienne to ride herd over the others.

"I heard we've got ourselves a beautiful new girl on the premises," Adrienne commented with a knowing look. "Are you ready for this?"

Lily laughed, "She took me by surprise I can tell you. But I can't wait for you to see her, Adrienne. She's grown so." Lily stopped, measuring her words. "Chantel is going to be a handful," she continued. "She's not only beautiful, she's as headstrong as I am."

"Uh-oh." Adrienne smiled. "We're in trouble."

Although she chuckled at her friend's lighthearted teasing, Lily couldn't help but agree. "I've already laid down some rules," she granted soberly. "Now I have to see if she chooses to abide by them. She's only sixteen."

"Just remember," Adrienne warned with an innocent laugh, "that you were only seventeen when Chantel was born." Then Adrienne, her short scarlet train trailing on the steps, continued her climb to the second-floor landing.

Lily, making her accustomed trek through the downstairs parlor, gave Brandy a pat on the shoulder as she passed by the piano. Brandy re-

23

turned her greeting with a warm, affectionate smile. Madame Lemogne had been good to him; she paid him generous wages and she was a considerate employer, respected by those who worked at *La Maison*.

Some people looked down their noses at Madame Lemogne because she ran a house of pleasure, but to Brandy she was a lady. And the girls who worked for Lily rarely complained. She had not filled her coffers at their expense, for they came to her seeking work and she never forced them. They had rooms furnished lavishly and Raul's fine cuisine to enjoy. Life at *La Maison*—despite its seamier moments—had a veneer of elegance that suited almost everyone just fine.

Andre Deverone appeared at *La Maison* that evening, for he was disturbed by her message. For a year he'd been Lily's lover, but he never felt he completely dominated her. Lily would not allow that. She had the same drive and force as he, which was what he liked about her.

He'd lost his wife five years ago, and he'd never sought to remarry. As beautiful as his wife had been, she was not the sensuous, hot-blooded lady Lily was; Lily Lemogne offered him the kind of tempestuous relationship he was ready for now. Since he had never been a father, Andre had no desire to father a baby at this late date. He was a wealthy, respected lawyer who lived a methodical life that pleased him well. What had made Lily such a comfortable lady to share this last year with was that she did not want to marry any more than he did. What a pleasure she was compared to the suburban widows and spinsters with their constant schemes to elicit a marriage proposal. Andre, considered an excellent catch, had remained the elusive bachelor. He was quite content to continue seeing Lily in one quiet compartment of his life indefinitely. They got along so well together.

Lily spotted him the minute she entered the small parlor as he sat alone in a secluded corner, sipping his inevitable glass of wine. She wasn't surprised to see him despite her note postponing their rendezvous.

She went directly to his table, and he rose up to greet her with a kiss. "You look as lovely as ever, *chèrie!*" He complimented her but moved quickly beyond the amenities. "Tell me what is wrong," he demanded in a tone of concern.

"My daughter, Andre—she arrived unannounced this morning and I'm a nervous wreck. Dear God, I've never told her the truth about this place. She thinks it's a restaurant for the upper crust." Lily moaned as she sank down beside him.

"My dear Lily, I expected something far more serious." Andre cupped her cold fingers in the warmth of his palms.

"It's serious to me, Andre." Lily sighed.

25

"She's an imp. She'll find out."

"Where is this *imp* as you call her?" Andre asked.

"Upstairs. Hopefully asleep."

"Well, I'm not going to linger here long tonight, so I'll see if I can come up with some ideas for you. Between the two of us we can surely solve this dilemma." He bent his head closer to her and whispered in her ear. "You could always marry me, *chèrie*. I am after all, an excellent catch." He flashed an elusive smile that made them conspirators in a game that pitted them against the rest of society.

Andre had a magnificent thick mane of hair that was silvery grey with a few hints of black. The first time Lily had seen him, she had been quite taken by his good looks. He was a striking gentleman, but she had never considered marriage to him or any other man.

She smiled and patted his hand. "We had an understanding about that, love, a long time ago."

"I know. But that was a year ago, and time changes things. I find I have become more than fond of you, Lily."

"Need I tell you how I feel about you, Andre?"

He leaned over for their ritual farewell kiss. "Perhaps, I might expect an invitation to an early dinner to meet this charming daughter of yours?" he wheedled, encircling her waist with his arm.

"Oh, I'm sure I could arrange that." She gave him an affectionate hug, and they ambled toward the foyer.

Lily managed to keep Chantel occupied the next day, and they didn't return from their shopping spree until four in the afternoon. At that time of day, the maids cleaned in a furor and Raul puttered in the kitchen, supporting her claim that *La Maison* offered the finest in dining in New Orleans.

Chantel was content to linger in her bedroom, examining her new acquisitions. Giggly and excited, she had fumbled with a stack of packages that towered above her forehead. "You must be a terribly wealthy woman, Mother, to spend as much as you did today," she observed guilelessly.

Lily laughed. "I do pretty well, sweetie," she affirmed. "But after all that spending, I'm ready for a relaxing bath. Shall I have Mimi prepare one for you, too?"

"Oh, yes, please." Chantel danced with excitement, pulling out the new lacy undergarments from one of the many boxes that spilled across her bed.

Lily stifled an indulgent smile, reflecting on her daughter's beauty. Everyone had stared at her in Madame Denise's Dress Shop. Her old friend Denise had raved about Chantel and then with a skeptical look asked, "Is she going to stay here now?"

"To tell you the truth, Denise, I don't know what I'm to do about Chantel," Lily had confessed. "I hadn't expected to be faced with this for another year at least."

"Oh you poor dear! I wish I could help you out."

"I'll think of something," Lily had replied blithely although inwardly she felt much less confident that she would come up with the right course of action.

When Lily arrived in her boudoir, a magnificent bouquet of yellow roses greeted her from the table. She didn't have to ask Mimi who had sent them. Andre always let her know he was thinking about her.

Mimi smiled at her pleasure. "He is such a nice man—Monsieur Deverone."

Lily, an incorrigible tease loved to make little Mimi blush. "You got your pretty eyes on my man, Mimi?" she asked and laughed companionably as a faint flush tinged the girl's cheeks.

"Oh, Madame Lily! Monsieur Deverone has eyes only for you," Mimi replied with the utmost sincerity.

"Well, I guess I can keep you around then—I can talk you into running me a nice warm tub with some of that gardenia bath oil in it."

From her armoire she chose the mauve gown for tonight. She liked the black braid trim, and she would wear the jet beads and earrings Andre had given her last week. And the black slippers.

Mimi styled Lily's hair as she sat in her satin dressing gown at the vanity table, and then Madame Lemogne joined her daughter for an early supper.

While Chantel and her mother ate, Mimi slipped down the back steps to have her dinner in a corner of the kitchen watching Raul and the downstairs staff moving at a furious pace.

No one was a better cook than Raul, Mimi would swear to it. Life had been good for her at *La Maison*. She'd been only fifteen when she'd come here in hopes of finding work as one of Madame Lemogne's girls. But Lily had instead asked the insecure child-woman to become her personal maid when Mimi confessed that she was nervous about the prospects of working as one of the girls. She'd never been with a man, she admitted, but she was desperate. Deserted by her mother, she had nowhere to go.

Since that fateful interview four years ago, she'd enjoyed the comforts of a cozy room of her own and good meals. And, as madame was not a lady who demanded her constant services, Mimi had plenty of free time every day and in the evenings, when Lily worked the downstairs crowd.

Mimi believed that Lily had saved her life and her virtue, and she worshipped her. She regarded Chantel with a jealousy born of admiration. The girl was the luckiest daughter in the world to have Lily Lemogne for her mother.

Mimi had never lived a better life than she had now. Madame Lily was always giving her cologne, stockings, and even pumps. They wore the same size slipper, and Mimi—who had once own one pair of shoes—was blessed with a fashionable selection.

The grandest gift madame had ever given her was a berry-colored cape with a black fur collar. Madame had urged her to take and enjoy it after Monsieur Deverone had presented her with a new cloak of French wool. Often, Mimi the young maid would unwrap her makeshift storage bag just for a look and the chance to touch and admire the luxury of the fur collar.

Mimi would shout it from the housetops: Madame Lily Lemogne was a saint—after her own fashion.

Three

"I wish you to meet my dear friend, Andre." Lily told Chantel with calculated casualness. "He'll be joining us for dinner tomorrow."

"Is he your fellow?" Chantel asked in the impulsive, candid manner that Lily was already recognizing as one of her daughter's unique traits.

"I guess you could call him my fellow," she agreed with propriety appropriate to the old-fashioned term. Later, she mentioned the conversation to Andre who, equally delighted, grew even more curious about Lily's sixteen-year-old daughter.

"I shall look forward to tomorrow night very much," Andre told Lily with grave reserve. "Chantel sounds absolutely enchanting," As he prepared to leave early once again, he paused as if struck by a sudden thought. "You know, Lily," he mused, "my sister Jacqueline would enjoy having Chantel out for a visit. Her daughter Nannette is about Chantel's age. They could go horseback riding—I bet she would enjoy that—and it would give you a few days to think about things."

"Let's just get through tomorrow night," Lily sighed, comfortable in his embrace. She found his efforts to help her out endearing. He was an unselfish lover, never demanding.

Promptly at eight the next evening, Andre was admitted to Lily's quarters. His arms were filled with flowers. He'd brought Lily her customary yellow roses, but for Chantel he'd selected a white bouquet.

His dark eyes appraised the two breathtakingly lovely ladies in the parlor. They were as different as day and night. Chantel was a vision in a floor-length pastel green dress with dainty pearls on her ears and encircling her throat. Lily was most attractive in her cerise gown, ruby earrings dangling almost to her shoulders.

Chantel was hardly prepared to be greeted by such an impressive man as Andre. He made an entrance gallantly placing the spray of flowers in her arms and handing the yellow roses to Lily with a bow.

Lily made the introductions, and Chantel gave a flustered curtsey, burying her face in the lush white bouquet. "I've never had flowers from a gentleman before," she avowed. "I thank you, *monsieur*." And she pulled out one of the white roses before relinquishing the spray to Mimi to arrange in a vase.

"Well, beautiful ladies deserve beautiful flowers, I think," Andre told her, giving her a warm, friendly smile.

Chantel felt very grown-up this evening. She ran the rose against her cheek, enjoying its delicate softness and its scent, and she sipped the glass of wine that Lily had permitted her for the occasion. They all gathered around the candlelit table to enjoy Raul's delicious specialty, *coquilles St. Jacques*, and Andre told her about his niece Nannette and her great love of horses. "Do you ride, Chantel?" he asked.

"I haven't ridden that much," she admitted with her truthful candor. "A couple of times I went out with my friend at boarding school in Boston."

"Perhaps, one day you can go out to my sister's place at the edge of the city and visit Nannette," Andre suggested. "The two of you are about the same age."

"Oh, that would be fun. I would enjoy that," she replied earnestly.

Lily leaned back, listening to the two of them talk. She could tell that Chantel approved of Andre, and she thought it sweet of him to direct so much of his conversation to her. She found it hard to end their meal and go downstairs this evening; they were so like a family—the three of them—sitting together around the table in her upstairs parlor. She delayed her departure from her second-floor quarters long past her usual time.

As Andre and Lily were going down the steps, he asked her, "Shall I speak to Jacqueline about having Chantel for this weekend?"

"Oh, Andre — you're too good to me. Are you sure your sister wouldn't mind?" Lily asked hesitantly.

Andre looked into Lily's eyes and drew her to him. "My sister and I have always been close," he told her. "She's known how I feel about you for months, and she would be delighted to have your daughter as her guest."

"Well, Chantel seemed excited about the idea, I have to admit. Oh, Andre," she sighed, "I don't even know what my daughter does or doesn't like."

"You'll learn. The two of you will come to know one another very well; I'm sure of it."

"Yes," she acknowledged with a wry smile. "But I've got a lot of catching up to do."

"I'll speak to Jacqueline tomorrow," he promised, wrapping her in his arms in a warm embrace.

"You're a dear, sweet man," she told him, but he shook his head in firm denial.

"The truth is I'm selfish," he confessed with a sheepish grin. "I want to be able to spend more time with you. I've missed it."

"Friday night will be ours, Andre," she assured him. "No matter what."

"Ah, *chèrie!*" He gave her a passionate kiss that told her how eager he was for them to have that intimate *rendezvous* they'd postponed for almost a week.

Early the next afternoon Lily made herself cozy at her desk. Her daughter's arrival at *La Maison* had proved to be a distraction in many ways, she observed. Her mind had not been on business, and—like Andre—she missed their intimate late-night dinners and making love in her boudoir before he left in the wee hours of the morning to go back to his own home.

Chantel, finding herself alone in her room, decided that she was ready to explore this place. Other than the front foyer and this wing of the second floor, she'd seen nothing.

She ran a brush through her hair and smoothed down the waistline of her gown. After she'd given a few gentle shakes to her full, gathered skirt, she was ready for adventure.

As she descended the steps she encountered two cleaning ladies busily polishing the black-and-white-tiled floors. She greeted them cordially, and as she sashayed by she overheard their whispered comments. "She has to be madame's daughter," one woman said, nudging the other. "Sure is a pretty little thing," the other replied. Although they could no longer see her face, Chantel blushed at the compliment, pleased.

Leisurely, she sauntered through the draped private dining rooms lavishly decorated in velvets and brocades. She noticed that the tables had only two chairs and that each intimate cubicle also featured a velvet settee. She was intrigued by the decorating scheme that alternated rooms done in rich scarlet shades with niches of bottle green.

Chantel's mother had certainly put a unique touch to her elegant restaurant, but perhaps that was why she'd been so successful. She had obviously prospered through the years.

Her aunt's house had none of the lavish furnishings she'd seen in her mother's quarters, and her own suite was far nicer than her little bedroom at Aunt Laurie's.

Roaming through the salons and parlors, she chanced upon Brandy's elegant music room with its large, inviting grand piano. Instantly, she seated herself on the richly padded bench to play one of the tunes Aunt Laurie had taught her.

How different her mother's lifestyle was from that of her older sister, Chantel mused. This mother she'd been away from so long was one to be admired more than she'd realized.

This flamboyant, exciting life that her mother lived appealed to Chantel and she vowed she would never go back to Boston.

Resuming her explorations, she didn't realize she had moved into a hallway where her mother was working behind one of the closed doors. Her hand on a doorknob, she drew back from the elegant studios to follow the enticing call of a melodious male voice raised in song.

She found herself at the threshold of the kitchen, mesmerized by Raul's *basso profondo*. To her amazement that deep bass voice bellowed from a diminutive black man with a white apron tied around his middle. He had to be the blackest man Chantel had ever beheld and he gave her a broad grin that displayed the whitest teeth—more pearly than any she had ever seen. "Good afternoon, Mademoiselle Chantel," he greeted her.

Her green eyes flashed, and a slow smile lit up her face as she gave a slight tilt to her blond head. "Now how do you have know that I'm Chantel?" she asked.

"Ah, but how could I not know this, mademoiselle? Eyes that sparkle like emeralds and hair as golden as a glorious sunrise, so I was told."

Chantel gave out a little laugh. "And I know who you are. You are Raul."

"And how would Mademoiselle Chantel know that?" he quizzed her in return.

"Because I smell all that good food you're cooking."

"*Alors,*" he sighed. "My *métier* gives me

away. Would you like a sample?" With a wave of his hand, he indicated the *crème brûlée* he'd just poured in dozens of little crocks for the evening meal.

"Oh, I'd love it, Raul," she enthused.

"Mademoiselle can tell me if she approves," he said, handing her a spoon.

For a few minutes Chantel said not a word, for she was too busy eating the delectable custard. Raul could see that she was enjoying every bite.

"Oh, Raul--can I have just one more?" she begged. "Please."

Nothing could have delighted him more than to hand her a second *pot de crème*. When she had finished, she entreated him with impish charm. "Would you mind," she asked demurely, "if I came here every so often to have myself an afternoon treat?"

"I would be most honored, mademoiselle." Raul, entranced by her, reluctantly returned to the management of his kitchen. This was a busy time.

"Would you excuse me, mademoiselle?" he requested politely. "I must get the bottles of wine that your mother wishes up from the cellar for tonight," he explained. "I shall be back shortly."

"Oh, don't worry about me, Raul. I've got to be going anyway for I've kept you from your work long enough already." She rose from the chair as Raul raced from the room but lingered when a good-looking young man entered the kitchen, his arms laden with a huge package.

He had hair as black as a raven's wing and the most devastating blue eyes she had ever seen. His eyes danced over her from the top of her head all the way down to her feet. Chantel had never before felt like a man was undressing her with his eyes as this young man was doing.

But then Chantel was a naive young girl who had yet to know a man's kiss. There was no question in her mind, however, that this handsome apparition in Raul's kitchen was a real man and one she might like to flirt with—and to kiss.

Her green eyes scrutinized him, taking in his broad shoulders and trim waistline. She saw how the faded pants molded to his firm, muscled body, and she noticed that the opened front of his blue shirt displayed ringlets of black that matched the hair on his head. An unruly wisp fell over his forehead. His shirtsleeves were rolled up so she could see the bulging muscles in his strong arms.

The glint in his blue eyes taunted her as he announced his business. "I've got Madame Lemogne's weekly order of fish for her," he said. "Where's Raul?"

"He's—he's gone to bring up the wine," she replied promptly.

He put the newspaper-wrapped package on

Raul's worktable, but his eyes quickly darted back to her. Boldly, he queried, "What's your name, honey?"

"Chantel. What's yours?" she retorted with a saucy air.

"Gabe O'Roarke, love. If I could be so bold, I've got to tell you that you're the prettiest girl I've ever seen around *La Maison*. And since I deliver Madame Lily's fish every week, what I think ought to count for something."

"You deliver fish every week?" Chantel asked.

Although Gabe assumed she was just another new girl at *La Maison,* she didn't look the type. To Gabe, she was a vision of sweet innocence that fired an instant desire in him. His blue eyes surveyed her hungrily, awed by the honeyed hair that flowed so freely over her shoulders. The simple afternoon frock she wore was attractive and flattering to her petite figure, but it didn't reveal the full, rounded flesh he knew was there. The scooped neckline gave only a hint of cleavage. Having a younger sister, Gabe knew that she could not possibly be more than seventeen or eighteen.

"I like your name, Chantel. It seems to fit you," Gabe told her. His outgoing nature had— since he was a boy on the bayou—endeared him to people and made them warm to him. Chantel found him infectious and gave herself up to his winning smile.

40

Gabe had another order to deliver, but before he left he could not resist asking Chantel, "Am I to assume that you are the new girl here at *La Maison?*"

Chantel, not knowing what he implied, thought she was answering him quite honestly when she said, "Yes, Gabe, I guess you could say that."

Although he believed her to be a girl of pleasure, Gabe could not get her out of his mind. She was too damned beautiful—an angel—to be one of Madame Lily's girls. She was dainty and petite, with a touch of class. Everything about her cried out that she was a lady. She shouldn't be at *La Maison.*

Long after he'd shared the evening meal with his family and retired to his own bedroom, he found himself thinking about the golden-haired Chantel, and she even haunted his dreams that night.

Four

Lily, finally leaving her office after a long afternoon of catching up on her neglected books, admonished herself that she couldn't allow the leisure of so much distraction, no matter how welcome Chantel's company.

"I need a bath," she told Mimi first thing. "A nice, leisurely soak." As Mimi scurried to run the water and add the soothing oils her mistress preferred, Lily called after her. "You might check with Chantel and see if she would like her bath prepared, too." Then she kicked off her slippers and collapsed on the settee.

But Mimi returned almost immediately. "Miss Chantel's not in her room," she panted breathlessly, and Lily came alive.

"You wish me to go looking for her, madame?"

"No, Mimi, I'd better go." Barefoot, Lily rushed down the carpeted hall only to see her preparing to mount the steps. Chantel swished her skirt to and fro to the tempo of a song she sang with gay abandon. As vexed as she had been, Lily smiled, worry and irritation evaporating at the sight of her.

"And just what have you been up to, Chantel?" she inquired playfully.

"Exploring, Mother. I figured that it was time I took a tour of *La Maison*, so I did," Chantel told her.

"Oh? And what do you think?" Lily asked her as the two of them walked down the hall together.

"It's fantastic. And so is Raul. He let me sample the custard, and it was great."

Lily threw back her head and laughed. "Did he sing for you?" she asked. "He has a voice like an opera star."

"His singing led me to the kitchen. I probably couldn't have found it if I'd been looking for it. This place is so big I was sure I'd get lost."

Lily gave her little daughter an affectionate embrace. "Ah, *chèrie*," she assured her, you would never have to be lost in *La Maison* for long."

"Oh, but Mother," Chantel interrupted, "I almost forgot to tell you the best part. I met a boy."

That got Lily's full attention. A part of her wanted to believe that Chantel was still just a child, but she had to admit that Chantel was a blossoming beauty. All too soon to please Lily, some young man was bound to enter Chantel's life. She wanted to protect her daughter from the pain of romance and the responsibility of motherhood that had turned around her own life when she was Chantel's age.

"Boy, Chantel?" Lily questioned. Where could she have encountered a young man at *La Maison?*

"His name is Gabe, and he has the most beautiful blue eyes I've ever seen," she told her mother, then ducked into her room to be alone with her daydreams.

Lily knew immediately she was talking about Gabe O'Roarke. He was a handsome young devil with an Irish wit that had even charmed her. Yes, he would certainly be exciting to a sixteen-year-old girl unversed in romance.

He was likeable and hard-working, but Chantel was too young to get involved with any man, Lily resolved as she sank into her perfumed bathwater.

Another realization struck Lily like a thunderbolt as she leisurely indulged herself in the heated tub. Gabe O'Roarke knew the truth about *La Maison.* One casual remark from him could give everything away to Chantel. But she could hardly lay rules down to him as she had to her employees.

Still, she acknowledged as Mimi draped a huge towel around her voluptuous body, Gabe O'Roarke could prove the biggest threat to her secret for he came to *La Maison* every week. Yet she would not like to have to discontinue ordering her fish from him. Gabe had dealt fairly with her and never failed to appear with her orders on the appointed day with the fresh catch of the day. Sternly, she reminded herself that everything couldn't change just because Chantel had suddenly come on the scene. She had to pull herself together and think clearly.

But she had only to voice her fears to Andre that evening and he was quickly consoling her. "Lily, I will be here tomorrow afternoon to pick up Chantel and take her out to Jacqueline's. Then you and I are going to have two glorious nights together." He took her hand in his and kissed the tips of her fingers. "Your world has been disrupted and you need to put it back together again," he said matter-of-factly—as if it could be that simple!

"I'm not as sharp as I thought I was, Andre," she confessed weakly. "I'm in a frenzy."

"No, Lily." He caressed her palm and stroked the inside of her wrist. "You are a woman who loves and cares very much what your daughter thinks of you. Chantel is a lucky young lady to be loved so much." Andre's adoring dark eyes easily persuaded her that she, too, was lucky.

"Andre! Oh, Andre, I thank you for you have eased such a heaviness in my heart this evening." She leaned closer to him and kissed his cheek.

"Then I am a very happy man, *chèrie*. If I have made my beautiful lady a little happier tonight then I, too, am happy. Notice that I do not say woman. There is a vast difference between a woman and a lady, and to me, Lily Lemogne, you are a lady!"

Lily had never adored Andre more than at that moment.

Gabe O'Roarke was unaware that his father had lain in his bed years ago before Gabe was born and pondered how he night meet the beautiful Angelique Dupree just as Gabe was engrossed with dreams of fair-haired, green-eyed Chantel. He did not wish to go to *La Maison* and engage her services for the evening. Oh, he could have given himself the pleasure of a single night, but Gabe didn't want to hold her in his arms in that sordid atmosphere. Nor did he want to kiss those tempting lips of hers just because his money had paid for that privilege. No, that was not the way he wanted to have her. Stubbornly, he refused to believe that she actually worked at the *bordello*. She didn't look or act the part and she was so young.

He slept restlessly, haunted by a vision of Chantel. He needed to sleep, he reminded himself in vain, for he faced a busy day tomorrow. He had promised to take Madame Jacqueline Basherone an extra order of fish for she was having weekend guests.

When Gabe finally managed to get to sleep,

it was almost time for him to get up. He left the bayou dragged out and weary, but the lakes and bays were teeming and he made a fine catch. By four thirty, Gabe was moving across the wharf, his order ready to deliver to Madame Basherone.

Out at the Basherone's country estate, Andre had already arrived with Chantel. Jacqueline nodded her approval of his young companion. Jacqueline had once lived in Paris, where she had known many exquisite beauties. Chantel possessed that kind of loveliness.

Her little Nannette didn't possess such beauty, Jacqueline had to privately confess to herself, and she had a retiring personality. She occupied herself with her thoroughbred, Prince, but she had no friends her own age.

Jacqueline sensed instinctively that Chantel's vivacious high spirits would be good for Nannette. Perhaps, she also ventured to reflect, her daughter might develop an interest in feminine attire when she saw the pretty gown Chantel had on. Nannette's preference was for her durable, practical riding habits.

The two young girls had gone immediately upstairs to settle Chantel into the guest room, leaving Jacqueline and Andre alone in the parlor.

"Andre, she is absolutely charming! I'm so glad you got the idea to bring her here. Now, you must bring your Lily." Jacqueline smiled.

They'd always been too close for Andre to conceal his feelings. Lily had been in his life for over a year, and Jacqueline was curious and concerned.

"Let me see what I might work out for this Sunday," he equivocated. "Perhaps I can get her to come with me to pick up Chantel."

A glint came into her eyes as she teased him. "Ah, Andre," she prodded, "when did you ever fail to work out anything you wanted?"

Andre surmised that it was because he was her older brother that Jacqueline had always admired and looked upon him as a hero. Perhaps it could have been that Jacqueline didn't get to know their father as he had. Phillip Deverone had died when she was only two-years-old, so Andre had played the role of father to her.

By the time he left, Chantel, dressed in one of Nannette's riding ensembles, was heading for the stables with his niece, definitely excited at the prospect of riding one of Jacqueline's choice thoroughbreds.

It was a wonderful summer day as Gabe guided his buggy down the winding dirt road toward the Basherone estate. He had rolled the sleeves of his cotton shirt well above his elbows to be more comfortable and—despite his tiredness—he felt good and whistled and sang as he rolled along.

Once he delivered this order, Gabe was heading for home. He and his parents were traveling up the bayou to a party this evening. Bayou people loved gathering together for a feast and an excuse to play their music.

He knew that his mother had probably been cooking all day and would be taking pies and cakes to the party. Yesterday, Gabe had brought a fine supply of fish to the Alred's cottage so Celine Alred could prepare them for tonight. That was the way of the bayou people and that was why their feasts were the grandest, for there was always more food than the crowd could possibly eat.

As Gabe guided his buggy around the last turn in the dirt road, he saw two riders coming toward him. Gabe's blue eyes focused on only one of the riders, a girl with golden hair that flowed back from her lovely face. He pulled up on the reins so that the bay would stop.

At the same moment, Chantel recognized him and reined in her mare while Nannette, oblivious, galloped on down the road.

As the spirited horse paced back and forth beside the buggy, Chantel looked down at Gabe. "Well, hello," she called out casually, as if her heart weren't racing like a thoroughbred trotter. "Gabe, isn't it?"

Entranced by her smile, he almost stammered his response. "This is a pleasant surprise," he said, at a loss for words.

"For me, too," she agreed. "Now don't tell me you're delivering fish out here."

"As a matter of fact, that's exactly what I'm doing. Madame Basherone ordered extra fish for weekend guests," he told her.

Chantel laughed. "Well, I am one of her guests, but I'll hardly eat as much as that." she indicated the package on the seat beside him with an impish grin.

"You're a guest at Madame Basherone's?" Gabe asked, skeptical.

With a tilt of her head, she met his gaze. "You seem surprised, Gabe," she commented, "but here I am, a *bona fide* guest." But before their conversation could go any further, Nannette turned her horse around and beckoned to Chantel.

"Well, nice to see you again, Gabe," she said as she spurred her horse into action and Gabe urged his bay to move forward.

Why, he wondered, would a girl from *La Maison* be a guest at Madame Basherone's country estate? Something didn't add up; and, by the time he reached the bayou, his interest and curiosity had peaked.

What was the mystery and the magic of this golden-haired goddess, Chantel? Gabe would not rest until he found out.

Five

Gabe knew that nothing would please his parents' friends, Sam and Celine Alred, more than for him to marry their daughter, Selena. Gabe would have been the first to admit that Selena was pretty and sweet, but she was not the woman he dreamed about having for his wife.

Flaming torches lit up the pathway from the wharf when Gabe and his family arrived. They could tell from a distance that the festivities had already started, for the music resounded through the grove of trees on the edge of the bayou.

His father carried the wicker basket of food his mother had prepared, but he also held Angelique's arm. Gabe had always been impressed by the great love that his parents shared. That was the love he wanted to know someday.

He also knew that the greatest despair of their life was the day his sister, Delphine, ran away with a riverboat man. She had been only sixteen, and that had been almost two years ago. They hadn't heard a word from her, and it was as if the earth had swallowed her up. His father had searched the city and the bayou for weeks after she disappeared, but he found few clues.

Gabe had his own ideas about Delphine's fate. The riverboat man who'd lured a pretty innocent girl away from her family and home had most likely deserted her by now. He suspected his sister was alone—or, even worse, had a child to support on her own. Delphine, stubborn with pride, would not come home or confess that she'd made an error in judgment.

He thought of her often, dejected that there was nothing he could do to bring her back to the bayou. Only she could make that decision.

As Gabe had expected, Selena came to his side immediately. He told her what he knew she wanted to hear. "You look mighty pretty tonight, Selena," he complimented, putting his hand to the fresh blossom pinned in her dark hair. He suspected that the floral dress was brand new and that Celine had probably made it for her this week, just for the gathering.

"Why, thank you, Gabe," she replied, a rosy blush coming to her cheeks.

Gabe ambled toward the crowd, not wanting to remain secluded in the shadows with Selena. He tried never to give Selena any false hope about their relationship. They were good friends and nothing more. The Alreds and his folks had been neighbors too long for him to do anything to offend them.

Gabe was quickly absorbed into the center of the party, though Selena continued to linger by his side, a shadow that moved wherever he moved and kept him from the hearty man talk he craved with his best buddy, Zack. It had been more than three weeks since they'd spent any time together. Gabe was always out on his fishing boat, and Zack worked at a mill on the outskirts of New Orleans.

Inspired, he pulled out a cheroot and handed it to Zack. "Got these fresh today, pal," he smiled. "Enjoy." He also lit one for himself, and the air was quickly permeated with cheroot aroma. A few minutes later, Selena began to cough and excused herself.

"Guess that's why men always walk out of the house to smoke," Zack said, breaking into a grin. "Women just can't take it."

"I guess so," Gabe agreed. "But my dad is the exception. Lucky for him Momma loves the smell of cheroot."

Now, with their hard-won privacy, they were free to talk. Zack teased him about Selena's dogged devotion. "There's more damn girls along the bayou that's got their hearts set on you, Gabe. You've got to tell me your secret."

"Oh, I don't have that many, Zack," Gabe

chortled. "Besides, I'm not ready to settle down yet."

Zack agreed and suggested they get themselves something stronger that Celine Alred's fruit punch, like Sam's jug of whiskey.

"Gabe, you had any word of Delphine?" Zack asked as they took their first sip.

"Not a word, Zack. We don't know where to go next to be honest with you."

Zack stared disconsolately into his paper cup half-filled with tawny whiskey. He studied the floor as if it might provide an answer to the mystery of Delphine's disappearance. "I had an eye for her," he confessed suddenly, "but I feared your pa wouldn't allow me to court her. I'd just about gathered up my courage when . . . she left."

"Delphine reached an age," Gabe said slowly, turning this new information over in his head. "And Dad would have approved of you." Zack had constantly come by their place, but he'd never given any indication that he was attracted to Delphine.

"I've kicked myself a dozen times," Zack admitted guiltily. "If I'd come to court Delphine, maybe this wouldn't have happened. Damn, I was such a coward."

Their cheroots had been thrown to the ground and Selena, seeing this, returned to Gabe and led him to the table spread with mountains of food. They shared the feast with

Zack and a bayou girl who had attached herself to him. But when two musicians picked up their fiddle and banjo, Gabe leaped to join them with his guitar.

Later, as the music played on, Gabe asked his mother to dance. He could well imagine what a ravishing beauty she must have been when she and his father had first met. He knew the story of how she'd defied her wealthy French Creole family to marry a lowly bayou fisherman, his father.

But his mother, Angelique Dupree had followed her heart's desires and she desired Scott O'Roarke so much that nothing else mattered to her. Gabe had every reason to believe that she'd never regretted that decision. His father had once told him that nothing or no one would ever stop him from having the woman he loved.

Gabe longed for a love as strong and consuming as theirs.

As he danced with his mother and held her in his arms, he noticed that she was the same size as the tantalizing Chantel. Someday, he would hold her in the circle of his arms, and his feelings would hardly be the same as now, when he whirled his petite mother around the dance floor.

Angelique was still graceful, and Gabe gave her an affectionate kiss on the cheek as they finished the dance. "Momma," he whispered, "you're a darn good dancer."

She smiled warmly up at the son who towered over her. "A lady can only dance as well as the man leading her, dear," she whispered back.

Gabe danced with Selena, her mother, and as many of the girls and ladies at the party as time allowed before the musicians finally stopped playing.

It was midnight by the time the O'Roarkes rowed back down the bayou to their cottage and dock, Tired, but still alert, Gabe's mother made an observation that her husband had probably missed. The Alreds, she said to herself, might just as well give up on Gabe. He would not be courting Selena. Although he was gracious and nice to her, he was definitely not interested in the Alreds' daughter.

Through the night on the bayou, Gabe's thoughts constantly drifted back to his encounters with Chantel. Meanwhile, out in the country, Chantel, could not escape the image of a handsome, young fisherman.

Chantel, having spent the entire afternoon at Jacqueline's country estate, prepared for dinner with dubious thoughts for the girl her age across the hall who might have become her friend.

But Nannette Basherone was dull and boring. Chantel had resented how she'd quizzed her about Gabe when Chantel had told her she'd met him yesterday afternoon.

"He delivers my mother fish, Chantel." Nannette said snobbishly. "He's a nobody."

"I found him nice," Chantel countered. "Does it make him a nobody just because he is a fisherman and sells fish to your mother?" she challenged.

"Oh, come on, Chantel. You know what I mean." Nannette cooed.

"No, I don't know at all. But we'll leave it where it is, because we probably have different opinions about people."

"It's a matter of class," Nannette said in an attempt to soothe Chantel's ruffled feathers, but her compromising statement merely convinced Chantel that the two of them had nothing in common. Nannette Basherone was a snob, but Chantel didn't find her mother, Jacqueline, that way at all. She had the same warm personality as Andre Deverone.

As they walked to the house, Nannette told her about the other guests who were coming to dinner tonight.

"The Chapelles have twin sons and mother thinks she's going to matchmake me with one or the other of them, but I've got news for her," Nannette said disdainfully. Chantel did not offer the opinion that poor Madame Basherone would have trouble matchmaking Nannette with any young man.

Since Nannette seemed to enjoy hearing herself talk, Chantel remained silent as the girl rambled on and on about Paris and how they'd lived there until her father had died.

"I gather you liked Paris better than here?" Chantel finally interjected.

"Mais oui," Nannette lamented. "And I miss my father. He and I were so much alike. He understood me." Chantel made no supportive comment. She had no father to be devoted to, for she'd never had one.

The gown she'd brought to wear this evening was one of the new ones her mother had bought for her. The stunning evening dress of emerald green matched her eyes to perfection, and she needed no jewelry to enhance her appearance.

She was a vision of loveliness as she joined Nannette to go downstairs. "You'll have Paul and Peter stumbling all over themselves to vie for your attention tonight." Nannette observed, impressed.

Chantel protested lightheartedly. "Oh, Nannette," she giggled.

"You'll know what I mean the minute they walk into our parlor and see you," Nannette declared resolutely.

The two young men were identical twins with thick manes of bright red hair and clear blue eyes, but Chantel noted fairly quickly that they had completely opposite personalities. Peter had an aggressive air of mischief about him. Paul was quieter and more reserved.

58

But from the minute she was introduced and the Chapelles were seated with their wine, Chantel realized that both young men were indeed vying for her attention. Neither of them paid Nannette any attention at all, and by the end of the evening she had to admit that Nannette had been right. Yet, although she'd been the center of attention as far as Peter and Paul Chapelle were concerned, another handsome, blue-eyed young man paraded insistently through her thoughts.

Six

Chantel would have been a liar to say that she didn't enjoy the attention of the two young men even though she wasn't attracted to either of them.

Before the Chapelles left, Paul suggested a picnic for the next day. The girls consented enthusiastically and—unbeknownst to Chantel—the twins got into a fierce debate as to which one of them would be her escort. Peter won the honor by the toss of a coin.

Chantel wore her green sprigged muslin. She loved the puffed sleeves and squared neckline. Atop her head perched a wide-brimmed straw hat with a band and streamers of green-velvet ribbon. She tied the saucy bow at the side of her face.

It was the perfect day for a picnic with a clear blue sky and a gentle breeze. Paul envied his twin in the back seat with Chantel as the buggy wound through the Chapelle property toward the lake. He would have liked to have done a "twin exchange"—he and Peter had had a lot of fun pretending to be each other—but he suspected his brother would want Chantel exclusively to himself. And he couldn't blame him for that.

Chantel had a wonderful time. She liked sitting on the ground by the side of the lake sampling the treats in the picnic basket. Toward the end of the afternoon Nannette and Paul went for a stroll and she and Peter talked about the end of summer and the unavoidable school year yet to come.

"I attended a boarding school back East," she told him. "Boston Girls Prep." She made a face but Peter was actually impressed.

"Well, that explains why you're so sophisticated," he remarked. "You're much more mature than, say, a girl like Nannette." He rubbed his chin as if trying to appear more mature himself. "You've only been here a month?" he asked.

"Yes." Her eyes sparkled. "But I was more than ready to come back. I love New Orleans."

"And I'll bet your mother and father are happy to have you home, too?"

"My mother is. My father is dead." She mentioned her father as a point of information and without remorse since she had never known him. "My mother owns *La Maison*," she added. "Do you know it? It's a restaurant."

Peter Chapelle's demeanor changed

abruptly. He mumbled that he'd heard of *La Maison* and plunged into a description of his father's work. He seemed quiet and remote as they traveled back to the Basherone house. Chantel was perplexed but undaunted. Boys—especially teenage boys—were impossible to understand.

Paul, ever-sensitive to his twin, sensed something had gone wrong for Peter and chalked it up to a refused kiss until they dropped the girls back at Jacqueline's country house and headed home.

"You and I both know what *La Maison* is," Peter muttered darkly. "Do you suppose Nannette's mother is aware of her background?"

"Perhaps. Madame Basherone is a woman of the world. She lived in Paris, so she might not be as offended as our mother would be," Paul pointed out.

"But it's a whorehouse," Peter protested.

"A *high-class* whorehouse," Paul corrected him. "There's a difference. Some of New Orleans' most elite gentlemen frequent *La Maison*."

But Peter would not be deterred. "Come on, brother," he retorted, "a whore is a whore being high class or low."

Chantel made no mention to Nannette about the sudden change in Peter Chapelle's manner, but it did occupy her thoughts the rest of the evening. She was convinced that it had something to do with *La Maison*, but the question was — what?

Nannette, who had actually enjoyed the outing, had changed her mind about Paul Chapelle. "He's really quite nice, Chantel," she admitted. "I guess I never gave him a chance. He wants to see me again." Her excitement was reflected on her face. "I think I could like him a lot."

Andre arrived to pick her up, and Jacqueline gave her a warm embrace. "You were a joy, *ma petite!*" she exclaimed. "Now you must promise to return soon, and tell your mother I'd like her to come, too, next time." Then she turned to her brother. "You bring Lily, Andre," she said firmly. "I want to meet her."

In the carriage going back to the city, Andre noted Chantel's preoccupation; but, although the weightiness of the quiet troubled him, he did not press her.

The sun had set by the time Andre's carriage pulled up at *La Maison*, but tonight there would be no music playing within the walls of the establishment nor would there be any crowds gathering to revel into the late night hours.

Lily had planned a quiet night for the three of them, and Raul had prepared a *truite mousse* with roasted pecans from the fish Gabe had delivered. But shortly after they finished their meal, Chantel excused herself. "I've got unpacking to do before I go to bed," she explained, hurrying to the door. But she paused before she left the parlor and turned to Andre. "Tell Madame Basherone I really did appreciate her invitation," she said. "It was a wonderful weekend."

"I'll tell her, Chantel," Andre promised. He watched fondly and blew her a good-night kiss as she slipped across the hall to her room. "You've got yourself a charmer," he told Lily. "Jacqueline thinks she's a good influence on Nannette." He chuckled. "She gets impatient with her daughter at times. Nannette is rather the tomboy type."

"I, too, appreciate your sister for being so nice to Chantel, Andre; but even with all these last three days free to think, I've still come up with no solution," Lily confessed.

"Then let's just take it one day at a time," Andre said cheerfully as if the matter were resolved.

"I guess all we can do is take our chances and hope for the best," Lily sighed.

Andre grabbed her hand mischievously and pulled her into his arms. "Let's take our chances," he suggested, "that Chantel will stay in her room the rest of the evening." He kissed her with barely restrained passion. "I'm aching to make love to you, Lily. Even with the weekend behind us, it still seems forever since we've been together."

64

They were not disturbed, and their lovemaking was fierce and passionate. With Andre's strong arms enclosing her and his sensuous lips caressing her, Lily realized that she had never had a man fulfill her as Andre Deverone did.

Chantel, up long before Lily, had a breakfast tray in her own bedroom. Although Mimi had warned her that her mother was still asleep, the little maid had discreetly hung Monsieur Deverone's waistcoat in madame's armoire. She had found it flung over the velvet chair, and Mimi took it as a sign that things were getting back to normal.

So when Chantel did breeze into the upstairs parlor, she saw nothing out of the ordinary and didn't linger long. Downstairs was ghostly quiet as well, typical of Mondays at *La Maison*. Bored, Chantel wandered through the deserted kitchen and out the back door.

Sitting in the sun, Jonah alternated between whittling and wiping the sweat from his forehead with the back of his hand. She watched for awhile, intrigued, before she spoke. "You're the only one awake in this place, Jonah," she commented, then bent closer to study his block of wood, "What are you making?"

Jonah chuckled. "Ain't sure yet, Miss Chantel. But I reckon it'll turn out to be something."

Chantel sat down beside him. "How long have you been at *La Maison*, Jonah?" she asked.

"Over five years now, miss," he replied, squinting at his handiwork with a frown.

She squatted quietly for another moment, watching him shape the wood with his knife, but then an impulse hit her and she voiced it instantly. "You know what I'd like to do this afternoon, Jonah?"

"No, ma'am, got no idea at all." He stopped his whittling to look up at her pretty face.

"I'd like to take a nice ride through the city. It's a glorious day, and I've been gone for five years. It would be fun to just drive around in the buggy. Could you take me? Would you want to?"

"I'm at your service, Miss Chantel," Jonah replied promptly, pocketing his knife and tossing the unfinished sculpting onto a wrought-iron table. Chantel was Madame Lemogne's daughter, and he would obey any reasonable request. "You wish me to prepare the buggy now, Miss Chantel?" he asked.

"Yes," she shouted gleefully, jumping to her feet. "I'll meet you back here in two minutes. I just need to get my hat." She dashed to the back entrance, and, within a matter of minutes, the widebrimmed straw hat bobbed atop her head, the velvet streamer tied under her chin. She'd also hastily picked up the bottle-green reticule from her dressing table, so she felt ready for any adventure.

66

So the buggy rolled away from *La Maison;* and, as Jonah guided the roan bay, he had no inkling that he was doing something that Madame Lily would not have approved of at all.

"Where do you wish me to go, Miss Chantel?" he queried respectfully.

"Let's drive by Lake Pontchartrain, Jonah," she suggested.

"Yes, ma'am, I'm heading in that direction." And Jonah executed a sharp turn at the nearest corner.

The extra-wide-brimmed hat she wore kept the bright afternoon sun from shining down on her face as they traveled first along the lake road and then down the streets where vendors hawked their wares on every corner. She had Jonah stop twice—once for roasted peanuts for the two of them and again for a basket of flowers that mingled blossoms of red, purple, white, and yellow.

"Down to the wharf next," she pleaded prettily. "I want to see if it's like I remember with all the ships and boats and hundreds of people milling around."

As Jonah drew up by the quay, Chantel spied Gabe O'Roarke jauntily swaggering up from the pier. Her heart beat a little faster as she realized that he had spotted her as well. A broad smile lit up his tanned face, and he waved as he quickened his pace to reach their buggy before they pulled away. His long strides rapidly closed the distance between them and he called to Jonah to wait.

"What a pretty sight you are," he told her, belatedly trying to affect a casual air. "To what do I owe this good luck that you'd chance to be here this afternoon?"

"A whim," she replied with a coquettish shrug.

"Good." He grinned foolishly, casting about for a topic of conversation. "Did you have a nice visit at the Basherones?"

"Very nice," she answered primly, wishing she dared tell him instead that the brilliant blue of his eyes stirred a heat inside her that made her flushed and ill-at-ease. "I guess I'd better go now," she stammered.

Gabe stepped back, but his bright eyes still devoured her as Jonah urged the bay forward. "Give Madame Lemogne my regards," Gabe called.

"I will," she promised. "I'll tell my mother you asked for her."

Her mother. Gabe grinned, pleased with the world. She was Madame Lemogne's daughter! Not one of her girls.

But why, he wondered later, would Lily Lemogne bring her daughter to *La Maison?* Chantel was too young, too beautiful. She had no business being in a house of pleasure.

How could Madame Lemogne allow it?

Seven

Just after four, Chantel, in a very gay mood, breezed into the parlor.

"Where's my mother, Mimi?" she asked. "I got her these flowers while I was out. Aren't they pretty?" Chantel held out the basket for the little maid's inspection, but Mimi was cool and reserved.

"Very pretty, mademoiselle," she said almost curtly, showing no interest. "Your mother is taking her bath." Mimi picked up madame's coffee cup and moved stiffly to the door.

"Well, I'll just sit here and wait for her to finish. Would you tell her I'm here, Mimi?" Chantel placed the basket of flowers on the table and laid her wide-brimmed hat on the settee.

Fluffing up her hair, she reflected that Mimi had acted strange, bothered. Was something wrong? she wondered. A few minutes later, she was certain.

Lily, deliberately nonchalant, strolled into

69

the parlor in her deep purple dressing gown, her dark hair streaming freely down her back. Mimi had not styled it in the upswept fashion she wore nightly.

"Well, Chantel," she observed coolly, "you've returned. May I ask just where you decided to go this afternoon?" Lily puffed savagely on one of Andre's slim Turkish cigarettes. Her voice was unmistakably sharp and angry.

"I just went for a drive," Chantel replied, bewildered. "I hadn't seen the city in years, and I really enjoyed it." She eyed her mother speculatively and gave her a timorous smile. "I bought these flowers for you."

She reached over to grasp the handle so she might hand them to Lily, and Lily melted. It was impossible to hold onto her fury. And there had, after all, been no harm done. Chantel had been safe with Jonah — and had not ventured into the forbidden wing where the girls lived and plied their trade.

"They're lovely," she capitulated, "but I was worried about you." She gave her daughter one last, stern admonishment. "No one knew where you were. Poor Mimi searched everywhere for you."

"I didn't mean to worry anyone," Chantel apologized. "I was bored and a jaunt around the city sounded like fun. And it was." Now she understood Mimi's displeasure. "I'll leave a message next time," she promised.

But Lily didn't like the sound of that. "Best you say something to me first, *chèrie*. I might have needed Jonah this afternoon. As it happened I didn't, but another time I might."

Chantel swayed by Lily's logic, gave in. "I'll ask you first," she said and her mother hugged her and the subject was dropped.

Chantel gave Mimi the little bag of roasted peanuts as a peace offering and like Lily, Mimi found it hard to stay out of sorts with the earnest little miss.

Chantel worried that her impulsive action might get Jonah in trouble, but she soon put away that heavy burden of thought in favor of reviewing what she knew about Gabe O'Roarke.

He was good looking. Too handsome. He probably had a bevy of girlfriends. And he had an exciting way of looking at you, his blue eyes flashing. Her stomach had been full of butterflies when he leaned into the buggy to talk to her.

On the way back to *La Maison,* Jonah had remarked, "Didn't know you knew Mister Gabe, ma'am."

"I met him in the kitchen," she'd said, remembering how her breath had caught in her throat at the sight of him, pulling up short to

71

gaze at her across the *petits pots de crème*.

"He's been delivering our fish for several months now," Jonah had noted. "He's a good man, Mister Gabe. Hard working and a capable fisherman, too."

"Sounds like you know him pretty well," Chantel had said, hoping he would go on.

"Yes, miss," he'd nodded. "And his father before him, long before I came to *La Maison*. He and his folks live out on the bayou."

Trying to sound casual, she tilted her head and asked if he were married. Jonah's chuckle burgeoned into a loud, long laugh.

"No ma'am, he ain't married. Not that one. He lives with his folks—last I heard."

Had jonah looked back at her lovely face, he would have seen the pleased glow of a smile for she was delighted to hear that Gabe wasn't married.

For the rest of the evening she dwelt in romantic whimsy, unable to forget the dashing Irish fisherman who devastated her with his piercing blue eyes and warm friendly smile.

Miles away from New Orleans, down on the bayou, that same Irishman was thinking about her. Her green eyes and golden hair haunted him. And his pleasure knew no bounds now that he knew she wasn't one of Lily's girls. Yet, even if she had been, it might not have mattered for he'd never met any girl who had set his heart fluttering so erratically. He vowed

72

that someday, somehow, he would make Chantel his lady.

The next day, assured that Jonah had not incurred Lily's wrath for his kindness to her daughter, Chantel fought the restlessness inside her. But by the time her mother went downstairs to charm her patrons, Chantel felt caged, like an animal.

She paced and found no contentment within the walls of her lavish bedroom. It was an oppressive, warm night and for the first time opened her window to look down at the street below.

Something struck her as strange as she observed the carriages arriving at the fancy entranceway of her mother's establishment as her clock chimed ten. Over and over again, only a lone gentleman would emerge to be welcomed by Jonah at the iron grillwork of the big front door.

Usually by this hour she would have been getting cozy in her bed, but the oddness of her mother's clientele whetted her curiosity. So she slipped the robin's egg-blue satin wrapper over her nightgown and went into the hall. She listened to the noises wafting up from below. The laughter and the soft sounds of the piano playing lured her to the stairway. Sweet-smelling perfumes mingled with the pungent odors of cheroot, enticing her. She sank down on the top step, an audience of one.

73

Adrienne knew the minute she saw her that she had to be Chantel.

Adrienne's curvaceous figure was molded into an emerald-green gown, and her dark hair was piled high on her head. Chantel, looking up, was struck by her beauty.

Adrienne joined her on the step. "You must be Chantel," she said simply. "I'm Adrienne. I work for your mother."

"You look absolutely stunning," Chantel breathed, restraining her as she rose to go. "What do you do here at *La Maison?*" she asked.

Not missing a beat, Adrienne "I sing, honey. That's what I do. And I got to get on downstairs, but it was nice to meet you."

The encounter with Chantel had unnerved her, especially since they had one of their "strange" gentlemen in the establishment tonight. Adrienne had never liked Justin St. Clair. He had a sadistic streak and a preference for young girls like Tanya or Colette. He was due to leave Tanya's room soon, and Adrienne didn't want Chantel in sight with him on the floor.

So it was Lily she first sought instead of her gentleman, but she wasn't fast enough. Justin St. Clair, his eyes lighting on the delectable golden beauty at the top of the stairs, was enflamed with an obsessive desire for her.

The sheer folds of her blue gown and wrapper fanned his passion as he folded himself onto the step beside her. "Where have they been hiding you, my pretty one?" he leered.

Chantel, caught by surprise, shrank from him. "I'm sorry, monsieur," she stammered. "I do not understand what you mean."

"Don't play innocent," he said, pressing himself close to her. "I'm a regular patron. You'll want to be good to me. The other girls will tell you."

Chantel tried to move away from him, but his arm had encircled her tiny waist and she was pinned against the balustrade.

"Monsieur, remove your arm," she demanded. *"Tout de suite."*

But Justin St. Clair did not intend to be denied the kiss he craved. His tall, reedlike body covered her and his arms encased her as his mouth sought her fresh, unsullied lips.

"You little bitch," he hissed. "Do you think you're too good for Justin St. Clair?" He gave her a venomous appraisal and spat. "Not the likes of you." He reached roughly for her. "Kiss me, damn you."

Lily took in everything as she and Andre raced frantically up the stairway. Andre surged ahead of her and grabbed Justin by the neck and yanked until the foul man was swept down the steps and through the foyer to the front entrance.

"You are no longer welcome at *La Maison*,"

75

Andre shouted at him. "That was Lily Le-mogne's daughter you molested."

Storming back inside, Andre ordered a shot of whiskey and then a double. He waited for Lily, afraid for her and the tenuous new relationship she had only just begun to forge with her daughter.

"God, she was as cool and calm as could be, Andre," Lily told him later in the privacy of her office. "I expected her to be upset, but she insisted I get back to you. Can you believe that?"

Downing his drink, Andre found it strange that Chantel had not burst into tears or admitted to fright. The girl had been accosted — by Justin St. Clair of all people, a lowlife lecher with too much money to spend. But he kept these thoughts to himself not wanting to upset Lily further.

"It's odd, Andre," Lily remarked, puzzled. "At a time like this all she wanted to know was how old I am."

But Chantel was hardly as calm as she'd seemed to Lily and Justin's words were etched in her mind. She would never forget what he'd said to her. Now she understood so many things that had not been clear before, fore-most among them the reason why she'd been shipped to her aunt's and boarding school. She and her roommate had exchanged whis-pered scraps of knowledge about men and women and sex. Her roommate had learned from the friend of a friend of her cousin that there were places where men paid to have their way with women. Places like *La Maison*.

Now Chantel knew beyond a shadow of a doubt that she was living in a house of pleasure. And she hated her mother.

Eight

Chantel lay in her bed, pretending to sleep. She had nothing to say to her mother. She was too angry.

For hours her head whirled as new information bred new thoughts and new questions. If her mother were thirty-two now, that meant she had been only sixteen when Chantel was born. Had Lily been married? Or had she been a "working" girl? A whore.

She made up her mind to go away, to go back to Boston and protect Aunt Laurie from the shocking truth.

In the morning she left *La Maison* on foot to find out the cost of traveling from New Orleans to Boston. The fares were more than she had in pocket money, but she felt no qualms about the little white lies that would grease Lily's guilt and supply Chantel with the wherewithal to get back home—to her real, respectable home with Aunt Laurie. Lily had told her repeatedly that if she needed money for something she wanted to buy, she had only to ask. As she wandered down the long wharf on her way back to *La Maison,* Chantel considered the dresses, bonnets, and jewelry that could provide her passage to freedom.

In her haste she had forgotten the wide-brimmed hat, and her golden hair flowed free and loose, glinting in the sunlight.

Gabe had just paid his crew their wages for the week's work, and all of them had left the boat to go into the city to spend it. Emerging onto the plank wharf, he spotted Chantel, as refreshing as a sunbeam in her pale-yellow frock with its full-flowing skirt and white, lace-edged pouf sleeves.

He called out to her, piercing the fog of her thoughts, and she whirled around and waited for him to catch up to her. "Where are you heading, little one?" he asked, his eyes pleading with her not to hurry off.

"Back to *La Maison* for now," she replied.

"Could I persuade you to accompany me to the tobacco shop? Then I'd like to invite you aboard my *Louisiana Lady.* Have you ever been aboard a fishing boat, Chantel?"

"No, I haven't," she said, "and I'd like to see yours."

Gabe, fairly bursting at this rare stroke of Irish luck, offered his arm and they strolled up the road to the tobacco shop and back. A packet of cheroots in hand for his dad, Gabe

79

stopped beside a flower vendor's cart.

"I'd better get my ma a bouquet or she might be peeved that I'm bringing dad something," he chuckled. But he also picked out a delicate white and yellow nosegay for Chantel.

"Thank you, Gabe," she said, taking the flowers in one hand. With a start she realized that Gabe held her other hand.

Proudly, Gabe took her on a tour of his boat, ending in his cabin. "I want you to share the basket of food my mother sent with me this morning," he told her, unwilling to relinquish her hand until she'd agreed to stay and eat with him.

Chantel didn't have to think twice about accepting his offer. She'd been too upset this morning to stomach breakfast, and now she was famished. While Gabe heated coffee on a little stove, Chantel arranged their meal on a small, wooden table. "Your mother was most generous," she laughed, amused, laying out the half-loaf of bread Gabe's mother had baked late the night before and a mound of golden-crusted chicken. Three fried pies filled with peaches—Gabe's favorite—completed the menu.

Time stood still for Chantel. She had never enjoyed herself so much and she wanted it to last. They ate every bite, every morsel, of the food Angelique had packed, and they cleared the table and repacked the hamper, and then there was no more reason—no excuse—for her to stay.

Chantel smiled, then lowered her eyes demurely. "That walk back to *La Maison* is going to be good for me after all I've eaten," she giggled. "You can tell your mother for me that she is an excellent cook."

"I want you to meet my folks," he said impulsively, and their eyes locked once more.

"I would like that." She nodded her appreciation, afraid her eagerness showed too much in her voice. "Jonah told me you live in the bayou."

"That old Jonah been telling you all about me, eh?" he teased.

"Jonah had only nice things to say about you," she retorted primly.

And then he laid aside his jesting manner. "And what about you, Chantel?" he asked, his expression serious. "What do you think about me?"

Chantel equally intense, replied honestly, "I think you are the nicest man I've ever met."

Instinctively, Gabe reached out and enveloped her in his arms. Gently, he urged her closer until his lips could claim hers in a tender, lingering kiss. As he released her, he murmured huskily "I've wanted to do that since that first day I saw you in the kitchen. You've haunted my dreams every night, Chantel Lemogne."

"Oh, Gabe, I think of you, too," she confessed.

"Do you, love?" But he didn't wait for her to answer him for he wanted to taste the honeyed lips again. He pulled her tight against him, and she wrapped her arms around his neck, overwhelmed.

It took all his willpower to control the burning desire consuming him but he forced himself to release her. "We better quit this," he said, his eyes continuing to devour her, "or you're going to think I'm not such a nice man after all."

Chantel understood only that she could not have denied him anything. She paused there at the cabin door, preparing to leave. "Could I come here again, Gabe?" she asked in a very low voice.

"Any time you want," he answered quickly. "I have no buggy to offer you a ride home, but I could walk with you if you'd like."

"No, Gabe." She was firm. "It would be better if I returned alone."

"As long as you get back before dark," he agreed. "It's almost five-thirty."

Like Cinderella she flew swiftly from the scene of her enchantment so that Lily—hovering anxiously by the window—wondered at her bold step and long absence. But she said nothing for she was at a disadvantage and Chantel remained cool and remote.

82

Relying on ritual and routine to get them out of the quicksand and onto firmer ground again, Lily dressed for dinner. Mimi—ever solicitous—helped her into a stunning scarlet taffeta. Lily's hand shook as she fastened the teardrop ruby earrings and dabbed her favorite toilet water on her throat. She walked quickly into the upstairs parlor and poured herself a glass of wine.

The help—like any close-knit family—had told and retold the story throughout the day, sharing the pain that separated mother from daughter. Raul prepared Lily's favorite grilled chicken breasts in an herbed cream sauce.

"I'll have to tell Raul how much I enjoyed it," Chantel raved. Then casually, between healthy bites of *crème brûlée*, she asked her mother for fifty dollars. "I saw a pair of divine blue slippers in a shop window," she exclaimed. "They're a perfect match for the party dress we bought at Madame Denise's. And there was some absolutely exquisite costume jewelry—a bracelet and a ring that I liked especially. Would it be too much, Mother?" She opened her eyes wide and gave a tiny pout. Lily took a bill from her purse, hearing the exuberance and not the falseness behind Chantel's entreaty.

Barricading herself in her room like a miser, Chantel counted and recounted her hoard before securing it in her reticule. She had more than enough to take a boat back to Boston.

But Mimi, turning down her bed and fluffing up her pillows, gave her another view of Lily Lemogne, proprietress of *La Maison,* as she prepared to leave. "You are a most fortunate young lady, Mademoiselle Chantel," she remarked, laying out the expensive nightgown and wrapper that Lily had insisted on for her daughter who was almost-all-grown-up. "You have a wonderful mother, and I envy you."

"Envy me?" Chantel asked bitterly, but the little maid would not be cowed and told her the story of her rescue by Lily from degradation. "I shall be forever grateful to her," Mimi said quietly and left Chantel almost swayed.

Mimi's revelation had made an impact; but once she had changed into her nightclothes and sauntered to the window to gaze at the street below, she had only to see a carriage approach and a gentleman descend in pursuit of pleasure to feel once again the horror and disgust and disillusionment of the night before.

She had to get away, and nothing would stop her.

Nine

She made her plans to leave New Orleans—
but not before she'd shared one more sweet
eternity with Gabe O'Roarke. It would be a
long time before she came this way again.

She helped herself to a bottle of fine white
wine while Raul selected herbs from his garden. Liberated from the kitchen, the wine
went into hiding in her armoire along with the
voile dress with the ruffled flounces and green
velvet bows at the shoulders. Gabe would like
the provocative neckline and the wide velvet
sash that emphasized her tiny waistline.

As she pulled out her soft crème-colored
pumps, she caught sight of Andre Deverone
from her window. Why, she questioned, did
this wonderful man seek Lily's company when
he knew how she made her living? And Jacqueline Basherone. She was a woman of the
world. She had to know about *La Maison*.

Nothing made sense anymore.

She left without fanfare the next day, making her way directly from *La Maison* to the docks. She recognized the *Louisiana Lady* instantly even though it bobbed in line with five other fishing boats. The quay teemed with carriages and buggies jammed on the road above while their drivers and passengers slipped down to the pier to buy their supply of fish.

She lingered for a moment watching him and his mate tying up packages and checking orders. This glimpse of him—bare-chested in faded blue pants—excited her. She saw that his broad chest was as tanned as his face, and his black hair fell onto his forehead as he busied himself on deck. The fisherman at his side was also well-endowed, but it was Gabe who captured Chantel's eyes and held them.

As if he felt her green eyes upon him, he glanced up and waved to her to come on board. She needed no further invitation and immediately darted through the crowds to the *Louisiana Lady*. He helped her onto the deck of his boat and wasted no time in giving her a warm embrace and kiss on the cheek even though they were still technically in public.

"Hey, pretty thing, don't tell me you came to buy my fish. I've an order to take to your mother when I shut down here."

"I came to see you," she told him without guile.

A broad smile came to Gabe's face as he replied, "Well, that's enough to make this fisherman's day."

In less than an hour, the crowd had dispersed and the crew had disappeared, leaving Gabe and Chantel alone on the boat.

She handed him the bottle of wine she'd brought from *La Maison*. "This is for you, Gabe."

"Why thank you, Chantel. You will have to share a glass of it with me," he told her.

They went to Gabe's cabin, and—suddenly self-conscious—he put on a clean shirt. "I wish I had some more good fried chicken to offer you, but I don't," he apologized. "Momma never packs me a basket on Fridays, because this is the day I get back to the bayou early."

"Then please don't let me keep you, Gabe," she interjected quickly. "I had an errand to run this afternoon so I came by to give you the wine."

He forgot about buttoning his shirt and, in two long strides, reached her side and took her dainty hands in his. He bent down to kiss her lips. "You're not keeping me from a thing," he whispered. "Besides, this time I'm taking you home. I've a buggy to deliver your mother's order, so you aren't going to walk today, Chantel."

But when he kissed her and gently urged her up to him, she felt the searing heat of his bare chest pressing against her sheer voile bodice. A liquid heat flowed through Chantel as Gabe's lips sought their fill of her honey-sweetness.

He was as breathless as she when he released her, but his hands still caressed her soft body and his eyes simmered with passion as he gazed down on her. "I could never tire of kissing those sweet lips of yours!" he exalted.

Suddenly, he swung her up in his arms and carried her to the bed. Sinking onto the bunk with her still fast in his arms, he freed one hand to brush her blond hair away from her face.

"You are the most beautiful girl I've ever seen," he said in awe, and then his lips found hers once more. His fingers, playing with the wisps of her long hair, trailed down to her throat. Without any warning, his hand cupped the firm roundness of her breast, and Chantel was fired with a new, unfamiliar sensation. She gave a soft moan of pleasure.

Wild desire blazed in Gabe, and his hand gently caressed her breasts under the ruffled flounce of the neckline. Her flesh was as soft and smooth as satin. Their eyes had only to meet for them both to know that this interlude would not end with just a kiss.

She offered no protest as Gabe's nimble fingers lowered the bodice of her dress for his lips were quickly tantalizing the tips of her breast, making her arch up to him. Her head was whirling with such giddiness that she didn't realize that he had removed his unbuttoned shirt and slipped out of his faded pants. Nothing separated them now. His bare flesh was pressed against her nude body. All she knew was that it felt wonderful, and she lay contented, her body undulating beneath him.

Suddenly his firm, muscled body buried itself between her thighs. At his first powerful thrust she felt a sensation of pain, but he reassured her with kisses and soft words. "That's it, love," he soothed. "That won't happen again. Come with me, love, and now it will feel good again."

With her passion mounting to loftier heights, Chantel thought she would surely die from the ecstasy of love, when she felt Gabe give forth a mighty quake that shook her to the core.

And then they lay, growing calmer in the circle of one another's arms. Gabe was the first to make a move as his hand reached over to brush the tousled hair from her face. He pulled her closer to him to kiss her still-flushed cheek. His deep husky voice whispered in her ear, "You're my girl, Chantel. I won't let anyone else have you. Tell me—tell me you're my girl!"

"I'm your girl, Gabe O'Roarke." The words came out easily for they were true.

He pulled her even closer to him. "I'm going to hold you to that, Chantel Lemogne," he exhorted. "You're my lady. My Louisiana Lady."

They never got around to the wine, for they had enjoyed a headier intoxicant. Chantel treasured each moment of the afternoon. It would be a memory to take with her when she left New Orleans, but it would be *hers*. She now knew what it meant to be made love to by a man.

But as much as she loved Gabe O'Roarke, she did not change her plans to leave *La Maison* and New Orleans. And he did not know about the money hidden in the pockets of her reticule and so, when he had delivered his fish to *La Maison* and told Chantel farewell, he headed for the bayou, a most happy man.

Chantel was happy, too, when she mounted the steps to the second-floor landing, unaware that her late afternoon return to *La Maison* had been observed by Tanya and Colette.

That evening, instead of her nightgown, Chantel changed into her fanciest gown. She pulled her golden tresses back with a jeweled comb, magnificently displaying the loveliness of her face.

She walked down the carpeted hallway toward the stairway no longer a sweet, innocent girl. Gabe had taught her as well as shown her a new world. She was a woman! Excitement and boldness churned within her, and she was determined to see what went on in the forbidden rooms downstairs.

Brandy's music resounded from the small parlor, and she yielded to its lure.

Adrienne saw her and, unable to stop her, followed her. She watched Chantel's bold stride and the warmth with which she greeted Brandy. She was young and inexperienced, but she was self-possessed with an air of assurance. No one could ever doubt that she was the daughter of the sensuous, sultry Lily Lemogne.

Ten

Brandy certainly had no doubt about the identity of the bewitching child in grown-up clothing and questionable surroundings. He did doubt, however, that Madame Lily had approved this public appearance. Quickly, he introduced himself and motioned for her to sit beside him on the plush, cushioned bench.

As Brandy played, she swayed with the music and unconsciously gave way to the urge to sing. Suddenly aware, she stopped singing, blushing with embarrassment. But Brandy whispered, "Keep singing. You sing like a bird, Mademoiselle. They love you."

Slowly, she began to sing again, encouraged by the outpouring of applause and eager requests for more. Brandy chuckled. "They do love you, Mademoiselle," he assured, praying he could keep her by his side, where she would be safe.

Brandy's long slender fingers launched into a popular tune, and Chantel waited for his cue and sang again. To her surprise, she found she was truly enjoying herself.

Brandy picked up the tempo and nodded to her to stand by the side of the piano where she would be free to move in time with the music.

Neither one of them noticed when Lily and Andre came to the archway, stunned by the spontaneous entertainment. "Lily," Andre whispered, barely able to contain his excitement. "Chantel has talent. Real talent."

Lily watched Andre watch her daughter. She wished Chantel could have had a doting father. Andre would have made such a perfect family man. What a shame it was that you couldn't be as wise at sixteen as you were at thirty-two!

The crowd roared with delight when Chantel took her bow and sat back on the bench with Brandy, a smug, happy smile lighting her face. "They did like me, didn't they Brandy?" she asked hesitantly, but she could tell the applause went beyond polite.

Brandy was a wiry little man, almost fragile-looking for he only stood five-and-a-half feet and weighed a hundred-thirty pounds, but Brandy's strength was in his nimble fingers. No piano player in New Orleans could tickle the ivories like he could, and Brandy knew music and he knew audiences.

"They loved you, honey. I told you that," he

declared, pleased with her — and with himself. He recognized talent when he heard it, and Chantel was a natural.

His attention intensely focused on Chantel, Brandy didn't notice Lily and Andre until they moved to the settee beside the piano. "Your mother's here," he said to Chantel, *sotto voce*.

Nervous, Chantel stole a look at her mother, unprepared for the obvious pride that glowed in Lily's eyes. Surely, she decided, she was misinterpreting Lily's reaction. On the other hand, Andre left no doubt about how he felt. "Chantel, you were terrific!" he praised, reaching over to squeeze her hand.

"Thank you, Andre," she responded softly and rose to make her exit. "I envy you, Brandy," she said wistfully. "I wish I could play like you do."

"Ah, my little canary," he countered "I wish I could sing like you. You made my night."

With a kiss for her mother and a hug for Andre, Chantel left the room, but not before she sent her mother whirling through a lifetime of memories to the moment long past but not forgotten when she'd surrendered her heart and her soul to a dashing young man with a mane of golden hair and the green eyes of a sorcerer. Never before had she encountered such a handsome, destructive man as Lucien Benoit.

His persuasive ways and silken tongue

worked a devastating magic on her. Lily, already a sultry beauty, had a full-bloom figure and a sensual air. The Lemogne family were not wealthy, but they were certainly not poor. Lily had been raised in a strict atmosphere by parents who adored her. She was their youngest and had come into their lives when her sister and brother were already married.

Lily had barely turned fifteen when both her parents fell victim to yellow fever and died. Bereft, a stranger in the home of her aunt, Lily needed to be loved and Lucien showed her that she was in a hundred tangible ways. A month later she was pregnant and Lucien was gone.

She had an inheritance that far exceeded the income of her aunt and uncle, and so—for five years—Lily and her baby lived in comfort and no one dared condemn her. But when her funds were gone, so, too, was the security she'd taken for granted.

She had no skills, and her one asset was her beauty. Men responded to her, providing she was ready to do some favors for favors. She justified her means of support with a logic borne of urgency. She would be doing nothing more than she'd done with Lucien—except that she would be paid for her services and paid handsomely.

Degraded by her work at *La Maison*, Lily rebuilt her self-esteem as her income increased and she realized that she had an inherent business sense and a flair for covering up the seamy with a gilt and glitter that almost made this back-street world fashionable.

When the old madame stepped down, Lily Lemogne stepped in and made *La Maison* her own. At last she could retire from the floor and concentrate on making her house and her girls the most desirable—and profitable—attraction on the dark side of New Orleans.

And as Chantel grew, Lily saw in her the father the girl had never known. She had his same emerald-green eyes, and—tonight—the flirting glint was painfully strong. "She'll be wanting to do this again," Lily said to Andre. "But I can't allow that."

"I know, *chèrie*. I'd already thought about it myself," he admitted. "Chantel enjoyed herself this evening. You saw her face. She was radiant."

But Chantel was already making her own plans.

In two days' time, she would be on her way to Boston, traveling light, the way she had come.

She would have liked to have been with Gabe one more time, but she would be gone before he returned to the docks. But she had the memory of him and the memory of singing tonight and the applause that was hers alone. She was no longer the wide-eyed inno-

96

cent girl who arrived from Boston only a matter of weeks ago. That girl was gone for good.

Chantel didn't fool herself about returning to Boston, school, and Aunt Laurie. Never again would she be content with what she had had after having seen this other side of life. She did not approve of *La Maison*, but she was frightened to know that her roots were there and that Gabe had unleashed within herself the sensuality that was her mother's trademark.

She had to get away.

Eleven

A pleasant atmosphere surrounded Chantel
and her mother the next morning as they had
an early luncheon together. How unfair,
Chantel thought, that now that she was leaving things should be this nice between them.

Chantel noticed that Lily was already
dressed in a very chic ensemble rather than
her usual dressing gown. Elegant and black,
the dress had a high neckline and bore no resemblance to her evening attire.

"You look very grand, Mother," she said as
Lily altered the tilt of her hat.

"Well, thank you, sweetie. I'll see you
later," Lily replied, picking up a pair of
gloves and rushing to the door. "I've got
some business details to attend to."

Chantel, left to her own devices, wandered
aimlessly through the cavernous house, always
so dead in the morning hours. She'd bought
a new whittling knife for Jonah, but he had
driven her mother into town so she couldn't

measure the progress of his still featureless sculpture.

There was no sign of Raul in the kitchen, and she was beginning to feel alone and lonely until she spotted Adrienne heading upstairs, a cup of tea sloshing on a small round tray. She rushed to catch up with her.

"You were great last night," Adrienne said right off. "We couldn't talk about anything else for the rest of the evening."

"Thank you," Chantel replied modestly, wishing Adrienne would stay and talk.

"I have to get this up to Tanya," Adrienne apologized, indicating the tea. "She's not feeling well at all."

"Could I go, too?" Chantel asked. Adrienne shook her head.

"Your mother wouldn't like it," she admonished.

"I'm a big girl," Chantel retorted. "I can go down that wing anytime I wish, and I wish to go now. I'm not a child."

"No, honey," Adrienne had to agree. "You are certainly no child—not with a figure like that. Come on then, but you tell Lily it was your idea not mine."

"What's the matter with Tanya?" Chantel asked as they moved into the forbidden second-floor wing.

"Just an upset stomach." Adrienne saw no

reason to tell Chantel that it happened every time Justin St. Clair took a turn with Tanya. Tanya had the right to say no—Lily was understanding about that—but Justin paid well and Tanya needed the money. All of them needed the money. They didn't work at *La Maison* for any other reason.

Tanya's auburn hair was fanned out on the pillow and her complexion was pale, but she raised up on her elbow when she saw Chantel, a quizzical look on her face.

"She wanted to come see you." Adrienne dismissed Chantel's presence tersely and gave Tanya the cup of hot tea. "Here, honey," she urged, "drink this."

"That's mighty sweet of you, Chantel," Tanya said between sips. "I'm glad you're here because I wanted to tell you that your singing was the one bright spot in the evening. I felt so awful all night, but I forgot for a little while how miserable I was when I heard you. You brought the parlor to life."

Chantel beamed, but her concern for Tanya overpowered her pride. "Maybe you shouldn't try to work tonight," she suggested. Her manner was practical and unembarrassed, and the two women realized that Lily's daughter knew the truth.

When Tanya closed her eyes and drifted off to sleep Chantel accompanied Adrienne into her room across the hall.

"Why do you work here?" Chantel asked with her customary directness, but Adrienne liked her candid, honest manner.

"For me," she confessed, feeling an honest question deserved an honest answer in return, "it was heaven to come to *La Maison*. I'd never lived in such lavish surroundings or had all the good food I could possibly want to eat. And your mother is a very nice lady to work for." She paused and took a deep breath. "I do no more than I was doing for a no-good husband, and I sure didn't get any money from him for the services I performed."

"You've been married?" Chantel asked, surprised.

"I still might be as far as I know, but that doesn't really matter to me. I don't care if I ever marry again." Her voice had taken on a hard, strident edge.

"But you're so beautiful, Adrienne," Chantel protested.

"I had to count on that, honey," she said bitterly. "I had nothing else with which to earn a living." She laughed a humorless laugh. "I was one of ten kids of a dirt-poor farmer. I had a new baby hanging on my hip every year from the time I was nine. By fifteen I was married and a slave to the farmer

101

next acreage over." A shadow crossed her face but she went on. "I had two miscarriages. You can't carry a baby when you're out plowing a field. But I guess it was for the best. I was growing old before my time and I hated the man I was married to, so I ran away. I figured anything would be better than what I had."

"Was it?" Chantel asked softly.

"Honey when you get that desperate, nothing else matters." She sat very still, remembering. "It was carnival time, and I've never seen the city that festive since. But I didn't have one red cent and I was cold and hungry and tired. I curled up on the steps of a place called Fat Fannie's. It was a house of pleasure but not high class like *La Maison*." She stared, unseeing, at the plush velvet overstuffed chairs and the rich brocade draperies in her room. "But I got fed and I had a roof over my head and I stayed there for the next six months. I made enough money to get myself some clothes, my looks improved, and I was happier than I'd ever been."

Looking up, she sensed Chantel's questions and answered them without having to be asked. "I never felt any shame, Chantel," she declared. "I still don't. That is the way it is for me. I was married to a man who thought he had the right to beat me any time the notion struck him just because he was my husband. I was scared then, but I don't have to be scared ever again. I'm safe here." Adrienne gave Chantel an encouraging smile. "I pray you're never taken down the path I had to walk."

Back in her room, getting ready for dinner, Chantel fought a wave of sadness that swept over her. She'd had great expectations when she'd arrived, but nothing had been as she'd anticipated.

She thought about Gabe O'Roarke and how she had felt when he made love to her. She'd allowed him to undress her, and his appraising eyes had seen her nude body. His hands had explored her most private places, and his flesh and hers had pressed together, becoming fused.

Aunt Laurie would have called her a wanton woman. Did that make her her mother's daughter? And what about Gabe? He'd spoken sweet words of love to her, but he'd not asked her to marry him.

She dismissed her questions and her guilt. While she was alone, she wanted to pack so she would be ready to leave when the time came.

She folded two simple gowns into her valise. One was a sprigged-muslin afternoon frock, and the other one was a blue-green

103

gown with a white lace collar and cuffs. She took her white wool shawl and her nightgowns. Her bag was bulging, but she put all her jewelry into a velvet pouch and tucked it inside the valise.

Next, she slipped into the pretty lavender gown she had laid on the bed to wear this evening. She pinned a cluster of matching velvet flowers in her hair above her ear. Checking her image in the mirror, she was reassured that she looked as beautiful as she felt. She was ready to make her appearance in her mother's upstairs parlor.

Lily was enjoying a glass of Chardonnay and she looked most elegant in her gold brocade gown. On the table next to the settee bloomed Andre's latest bouquet of yellow roses.

Lily invited her to share a glass of wine with her. "Andre will be dining with us tonight," she told Chantel. "I hope you don't mind."

"Oh, you know I don't, mother. I'm very fond of Andre," she smiled. In fact, she considered the smartest thing her mother could do would be to marry Andre Deverone. There was no question in Chantel's mind that he adored her mother. One of these days Lily Lemogne was going to grow too old to run *La Maison* and she would no longer be the striking looking lady she was today; Andre would be a good man to have at her side when the bloom was off the rose.

Since this would be her last evening at *La Maison,* she was glad that Andre would be joining them. He would always have a very dear spot in her heart.

Twelve

Chantel woke up early, dressed, and dashed down the back stairs to find Jonah. She had the knife to give to him, but she also had another reason for seeking him out.

She had lain awake through the night until she'd come up with a plan to get her from *La Maison* to the *Southern Belle* in time for its four o'clock departure. Jonah was an essential ingredient. She found him on his usual bench under the oak tree.

"A good morning to you, miss," he greeted her. "You are as bright and pretty as that nice sunshine warming me."

She sat down beside him and, with an impish grin, told him, "Well, just because you're so nice, I got something for you." She handed him the velvet-lined case. He didn't open the box right away, but looked at it for a few moments and then remarked, "And you went and got this for me? Now, ain't you a sweet, thoughtful child. Bless your heart,

Miss Chantel. I surely thank you."

"My pleasure, Jonah," she said, pleased at his delight. She watched him lift the lid, shake his head in amazement and examine the blade.

"My, my, my," he breathed, "that's one fine knife. I'll whittle something special for you, Miss Chantel."

While he tested the metal against his block of wood, Chantel asked casually, "Do you think my mother will be needing you this afternoon, Jonah?"

"No, ma'am, not that I know of." He fixed an eye on her. "You need me to drive you somewhere?"

"Yes. I want to take a valise down to the dock to ship back to Boston. Could you take me there about three?"

"About three?" He rubbed his chin, contemplating the day ahead. "Sure I can, miss," he said at last. "I don't see why not."

That settled, all she had to worry about was getting out to the buggy without being seen. But afternoons at *La Maison* tended to be quiet, a routine she was counting on.

She went through the ritual of a late brunch with her mother and it was almost two when Chantel left her mother's rooms. Lily surprised her when she followed her into the hall.

"Are you going somewhere, mother?" Chantel asked, her heart pounding in alarm. If Lily needed Jonah, Chantel would be stranded.

"I've got a couple of hours to put in down in my office," Lily told her. "Budgets and accounts, the evils of running a business—any business."

Chantel almost sighed with relief. Barricaded in her office, Lily would be oblivious and out of the way. Her plan was working.

In her room, she changed into her traveling outfit. She'd laid the jacket out on the bed, her reticule on top of it. The bottle-green bonnet was on the chair.

The hands of the clock told her that it was almost three. She placed the note she had written to her mother on her dressing table. When she had tied the ribbons of her bonnet, she was ready to make her exit from her room and leave *La Maison*. She could hardly breathe as she opened the door and struggled with the heavy valise. What would she say if she encountered Mimi in the hallway?

But she didn't. Chantel laboriously made her way through the hall to the back stairway and down the steps. She didn't run into anyone until she emerged from the back door and Jonah scurried to meet her. "Missy, missy," he chided, "that's too heavy for a tiny little lady like you."

He took charge immediately and Chantel, grateful, worried that she had packed too much. But a few minutes later, they were rolling down the street toward the docks.

Chantel's green eyes scanned the quay for the *Louisiana Lady,* but Gabe's boat wasn't in port. She felt a prick of disappointment, even though she had known he would be in the bayou at midweek.

So far everything had gone smoothly, and Chantel was elated, but now she faced the last barrier.

She allowed Jonah to carry the valise into the office, but she quickly dismissed him as soon as he had the valise inside the door. "I'll join you shortly, Jonah," she promised, "as soon as I attend to this."

"Yes, ma'am," he replied, unquestioning— at least on the surface.

Jonah didn't have to wait long. In fact, he had barely climbed back into the buggy, when Chantel came out the door. She had lingered inside long enough to take a deep intake of breath and prepare for the lie she was about to tell.

She was a grand little actress as she dashed out to Jonah. "I met up with my friend, Gabe," she said with girlish excitement. "He'll see that I get back to *La Maison.*"

There was a skeptical look on the old black man's face, but he did not argue with her. Yet, he could not resist asking, "Are you sure, Miss Chantel, that I should go on back?" She flashed him one of her loveliest smiles, and her dainty hand covered his weathered one as she reassured him.

"It will be just fine, Jonah," she affirmed. "Believe me. You go on back to *La Maison*."

She watched until he had turned the buggy around and headed back home. Only then did she reenter the office. A short time later, she was boarding the *Southern Belle* along with the other passengers who were going to be traveling up the eastern coastline.

As the port of New Orleans receded into the distance, she felt another wave of sadness wash over her. The handsome Irishman who'd stolen her heart would be at the levee on Friday looking for her. She was leaving many people she'd become fond of and she would remember forever the night she'd sung downstairs while Brandy played his piano.

She thought of Andre and his sister, Jacqueline, who'd been kind and gracious to her. She'd liked chatting with Adrienne — just as if she were one of her friends at boarding school. Old Jonah was very dear to her and it had pained her to lie to him, although — from the look in his dark, concerned eyes —

she doubted that she'd fooled him.

As for her mother, whether she approved or disapproved of *La Maison,* Chantel had never known any woman more vivacious or exciting than Lily Lemogne.

By the time the sun had set, Chantel could no longer see New Orleans. She finally moved away from the railing to go to her cabin. She could be calling the *Southern Belle* home for the next few days.

She took out her two gowns and gave them a couple of shakes before hanging them up. She would have to wear those three dresses over and over until she got back to Boston.

She decided on the bottle-green frock with the white-lace collar to wear to the ship's dining room for dinner. She let her mind dwell only briefly on tonight's evening meal at *La Maison*. Lily would have surely read her note by now, and there would be no mystery as to where she was. The *Southern Belle* had been traveling through the gulf waters for almost four hours.

Chantel, looking over the schedule, knew that their first port would be Biloxi, Mississippi, for a brief stopover. But in Mobile, Alabama, they were in port for an hour.

Refreshed, her golden hair shining, she put

111

aside thoughts of home and her itinerary. She was ready to go to the dining room for dinner.

She made a fetching sight as she swayed into the already-crowded dining room, and more than one gent's eyes ogled her. Chantel was very aware of the attention she aroused.

Carter Bascombe found himself mesmerized by her, his interest whetted when he realized she was alone. What a streak of luck, he thought.

He was a dapper dandy that always searched for a pretty, young thing traveling unattended. Clever and cunning, he had a way about him that encouraged young ladies to trust him. They believed him a most gallant gentleman, but Carter was hardly that.

He abandoned his glass of wine and sauntered to Chantel's table.

Graciously, he introduced himself. "Since I am alone and so are you," he said, assuming a hesitant air, "I wondered if it would offend you if I sat at your table. The room is crowded tonight, and couples are waiting to be seated."

Her back to the entrance, Chantel never thought to question what he told her. How considerate, she thought, noting that he was as impeccably dressed as Andre Deverone. She agreed to his suggestion.

112

"Ah, thank you, Mademoiselle. You're very kind," Bascombe smiled as he pulled out a chair and sat down. Gazing across the table at her lovely face, Carter realized that she was even more beautiful then he'd first thought.

He found her a delightful and talkative dinner companion. He liked her soft laugh and twinkling eyes so alive and flashing with spirit. By the time they'd finished dessert, he knew she was heading for Boston.

"And where are you bound for, Carter," she asked.

"Charleston, South Carolina," he replied.

"Do you live there?"

"Yes, I do." Chantel had no reason to doubt him, but she should have because his easy conversation was filled with lies.

She rose to leave with a friendly smile. "It was nice to meet you," she said, "but I must go back to my cabin now. It's been a long day." When Carter offered to escort her, she politely refused.

He had expected her to accept, but he did not allow his disappointment to reflect on his face. "Well, perhaps we will see one another on the deck tomorrow afternoon," he said and stood — every inch the gentleman — as she made her exit.

As she walked down the long passageway

113

to her cabin, she speculated about Carter Bascombe. He was a most charming, entertaining man—older than Gabe but not as old as Andre. He had Andre's polish, but she had been very aware of how his eyes continually appraised her throughout dinner. Perhaps that was what had prompted her to refuse him to escort her to her cabin. She had learned well from Gabe O'Roarke, and instinctively she had known that Carter Bascombe was attracted to her. But not just Carter.

As she'd left the dining room, she had moved past the other tables, and had seen the other men. She had seen the appreciation on their faces and she would not have been human if she had not felt a little smug.

Men found her attractive. She smiled to herself. Their response did not offend her at all.

There was no question about it, the innocent girl who'd arrived in New Orleans in the early summer was not the same knowledgeable young woman who left the city late in August.

Well, she thought, thankful for the guardian angel that had protected her in her inexperience, she wasn't naive anymore.

Part Two

Escapade

Thirteen

Mimi had never seen Madame Lily in such a state. Returning from her daughter's bedroom, a piece of stationery in her hand, she literally barked at Mimi. "Go fetch Jonah," she told her tersely and poured herself a stiff drink and lit one of her Turkish cigarettes.

She read Chantel's note again. *La Maison* wasn't for her, she had written. She was returning to Boston.

Lily understood, and she was hurt and angry. A raging tigress, she flung the note on the table and began to pace the room. She might not have been a conventional mother, but she loved her daughter and had never once thought of giving her up. Although she had been young, pregnant, and without a husband, through blood, sweat, and tears, she'd managed. More than managed — Chantel lived in the lap of luxury. Pouring herself another whiskey, Lily allowed the hurt to fester. Nothing she'd done had been appreciated.

117

Her daughter was a snob who turned her nose up at her.

Well, her secrets were all out now, and soon Laurie, too, would know everything. "I don't care," Lily muttered, stubbing out her cigarette. "I really don't give a damn."

When Jonah tentatively entered the parlor, she ordered him to sit down.

"You took my daughter to the wharf today, Jonah?" she asked in a brusque voice.

"Sure did, ma'am," he answered with forced brightness. "She told me she had to get a valise shipped back to her aunt. But I didn't bring her back home because she met up with a friend who was going to bring her back." His weathered, wrinkled face took on a look of concern. "Did I do something wrong, madame?"

"No, Jonah, you did absolutely nothing wrong," Lily assured him. "Everything is all right, and tomorrow you are going to have a nice, quiet day to enjoy the gardens and carve your wooden figures."

A broad grin sprang across Jonah's face. "I sure will, ma'am," he said. "Miss Chantel gave me a fine new knife this morning. She's one sweet child, she is." He fumbled in his pocket and pulled out the knife to show to Lily, who nodded vaguely and then dismissed him.

Lily, adhering to her usual routine, said nothing to Mimi until the little maid was styling her hair. "I'll be having my late night dinner with Andre tonight," she advised her. "My daughter has returned to Boston."

"Oh, no madame! I am sorry to hear that." Mimi sighed, for she heard the pain in Madame Lily's voice. Chantel, she thought, had acted foolishly. She was so lucky and didn't know it. But one day—Mimi shivered with a sense of foreboding—she would realize how much love she had waiting for her at *La Maison*. In the meantime, everything was the way it had been before the young miss had changed them all.

Carter Bascombe had a sharp, calculating mind which contributed to his success in his profession. He had recognized immediately that the little pearls Chantel had worn on her ears were the real thing and not fakes. Her gown had an exclusive, salon design, and the collar was of French or Belgian lace. He had only to look at the softness of her hands to know that she was pampered and unaccustomed to hard work. And her flawless complexion also told him that this little creature was a rare gem.

But there was so much more that his piercing eyes had surveyed in his brief time with her. He'd seen the wasplike waist and the full breasts pressing against the bodice of her gown. The soft, flowing skirt had not concealed the firmness of her hips, and he could imagine their appeal if she were bare of those folds of material in the skirt. She was, he assessed, a golden goddess.

Carter Balcombe had been a jewelry salesman for the last fifteen years, but very early on he had expanded his business to include more lucrative services as a procurer for a wealthy restauranteur in Charleston, South Carolina. His client had an insatiable appetite for young ladies of rare beauty. Since none ever held his interest long, Carter was constantly in the market for a new enchantress to excite Antoine Savanti. Savanti's fees for a belle that pleased him made it well worth the effort.

About a year ago Carter had found a most exciting nymph in the bayou just outside New Orleans. She'd had a dark, haunting bloom and a wild, earthy spirit that had thrilled Antoine for many months. But eventually he'd tired of her and told Carter to look for a new girl.

And Carter had been looking, but he had not been able to find a young woman so lovely that she could outshine the dark beauty of Delphine. An ordinary pretty girl

120

was not what Antoine wanted. Chantel, Carter had sensed instantly, was and he was already looking forward to the handsome compensation she would bring.

He began his campaign that very afternoon, rushing to her side pretending that he had just spotted her. She consented to a leisurely stroll around the deck and sat beside him in a lounge chair looking out over the water.

By the time he escorted her back to her cabin, Carter had managed to get a promise from her to join him for dinner.

"A beautiful lady like you should be escorted to the dining room," he admonished gently. "You can't possibly know what kind of characters you might encounter on a ship like this."

Chantel found herself appreciating Carter Bascombe's concern for her aboard the ship. So she agreed that he could pick her up at seven.

Back in his own cabin, Carter hunted through his jewelry display case. Women of all ages loved receiving trinkets, he'd discovered, so he checked his strings of beads for the perfect gift to present to Chantel. He selected a strand of clear crystal that would go with any color of gown she might be wearing that night.

121

He lifted the necklace from the case and coiled it into a velvet pouch, a smug grin on his face. The jewelry would help lay the groundwork to entice her from the ship when they reached Charleston.

He chose his evening wear with equal exactitude, for Carter Bascombe was a fastidious dresser. He knew how to create the exact impression he desired, a technique he had perfected over the years.

Chantel, trusting and unaware of his cunning, was grateful to have an older man looking out for her welfare aboard the *Southern Belle*.

She wore the bottle-green silk gown but didn't need the matching light wool jacket. As she had promised, she was ready when Carter knocked on her door. She picked up her velvet green reticule from the bunk and slipped into the passageway. There was no reason for Carter to enter her cabin.

She didn't protest when he took her arm, convinced by now of his gallantry. He was polite and well-mannered and made no untoward advances. She enjoyed his company and conversation and relaxed over a glass of wine before dinner. And even the meal was delicious. She had the roast duck with an orange marmalade sauce over a bed of herbed rice and found that it rivaled Raul's talents.

"I also stop along the Florida coastline and at Savannah," Carter told her, describing his jewelry route which frequently took him to Mobile and New Orleans.

"You are truly a traveling man, aren't you Carter?" Chantel remarked as she took another sip of her wine.

He laughed. "Constantly, Chantel. I get home in Charleston for only a few days before I'm off again, but then I have no wife or family so everything works out quite well."

"I suppose it would," she mused. "It wouldn't be a very happy life if there were a wife and children to constantly be left behind."

"It would be impossible to leave a family." He affected a sad air, held onto the sense of dreams lost, and then brightened as if for her benefit.

"I have a little gift to give you tonight," he told her. Pulling the velvet pouch from his pocket, he handed it to her.

As she withdrew the strand of crystals, the beads reflected a rainbow of colors as the light from the dining-room chandelier gleamed on them. "They're beautiful, Carter," she said slowly, examining the necklace. "I thank you very much."

"It's a token," he explained. "A memento of this night when we've gone our separate ways." He immediately rose up from his chair to go around the table to assist her in fastening the clasp of the crystal beads.

Her gown had a high neckline, and Carter congratulated himself for he had picked out the perfect piece of jewelry to present to her. He looked down at her with a warm smile on his face. "They look very pretty against your lovely green gown, Chantel," he told her in all honesty.

"They are lovely and I thank you again," she replied, fingering the strand. "That was very thoughtful of you."

Even though Carter had made sure that he had done everything just right, Chantel declined a moonlit stroll and asked to be escorted directly to her cabin.

Had Carter been anticipating a good-night kiss at the door, he would have been sadly disappointed. She became distant and formal the minute they left the dining room for the darkness of the deck.

After he'd seen her to her room he went back on deck and stood by the railing, inhaling the smoke from one of his favorite cheroots. How would he get this prim package out to Antoine's mansion? The *Southern Belle* had a two-hour stay in port in Charleston before sailing on to Wilmington and Norfolk.

But he had begun to suspect that Chantel would prove more difficult than the gullible Delphine. Delphine hadn't questioned his assurance that they could be back long before her departure time.

But this green-eyed vixen Chantel was a challenge.

Fourteen

All day Friday Gabe kept searching the wharves for some sign of the golden-haired schoolgirl he had lost his heart to just a few weeks ago. He wanted time alone with her again in his quarters on the *Louisiana Lady,* but she never appeared. So he was impatient when he prepared the delivery order for *La Maison* late that afternoon.

He encountered old Jonah in the back gardens and heard the startling news about Chantel. A frown creased his brow as he quizzed the old black man, certain he must be confused. But Jonah insisted Chantel had returned to Boston, and Gabe's head was whirling as if he were giddy from drinking too much liquor as he marched into the back door of the two-story house.

Raul gave him a warm greeting. "Ah, Gabe," he said, "you got me some more of that fresh-caught fish of yours."

"That I have, Raul." Gabe forced a carefree smile onto his face. He set the huge pile of fish on the worktable in the kitchen. Raul took the money out of his apron pocket for the fish delivery, but Gabe wasn't ready to leave until he had verified old Jonah's claim. "Is it true about Chantel?" he asked.

Raul nodded soberly, confirming the awful truth. "She left without a word to anyone."

Devastated, Gabe left without comment, and it took Raul awhile to comprehend. It was only when he turned his attention back to his pots and pans that Raul realized that the handsome young Gabe was infatuated with Mademoiselle Chantel.

More fortunate than Gabe, Lily had Andre's devoted love and strength to help her come to terms with Chantel's defection. "She has to stretch her wings," he reminded her. "There is nothing you can do but wait. She'll either find what she's searching for or she'll return, possibly wounded. But no matter what, you'll be here ready to give her your love."

She had mailed off a letter to Laurie telling her what had happened and urging her to let her know the minute Chantel arrived in Boston. And, with—as Andre had said— nothing else to do, she resumed her role as hostess of *La Maison*. Once again, Andre spent whatever nights he could with her.

"Damn, Lily," he teased her as he prepared

to leave early one morning at dawn, "why don't we make this simple and just get married?" She stared at him in sleepy surprise and, encouraged, he went on. "I've got more than enough to support us the rest of our lives, and you could be a lady of leisure and my loving wife. I'm getting too damned old for these nocturnal jaunts down the streets when I should darn well be in bed for the night."

"You are tempting me," she granted, giving him a kiss on the cheek. "Perhaps, I'm ready."

Andre's strong arms encircled her as he pulled her to his broad chest. "Lily, it could be the answer to everything," he pledged. "You know we could be happy, and I do adore you."

Her dark eyes warmed as she gazed up at him. "It has been enough for me to love and be loved by you, honey," she affirmed.

"I'm greedy," he grinned. "I want us to have more time together. I will never have it until you marry me and give up *La Maison*."

She had much to consider for another man like Andre might never come her way again and she hardly looked forward to operating *La Maison* into her dotage. "A month," she whispered. "Give me six weeks at the most and then we'll be married."

* * *

It was an oppressive, hot day as the *Southern Belle* plowed southward along the coast of Florida and Chantel sought the comfort of the cool cabin instead of the ship's sun deck.

Carter had made three trips out on the deck in search of her, all to no avail. But a visit to Chantel's cabin, couched in friendly, adult solicitude, proved equally unrewarding.

When he knocked on her door and called out her name about three o'clock in the afternoon, he got no response. Chantel was stretched out across her bunk wearing only her undergarments, allowing the breeze coming through the small window to cool her. She lay still, making no sound or effort to answer Carter's rap. After awhile, everything was silent once more and she fell asleep.

She awoke famished and headed immediately for the dining room and an early supper.

She decided on the light sprigged-muslin gown with its short pouf sleeves. It was her coolest dress. If it continued to be this hot along the Florida coast then, her clothes would be stained and damp from the muggy air before they rounded the peninsula and headed north again.

She pulled her thick hair away from her

129

face and tied a black velvet ribbon around it. She had meant to look older and worldly on this trip, but with her hair done up like Alice in Wonderland and her simple frock suggestive of little-girl fashion, she looked even younger.

As she had done the first evening on the ship, she entered the dining room alone to take her seat at a table, receiving many admiring glances. Tonight, she didn't linger over a glass of wine, but ordered dinner immediately. The roast chicken and stuffing sounded divine and the generous serving was in line with her ravenous appetite.

She had almost finished her dinner by the time Carter sauntered into the spacious dining room. Her back was to the door and her hairstyle was different, but he recognized her immediately and went directly to her table.

"I'm glad to see that you are all right," he said, relief evident in his voice. "I was concerned that you might be ailing when I didn't see you. I even came by your cabin to check on you, but I didn't get a response when I knocked."

"It was so miserable and hot that I slept all afternoon. I didn't hear you knock," she lied.

He saw that she had finished her meal but urged her to have a glass of wine while he

130

ate. "I'd enjoy your pleasant company, Chantel," he asserted.

"Well, I suppose I could," she replied. It was sweet of him to be concerned about her. He ordered her a liqueur and then a delectable little dessert she couldn't refuse—a pastry shell filled with custard that reminded her of Raul's specialties. When they finished, she accepted Carter's invitation for a stroll.

As they left the dining room to go out on deck, a cooling breeze greeted them. Several couples had obviously had the same idea now that the scorching sun had set and a light wind blew in over the water.

Chantel found that she was enjoying walking with Carter. He was an entertaining man with a repertoire of funny anecdotes about the jewelry business.

She had to say that he was certainly a nice man by the time he had seen her to her cabin an hour later. He had not sought to take advantage of her in the darkness as some men might have. He made no attempt on the dimly lit deck or in the isolated passageway as they'd said good night at her door. He had been gallant and attentive and had not once taken advantage of a young lady traveling alone.

By the time the *Southern Belle* had gone to the southern tip of the coastline of Florida and veered back toward St. Augustine, Carter was encouraged. He was certain that he'd won Chantel's trust. Now he could move on to stage two: The fabrication of a convincing story to lure his unsuspecting victim into his trap.

Tomorrow they would dock in Savannah, and then it was only a short distance on to Charleston. He had no time to waste.

During dinner he turned on the charm. "I can't believe that I'm going to be parting company with you, Chantel," he lamented. "This trip has gone by far too fast."

"You've made it a very pleasant trip for me, too, Carter," she told him.

"I'm glad to hear you say that," he enthused. "I know it can't be, but it would be nice if I could show you around Charleston. Your city of New Orleans is fabulous, but so is Charleston. It is picturesque and quaint."

Chantel listened as he described the historic district that made the past live again as part of the present. "You make me want to see your city," Chantel admitted, "but I fear I can't do that on this trip."

"I know, Chantel. I really do." Carter assumed a wistful mien. "It was just wishful thinking. But you could see some of the city. You've a long layover in Charleston, and I'd welcome your spending a couple of hours as my guest." Carter seemed to be excited as if seized with an idea. "I'd love for you to meet my uncle. He lives only about fifteen minutes from the harbor in one of the finest old houses in Charleston. We'd have time for an hour's visit and I could still have you back to the *Southern Belle* long before it sailed."

"I'll think about it," she said, wavering, and gave him hope.

"Most of the passengers take advantage of the opportunity to get their feet on the ground during the long wait," Carter went on. "However I wouldn't want you to go out on your own in Charleston." Carter shook his head, a serious, concerned look darkening his face. "A young girl alone can't be too careful."

Chantel saw that she had two options. She could remain in her cabin during the long stopover in Charleston or she could accept Carter's gracious invitation.

She certainly didn't wish to wander around a strange city by herself. She wasn't that foolhardy anymore.

Fifteen

A heavy downpour of rain moved in over the entire eastern coastline in the next few hours. Passengers boarding the ship in Savannah were drenched, as were the passengers disembarking for the carriages below.

Chantel had remained in her cabin throughout the afternoon, and when she joined Carter that evening for dinner, she wore her blue-green gown with the white-lace collar. Around her shoulders she had draped her wool shawl, for the rains had brought a chill to the night air.

She chided herself for not remembering that it was much cooler in Boston this time of the year. She should have packed her wool cape, but she could hardly fret about that now.

Despite the dismal rain outside, a gay atmosphere permeated the dining room. Carter, anticipating the handsome fee Antoine would pay him, could not have been in higher spirits. Chantel had told him that she would accompany him to his uncle's house when they docked in

Charleston. "But I don't want to impose upon him, Carter. After all, I would be arriving there with you unannounced."

"Ah, Uncle Antoine will be delighted, Chantel. He's an old man, and he gets lonely in that big old mansion by himself. You don't have to worry about that." Carter Bascombe could be a most convincing liar.

When Carter returned to his own cabin that evening, he was full of congratulations for himself. He pulled out the flask from the drawer of the chest by his bed and took a hearty gulp from it and thought about tomorrow.

When they arrived at Antoine's estate, his housekeeper, Jessamine, would meet them at the big front door and guide Chantel to a particular bedroom to refresh herself. Carter would be taken to Antoine to discuss particulars.

Antoine would excuse himself after their brief conversation to go to an adjoining room where he could look through a peephole he'd had installed in order to preview the merchandise.

If she met with his requirements, then Antoine would return to Carter and close the deal in cash. Carter would quickly take his leave. He never looked back and he had never lost sleep over any of the girls who'd remained behind in the sadistic hands of Antoine Savanti!

The rains that had pelted the *Southern Belle*

that evening in Savannah had produced torrents of rain up the coast in Charleston.

Once Jessamine was through with her duties in the big house, she was free to go to her own quarters over the carriage house. She was always glad to get to her own little haven.

The black woman didn't like or approve of the goings on inside Antoine Savanti's house. If she had been younger, she would have left long ago, but she had nowhere to go. She'd lost track of her older brother, and her husband had died almost eight years ago.

She'd had no inkling, when she'd first hired on as Monsieur Savanti's housekeeper, the kind of man he was. She'd known that wealthy white men had their pretty mistresses, whether they were white or the lovely octoroons and quadroons. So she'd not been too shocked when two or three young beauties had taken up residence in the palatial mansion.

Later, she began to question why they never stayed long and suddenly disappeared. But Jessamine, with no alternative for herself, merely attended to the job she'd been hired to do.

Monsieur Savanti could be a most generous man, and he was to her. One night, when she had fixed him her special oysters à la Jessamine, he had presented her with a magnificent string of pearls.

And another time, when he had spilled wine on his favorite velvet robe and she'd managed to clean it successfully for him, he was so grateful that he'd told her to hold out her hand. When she had, he had filled her palm with gold coins and told her, "Jessamine, you are worth all this gold to me."

But Monsieur Savanti was also disturbingly eccentric, bizarre. Jessamine had become all the more aware of his monstrous capabilities over the last year. His latest conquest struck a nerve in her, and the first time she saw her bruised, lovely face, Jessamine was fired with a drive to protect her.

She was a tiny little thing who insisted that she was almost nineteen.

Delphine was from New Orleans, and so was Jessamine—born and raised in the bayou.

It had been a miserable two months, Delphine bearing the bruises of Monsieur Savanti's brutal treatment. Finding a private moment alone with Delphine, Jessamine had urged her to escape. "You got to get out of here, honey," she'd whispered urgently, "or that man's going to kill you."

"I know, Jessamine, and I'm going to," the girl had replied, "but I've got to save enough to get back to New Orleans. Did you know that old bastard has money hidden all over this house?"

"Honey, you don't have that long to hunt it up." Jessamine had warned. "You make a plan," she'd said, "and I'll help you."

But they never had the luxury of a plan, for late the next night Jessamine found Delphine

137

battered and bleeding on the carriage-house stairs.

Her lips were swollen and caked with blood. Bloodstains covered her sheer, blue nightgown. Jessamine tugged the girl's limp body into her room. She removed the wet gown from her bleeding body and with difficulty hefted her onto the bed and tucked a blanket around her trembling frame. "You're safe here, Miss Delphine," she soothed. "Jessamine is going to take care of you. When you're able to travel we're going to get you back to New Orleans where you belong."

Jessamine noticed that her words seemed to calm the girl so she left her to put a fire under her teakettle and mix a healing balm for her wounds. In the bedroom she took one of her own clean gowns to replace the stained and torn negligee.

They could hear the heavy downpour of rain on the carriage house roof, but Jessamine's quarters were warm and cozy; and Delphine, propped up on pillows, drank the healing cup of tea Jessamine had brewed for her.

Before she dimmed the lamp, Jessamine assured Delphine that she was safe. "But you must stay hidden until we can slip you out," she warned. "Do you hear me, Miss Delphine?"

"I hear you, Jessamine, and I'll do whatever you say," Delphine replied, her eyes closing against her will.

The black woman crawled into the bed beside her. "Tomorrow's another day, Miss Delphine," she murmured almost as she would a prayer. "And we're going to greet it just being grateful you lived through this night. You could surely be dead right now."

"And I thank God for you, Jessamine," Delphine prayed, her hand reaching out for Jessamine's.

Jessamine held her hand until she was certain that Delphine had drifted off to sleep. Never in her life had she hated anyone, but tonight she despised Antoine Savanti.

Morning came far too soon, and Delphine was still sleeping when Jessamine left for the big house. She'd propped a note on the table next to the bed cautioning Delphine to remain secreted inside the carriage-house apartment. She doubted, however, that Delphine was strong enough to even make it to the door.

Jessamine was well aware of the gamble she was taking. She had witnessed Monsieur Savanti's rages and did not wish to have his anger directed at her. But she would not turn her back on the pretty little girl from the bayou.

She put in her usual morning routine at the big house and saw that the cook had the menu for Antoine's evening meal. But she didn't see her employer until late afternoon when she was summoned to his office. Occupied with thoughts of Delphine, Jessamine had forgotten that this was the day of the month when Monsieur Savanti paid her wages.

As she prepared to leave the study, she paused and cleared her throat. "Would it be all right if Enos drives me into the city one afternoon this week to get this money in the bank?" she asked guilelessly.

"Any afternoon you like, Jessamine," he told her without looking up from his desk. She noticed that he was in a sullen mood and unusually quiet.

"Thank you, sir," she replied politely. She was glad to made a quick exit from the room and the sight of him.

But he was generous with her and allowed her special privileges because she was his dutiful housekeeper. By nature, Antoine was a selfish man. However he recognized that Jessamine was the most capable, hardworking housekeeper he'd ever had. And, even more important, she tended to her own business. She was not snoopy or nosey, and Antoine liked that.

So when she left the big house, Jessamine was smug in the knowledge that she had laid the groundwork to get into the city to buy Miss Delphine a ticket for home.

As she had made her way through the kitchen, she helped herself to a nice little crock of the beans simmering in Selma's pot and sliced four thick slices of the ham. Selma, amused, told her to take a cherry pie as well. "You might

140

as well," she chortled, "because the mister's goin' to be eating all by himself tonight."

"Oh?" Jessamine asked, playing dumb. "Monsieur Savanti is dining *alone?*"

Selma glided across the kitchen and bent down to tell Jessamine in a confidential tone. "His latest honey disappeared last night," she whispered. "And you know what, Jessamine? I'm glad she did. I just hope she's all right."

"So do I, Selma," Jessamine concurred and carried her feast home to share with Delphine.

The next day, the old black housekeeper slipped into Delphine's room in the big house. She gathered up some undergarments and a pair of slippers, for Delphine had run out in her bare feet. She passed by the stylish gowns Antoine had bought for the girl and instead picked out two simple dresses suitable for long-distance travel and a cape of black wool.

Three days went by, and Delphine was still weak and weary, but her mind was alert. "There's a velvet pouch in a drawer of the chest in my bedroom," she told Jessamine. "It's filled with gems which Antoine gave me when that despicable Carter brought me here. He's probably forgotten about them, but they could bring a huge amount of money." She looked squarely at Jessamine. "But please, please don't chance anything."

Jessamine laughed. "Honey, I'm the housekeeper. I could have already had them for you, and God knows you deserve them."

The next evening Delphine emptied her bounty of exquisite jewels onto the bed.

"This should more than pay for my passage home," she cried, delighted.

"No, missy," Jessamine objected sagely. "I'll buy your passage. Sell those when you get back to New Orleans and repay me then. You know what power Monsieur Savanti has here in Charleston."

"I wish I were as smart as you," Delphine sighed.

Jessamine chuckled. "The years make us all smarter, Miss Delphine, and when you've lived as long as I have, you're going to end up smarter than me."

"I sure hope so, Jessamine," Delphine confessed, "because I didn't realize what a good life I had on the bayou until I was away from it."

"We're going to get you back there, too, Miss Delphine," Jessamine assured her. "I promise you that."

Sixteen

The rain had moved away from the east coastline by the time the *Southern Belle* docked in Charleston. The sun shone through a cloudless sky as Chantel Lemogne and Carter Bascombe boarded the carriage to take them to the Savanti estate about a half-mile out of the city.

Chantel's bottle-green gown with its light wool jacket felt just right for the cooler late afternoon air that had settled in after the rains.

Jessamine was just about to leave the big house, for she had given the cook orders to serve Monsieur Savanti a tray in his bedroom suite tonight. "He is feeling poorly," she had instructed Selma as she prepared to leave.

But suddenly she found herself greeting guests at the front door — Carter Bascombe and a charming girl who Jessamine knew was destined to be Delphine's replacement.

"Good evening, Monsieur Bascombe," Jessamine said graciously despite the loathing that surged up in her.

She escorted him and his beautiful young companion to the parlor. She could tell that he was confused by this break from routine. But she quickly explained that Monsieur Savanti was ailing.

Carter nervously waited in the parlor for Jessamine's return. Would Antoine see him? Was it conceivable that he wouldn't?

When she had announced to Antoine that Carter Bascombe was downstairs, he revived quickly and ordered Jessamine to bring Carter up to his bedroom.

"Send Carter up here and see to the young lady's comforts in the guest room," he told her. Jessamine knew this procedure too well by now.

"Yes, Monsieur Savanti," she told him decorously and withdrew from the room. She carried out his dictates as she had always done, but with a different attitude.

When Jessamine returned to the parlor to announce to Carter that Monsieur Savanti would see him in his bedroom and she would see to mademoiselle, a relaxed smile came to Carter's face. So he spritely mounted the steps to Antoine's bedroom as Jessamine guided Chantel to the stairway.

As they mounted the steps, Jessamine noticed a curiosity in this young lady that she had not seen in Delphine. Chantel Lemogne did not hesitate to ask questions. "I'm sorry to hear Carter's uncle is ill," she remarked.

Jessamine, unnerved by the blatancy of Carter's deception, could no longer remain aloof. She didn't care what the future held for her. She'd had enough of the duplicity and evil in this household.

Before she left Chantel, she offered her a cup of coffee or tea and Chantel thanked her as she removed her jacket.

"Where are you from, mademoiselle?" Jessamine asked, trying to place her accent, which was a blend of North and South.

"I'm from New Orleans," Chantel told her.

"Ah, New Orleans! I lived there once," Jessamine confided.

Antoine Savanti, having gathered enough strength to peer through the peephole, was fired with eager anticipation as he gazed upon the golden-haired goddess in the adjoining room. He appraised her burnished tresses and brilliant green eyes and noted the sensuous curves of her youthful figure. Carter had certainly earned his fee this time, and Antoine paid the money willingly and dispatched the procurer from his house.

Antoine found himself so weak when he returned to his room that he collapsed on the bed. Regretfully, he consigned his lusty dreams till tomorrow.

Tomorrow he would be feeling better, he was certain, for he had the proper incentive just down the hall. She would be a tonic to heal his infirmity. So he ordered a dinner tray for himself and for his guest.

Chantel was becoming impatient after she had been waiting in the guest bedroom for almost a half-hour. What was taking Carter so long to come for her? Didn't he realize that she had to get back to the *Southern Belle?* She had no intentions of playing it close for time.

When Jessamine came into the room again, she immediately inquired about Carter. "Is he still with his uncle? I can't wait around here too much longer for I've a ship to be back on."

This young lady was not the docile type, Jessamine saw. Her eyes flashed with green fire. This little miss had spirit and wasn't going to accept for a minute that a dinner tray would be served to her. This young lady had not made plans to be here that long.

So Jessamine could do nothing but tell her the truth: That Carter Bascombe had left already and that she was now the property of Antoine Savanti. She barely had the words out before Chantel showed her fury. "I'll not stay here one minute!" she shrieked. "I'm getting out of here if I have to walk all the way back to Charleston." She picked up her jacket and reticule from the bed.

"Listen to me, mademoiselle," Jessamine pleaded, her voice low. "You wouldn't get past Monte, Monsieur Savanti's manservant and bodyguard. He's a giant of a man."

Jessamine urged her to sit back down on the bed so they might talk, and Chantel did as the black woman bade her. "Now, listen to me, child, for I'll try to help you. It's not long before dark and, lucky for you, Monsieur Savanti is ill tonight or there would be nothing I could do."

"Dear God, Jessamine, what kind of crazy house is this?" Chantel asked, apprehension settling on her lovely face.

"Later," Jessamine promised. "I'll answer what I can when there's time, but right now you do what I say and, God willing, I'll slip you out the backstairs, for you'll never make it out that front door." Hurriedly, Jessamine contrived a course of action.

"I'll go into the kitchen and distract Selma, the cook," she improvised. "Then you come down the stairs and make a run for the back door. Wait for me outside, and I'll take you to safety in my quarters above the carriage house."

Jessamine peered into the hall to see if the coast were clear. "You ready, miss?" she asked.

Chantel nodded and moved cautiously down the long hallway behind the black woman. She inched down the stairs, halting at Jessamine's

147

signal on the third step from the base. Jessamine went ahead into the kitchen.

Poised on the shadowy staircase, Chantel listened as the two women talked. When she heard Jessamine ask Selma for one of her fresh-baked loaves of bread, she held her breath. "Sure," the other woman agreed readily. "Let me go in the pantry to get it for you."

Chantel took this as her cue and dashed out the door. She had only long enough to take a deep breath of fresh air before Jessamine joined her, but it was still enough time for Chantel to wonder why the housekeeper was risking her own safety for a stranger.

"Come on, child, quick — to the carriage house," Jessamine urged her. Chantel took her arm and tried to thank her, but Jessamine waved her appreciation aside.

"I couldn't stand by and see it happen again," she said. "You'll understand better when you meet Delphine, the girl who came before you. Hurry now."

More than once Jessamine looked back over her shoulders to see if Monte were roaming the back gardens. He could slip up behind you and take you unaware. She breathed more easily once they'd begun the climb up the stairs to her quarters.

The unexpected sight of the beautiful girl coming through the door with Jessamine startled Delphine. She had just put on a pot of coffee anticipating Jessamine's arrival, and was resting in a large, soft chair.

Jessamine said simply, "Delphine, meet Chantel. Chantel, this is Delphine." Jessamine put her loaf of bread on the table after she'd taken the time to secure her door and cast a final glance out over the back grounds of the house a short distance away. She was glad to see that Delphine had drawn the curtains on the south and east side of the little apartment.

Jessamine quickly filled in the gaps of her introductions, and Delphine shook her head and sighed. "You're lucky, Chantel," she said. "You got away the first night. I wasn't as fortunate, as you can see."

Chantel's head was whirling with so much confusion that only one thing seemed clear: There was no hope of her catching the *Southern Belle* tonight.

Over fresh-brewed coffee, Delphine filled Chantel in on the finer points of Carter Bascombe's procurement scheme and Antoine Savanti's treatment of his young sex objects.

"How long were you here, Delphine? How did you stand it?" Chantel asked. "It's frightening just to listen to you."

"I was frightened," the dark-haired girl admitted. "And many a night I trembled from the revulsion and the pain he inflicted. It's been the longest year of my life."

Ostensibly puttering in her kitchen, Jessa-

149

mine was listening to the two girls talk. She had already made up her mind that since both girls were from New Orleans they should travel back there together. There was safety in numbers, and they were bound to have a comradely, protective feeling for one another.

Delphine, learning that Chantel was also from New Orleans, had only to scrutinize the girl's exquisite green gown to know that it didn't come cheap. It was like none of the simple little frocks she'd had when she'd left New Orleans, although after she'd become Antoine's playtoy, she'd had the pleasure of donning the fancy gowns he enjoyed seeing her wear.

"Where were you heading, Chantel?" Delphine asked curiously when they'd finished dinner and moved back into Jessamine's small parlor.

"Boston," Chantel told her. "My aunt lives there."

"But your mother lives in New Orleans," Delphine probed. "Were you going for a visit — or running away?"

"I didn't care to live with my mother anymore," Chantel said shortly, but she liked Delphine and added, almost in apology, "My mother owns *La Maison*. Perhaps, you've heard of it."

Delphine laughed. "I don't think anyone could live in New Orleans and not know about

La Maison," she said. "It is almost a land-mark! A gathering place New Orleans' most elite gents."

"I have no doubt of that," Chantel conceded. "But *La Maison* was not for me, so I decided to go back to my aunt's."

Jessamine left the girls to talk into the night once Chantel had assured her that she could sleep comfortably on the narrow settee in the front room.

The next morning Jessamine expected a furor at the big house once Chantel's disappearance was made known. She couldn't be sure how soon her escape would be discovered and the word would get back to Antoine.

She knew that she would delay it as long as possible. But to her amazement the atmosphere was calm when she entered the kitchen. Selma perused a dog-eared magazine, and the aroma of coffee permeated the room.

"Monsieur Savanti must be awfully ill," Selma commented, not looking up. "He didn't want any breakfast when I sent Cora up to his room."

Let him die, Jessamine thought, but kept the sentiment to herself. It would rid the world of vermin.

She planned to go into Charleston that afternoon to book Delphine's passage to New Orleans. But now she had two young girls to conceal and was uncertain what plan would be

151

best.

But in her absence, Delphine had convinced Chantel to accompany her back to the bayou. "Chantel, we're sisters in a way now," she said persuasively. "I'll take you to my home, and you'll find the answer to all your problems. I had to have been crazy to leave."

Chantel found Delphine's solution acceptable. She didn't have enough money now to replace her ticket to Boston, and she had only the clothes on her back.

Delphine quickly eased her concerns. Proudly she displayed the jewels that would cover both their passage. "Jessamine told me to wait to sell it until I got back to New Orleans," she said. "But I won't leave now without you."

That night they presented their plan to Jessamine, who approved at least in theory. But she insisted firmly that she handle all the arrangements. "I'm buying the passage for the two of you and you can pay me back later," she reiterated. "I've gotten you two young ladies this far, so don't you give me any arguments."

Impishly, they chimed in like twins, "Yes, ma'am."

Seventeen

Jessamine made her trip into the city and deposited her wages to her account at the bank, but she walked out the side door to go to buy the passage for Chantel and Delphine before she came out the door of the bank again. It took awhile, but she was protecting both herself and Enos. Should Enos ever be questioned, all he could say was that he had taken her to the bank.

However, when she and Enos returned to the Savanti estate that evening, she had the girls' tickets to freedom secured in her bag. She had chosen an early departure the next morning aboard the *Delta Queen*. They would have to walk into the city, but at least they would have the cover of darkness in leaving the grounds. That would work to their advantage.

Chantel and Delphine slept restlessly, both eager to be on their way. Jessamine didn't sleep much either, consumed with worry for these two young girls who'd become so important to her. How different they were, as different as day and night.

That night as the lamps were dimmed she embraced them both and kissed them soundly. "Don't wake me when you leave," she cautioned. "It's better if I don't see you go, but let me know when you get to New Orleans."

"You'll hear from us," Chantel promised, and Delphine nodded faithfully, not trusting herself to speak for she was close to tears at leaving the woman who had saved her life.

It was still dark when the two young girls dressed by the dimly lit lamp in the kitchen. Delphine had placed her two small bags by the door, but Chantel had no luggage, for all her belongings were on their way to Boston. Delphine had already determined that they would share.

"Are we ready, Delphine?" Chantel asked, her hand on the door latch.

"Just a minute, Chantel," her dark twin said warily. "Let me put out this lamp and take a peep outside to be sure that Monte isn't prowling the back gardens." Delphine, cloaked in black with her long ebony hair flowing over her shoulders, blended into the shades of the night. She carefully scrutinized the area until she was satisfied that it was safe to go down the steps, then motioned to Chantel. They each carried one of the bags.

Like two young gazelles they moved swiftly over the grounds, not daring to look back. Delphine guided them toward the dirt road that went by the front of the old mansion. They didn't stop to catch their breath until they had covered a fair distance. Breathlessly, they stopped in unison and broke into a gale of joyous laughter.

"We're free," Chantel declared. "Free and out of there!"

"Yes," sighed Delphine. "But I'm not going to relax until the *Delta Queen* pulls out of Charleston. You can't imagine the power that old man has around here."

Stealthily, they moved on, and it was still dark when they reached the outskirts of Charleston. Limping, their tired feet burning with blisters, they crept across the wharf. Suddenly, Delphine grabbed Chantel's arm. "There she is," she whispered, pointing. "The *Delta Queen*." Just the sight of the ship was enough to make both of them hasten their pace.

Within a half-hour they were in their assigned cabin and, to Delphine's delight, there was no delay in the departure of the *Delta Queen*.

"Now I feel I can breathe," Delphine declared as she slipped out of her slippers and rubbed her feet. Chantel did the same.

Chantel stretched out on the bunk to rest and lazily drifted off to sleep. Delphine,

155

propped up on a pillow, sat deep in thought. More than a year had passed, and now she was heading back to the home she'd run away from.

She held a little hand mirror close to her face and surveyed the bruises that were almost gone. The big ugly welts across her thighs and hips were still visible but she could keep them covered. And the pain inside her would be there forever.

But she was going back home a wiser girl and that quiet serenity of the bayou was welcoming. She would never again find it dull to be surrounded by her devoted family.

No smooth-talking stranger would dupe her again. In fact, she didn't know whether she'd ever be able to fall in love again. After all that had happened, how could she trust any man?

The torrid love affair that had impelled her to leave her home and run off with a young man she'd hardly known had lasted two months. Deserted in Savannah, Georgia, with no money and the rent paid up for only the rest of the week, Delphine had had to fend for herself.

The rest of that week she'd looked up and down the streets of Savannah for a job in the bakery and flower shops. She'd also tried the inns and a hotel to see if they needed a cleaning lady or a cook, but no one had hired the young inexperienced girl whose best asset was her striking good looks.

She hesitated in the lobby of the hotel, uncertain where to turn next. But as she headed toward the door, a well-dressed woman called to her. "Young lady," she queried, "did you say you were looking for work?"

"Yes, ma'am. I surely am." Delphine declared and promptly presented herself before the woman, who set aside her magazine and surveyed her carefully. Delphine tried to look bright and eager, but her weariness and hunger made a stronger plea.

Constance Monroe gave her a warm smile. "Let's you and I go down to one of Savannah's famous tearooms and talk about this dilemma you seem to be in."

How trusting and naive she'd been back then! But the lady was kind and had bought her a meal. Desperate and alone, Delphine had told her everything that had happened to her since she had left home. And when Constance Monroe had suggested she come to work for her, she had accepted with only fleeting reservations.

At least she had a roof over her head and good meals to eat at the Paradise Club. She wore lavish gowns in the evening as she moved around the club encouraging the gents to drink more, and later there were those who paid a fine fee for an hour or so of pleasure with her. And, as Constance had reminded her, Delphine

157

had already given up her virginity to the swarthy youth who'd left her when times got bad and the love ran out.

Delphine had decided that she didn't have to stay there long. But while she *was* at the Paradise, she was going to make all the money she could. After she had been there two or three weeks, she didn't find it too difficult to play the role; and Constance could not have been more pleased about her new girl. Delphine's sultry dark looks and curvaceous figure certainly attracted the gentlemen. In fact, she became so popular that Constance realized that some of her other girls were jealous. But that didn't bother her. Competition was good for business.

Delphine enjoyed having money in her reticule and began to add to her meager wardrobe. One of the first things she bought for herself was a warm wool cape, for she had only the knit shawl her mother had made for her. By the time she had worked at the Paradise Club for a month she had become a regular shopper at a pricey boutique, but Delphine always kept enough in her reticule to get her back to New Orleans.

She liked having a supply of lacy undergarments and five nice afternoon frocks.

Each girl at the Paradise had her own room, which was also to Delphine's liking. She remained aloof from everyone except for the girl who called herself Marline.

Marline came to her room late one afternoon and confided that she was leaving in a week. "I'm going to Norfolk, Delphine," she said, "and you ought to think about coming with me." Delphine shook her head, but Marline went on. "I got a letter yesterday from a friend of mine, and she's got me a deal at this new place called Southern Mansions. She's making double what we're making here with Constance."

"I'll think about it, Marline," Delphine had told her, but she didn't really want to go to a new place. Constance had been good to her, and she knew what to expect at the Paradise Club.

"Well, don't say anything to the others. You're the only one who knows, and I don't intend to tell Constance until I'm ready to leave. She can be a bitch when she gets riled as you'll find out if you stay here long enough," Marline warned her.

A week later Marline had left with a last reminder to Delphine to get in touch with her if she decided to come to Norfolk, so she could get her on at Southern Mansions.

Constance was in a waspish mood after Marline left, and that mood remained with her for the next month, for she found no one to replace the pretty Marline. But although Constance's coffers suffered the loss, Delphine's nightly fees were enriched. Soon she had actually saved much more than the cost of her passage back to New Orleans and indulged in a shopping spree and a mid-afternoon repast at her favorite tearoom.

Back at her room, after she had stowed away her purchases and picked out a wine-colored gown to wear that evening, she enjoyed the luxury of a rose-scented bath. But as she sat at her dressing table brushing out her hair, a sharp spasm of pain seized her until she was doubled over in agony.

Moaning from the fierce and sudden twinges and cramps, she staggered across the hall to Francie's room. "Tell Constance I can't work tonight," she mumbled, hardly able to speak. "I'm so darn sick I can't even walk, much less get myself dressed. I can't make myself or Constance any money tonight."

"Can I get you something, honey?" Francie asked her. "Could you use a cup of tea?"

"No thanks, Francie. I've just got to get back to my bed," Delphine stammered and struggled across the hall.

Eventually, when the sharpness of the pain dulled slightly, she drifted off to sleep. But it was an angry Constance who stormed into her room accusing her of laziness.

Weak and still half-asleep, Delphine protested her innocence. "It's something I ate," she said, but she did not erase the look of disbelief on Constance's face as she marched from the room, slamming the door behind her.

The sharp pains in her stomach had eased, but Delphine still felt weak, so she dimmed her lamp and scooted down in the bed, pulling the sheet up over her. For the first time in over two months she was sleeping soundly by ten-thirty.

Early the next morning, she made her way to the kitchen. She could use a hot cup of the strong coffee which she knew Tilda would have brewed.

Tilda saw her coming through the door, and she frowned, a quizzical look on her face, as she asked, "What you doin' up at this hour, Miss Delphine?"

"Didn't work last night, Tilda. I was sick."

Delphine helped herself to a cup of coffee, and Tilda fixed her a couple of eggs and fried a slab of ham. Tilda chuckled. "Miss Constance was madder than a wet hen," she commented.

"I couldn't have come downstairs if my life had depended on it," Delphine defended herself.

"Miss Constance don't figure it that way, sugar," Tilda told her. "You'd best watch your step around her for awhile."

Delphine nodded. She'd learned to heed her friend's warnings, and she recalled that Marline had told her just before she left for Nor-

161

folk to watch out for Constance when she got riled.

Delphine went back to work that night and the night after, but Constance was cold and obstinate. Giving way to her impulsive nature, Delphine decided to follow Marline's advice and join her in Norfolk.

Lying on her bunk aboard the *Delta Queen*, Delphine realized that it was to New Orleans she should have bought passage instead of Norfolk, Virginia.

Traveling from Savannah to Charleston, fate was to play a cruel trick on her when she crossed paths with the silken-tongued Carter Bascombe, and the months that followed had been a nightmare that Delphine had thought would never end.

Eighteen

Jessamine made sure before she went to work at the big house that there was no evidence anywhere in her quarters that two renegade girls had stayed with her.

She was apprehensive about Monsieur Savanti's reaction to Chantel's exodus, but she didn't catch even a whisper of gossip from Selma. She assumed her employer was still feeling poorly.

In the late afternoon when she opened the door and walked inside her quiet apartment, it seemed almost ghostly. As much danger as they had posed for her, Jessamine had enjoyed the girls' company. Now, sitting down to have her dinner all alone, she realized that she had nothing to hold her to this place. God knows, it was not a place of happiness. Maybe, it was time for her to think seriously about her own flight to freedom. But, she asked herself, where would she go?

The happy times she remembered most vividly were those days in New Orleans when she'd left her family to go with her new husband. But now she had no husband, and her family had scattered over the years.

Still, perhaps she might take the *Delta Queen* back to New Orleans and recapture some of the magic and happiness of the young years of her life.

She could be a housekeeper there as easily as in Charleston. And her bank account was large enough to carry her for a few weeks if it took that long for her to find a job.

Jessamine reminded herself that if she did decide to leave she should book her passage before the winter months set in. She wouldn't want to be sailing in the boisterous winds of the cold season.

Two tantalizing temptresses made an entrance in the ship's dining room that first evening and drew the attention of more than one gentleman. They were a vision: the dark sultry Delphine and Chantel, a breathtaking blonde.

Delphine was aware of the stir they'd caused, and she expected that before they finished their meal they would be approached by at least one of the ship's gallant hopefuls.

She also knew that the look in a lady's eyes and the way she moved her body when she entered a room could excite immediate interest. She'd learned a lot at the Paradise Club, but she noticed that Chantel's allure came as naturally as breathing. It was no wonder she had caught Carter's appraising eye.

Now that they were both long gone from Charleston and safe, she'd love to encounter him and see the flabbergasted look on his face when he found her and Chantel together. Oh, what a feeling of sweet revenge that would create!

The two girls were in a festive mood that late summer evening, so they each had a glass of wine and toasted themselves and enjoyed the fresh-caught fish fillet. They sipped slowly on their wine as they talked, pleased with one another's company to the exclusion of the eager swains who tried to catch their attention.

But one of the more determined, bolder youths refused to be discouraged and sent them complimentary wine.

"Compliments of Monsieur Charles Trehurne, ladies," their waiter told them.

"Thank Monsieur Trehurne for us," Delphine replied smoothly. She chanced to glance over at Chantel and saw a frightened look in the wary green eyes. She knew immediately that Chantel feared another Carter Bascombe.

As soon as the waiter moved away from the table, Delphine consoled her. "Don't worry," she whispered. "You have me and I have you, and nothing is going to happen to us this time."

An uneasy, almost guilty, smile crossed Chantel's face. "You saw it immediately," she said. "The fear, I mean."

"Why shouldn't I?" Delphine replied. "We're sisters in spirit now, and we understand one another. How could we not? I'll always be there for you, Chantel, after what we've shared," Delphine reassured her.

"And I feel the same," Chantel acknowledged. "I — I just wish I were feeling as thrilled about returning to New Orleans as you are. Oh, don't get me wrong, I'm thrilled to be away from Savanti."

"But you don't want to go back to *La Maison?*"

Chantel nodded.

"Then you just quit fretting, honey, 'cause you don't have to go back," Delphine reminded her. "You're coming home with me to the bayou. You'll love it. I promise."

"Oh, Delphine," Chantel sighed. "I couldn't impose on your family like that."

Delphine gave out a lilting laugh. "Ah, Chantel, you don't know my beautiful family. The welcome mat is always out; my home is warm with love." She went on to tell her how her very beautiful French Creole mother had married her Irish father, who was a fisherman on the lakes and bays.

"My mother came from a wealthy family in New Orleans," she explained, "and my father was hardly what they planned for her future, but nothing stopped them once they'd met and fell in love. My mother had been so pampered that she didn't know how to cook when she married my father, but now she gets in her canoe and travels up and down the bayou taking her bread and pots of soups to the ailing."

"She sounds like a most wonderful lady," Chantel declared.

"She is. Everyone adores her, but no one as much as my father. He calls her his Bayou Queen, which is also the name of his fishing boat."

Chantel found Delphine's story intriguing, and she could certainly understand why she was excited about traveling home. She had no wonderful story about her family to tell, and she envied Delphine.

"I want you to come home with me, Chantel. I want you to meet my family. Please say you'll come."

"All right," Chantel agreed, not needing much coaxing. "For a few days I will go to the bayou with you and perhaps, as you said, I will find an answer — or at least know the question."

Delighted, Delphine exclaimed, "You won't be sorry." And she made a mental note to cau-

167

tion that tease of a brother of hers not to come on strong with the gun-shy Chantel.

Charles Trehurne's eyes had been constantly on the table where the two lovely young ladies had been sitting for over the last hour. He figured if he were going to make a move to introduce himself he had to do it quickly for they had finished their meal.

Just the name Trehurne opened doors for him and his arrogance settled about him like a cloak for he had been born with a silver spoon in his mouth and he'd never known what it meant to earn one cent of the dollars he so lavishly spent. When he was home in New Orleans, he squired the debutantes to elegant soirees and social affairs. He was used to ladies fawning over him.

There were two houses in New Orleans he called home. The two-story mansion in the city was embellished in elaborate iron grillwork. At the country estate just outside the city, his father had bred his prized thoroughbreds. Charles was used to being sought after, and so he naturally assumed that any young lady would be flattered by his attention.

When he introduced himself, Delphine immediately sensed that he expected them to recognize his name. She had met his kind before and she'd learned at the Paradise Club how to flatter their egos.

"Ah, monsieur," she sighed expressively, "we

are two very weary ladies tonight, but we would be delighted to have you escort us to our cabin. Tomorrow night perhaps we shall be more rested."

It soothed his vanity for all the other men to watch him escort the two pretty ladies from the dining room, and by the time they reached their cabin, he had invited them to be his guests for dinner the next night. Delphine accepted sweetly.

Later she told Chantel, "Why not? Let him fete us. Remember we're safe as long as the two of us are together."

Chantel gave her no argument for she was beginning to realize that Delphine was far wiser and more experienced than she was where men were concerned. In fact, she was realizing that she was very naive.

That night as they talked before going to sleep, she asked Delphine how old she was. Delphine smiled slyly, "I'm only eighteen going on nineteen," she admitted, "but I feel like I'm going on forty."

Chantel understood what she was trying to tell her and thanked God—and Jessamine—that she'd been saved from the hellish torment Delphine had endured. Yet, that stubborn streak in Chantel told her that she would not have resigned herself to the abuse and punishment as Delphine had for a year. She would have fought to the death before Savanti would

169

have subdued her, she believed.

And yet she could not have felt closer to a sister then she did to Delphine. Forever they would be bound together.

Chantel knew now that going back to Boston would not have solved her problems or answered her questions about life. There was a driving force back in New Orleans that had made a forceful impact on her dreams, and that had been Gabe O'Roarke. Quite often over the last few days, she had yearned for his strong arms to hold and comfort her as they had in the brief interludes they'd shared. She had not wanted to leave him although she'd felt compelled to leave New Orleans.

Meanwhile, the *Delta Queen* plowed through the waters along the Florida coastline, veering to the gulf coast to turn into the Mississippi River and make port in New Orleans.

By now, there was no question in Delphine's mind that it was her beautiful companion, Chantel, who sparked Charles' interest. She could understand why. There was an aura of sweet innocence about Chantel. That year of being Antoine Savanti's playtoy and those months of working for Constance at the Paradise Club had to reflect on Delphine's face and Charles, she was certain, could see it. Chantel was far more intriguing to him.

But because she was aware of his interest, she was constantly by Chantel's side whenever they went on the deck or down to the dining room.

When the *Delta Queen* docked in New Orleans, it was a Friday and Delphine could not have been more pleased for she knew that she and Chantel had themselves a way out to her bayou home.

As they left the *Delta Queen* and made their way along the familiar wharf, Delphine swore she'd never leave again. It was so good to be back home.

Delphine spied her bare-chested brother on the deck of the *Louisiana Lady* and she assumed that he saw her, too, when he flung down the fish he was holding and dashed off the boat.

But just as suddenly Chantel broke stride, running directly toward Gabe. She froze and gasped in amazement as the two of them eagerly embraced one another. Chantel threw herself into Gabe's arms and clung to him, and Gabe's strong arms enclosed her, holding her close to him as though he never intended to let her go.

Delphine picked up the valise Chantel had dropped and walked on up the levee. When she reached the two of them, still locked in an embrace, she laughed. "Guess I got to figure you two know one another," she observed loudly.

Gabe released Chantel and took his sister in his arms as if it had been yesterday and not more than a year since he had last seen her. "It's good to have you home, little sister," he murmured into her hair, choking back the emotion that overpowered him.

His one arm remained around his sister and his other arm reached out to pull Chantel back close to him. Now it was Chantel who had a quizzical look on her pretty face as she looked from Gabe to Delphine, tongue-tied. "You mean Gabe is your brother, Delphine?" Chantel stammered.

"My one and only."

He picked up the two bags. "Can't wait to hear how the two of you got together, but let's get down to the boat. I've got fish to sell."

Delphine took Chantel's arm to guide her down the deck toward Gabe's cabin, but it was apparent that Chantel knew which way to go. She'd been on the boat before, Delphine realized.

Delphine wasted no time making herself at home in the cabin. She kicked off her slippers and then started to brew a pot of coffee.

Sweet, sweet memories flooded Chantel as she sat on the bunk where Gabe had made love to her for the first time. Delphine couldn't help but notice her starry reverie.

Gabe, impatient, hurried his customers and left the last few sales in his mate's capable hands. He breezed into the cabin, sniffing the coffee Delphine had brewed. "Ah, bless you,"

172

he said, "I'm ready for a cup." He reached up to grab his cotton shirt off the peg and slipped into it.

With his cup filled, he sat down beside Chantel with no pretense of hiding his feelings about her. His tanned hand closed over hers, and their eyes locked. "Now tell me where you ran away to, love," he demanded with tender concern.

"I started out for Boston, but I never got there," she explained hurriedly, condensing her adventure into a few inadequate words. "I only got as far as Charleston."

His eyes then turned in Delphine's direction. "And is that where the two of you met?"

"Yes," she confirmed. She would tell him more later, when they got home.

"I still have fish to deliver to *La Maison*," he lamented, draining his coffee cup.

"So take your fish to *La Maison*," Delphine laughed, a teasing glint in her eyes.

"But I don't want to part with Chantel this soon," he responded instantly.

"Chantel is coming home with me for awhile, Gabe."

His eyes darted back to Chantel, and she sensed that he was pleased to hear that. "Please don't tell anyone I'm back," she cautioned Gabe. "I don't want them to know, not just yet."

"Whatever you want, honey. But, in that

case, I'm going to gather up my fish and get that delivery out of the way so we can be on our way home." He buttoned up the front of his shirt and set his empty cup on the table.

Gabe drove the buggy to *La Maison* with great haste and eagerly sped back toward the docks. But he did make one stop, where he bought three colorful baskets of flowers. One was for the girl he loved, one for his beloved sister, and pink rosebuds for his dear mother, whose happiness would be transformed when she saw her daughter again after all these many months of fearing that she might be dead.

What a glorious homecoming it was going to be tonight!

Nineteen

There was a beautiful sunset in the western skies as the *Louisiana Lady* plowed through the waters toward Gabe and Delphine's home in the bayou that late afternoon.

To Chantel a certain serenity was already settling in on her for she was not the least bit apprehensive about going to stay with the O'Roarkes for she and Delphine had become so close and had spent so much time talking she felt she knew her parents. But in all their long chats Delphine had never mentioned her last name nor had she mentioned her older brother's name although she'd spoken about him frequently.

At Gabe's urging, Delphine began the tale of her crazy odyssey.

"Why didn't you get yourself back here to New Orleans?" Gabe asked when she told him of her young man's shipping out and leaving her stranded in Savannah.

"No money for passage, my dear brother," she

said simply. "I had to get work." She didn't tell him where she got work. And she didn't give him the particulars of the job she'd sought in Norfolk. She did tell him about Carter Bascombe, and Chantel listened, amazed at the similarity of their experiences. Bascombe was a cunning con man with a formula for success.

She knew that Delphine was sparing him the worst of her story, but Chantel sensed the rage churning within Gabe as his sister related the sordid debasement she had endured.

When she came to the night she escaped from the sadistic Antoine Savanti and was hidden by Jessamine, Chantel picked up the story, filling in the details of how she and Delphine had chanced to meet.

Gabe's strong arms enclosed his sister and he listened intently to the final chapter of their flight to safety. Then he moved away from Delphine's side to embrace Chantel. He kissed her forehead with a sweet tenderness. "You're safe now, love, and I intend to see that you stay that way," he vowed. "You two have lived a lifetime already. The bayou is the tonic you both need right now."

The *Louisiana Lady* wound through the turns and bends of the marsh, and Delphine became suddenly alert to the night sounds of the bayou. "It's music," she cried, her eyes filling with happy tears. "It's the most wonderful music." Rushing out of the cabin, she limbed eagerly up on deck. "I've missed all of this," she called back to them. "I've smelled the wild jasmine and heard the night birds singing in my sleep. And in my dreams I've watched the bayou moon peering out of the dark sky, its beams shining over the rippling waters."

Back in the cabin, Gabe's arms still encircled Chantel. "I'm glad you're coming home with us," he whispered. "Our home is your home for as long as you wish. That's the way of the bayou."

Her green eyes gazed up at him. "I wish I had been born and raised in the bayou like you and Delphine," she murmured softly.

"Being born and raised in the bayou didn't spare Delphine, Chantel," he reminded her. "But the past is behind you. The future is all that matters now." He took her by the hand and led her up on the deck of his boat.

"We're almost home," he announced, positioning her at the railing beside his sister. "When we round that next bend, we'll see mom's lamplight gleaming out the windows." He placed his hand on Delphine's shoulder. "I'll tell your story to the folks, honey," he said, sensitive to the tension he could feel welling up in her again. "One telling is enough to have to relive that horrible time in your life."

"Thank you," she sighed, melting against his side in gratitude.

A few minutes later the trio were at the small dock that jutted out from Gabe's father's property. With the two bags and three baskets of flowers, they moved up the path through the grove of trees surrounding the cottage that the O'Roarke family called home.

Chantel felt a kind of magic emanating from the front door of the cottage. From every window a lamp beckoned, welcoming all visitors.

Neither of the young girls by his side completely realized the fury they'd stirred in Gabe O'Roarke with their tales of Carter Bascombe and Antoine Savanti. His sister and the lady he loved had been sorely used, and that was enough to make the hot-blooded Irishman seek revenge. He would not rest until the score was settled. But his happy-go-lucky air gave no hint of his private musings as they went up the two front steps to the porch.

Delphine entered first, and Chantel held back until Gabe nudged her. Towering over the petite Chantel, he could see his father's face as Delphine moved into his line of vision. Scott O'Roarke sat up straight in his favorite chair like a man in a trance. Then he gave out a moan. "Dear God Almighty! Oh, Delphine! Delphine!" His arms embraced the daughter he had feared he would never see again.

Gabe's mother flew from the kitchen when she'd heard her husband, and at the sight of the two of them embracing, tears streamed down her lovely face. Chantel and Gabe exchanged smiles. It was a tender, emotional moment for the

O'Roarke family, and Chantel would have felt like an intruder but Gabe was affectionately holding her hand. Chantel could see that Delphine's dark, sultry beauty came from her mother. Angelique O'Roarke was one of the loveliest women she'd ever seen, all the more striking because her light tawny complexion was accented by ebony eyes and jet-black hair.

Delphine introduced Chantel. "She is my dearest friend and I invited her to spend a few days with us because I wanted her to meet my wonderful family," she said all in one breath.

Angelique O'Roarke smiled warmly at Chantel. "You are most welcome here," she began, but her pleasant smile suddenly faded. "Oh, *mon Dieu!* I smell our dinner burning," she cried, racing back into her kitchen.

Scott chuckled. "So we eat a burnt supper tonight. Who cares? It is too glorious a night to worry about that."

Chantel noticed that Scott had the same flashing blue eyes as his son, and she envied the adoring look that radiated across his face each time he gazed at his daughter—incredulous that she had actually returned home. He told her, "Delphine, your room is exactly as you left it. Perhaps you and Chantel would like to settle in while your mother finishes burning our dinner."

While the girls retired to Delphine's back room, Gabe took his mother the basket of flowers he'd bought for her.

"Mother, these are for you," he said, stopping to stare at her. What a beautiful sight she made, he thought, stirring the food in the pots while tears of joy streamed down her cheeks.

"Oh, Gabe, you are a dear son." she sniffed happily. "They're beautiful! Put them on that table by the window for me, will you?"

He did as she requested and went over to give her damp cheek a kiss. "It's good to see you so happy, Mother," he commented. "I'll fill you and Dad in later when the three of us are alone."

"Ah, Gabe dear, it is enough to have her here under our roof again. All of that can come later," she replied, brushing at the edges of her eyes with the back of her hand.

Standing by the stove for those few brief moments whetted Gabe's appetite. He looked over her shoulder to preview the menu. It seemed appropriate that she had prepared chicken and dumplings, his favorite meal. He also spotted a huge pan of biscuits and two peach cobblers on the cupboard. He was more than ready to sit down at their dinner table, famished after the very busy, eventful day he'd had.

Chantel watched Delphine as she quietly surveyed every corner of her bedroom. It was a cozy, neat little room with pink ruffled curtains at the windows and a pink coverlet on the bed. As her father had told her, it was just as she'd left it. On the dressing table were her hand mirror, brush, and comb. Her little wooden stool with its cushioned pad of pink chintz was tucked beneath the shelf.

They unpacked quickly, hanging Delphine's dresses in the closet and filling the chest with the more intimate wear. Delphine gazed with delight at the clothes she had left home, still neatly folded in her bureau drawers. Impulsively she gave Chantel the two expensive nightgowns they had brought from Charleston. Her simple batiste gowns looked good to Delphine—like everything else in her room. She suggested Chantel change into one of her muslin frocks for the evening.

"That beautiful green gown is going to be worn out, Chantel," she giggled.

Chantel laughed, too. "You know, I was just thinking," she said, "that I have beautiful clothes scattered everywhere. I've an armoire filled to overflowing in Boston *and* in New Orleans. Who knows what will happen to that valise aboard the ship? Yet I wouldn't have even had a change of underwear if it weren't for Jessamine."

Like a miser, Delphine emptied out the contents of her velvet pouch. "I managed to hold on to all of this," she gloated. "We can sell it here in New Orleans and send Jessamine what she laid out for our passage.

"They're so exquisite," Chantel gasped as she viewed the sparkling gems for the second time. In the safety of the bayou, curled on Delphine's bed, she could take more time to examine each piece.

181

"Oh, the old devil gives you these in the beginning. He invests a fortune because it allows him to play out his fantasy. An hour later, that expensive designer gown he lavished on you could be torn to rags. He's crazy, Chantel."

"But it's over, Delphine," Chantel reminded her.

"It will never be over," Delphine objected. "But it's why I'm more than delighted to be back home where I can wear my simple cotton frocks and my plain batiste nightgowns."

Chantel understood, for she shared Delphine's relief.

When the two of them emerged from Delphine's bedroom they looked like typical bayou girls. Their long hair flowed free and loose over their shoulders, and they wore modest muslin frocks—Delphine in pale pink and Chantel in a creme-colored dress with a green sprigged pattern.

Delphine gave her mother a warm embrace as they met again in the front room. "Oh, Momma," she breathed, "it is so good to be home again."

"And are you two ready for some chicken and dumplings?" Angelique asked to cover the quaver in her voice.

Both of them were wee little ladies, but their appetites seemed as hearty as Gabe's. But Angelique didn't mind that at all. She watched the two girls at the dinner table and she knew not what bound them together but she could tell their devotion to each other went very deep.

Her all-knowing eyes had also observed something else during the evening meal they'd shared and after dinner as the five of them returned to the parlor. It was her son Gabe who'd caught her interest this evening for his eyes were constantly on the beautiful Chantel. There was an intimacy between them that could not have developed this afternoon. They had obviously known each other before, and she found it puzzling that Gabe had never mentioned their meeting.

Unless she was badly mistaken Angelique saw on the face of her twenty-five year old son the look of love.

Although she had only met Chantel a few hours ago, she had instantly liked her. It had always been Angelique's nature that she either liked or disliked someone on her first meeting of them.

It was about time that Gabe took himself a pretty bride, Angelique mused as she sat in her front room that evening. Would that bride be Chantel?

Twenty

It was only after Chantel and Delphine had retired to Delphine's room that Gabe sat in the front room with his parents and related the girls' grim tale.

Scott O'Roarke, feeling the need of a glass of his Irish whiskey, poured a generous tumblerful for himself and his son and brought his wife a glass of wine.

Gabe watched the mixed emotions reflected on both his parents' faces, unaware that he had unwittingly set them both to thinking about their younger days and the history that was in a way repeating itself.

Angelique had had no inkling when she was only sixteen that her beauty had inspired an obsession in François La Tour. Since she was the daughter of a wealthy French Creole, La Tour knew he'd never be accepted as her suitor, so he abducted her. He took her miles away from New Orleans to his private fortress down the Mississippi River at Pointe à la Hache.

184

She had become his captive, but he had not known of the young, bold fisherman who'd loved her enough to dare to rescue her. It was to his home in the bayou he'd taken her, and Angelique had found such serenity there that she never wished to leave.

Scott O'Roarke remembered that once she'd gone back to New Orleans she had had to face the determined, obsessed La Tour. Scott had realized that she would never be free of him until he was dead.

The second time he rescued Angelique Dupree, he killed François La Tour.

A short time later they had been married, and he'd never had any qualms of conscience about what he'd done. Even the law had found his action justified.

As Gabe told the sordid tale of Delphine and Antoine Savanti, Scott wished he were once more the intrepid young man he'd been. If he were twenty again, he'd settle the score and track down Carter Bascombe.

In her bedroom with Chantel lying in the bed beside her, Delphine asked, "Are you going to tell me about you and Gabe? How'd the two of you meet?"

Chantel gave her a hurried account of their meeting and was startled when Delphine said, "Well, I know one thing for sure and that's that Gabe's head over heels in love with you." Chantel shook her head, but her friend persisted. "He can't take his eyes off you." She paused briefly, then asked, "Are you in love with him?"

"I've never felt about any man as I feel about Gabe, so I suppose you could say I am," Chantel answered her honestly.

"Oh, I hope so. I think it would be perfect if you and Gabe got married. Think about it, Chantel—we'd truly be sisters," she exclaimed excitedly.

Chantel laughed softly. "Oh, Delphine," she protested, "he's not asked me to marry him."

But Delphine was undaunted by that. "Oh, but he will."

At early dawn father and son boarded their fishing boats and traveled through the bayou, picking up their crew along the way.

The O'Roarkes provided a livelihood for several families, and Scott had found a young man who could take over for him when he was not able to make the daily trips out on the lakes.

Terry Monroe was hardworking and dependable. He put in a good day's work for his wages, but what impressed Scott most was that he was always willing to give extra of himself. Scott trusted him and he admired Terry's loyalty to his widowed mother and fourteen-year-old sister. At twenty-one, the boy was shouldering a big responsibility and handling it very well.

While the men worked the bayou, Angelique finished her morning's baking and set some herbs out to dry, letting the two girls sleep well into the morning. She peeked into Delphine's pink-and-white room just before they woke up and the deepness of their sleep made her realize how exhausted they must be from their ordeal.

"Fix yourselves breakfast," she urged them when they finally emerged—sheepishly—from beneath the covers. "Mrs. Monroe is ailing again and I've a pot of stew and some bread to deliver to them."

Delphine thought nothing about it when her mother left the cottage with the kettle in one hand and two loaves of fresh-baked bread under her arm. But Chantel was amazed as she watched the petite lady climb into her canoe and paddle upstream.

"Isn't she afraid?" she asked Delphine.

"Oh Lord, no. She was taking Gabe and me up and down this bayou when we were only knee-high to a duck."

"I wouldn't do it. I'd be scared out of my wits," Chantel declared. "The snakes alone are enough to keep me on land."

"I don't like snakes either," Delphine agreed, "but they've never seemed to bother Mother."

The two girls fell silent, concentrating on a

plate of eggs and homemade jam. Then they worked together to put Angelique's kitchen back in order. Delphine laughed as she told Chantel, "Mom taught me real young that what I messed up I could clean up. As sweet and gentle as she usually is, when I dared to test her she could be firm and strict."

"But you knew she loved you, didn't you?" Chantel asked.

"Oh, Gabe and I had to be the most-loved kids in the world. We never had any doubts about that."

Housework completed, they raced joyously from the cottage and into the dense woods that extended to the banks of the bayou.

Chantel stopped beneath a tall, majestic tree and listened intently to the unfamiliar calls of the birds fluttering through the branches above her. Amid the boulders along the pathway, she spotted wild ferns flourishing in the shade. Attracted by a fragrant aroma, Chantel bend down to pluck a yellow blossom from a trailing vine. "That's wild Jasmine," Delphine told her. "That should be your flower. It matches your pale gold hair. The blossoms are beautiful when they are in full bloom."

With a finger to her lips, Delphine pointed to a large rock where they could sit and watch two young raccoons at play. Beyond them, canoes navigated the stream.

"In the bayou, people would not know what

to do without their boats," Delphine explained. "Our canoes make it possible to visit neighbors, take goods into the city, and bring home supplies."

"It's paradise," Chantel breathed. "How could you have left it?"

"Crazy, I guess." Delphine studied her hands and the sky and shook her head in disbelief. "I thought I was being smothered by too much love. I had two doting parents and a very protective older brother, and I was curious about the world outside my bayou." Delphine sighed. "I found out more than I needed to know."

Then, freeing herself of her reverie with a determined giggle, she grabbed Chantel's hand. "I've decided," she said with a definite nod, "that I shall marry for the rest of my life. And you shall be my maid of honor and my best friend for always." Their hands and eyes locked in an affirmation of friendship and then, suddenly, Delphine raised up and nudged Chantel. "Look at the old cypress tree," she whispered. "The one with its trunk jutting out over the water."

Chantel pivoted on her heels until she could see a blue heron that stood long-legged and motionless in the water beside the cypress. "He's magnificent," she murmured as quietly as she could so the sound of her voice wouldn't disturb him as he stalked his prey in the stream. "I've never seen one up close before."

"Watch him," Delphine said in an undertone. "He's going to catch himself a bayou fish—just like me." She muffled her laughter until the patient bird grabbed the exact fish he wanted and flew into the sun, his massive wings burnished by the light "You'd make a good bayou girl, Chantel," Delphine commented as the heron disappeared in the distance.

"Me?" Chantel was surprised.

"I've been watching you," Delphine confessed. "You're taking it all in and enjoying it. Look, you've even gathered an armful of wildflowers."

"I have enjoyed myself," Chantel granted cautiously. "I do like your bayou, but I could never make it mine the way your mother has. You'd never get me out there alone in a canoe."

There was a twinkle in Delphine's dark eyes. "We'll see," was all she said, and the girls left it at that.

When the two of them got up from the spot where they'd been sitting for more than a half hour, Delphine ran her fingers through her thick black hair pushing it away from her forehead. A big smile came to her face. "This is Saturday," she told Chantel. "We'll probably have visitors tonight, since the men don't have to work on Sunday."

"It's a good life here," she added as they retraced their steps to the cottage. "I can't remember a time in my life that our dinner table wasn't overflowing with food." She showed Chantel some fresh tracks in the underbrush.

"My dad and Gabe can hunt for quail, turkey or duck if we don't feel like fish." She spun around like a little girl, gleeful, with a sudden new thought. "But tonight," she laughed happily, "just might be a crawfish night!"

Chantel found herself completely absorbed as Delphine spoke of her life in the bayou. The O'Roarkes and their ways seemed so different from the lifestyle she'd lived with her aunt in Boston or the time she'd spent with her mother at *La Maison*. The more she learned about this wonderful family, the more she understood why she found Gabe O'Roarke so completely different from any other young man she'd ever met.

They were a different breed of people from those she had always known, and she thought she could easily love these men and women of the bayou.

Twenty-one

It was past midday when Angelique O'Roarke returned from her visit up the bayou. But her empty kettle had been refilled with okra from the Monroe's garden. she also had a paper sack heavy with green peppers and onions.

"That's the way it is out here." Delphine told Chantel. "We look out for one another."

During the afternoon Delphine observed her mother in the kitchen, chopping the onions and peppers. She saw her go out to her garden near her back door to gather up herbs, and Delphine became more certain of the treat in store for them this evening. "It's my mother's crawfish *étouffée*," she whispered to Chantel. "Even the aroma is delicious!"

When Gabe and his father came through the front door, Scott had the wine and Gabe carried a bucket filled with fresh crawfish.

The O'Roarkes were an affectionate family who displayed their emotions freely. Scott bent

192

down to embrace his wife. His touched his lips to his daughter's cheek and gave Chantel a fatherly kiss on the forehead. Chantel appreciated being included.

Gabe in turn hugged his mother and his sister. He kissed Chantel on the lips; but due to the warm atmosphere of the O'Roarke's cottage, she did not feel embarrassed or ill-at-ease. It seemed only natural and right.

Angelique immediately took charge of the crawfish, admonishing the men to get themselves cleaned up to sit down at her table. It was apparent that both husband and son adored this bossy little lady who now busied herself at her stove.

Chantel found her fascinating. She moved with expertise, adding the crawfish to the one pot, rice to the other. Her table was already set, but she hastily lit a candle for a centerpiece and rapidly turned up the lamps in the front room.

She recalled Gabe's comment when they'd arrived—that his mother's lamps beckoned from the front windows.

Angelique was so completely in charge in her kitchen that Delphine did not even offer to help her. She laughed, "Momma'll let it all steep slowly for thirty minutes and then she'll scoop it onto a platter for us to enjoy." As if to prove her daughter's point, Angelique relaxed over a glass of wine while her rice and crawfish simmered.

Gabe poured himself a glass of the wine and sat beside Chantel. "Beware of the cayenne pepper," he warned. "It can be wicked."

"Gabe, you let Chantel find out for herself if she likes it," Angelique scolded.

"Had to warn her, Momma. It wouldn't have been fair to not prepare her for your *étouffée*," he teased. Angelique, contemplating the twinkle in his blue eyes, thought that he'd not changed much from the towheaded tot she had taken with her up and down the bayou when he was only three or four. Everyone had adored little Gabe, and she sometimes found it hard to believe that he was twenty-five years old. How quickly the years had gone for her — and how happy she was!

Nothing was needed at Angelique's dinner table that evening except for the huge loaf of her fresh-baked bread and the large platter with the white bed of rice lavishly covered with the exquisite mixture of crawfish, onions, and peppers simmered in her extra-spicy hot sauce.

"Oh, it is wonderful, Mrs. O'Roarke," Chantel declared, but she did see what Gabe had meant about the cayenne and immediately bit into a huge slice of bread.

Angelique was pleased, and her dark eyes sought Gabe's across the table. "You see," she gloated, "Chantel does like my *étouffée*."

When the meal was over, Delphine and

Chantel insisted that they would clean the kitchen. "For the rest of the night you're a lady of leisure," Delphine had decreed.

Angelique didn't even put up a show of protest, content to accompany her husband back to the front room. She was well aware, however, that Gabe lingered in the kitchen with the girls and wasted no time asking Chantel to take a walk with him. Delphine, not in the least insulted by the exclusion, joined her parents.

Glad to have a private time with her daughter, Angelique remarked on Chantel's delicate beauty. "Did she have nowhere to go?" she asked. "Is that why you had her come home with you?" Delphine shook her head and explained about *La Maison* and Chantel's confusion.

"I understand," Angelique nodded, remembering the rumors that had circulated about *La Maison* long before Lily Lemogne's reign as madame, back when Angelique had been younger than either Delphine or Chantel. She sighed. "Chantel's mother must be concerned," she said softly, "to have her daughter disappear. Imagine how afraid she must be for her."

"Guess I hadn't thought about it that way." Delphine considered this new point of view. "Chantel was disillusioned when she learned the truth about *La Maison*. Perhaps her mother wanted to spare her. Who am I to judge?"

"It is not our place to do so," Angelique agreed. "But there is nothing as terrible as a mother worrying about a daughter's welfare." Delphine could not meet her mother's eyes, knowing that she spoke from experience.

"Does Chantel ever talk about her mother to you?" Angelique asked after a moment.

"She says she is very beautiful and must have been very young when Chantel was born," Delphine replied.

"She is welcome here as long as she wishes to stay," Angelique said slowly. "But I do think that her mother deserves to know she is well and safe. Perhaps you might persuade Chantel to give this some thought."

"I'll see what I can do." Delphine, seeing the situation now from her mother's vantage point, agreed with Angelique. Besides, she could hardly look down her nose at Lily Lemogne after what she herself had done in Savannah at the Paradise Club.

As close as they had become, Delphine had not yet told Chantel the entire truth about Savannah. One day she knew Chantel would be as shocked by the Paradise Club as she had been by *La Maison*. Someday, perhaps Delphine could risk her condemnation, but not now.

It was a glorious night on the bayou, with

silvery moonbeams shining through the branches of the tall trees that lined the banks of the stream. Gabe held her hand as they ambled along the path. When they reached the small dock, they sat down and dangled their legs over the side. Gabe's arm urged her closer to him. "Do you know," he asked, his lips close to her ear, "how good it feels to have you so close to me?"

"I think I do because I feel the same way, Gabe. I feared I might never see you again," she confessed.

He pulled her into his arms and gave her a long, lingering kiss. He knew that he could not make love to her as he so desperately yearned to do. He had to settle for a few kisses from her sweet lips. His deep husky voice urged her, "Don't ever run away from me again, love! There's always a solution for any dilemma, and I'll always be here for you. Remember that."

"Oh, I'll never run away again, Gabe. I can promise you that," she assured him quickly.

"You and Delphine were very lucky," he reminded her solemnly. He kissed her forehead as if he could impart protection with his love.

Knowing what a hellish torment his own mother had gone through worrying about Delphine, Gabe felt guilty that Lily Lemogne did not know that her daughter was safe and secure in the bayou. He liked Lily. He wasn't sure how to approach the subject, so he just plunged in as they began to walk back toward the cottage.

"Chantel," he began, "you must let your mother know you're all right. I remember how my mother grieved over Delphine."

He felt her suddenly stiffening against him, but that didn't stop him from talking. "Don't judge her so harshly, Chantel, until you know her side of the story. I know you must have been shocked, but you might not find it so startling now, knowing what you and Delphine experienced."

Chantel said nothing, but she listened. She absorbed the import of his comments, reflecting on the news that Raul and Jonah had nothing but the highest praise for Lily Lemogne. As for the girls who worked for Lily, they chose to be there.

"They *ask* for the opportunity to work at *La Maison*," he continued, taking her hand as they entered the woods. "Raul told me that your mother turns girls away weekly."

Chantel stopped suddenly to gaze up at Gabe. "Are you telling me that you approve of a place like *La Maison*?" she asked.

A slow, easy smile came to his face as he responded. "I don't approve or disapprove," he explained. "It's a man's or lady's choice what they do. What I don't approve of is forcing people against their will. What happened to you and Delphine makes me very angry."

She stood frozen in the same spot and stared at him. With a childlike curiosity, she asked, "And have you ever spent an evening at *La Maison*, Gabe?"

The moonlight illuminated her face in the darkness, and he was once again overwhelmed by her loveliness—and by her innocence. From the shadows of the night, he confessed, "I was tempted once."

"Oh?" Her long lashes fluttered nervously as she waited for him to go on.

"Yes," he nodded, a chortle escaping his throat as he pulled her to him. "I surely was tempted that afternoon I came into Raul's kitchen and saw you there. I thought you were a new girl, and I would have gone back that very night, but I couldn't afford an evening at *La Maison*."

Chantel broke into a gale of laughter. She, too, recalled that afternoon vividly, for she'd thought he was so very handsome. He had taken her breath away when she'd first seen him.

"When I found out that you were Madame Lily's daughter," Gabe continued, "I was one happy fellow."

"And had I not been Madame Lily's daughter, would you have still wanted to see me again, Gabe?"

He answered immediately without even an instant of hesitation. "Chantel," he said with forthright conviction, "nothing—absolutely nothing—would have stopped me from trying to see you again."

"Not even if I'd have been a working girl?"

"Not even that! That would not have mattered that much to have stopped me, Chantel. I'm a determined man when I want something bad enough."

She raised herself up on tiptoe. "Kiss me, Gabe," she urged him. More than willing to oblige her, he bent down to capture her half-parted lips.

Reluctantly, he forced himself to release her. He wanted to pour out all his love, but it was not possible tonight. So they walked back to the cottage with the flame of passion fired within them.

Twenty-two

Sundays were lazy, relaxed days on the bayou, and by the time Chantel emerged from the bedroom still dressed in her gown and wrapper, she moved through a ghostly quiet house.

She found Angelique O'Roarke engulfed in a bathrobe at the kitchen table, sipping coffee.

"Too much wine last night," she grimaced wryly. "And ate too heartily too much crawfish."

"Me, too," Chantel acknowledged conspiratorially, accepting a mug of coffee.

"Scott and Gabe took off to go hunting, and Delphine has gone for a canoe ride with her friend Terry to see some old friends," Angelique said. "So you and I are left here alone this late morning."

Chantel quickly discovered that Gabe and his mother thought very much alike. Chantel couldn't resist Angelique's generous offer. "I am going into New Orleans in the morning with my husband," she said. "Would you mind if I went to *La Maison* and spoke with your mother? I don't like to think of her worrying about you." She patted Chantel's hand comfortingly. "I will make her understand that you need to stay with us for awhile. Let me do this for you and for her, Chantel."

Chantel could hardly refuse her. Gabe's mother had a persuasive charm and grace.

"You would go to *La Maison?*" Chantel asked her.

"Of course, I would, *ma petite.*"

"Well, I suppose I must say yes, but I would like to stay here a little longer," Chantel stammered.

Angelique's hand went out to clasp hers. "You can stay here as long as you like, Chantel. We love you already. Don't you know that by now?"

Chantel laughed. "Oh, I've never known a family like the O'Roarkes before, I must say. First I met Gabe, then Delphine and I crossed paths and she brought me here to meet you and Mr. O'Roarke. I had no inkling that she was Gabe's sister. Life's crazy."

"Ah, it is that, Chantel. But you and Delphine have the best of lives to live yet. Believe me."

"I want to believe that," Chantel admitted cautiously.

"The best of life," Angelique repeated emphatically. "Well," she sighed, "I suppose it's time I got dressed. Before I know it Scott and Gabe are going to come in with something for me to fix for our dinner tonight."

Chantel noticed that when she spoke of her husband or her son her voice warmed with affection. In the encompasing glow of O'Roarke love, she, too, decided to get dressed.   She selected a bright green muslin gown with a black-braid trim from Delphine's armoire, and she pulled her hair back with a black-velvet ribbon.

Delphine and Terry returned to the cottage in the late afternoon. Chantel could tell Delphine had enjoyed her Sunday outing, and she was glad to see her in such a gay mood.

"We'll have to take Chantel with us next time," she said to Terry.

"Anytime you say, Delphine," he agreed obligingly. "Any Sunday, that is. It's about the only day off I have. Saturdays I'm hoping to get chores done for ma and my sister before I go back to work for your pa." He didn't sit down, even though Delphine invited him to. "I need to help Sis cook supper," he apologized. "But it sure was fun, Delphine. It's good to have you back; it seems like old times again."

"I'll look in on your mother this week, Terry," she told him as she walked him to the door. He beamed with gratitude.

"Oh, she'd enjoy that, Delphine," he responded eagerly. "She surely would."

When Delphine returned to the front room, she sank into a chair beside Chantel. "Now, there went a good man," she said. "Terry is one man I trust."

"He seems awfully nice, Delphine," Chantel agreed. "It's obvious that the two of you had a really nice afternoon."

"Is it?" Delphine looked startled. "Well, I guess we did." She seemed lost in thought for a moment then pulled herself back to the present almost as if by force. "Where's Gabe?" she asked.

"He and your dad went hunting," Chantel said, "so your mother and I had a chance to get more acquainted." She looked wistful. "You have a wonderful family, Delphine. I envy you."

Delphine smiled as she gave Chantel's hand an affectionate pat. "Oh, honey, I can't argue with you about my family," she said, "but don't envy me."

It was about this moment that Angelique O'Roarke came into the room, a fresh frock on and her thick dark hair piled atop her head in one large coil. "Well, if that son and husband of mine don't strike it lucky after all this time, we may have to settle for ham and eggs for our supper." She laughed, not doubting in the least that they would provide.

"Oh, they'll bring something home. They always do, Momma," Delphine reminded her unnecessarily.

On the heels of their speculation, Scott sauntered into the front room. "You think fourteen quail will provide us a tasty feast tonight, love?" he asked, affecting an air of innocence.

"Fourteen, Scott?"

"That's right," he grinned. "And if you could get us started with a pan full of hot water, we'll get busy preparing them for you to cook."

Angelique laughed as she started toward her kitchen, for she already had a kettle of water steaming on her stove.

Two hours later, the O'Roarke table groaned beneath a huge platter of golden-brown quail and a large bowl of fluffy rice. With a crock of butter and a pan of corn bread on the sideboard, Angelique took her seat to enjoy this feast while planning another grand meal for the next night. Gabe's sharpshooting this afternoon had also targeted a fine duck. Chantel was beginning to see how the bayou provided the O'Roarkes with most of the meat served at their table.

As she and Delphine were washing the dishes, Delphine told her, "Wait until you eat Momma's fried frog legs!"

Chantel frowned, unable to hide her aversion. "Oh, no," she declared. "I couldn't eat a frog."

"Bet you've never had one."

"No, I haven't and I don't think I care to either."

Delphine laughed. "Chantel, it's as good as chicken — really. Besides, how is a frog any worse than a crawfish. You loved my mother's *étouffée*."

"Crawfish are different from frogs," Chantel protested.

Gabe, standing in the doorway, listened to the two of them with a grin. He well remembered the trick his father had played on Delphine when she was little to convince her that rabbit meat was fine eating. He'd let her think it was chicken until she'd asked for seconds.

When the two of them were taking their aprons off and ready to leave the kitchen, Gabe invited Chantel to go for a stroll with him. He'd been gone practically all day, and tomorrow he would be leaving to get back on the lakes.

Today as he and his father had shared the day, they had engaged in their usual father and son talk. It didn't exactly surprise Scott O'Roarke when his son confessed to him that the golden-haired girl back at the cottage had captured his heart in the first minute he'd met her.

"I know the feeling, son. I felt the same way about your mother. And I still do."

"It's like an omen that she and Delphine returned to New Orleans together. Why, they're closer than sisters."

"We think alike, son," Scott mused. "I would have figured it that way too."

"Dad." Gabe poked at the ground with the butt of his gun. "Delphine wants me to take her into New Orleans to sell some jewelry Savanti gave her. She wants to use the money to pay back the old black woman who bought their passage from her own savings. What do you think?"

"Take her," Scott said without reservation. "Delphine wants to honor a debt she feels she owes. I'm proud of her."

"And what would you think about my personally delivering the money to this Jessamine in Charleston?"

The two Irishmen's eyes locked. Scott knew exactly the thoughts occupying his son's mind. He'd walked in Gabe's shoes some twenty-six years before, and nothing could have stopped him from seeking his revenge against the despicable François La Tour.

"I would say that delivering the money would be a nice gesture on your part, Gabe. I'm sure Jessamine would be pleased to hear from Delphine's brother that the girls are safe and sound."

They had no need to talk further, for they understood one another. The two of them got up from the old fallen tree trunk where they'd been sitting. Gabe picked up the duck he'd already shot, and they moved into the open field to bag themselves some quail.

Later that evening walking with Chantel, he made no mention to her about Charleston. But he did take the opportunity to speak to her about taking Delphine into the city to sell the gems. "Do you want to go with us, Chantel?" he asked. "You could go to *La Maison* to see your mother. That doesn't mean that you can't come back to the bayou with us in the afternoon."

For a moment she didn't answer him, and he noticed that she was hesitant to respond. Finally, she stammered, "I'll think about it, Gabe. Is Delphine going with you in the morning?"

"Not tomorrow," he assured her. "Perhaps Tuesday or Wednesday, so you have time to think about it, love."

"I will, Gabe," she promised.

His arm pulled her closer to him, and he turned to plant a kiss on her cheek. "Hey, honey," he added, "you don't think for a minute that I'd come back here to the bayou and leave you at *La Maison* unless you assured me you wanted to stay there, do you?" He looked intently into her eyes. "Chantel, I love you. You must know that. Tell me you know that, Chantel."

Her green eyes looked up at him with complete trust as she faltered, "I want to believe that, Gabe. I do want to."

He shifted her so he could enclose her in the circle of his arms. His head bent down so that his lips could meet with hers. His heated lips joined with hers in a kiss that confirmed his love to Chantel. She felt the beat of his heart pounding against her breasts. The long, torrid kiss left them both breathless.

In a deep, husky voice he murmured in her ear, "Chantel, oh Chantel, I've never known such love as I feel for you. If you don't feel the same way, then tell me now so I won't make a fool of myself."

Her arms tightened around him. "Oh, Gabe O'Roarke, I would be playing the fool if I tried to deny that I loved you. You know that I love you."

It was all Gabe needed to hear. But it was also enough to make him realize that they had to be married. Soon!

He could not be satisfied to just be Chantel's lover. He wanted to be her husband.

Twenty-three

Gabe put in a long day out on the lakes for he wanted to enrich his father's coffers as much as he could before he and the *Louisiana Lady* put out from New Orleans. When he returned to the bayou that evening, he had made a good catch.

Scott knew why his son was leaving an hour earlier than usual and arriving home an hour later than he normally did. Nevermore had he admired this son he had sired. Gabe's devotion to his family made Scott swell with pride.

After he had put in two long days out on the lakes, Gabe told Delphine Tuesday night after dinner that if she wished to accompany him into the city in the morning she'd have to get up early. While he and his sister were alone, he quizzed her about Chantel. "Has she said anything about coming with us, Delphine?" he asked.

"No. Did you ask her to come with us, Gabe?" Delphine eyed her brother with curiosity.

"I suggested that she might want to visit her mother while you conducted your business. Madame Lamogne is not a bad sort of woman, Delphine. At least, she doesn't appear to be."

It pleased Delphine to hear her brother talk like that. It made her realize that the day might come when she and Gabe could have a talk and she'd be free to tell him about her days at the Paradise Club without feeling shamed.

"Shall I say something to her, Gabe?" she asked, but he shook his head.

"No," he said. "I'll talk to her myself later."

He waited until they were returning to the cottage from their evening stroll. "I'm taking Delphine into New Orleans tomorrow," he said casually. "Have you thought about going in with us?"

Her manner was serious. "Yes, Gabe," she said, "I've thought about it."

"And?"

"I'll go to see my mother, but I'd like to return to the bayou with you and Delphine if that's all right."

"You know it is, Chantel." But he sought to advise her as he had his sister that she'd have to rise and shine early.

"I'll be ready," she assured him. "We'll go to bed early so we can be up at dawn."

The next morning the three of them boarded the *Louisiana Lady* at seven. An hour later they were approaching the docks in the city. "It's early," Chantel said suddenly. "My mother will still be sleeping."

"Come with me, then," urged Delphine. "We'll sell the jewelry and then Gabe can take you to *La Maison* while I get some shopping done for Momma."

But Delphine's transaction didn't take long—the jeweler made a handsome offer for the few pieces she had brought—and it was still far too early for Chantel to arrive at *La Maison*.

Once again, Delphine had the answer. She and Chantel would shop while Gabe attended to his errands.

Later, when Gabe pulled the buggy up in front of the emporium, the two girls were waiting for him, their arms loaded with packages. Gabe leaped to help them, a grin spreading across his face. "What did you do, Delphine—buy out the emporium? I know Momma didn't give you that long a list of supplies."

The two of them were in a lighthearted, giggling mood for they'd had themselves a grand shopping spree with the jewelry money. First Delphine had set aside the money she owed Jessamine. Then she had purchased a gift for her parents and Gabe, and she and Chantel had picked out a bottle of sweet-smelling toilet water for themselves.

Chantel was feeling more relaxed about going to *La Maison* after she and Delphine had enjoyed such a gay time.

As Gabe pulled up at the entrance, he asked her, "When shall I pick you up, Chantel?"

"Could you come back about two?" She wasn't sure how her mother would react to her arrival after the way she'd left.

"I'll be here, honey." He wanted to escort her to the door, but Chantel insisted on going up to the house by herself. But Gabe didn't put the buggy into motion until he saw Jonah open the door.

211

"You ain't no ghost are you, Miss Chantel?" Jonah stammered with utter surprise at the sight of her. "I'm very much alive," Chantel replied, laughing.

"Lordy, Miss Chantel, I was afraid I'd never see you again. Mighty good to see you back here," he declared. "Your ma is going to be one happy lady."

Old Jonah accompanied her to the foot of the stairs. "There's no need for you to climb the steps, Jonah," she told him with a warm smile. "I know my way this time."

Jonah chuckled. "Guess you do, ma'am," he agreed and shuffled off as Chantel prepared to mount the stairs. As usual at this time of day, the long hallway on the second floor was deserted and quiet.

When she reached her mother's *boudoir*, she knocked, and Mimi opened the door immediately. She greeted Chantel with an excited gasp. "You're safe, mademoiselle!" she exclaimed.

"I'm just fine," Chantel acknowledged, moving through the door. "Mother still asleep, Mimi?" she asked.

Aflutter, she stammered, "No, mademoiselle. I'll tell her you are here." She dashed out of the parlor and through the bedroom door. Immediately, Lily came out of the bedroom and rushed to embrace her daughter.

"Oh, Chantel, you are all right and that's all that matters," Lily declared as she led Chantel to the settee so the two of them could sit down.

"I never set out to cause you any concern, Mother. That's why I wrote you the note telling you my plans to go back to Aunt Laurie's. I—I just felt the need to get away," Chantel tried to explain.

"Your Aunt Laurie was just as frantic," Lily told her as she reached for one of her cigarettes.

"My plans went awry, I fear," Chantel confessed.

"So where have you been all this time?" Lily wanted to know. Chantel hedged, uncertain where to begin her complicated story.

Over a brunch tray Chantel told Lily every detail of her escapade from the minute she'd first encountered Carter on the boat up to the night she and Delphine O'Roarke had escaped the clutches of Antoine Savanti.

The worldly Lily Lemogne did not figure that much of anything could shock her, but she did find Chantel's tale upsetting. Lily certainly knew about men like the sadistic Savanti, but to think that her own beautiful daughter had almost been his victim chilled her bones. And her heart went out to Delphine O'Roarke, who had endured so much for so many months.

When Chantel finished her tale, Lily asked her solemnly, "Why didn't you come to me when you arrived back in New Orleans?"

"I—I wanted to go home with Delphine to that quiet little bayou where she lives, Mother. I felt I needed that kind of atmosphere," Chantel declared candidly.

Lily took a sip of her coffee before she said anything more to her daughter. She could not deny that it hurt to know that her daughter preferred the familiarity of strangers to the love and comfort of her own home. But she tried to not show this hurt to Chantel.

"Have you been with the O'Roarkes all this time?" she asked, steadying her voice and inhaling on her cigarette.

"Yes, Mother," Chantel admitted. "Ever since we got back. Delphine and I formed a very strong bond of friendship, but I had no inkling until we arrived in New Orleans that her brother is Gabe O'Roarke."

"Gabe's Delphine's brother?" Lily asked, stunned.

"That's right. I met Gabe here before I left for Boston," Chantel told her.

Those all-knowing, experienced eyes of Lily Lemogne had been intensely scrutinizing her daughter during the last hour they'd spent together. Lily saw changes in her daughter. She had an independence about her now that had not been there this summer. Now Chantel talked openly and frankly with Lily.

They finished their brunch and had several cups of coffee. Lily lit another cigarette, but Chantel stood up. "I need to get a few things before Gabe comes to pick me up," she announced. "I left Charleston with nothing but the dress I have on now."

Taken aback, Lily whirled, her dressing gown flowing about her as she followed Chantel through the parlor and across the hallway to the room she'd occupied only a few weeks before.

It had been a long time since Lily Lemogne had been as confused and perplexed as she was now. Her daughter had a mind of her own and was willfully determined to use it.

"Are you telling me, Chantel, that you only came here this afternoon to pay me a visit and that you are going to go back to the bayou to stay?" Indignant, Lily could not disguise the resentment that churned within her.

Chantel had anticipated her mother's reaction. In fact, that was the only reason that she had hesitated to come here today. But she knew that she was not ready to return to *La Maison*—not yet.

She turned to her distraught mother and addressed her with a calm self-assurance. "Believe me, Mother, it will be best for you and me if I do—at least for a while." As she spoke, she placed a neat pile of undergarments, nightgowns, and wrappers on the bed. She pulled a few garments from the armoire although it bulged with gowns and wraps. She chose simple afternoon frocks and the crème-colored, short wool cape.

Lily's dark eyes flashed with the fire that sparked her daughter's green eyes. "Well, I'll leave you to your packing, Chantel," she said frostily. "I'll be in my bedroom."

At a few minutes before two, Chantel went back across the hall to tell her mother goodbye before she descended the stairway.

She gave Lily a warm embrace despite her stiff, unresponsing air. Chantel didn't allow Lily to weaken her resolve, although her own words upset Lily when she realized she could give Chantel no argument.

"You know where I am, Mother, and I will come back to see you. In fact, I'll see you more often than I did in the past. Twice a year isn't much, Mother."

Lily found that it was one of those rare times in her life that she didn't have a quick retort. Chastened, she merely remarked, "And you know where I'll be, Chantel."

Chantel kissed her mother's cheek and turned to leave the room. She went down the steps with the valise in her hand. The minute she walked out the front entrance she was greeted warmly by Gabe.

"Ready to go home, love?" he called out to her. Jauntily leaping down from the buggy, he rushed up to take the valise. With his free hand, he reached out for hers.

"I'm ready, Gabe," she told him, flashing a radiant smile just for him.

Lily happened at that moment to look out the window at the street below and saw her golden-haired daughter being helped into the buggy by the handsome young Irish fisherman. She also saw something else: the two young people were in love.

Twenty-four

Little Mimi knew that something had not worked out right between Madame Lily and her daughter but she dared not say anything. However, she had slipped across the hall to see if Mademoiselle Chantel were in her room and she wasn't so Mimi understood that she'd left *La Maison* as swiftly as she'd appeared some three hours ago.

She also noticed that throughout the rest of the afternoon her mistress was unusually quiet and pre-occupied. Chantel's departing words had pricked her to the core of her being. Her daughter had not wanted fancy gowns and clothes to wear or an elegant house to live in. She had wanted her mother's time, something Lily had not given her for five years.

She had had the best that Boston could offer — but no mother. For five years she had smoldered with resentment. And Lily had been unaware.

To see a little girl only once every six months wasn't enough to make much of an impact on her, Lily had to admit. She had to be fair with her daughter at this late date, now that she'd been made to face the unpleasant truth today. It was apparent to Lily that that little cottage on the bayou offered a home and haven to Chantel that she did not find here in the lavish *La Maison* where she had her own private bedroom and an armoire filled with fancy clothes.

She'd noted the simple gowns Chantel had selected to take with her. Her choices told Lily a lot about what Chantel wanted and what she had failed miserably to give to her one and only daughter.

At the usual appointed hour, Lily asked Mimi to prepare her bath. She had sorted out everything in her mind and was ready to get on with her own life and routine.

That evening Andre Deverone listened intensely as she told him about the afternoon she'd spent with her daughter and what had actually happened to her.

"Oh, Lily, she'll be all right," he consoled her. "Just thank God she's alive and well. These people must be awfully good if Chantel admires them so much."

Andre's heart went out to Lily for he could not miss the pain in her voice as she spoke about Chantel. A forced smile came to her lovely face as she declared, "Obviously she prefers the O'Roarke's way of life."

"We could remedy that *chèrie,*" he reminded her. "You know I'm more than willing to share that spacious house of mine with you and your daughter. You've promised to marry me in six months, but why should we wait?"

"Now, Andre Deverone, don't you give me a rough time, too," she admonished and then reached out and held on tightly to his hand.

A feeling of blissful contentment engulfed her as Chantel sat beside Gabe in the buggy and they headed for the wharf.

She seemed in such a happy mood that Gabe assumed she had had a pleasant visit with her mother. He was glad she'd decided to see Lily and hoped that Lily bore no resentment toward him or his family. He knew his mother would have been very hurt if Delphine had wanted to stay with someone else.

"Everything was fine," Chantel mumbled in response to his questioning look, she couldn't bring herself to tell him the truth.

"Well, I've always liked Madame Lemogne," Gabe repeated as they pulled up near the wharf. He helped Chantel out of the buggy and set her luggage on the ground. When he had paid the young man from the livery for the use of the buggy, he took Chantel's arm and escorted her to the boat where Delphine was waiting for them.

It was early for Gabe to be heading for the bayou, but he had set this day aside for Delphine and Chantel. Tomorrow he'd put in another long day; and if things went the way he planned, he would leave Friday morning for Charleston.

"Oh, Gabe," Delphine had suggested when he'd told her of his plan to personally pay back Jessamine, "if she wants to get out of there, you bring her here. Bring her to the bayou if she'll come with you."

"I will," he'd promised her. "Now, please, don't tell mother or Chantel about my going to Charleston. I don't want them to worry. Dad knows, though. He and I have already discussed it and he approves."

He wasn't dealing with the younger sister that he'd always outsmarted in the past. Her dark eyes locked with his. "You're going to do more in Charleston than repay my debt to Jessamine, aren't you? Don't you try to lie to me, Gabe O'Roarke."

There was a serious look on Gabe's face that Delphine had not seen often. His blue eyes looked at her in anguish and his voice was husky with emotion. "That man in Charleston sullied my sister and planned the same fate for the lady I love. I can't dismiss that."

"I'm fine now, Gabe, and so is Chantel," Delphine objected. "Neither of us wants you to put yourself in danger. You can't imagine the power Savanti has in Charleston, Gabe."

"I'll be careful," Gabe affirmed. "But I'll not rest until I settle this score. I want it over and done with once and for all."

Delphine saw there was no point in trying to talk him out of going to Charleston. He was just like her father and Grandpa O'Roarke before him.

So she merely nodded her head and cautioned him. "Just remember what I've told you about Savanti. He's a dangerous, ruthless man. No, not a man, a fiend."

When the *Louisiana Lady* turned back toward the bayou, the sun was still high in the sky. On a workday Gabe would have spent another two hours on the waters.

He had the girls back at the cottage, Delphine's packages and Chantel's valise unloaded, long before Scott arrived at the dock. The girls were preoccupied in Delphine's room, unpacking, when Gabe sauntered into his mother's kitchen.

"Do you think it went all right?" Angelique asked anxiously and he knew she meant Chantel's reunion with Lily Lemogne.

"It must have, Momma," he replied. "She was there for three hours and she brought back a heavy valise." Gabe lifted the lid of each pot on the stove, sniffing hungrily.

Angelique smiled with amusement. "Roast duck," she confirmed, "with your favorite orange marmalade sauce."

"Ah, it smells wonderful!" He hugged her and gave her a wink. "I don't think I'll ever get married. That way I can stay here and enjoy your good cooking the rest of my life." He grinned unabashedly.

"Tell that to someone else, Gabe O'Roarke, for I don't believe you for one minute. You inherited that silken tongue of yours from your dad," she said, her black Creole eyes sparkling mischievously.

Seeing his father's boat nearing the dock, Gabe left the kitchen and went outside. He wanted a few private moments with Scott before he came in.

"Delphine sold the jewelry and Chantel saw her mother," he filled his father in quickly. "But I almost forgot—I have to run up to Terry's before momma has supper ready. I need to have him make the delivery to Madame Lemogne on Friday."

Scott O'Roarke studied his son. "I presume that means you are leaving before Friday afternoon," he said quietly.

"Yes, sir, I'm going to be leaving bright and early Friday morning. Plan to put in a long day tomorrow since I got nothing done today."

"Don't worry about that," Scott said. "We'll be fine. Terry and I will have ourselves a fine catch. You just go do what you got to do and then get your butt back here safe and sound."

"Oh, I'll get back. You don't have to worry about that," his son told him with a cocky air and shoved off from the dock in the canoe. "Tell Momma I'll be back in time to eat that duck," he called, dipping his paddle into the stream.

Scott grinned and waved, but Gabe's strong, muscled arms had already taken him a good distance away.

He found Terry in the kitchen, a white apron tied around his middle. His sister was setting the table.

Gabe stated his business quickly. "It's a rather large weekly order so I wouldn't want to lose it," Gabe explained.

"I'll have it there for you," Terry promised. "You can count on me."

Gabe, not wanting to miss his own supper, turned to make a hasty departure. Terry handed his spatula to his sister and followed Gabe.

Wiping his hand on the apron, he ran his long fingers through the unruly brown hair that fell across his face. When they reached the front porch,

Terry stopped Gabe with a hesitant question. "Just another minute, Gabe," he began.

"Sure, Terry, what is it?" Gabe's stomach grumbled and he covered the sound and his anxiousness to leave with a shuffle of his feet. Then he noticed that Terry, a tall man who measured four inches over six feet, was as nervous and bashful as a school boy.

He cleared hiss throat and looked down at the stoop. "Would it be all right with you if I courted your sister?" he faltered. "I've loved her since we were all just kids."

Without missing a beat, Gabe gave his approval. "But it's Delphine you need to talk to, Terry," he reminded the jittery suitor. "But, for what it's worth, my dad and I will be rooting for you. Good luck."

A grin of relief illuminated Terry's rugged face, and he pumped Gabe's arm in gratitude. "Thanks," he said. "Thanks."

Back in the kitchen, he fried his fish and the skillet of potatoes with a gleeful flick of the wrist. And when he sat down and spread his napkin across his lap, he found that he was ravenously hungry.

Part Three

Rendezvous in Charleston

Twenty-five

As Gabe was getting out of the canoe at his father's dock, a sudden shower pelted him with a cold biting rain. By the time he got to the porch, his shirt was spotted by the raindrops.

His father was the only one in the front room, and he looked up from his paper. "Get your business taken care of?" he asked.

"Yes sir, I did." He sat down and ran his hands over his damp hair. "Rain's coming down outside," he added.

"I didn't know that," Scott declared keeping a straight face as he handed his son a towel to dry off.

"I don't need that for tomorrow, Dad."

"We don't have any say about it," Scott told his son. "Worry about those things you can change."

"The platters are on the table," his mother interrupted. "Dinner is served, gentlemen."

She didn't have to tell them twice, for both of them eagerly leaped out of their chairs to follow her back into the kitchen.

The light rains came more steadily, and as they

ate they could hear the sound of the drops drumming against the windows and on the roof. Reluctantly Gabe conceded that he and Chantel would enjoy no leisurely woodland stroll together this evening.

But Delphine added spice to the after-dinner hours once they had gathered in the front room and the lamps in the kitchen were dimmed.

She brought out the gifts she'd purchased in New Orleans — a blue pullover for Gabe and a pearl-grey cotton shirt for Scott. For her mother, she had picked out a knit vest in a pale pink that would complement her dark coloring.

At least, Savanti's gems had brought smiles to her family tonight, Delphine thought with pleasure. She and Chantel had the luxury of magnolia-sweet toilet water, and Gabe had the rest of the money in his pocket to give to Jessamine.

Oh, she knew that the jewels were worth far more than she'd received, but she didn't care about that.

Everyone retired early, perhaps because they'd all eaten heartily of Angelique's roast duck or perhaps because the pitter-patter of the rains outside had a soothing, relaxing effect.

For awhile after Gabe went to his own room, he lay on the bed pondering how naturally Chantel fit into his family — as if she belonged with them. Taking refuge in Irish superstition, he chose to believe that their paths had crossed as part of a broader plan: Chantel was meant to be his.

By dawn the rains had moved out of the area and

Gabe had a perfect day to work the lakes. Meanwhile, Delphine wondered how he would tell Chantel and what her reaction would be. He might be able to fool Chantel, she considered, but Angelique would not be easily deceived. She would question him—and question her husband. Scott would find it impossible to lie to her. They'd lived together too long and knew one another too well. He'd have to tell her the truth.

As Delphine had suspected, the minute Angelique and Scott were in the privacy of their own bedroom she insisted that Scott tell her what Gabe was really up to.

"You're not to mention a word of this to Chantel," he cautioned. "Gabe's going to Charleston."

He didn't need to say more. Gabe was his father's son, and she understood. But the next morning she got up as dawn was breaking to have a private talk with him before he left. Scott, only half-asleep, smiled to himself when she slipped out of their bed. He had expected as much.

She was in the kitchen with a pot of coffee brewing before Gabe entered, and took him by surprise. "What are you up to?" he asked as she bolted into the pantry, returning with the extra pie she'd baked last night and two loaves of her home-baked bread. Piling them in his arms, she reached back into the pantry for a ham.

"You get all this stuff down to your boat, Gabe," she directed. "Then we'll have some coffee."

"Just coffee, Momma," he said firmly. "Nothing to eat." He accepted the foodstuff for the trip and stowed it on board.

When he returned, he sipped the coffee to placate her. He sensed that she knew his mission and was determined to worry. At last he pushed back his chair from the table and patted her hand. "I've a long way to go and the sooner I leave, the sooner I can get back," he reminded her. He could have all the coffee he wanted once he got on the *Louisiana Lady*.

She inclined her head in a nod of acceptance. "Son," she said, placing a hand on each side of his head, "I appreciate why you're going, but you just make sure you get back to this bayou. You're the only son I've got."

He bent down and gave her a kiss on the cheek and a promise that she had nothing to worry about. "I'll be back here to pester you before you know it," he threatened playfully.

Angelique watched his tall, towering figure glide down the pathway through the grove of trees that sloped to the banks of the bayou. A short time later she could see the *Louisiana Lady* moving away from their dock and navigating up the bayou.

She glanced at the sky and saw the sun rising from the horizon. Her day had begun and soon Scott would be up as well. Dabbing at the dampness in the corners of her eyes, she focused her attention on a man who never turned down breakfast.

From the bedroom he could smell the inviting aroma of slab bacon frying in the iron skillet. So his appetite was whetted by the time he entered the kitchen to greet her with a warm kiss on the cheek. "Gabe is off, I guess," he commented, pouring his own coffee as she slid the bacon from skillet to platter and dropped four eggs into the drippings.

By seven, contented and well-fed, he was ready to be on his way on the *Bayou Queen*. "We'll put in an extra hour today if we can," he told Angelique, crumpling his napkin beside his plate. "Expect us when we get here."

"So we'll eat a little later than usual." She flicked a bit of dried egg from his cheek with her fingertip, then kissed the spot on his cheek. "Have a good day, dear."

And he walked down the same pathway as Gabe. Her two men . . . so much alike . . . so much in love.

Several hours passed before the two girls stumbled sleepily into the kitchen. Angelique had found that Chantel was exactly like her Delphine. She didn't eat much in the morning. They were both nibblers at the breakfast table—a nibble of ham or a half of a biscuit with a dab of jelly was about it.

Chantel wanted even less this morning, barely touching her coffee, staring idly into space while Delphine chattered and Angelique, just outside the back door, worked in her vegetable garden.

Gabe's announcement after dinner last night had caught her completely unprepared. Stunned, she'd not even asked him where he was going. "I'll be back as soon as I can," he'd vowed, but she'd hardly heard him.

Trancelike, she'd paid little attention to anyone else. Even after she and Delphine had retired to the bedroom, she'd remained remote, untouched by Delphine's endearing prattle.

231

Delphine knew that long after she'd dimmed the lamp Chantel had lain quietly in the darkness, unable to close her eyes and go to sleep.

Because she was aware of his intentions, Delphine, too, was concerned about Gabe. Listening to the uneven breathing that signified Chantel's sleeplessness, she realized a few white lies might be in order if Chantel were to be protected from learning Gabe's whereabouts—as he had wished.

Feigning a deep interest in her coffee and biscuit, Delphine taxed her brain for something to get Chantel's mind off Gabe's seeming desertion.

"Ever been fishing?" she asked abruptly.

Chantel raised a skeptical eyebrow. "Fishing?"

"That's right."

"No, never."

"Do you want to try your hand at it?" Delphine coaxed. "If you're going to be a bayou girl, you've got to try fishing." Chantel shook her head doubtfully, but Delphine was insistent. "We'll sit on the dock with a couple of old poles and see if we can land ourselves a fish. By the time Gabe gets back, you'll be a pro."

A slow smile came to Chantel's face as she gave in. "I guess I could give it a try."

Delphine giggled. "Then come on. I've got some old pants of Gabe's I used to wear somewhere upstairs."

Chantel tagged along behind her, enthusiasm building. "Did you say pants?" she questioned curiously.

"Exactly. Momma would cut off Gabe's old pants for me. Now all I've got to do is find the darn things — and my plaid shirts. You'd better wear Gabe's straw hat or, with that fair complexion of yours, you'll burn to a crisp."

In her room, Delphine rummaged through the drawers of the highboy. Chantel sat on the bed watching her toss outgrown clothing to the floor until she finally gave out a shriek of delight. "Ah, I found them!"

A half-hour later they had changed into the baggy dark-blue pants and loose, comfortable shirts.

Delphine sat down at her dressing table and began to plait her long black hair. "You ought to braid yours, too," she suggested, studying her friend in the mirror.

In a playful mood, Delphine flopped the old straw hat atop Chantel's head and pulled her out to the old shed to find the fishing poles.

Angelique, eyeing them from her kitchen sink where she was rinsing the vegetables she'd just picked in her garden, laughed with gusto.

"Do we look that funny?" Chantel asked. Angelique nodded, holding her sides, and the girls broke into laughter, too.

"Good luck," she bade them. "I'll be expecting a couple of big ones for my dinner tonight."

Watching the two of them breeze down to the dock, Angelique submitted to another wave of laughter. They reminded her of the two scarecrows in Mrs. Munson's garden.

She hoped that Chantel would land her first fish today. She'd never forget Delphine's first catch. She'd run all the way up the path screaming with excitement and smug with pride. And she'd been almost incredulous when Angelique had served *her* fish on a platter for dinner that night.

"Am I getting old?" Angelique wondered, catching herself in her reverie. Sometimes it seemed like only yesterday the children had been little and then again it seemed like a lifetime ago.

Twenty-six

Sitting with her legs dangling over the edge of the dock was the best tonic Chantel could have had that late summer afternoon. Delphine was to realize that she'd made a wise decision to persuade Chantel to go fishing with her. She was enjoying herself and Delphine would never forget how wide her green eyes were the first time she'd felt the nudging of a fish about to take her bait.

"Delphine! Delphine, I think I've got a bite," she'd whispered, amazement reflecting on her face.

"Let him take the whole thing before you yank that pole, Chantel, and you will have caught yourself a fish," she cautioned her.

But Chantel got over-anxious and yanked her line too soon. "The fish is gone," she said in surprise when she checked her line.

"Part of your bait, too," Delphine observed. "Fishing takes patience."

But Chantel had no use for patience, especially when Delphine landed a very nice-sized bass.

"You'll likely get one, too, before we go back to

the cabin," Delphine told her. "It just takes time."

They had been on the dock for almost three hours when Delphine noticed that Chantel had finally hooked a fish. "Yank that pole, Chantel," she cried. "You've got one this time."

So she gave a wild yank and to her delight a bass dangled in the air. Delphine helped her maneuver the pole so they could grab the line to get hold of the fish. Chantel's green eyes were sparkling. "My fish is bigger than yours," she taunted.

They laughed together as Delphine added Chantel's bass to the bucket. "Well, let's take these to Momma and demand that we have them for dinner tonight. You take the bucket and I'll take the poles, Chantel," Delphine told her as they got up from the dock.

Angelique was as thrilled as the girls when they displayed their catch. But she was working up the dough for her bread so she told Delphine that she would have to get busy scaling them. Delphine frowned. "I've got to scale them?" she asked.

"Well, you'd better if you want them for dinner tonight," Angelique said. "I can't stop in the middle of the bread. You caught them, you scale them."

Delphine knew how to scale a fish, but it was just a job she didn't relish. Her father or Gabe usually did it.

The procedure intrigued Chantel, but then the entire afternoon had been a new experience for her. By the time the bass were cleaned and washed, Delphine was more than ready to have a bath and get out of her fishing clothes and Chantel felt the same way.

The girls were still in their room when Scott O'Roarke docked the *Bayou Queen*. It was such a beautiful late afternoon that Angelique had left her kitchen to sit on the front steps.

Her bread and the pan of cornbread for their supper were already baked. The bass, cleaned and scaled, were waiting to be fried. Nothing required her immediate attention, and she found it nice to just sit and enjoy the gentle breeze blowing through the tall oak trees. Released from the confines of her kitchen, stuffy from the heat of baking, she breathed in the fresh air in greedy gulps.

She saw the *Bayou Queen* when it inched around the twist in the stream and she was pleased that Scott was getting home not much later than usual. So she walked down to the dock to greet him.

"Well, this is a nice welcome, love. What did I do to deserve this?" Scott teased, a twinkle in his blue eyes.

"You got home sooner than I'd expected." She took hold of his arm, and the two of them started up the path. "Chantel caught her first fish this afternoon," she told him, filling in the details of the day. "Can you guess what we're having for dinner?"

"Terry's mother's feeling poorly," he told her in their exchange of news. "I knew he wanted to get home to her, so I figured that we didn't need what another hour would have given us in extra fish."

Angelique smiled up at him as she declared, "And you, Scott O'Roarke, are a most understanding, generous man. That's why I love you so very much."

He bent over to give her a kiss and a compliment.

"I might as well confess that I'm always more than ready to get back to this bayou and you. It has nothing to do with my being generous."

The two of them were in a gay, carefree mood as they entered the cottage, and Scott's arm encircled her.

Chantel, observing them, envied the love she saw reflected in their eyes It must be wonderful to feel that way about someone after you've been married for over twenty-five years, she thought with a happy sigh.

Perhaps that was why she had so desperately wanted to return. There was warmth and love within the walls of this little cottage, and that as much as Gabe had drawn her back here. Oh, she'd not deny to herself that being around and near Gabe gave her a feeling of bliss like nothing she'd ever known before.

She wondered if Delphine suspected that she and Gabe had been lovers. Delphine was so much more experienced than she was that it wouldn't surprise her if she did sense that they'd been intimate.

The four of them enjoyed the delicious fish that evening, but beneath the lighthearted banter, each of them was aware that something was missing. And they each knew that that something was Gabe.

Gabe had taken a light crew with him, including a young man named Denny who had just hired on a week ago. Denny had been sleeping on the boat to escape the wrath of his drunken father, but he was so new to the crew that Gabe had not even told

Scott about him yet.

Caleb who had been with him since the day he'd taken charge of the *Louisiana Lady*, was automatically included on his skeleton crew along with the pot-bellied Jean Paul, who had also been around since day one. An Acadian, he'd lost his wife and children to yellow fever when it had struck a brutal blow around New Orleans seven years before.

Often, Gabe had taken Jean Paul and Caleb to his home in the bayou to enjoy the hospitality of his family. All the O'Roarkes liked the two men, and Gabe took them into his confidence about his mission in Charleston. They in turn pledged their support.

It had been smooth-sailing, and the *Louisiana Lady* had made good time from New Orleans to Mobile. By the second day, they were cruising the northern coastline of Florida.

They encountered rain on the third day and covered less distance, but the next morning the sun shone bright in the eastern sky.

As he plotted his course in the waters, Gabe also plotted his course of action in Charleston. Delphine had given him the layout of Savanti's estate and had warned him to stay clear of the bodyguard that patrolled the mansion.

He knew it wasn't going to be an easy task, and he had no intention of taking any of his crew with him into Charleston. When he went out to the Savanti estate, he would be alone. This was his vendetta, and he would not involve his crew in his personal feud.

But his thoughts kept drifting back to the bayou.

He would not linger in Charleston. He was there to do a job and nothing more.

When he pulled into Savannah, Gabe recalled all that Chantel and Delphine had told him of the city. Delphine had been deserted in Savannah by the riverboat dude who'd lured her from her bayou home. And it was in Savannah that Chantel had met that vermin Carter Bascombe.

Ironically, the *Delta Queen*, the ship that had brought Chantel and Delphine back to New Orleans, was docked in Savannah. Gabe studied the passengers as they boarded the vessel.

He shook his head at the sight of the elegantly clad couples and the dapper fellows who strode up the gangplank alone. Any one of them might be the foul Bascombe.

But Gabe didn't make a stop in Savannah, so he guided the *Louisiana Lady* on up the coast. He would have liked to have wreaked his revenge on both Antoine Savanti and Carter Bascombe. But, since Bascombe was out of his reach, he decided that settling the score with Savanti would be enough to satisfy him.

His *Louisiana Lady* was almost an hour ahead of the *Delta Queen* that late afternoon in August.

What Gabe could not know was that one of the dapper gentlemen *was* Carter Bascome, making his routine sales trip and also on the lookout for a new lady for Antoine's boudoir.

Savanti had been exceptionally cantankerous since his last purchase had managed to escape before he'd had even one night's pleasure with her. He was all the more vexed because he could recall her

The Publishers of Zebra Books Make This Special Offer to Zebra Romance Readers...

AFTER YOU HAVE READ THIS BOOK WE'D LIKE TO SEND YOU 4 MORE FOR *FREE* AN $18.00 VALUE

No Obligation!

4 FREE BOOKS

TO GET YOUR 4 FREE BOOKS WORTH $18.00 — MAIL IN THE FREE BOOK CERTIFICATE T O D A Y

Fill in the Free Book Certificate below, and we'll send your FREE BOOKS to you as soon as we receive it.

If the certificate is missing below, write to: Zebra Home Subscription Service, Inc., P.O. Box 5214, 120 Brighton Road, Clifton, New Jersey 07015-5214.

FREE BOOK CERTIFICATE

4 FREE BOOKS

ZEBRA HOME SUBSCRIPTION SERVICE, INC.

YES! Please start my subscription to Zebra Historical Romances and send me my first 4 books absolutely FREE. I understand that each month I may preview four new Zebra Historical Romances free for 10 days. If I'm not satisfied with them, I may return the four books within 10 days and owe nothing. Otherwise, I will pay the low preferred subscriber's price of just $3.75 each; a total of $15.00, *a savings off the publisher's price of $3.00.* I may return any shipment and I may cancel this subscription at any time. There is no obligation to buy any shipment and there are no shipping, handling or other hidden charges. Regardless of what I decide, the four free books are mine to keep.

NAME

ADDRESS _____ APT _____

CITY _____ STATE _____ ZIP _____

TELEPHONE
(   )

SIGNATURE _____
(if under 18, parent or guardian must sign)

Terms, offer and prices subject to change without notice. Subscription subject to acceptance by Zebra Books. Zebra Books reserves the right to reject any order or cancel any subscription.

ZB0993

GET
FOUR
FREE
BOOKS
(AN $18.00 VALUE)

ZEBRA HOME SUBSCRIPTION
SERVICE, INC.
120 BRIGHTON ROAD
P.O. Box 5214
CLIFTON, NEW JERSEY 07015-5214

breathtaking beauty. If only he'd not been so ill that night, he fumed, she would have been his—completely.

Not for one minute had he suspected his trusted servant Jessamine of conspiring against him. But not a day went by that Jessamine did not think about the girls she had helped to flee. Soon, she thought, she would hear from them. They had to be back in New Orleans by now.

Savanti had found no replacement yet for Delphine and Chantel, but Jessamine knew that sooner or later Carter Bascombe would exchange another beautiful young girl for a pot of money. Scum, Jessamine whispered to herself with loathing whenever she thought of either man.

Jessamine, privileged to move freely throughout the house, had slipped into Delphine's suite only to find that all trace of the girl had been erased.

Her subtle queries soon disclosed that the young mulatto Dahlia had disposed of Miss Delphine's personal effects. So, Jessamine suspected Savanti was using young Dahlia until Bascombe chanced upon a suitable new toy.

Poor naive Dahlia readily responded to Jessamine's proddings. At Savanti's direction, she confided, she'd burned the contents of the armoire and chests.

"All those beautiful silk gowns went up in smoke," Dahlia lamented. "Such pretty lace and satin—all destroyed. It's a waste." She gazed at Jessamine with wide-eyed innocence, confused. "Why would he want me to do that?"

"I'm only the housekeeper," Jessamine had answered shortly. "Monsieur Savanti doesn't defend his actions to me."

That night when she got to her quarters she told herself that she could not allow herself to become Dahlia's protector, too. She was getting old, and rescue missions were too risky. More than ever she yearned to leave this place and get back where she belonged. The New Orleans of a happier time beckoned to her.

Somehow, the calling had been so constant lately that Jessamine could not ignore it. She was thinking seriously about leaving before another poor angel came into that mansion and pulled at the strings of her heart. She had enough money to buy herself passage to New Orleans and she figured that she had two good friends waiting for her even though she didn't know exactly where Miss Delphine or Miss Chantel were.

But Jessamine knew that she could always find herself a fine house to clean or someone in need of a good cook, so she didn't worry that she'd be idle long.

"Perhaps," she thought, "it's destiny." And as the idea of unseen forces directing her life took hold, she became convinced that she should return to New Orleans. Tomorrow.

Twenty-seven

Clouds had settled in on the Charleston coastline by the time Gabe approached the harbor. Before he left the *Louisiana Lady,* he put Caleb in charge, advising him that he might be absent through the next day. How long would his business in this city take? He did not know.

Fog and drizzly rain misted the city, hindering Gabe's progress. At the livery where he hired a buggy, the manager recognized the name Savanti instantly provided clear directions to the estate. Gabe remembered that Delphine had cautioned him about Savanti's power in Charleston.

As he'd guided the buggy to the outskirts of the city, Gabe determined the ploy he'd use to gain audience with the black woman Jessamine. He had two goals to accomplish. He would pay Jessamine back the money Delphine owed her and take her with him if she wished to leave. But he also intended to prevent Savanti from ever taking advantage of another innocent girl.

When he leaped from the buggy, a giant of a

black man met him at the front door, and Gabe knew instantly that he had to be Monte. A fierce-looking brute, he glowered at Gabe, who claimed to have brought word to Jessamine of her brother. "Her bother Jonah," he said facilely, adding a personal touch and conjuring an image of old Jonah at *La Maison*.

Unquestioning but silent, Monte guided him to the kitchen and Jessamine. "News of your family," Monte growled succinctly in a deep bass voice. Jessamine's brow knitted in a quizzical frown as she dried her hands and faced him.

Please don't give me away, he prayed beneath his bland pose of messenger. "Yes, ma'am," he interjected quickly. "I've come from New Orleans."

"Have a seat, young man," she offered, pulling a straight-backed chair out from the table. "I'm most anxious to hear any news from New Orleans." Gabe relaxed and gratefully accepted the cup of coffee she poured for him, grasping the mug tightly for moral support. "Do you want something, Monte?" she asked curtly, and Monte retreated, dismissed. She noted with amusement the scowl on his face. Their dislike of one another had always been apparent — and mutual.

Mindful that he might linger in the corridor, listening, Jessamine wasn't going to take any chances. She bent close to Gabe and asked in a whisper, "Who are you really, monsieur?"

Gabe, keeping his voice low, spoke quickly, "My name's Gabe O'Roarke. I'm Delphine's brother."

"Well, dear God Almighty," she sighed. She motioned for him to follow her into the pantry. When they were inside the small room, she asked him, "Are they safe?"

"Thanks to you, Jessamine," he affirmed. "My family and I are very grateful for what you did, and I've brought you the money they owe you."

"You made this a happy day for me, monsieur," she said, "but I don't like the way Monte was sizing you up."

"Delphine warned me about him" he said, "I'm prepared for anything."

"I'm sure you are," she agreed. "We need to talk more, but not here." With a jerk of her head toward the corridor and the possibly eavesdropping Monte, she indicated danger. "Meet me in my quarters over the carriage house in an hour. But for now, get in your buggy and leave." She thought quickly. "Go back down the main road, but turn south on the first side road. You'll come to another lane that veers to the east. That will take you to the back of the carriage house. There is a thick grove of trees where you can hide the buggy. The carriage house steps lead directly to my apartment. The door's unlocked." She ushered him back into the kitchen, carrying a plate of biscuits as camouflage.

"I'll be there, Jessamine," he agreed readily.

The housekeeper had been wise to take him into the seclusion of the pantry, he realized for as she led him back through the house to the front entrance it was obvious that the seven-foot giant lurking in the hall had been trying to overhear their conversation.

With the cockiness of youth, Gabe sauntered past Monte and gave him a flip of his hand as a farewell gesture. He repeated Jessamine's instructions to himself as he guided buggy and bay down the drive to the main road. He checked frequently over his shoulder to make certain he was not being followed.

The road behind him was deserted, so he made his turn onto the side road and traveled the short distance down the lane to the grove of trees. From the buggy, he could see the roof of the carriage house jutting through the tree branches.

The sun was sinking in the western sky, but Gabe had another hour to wait before Jessamine could leave the big house. To fill the time, he lit up one of his cheroots. The lower the sun, the greater his advantage.

But when he stubbed out his cigar and slipped through the grove of trees for a survey of the carriage house and the surrounding grounds, he saw that it would have been difficult for anyone to see him climbing Jessamine's stairway. A row of ancient evergreens towering over thirty feet effectively blocked the view from the big house.

So he didn't hesitate any longer to leave the security of the grove and walk the short distance to the steps. Once inside the quarters, he remained in darkness. He filled the coffeepot with water and put kindling in the cookstove so the coffee could start brewing once Jessamine entered the door.

When she arrived, he was puffing on one of his cheroots. Already at home, he lit the kindling for her and she set a wicker basket of food on her kitchen table.

"Got us a nice supper here, Monsieur Gabe," she said with a welcoming smile.

"What all you got in that basket?" he asked, realizing with surprise that he was indeed hungry.

"Fried chicken," she said. "And roasted sweet potatoes. A fresh-baked loaf of bread. And, oh yes, a cherry pie."

Gabe grinned. "You're tempting me sorely. What do you want of me?"

"I want you to stay awhile, monsieur," she replied promptly, dead serious. "I've got a question for you. Monte came back in the kitchen after you left. He said you had told him you had news of my brother Jonah."

Gabe laughed. "I just made that up, Jessamine."

"But Monsieur Gabe," she said earnestly, "I *do* have a brother named Jonah."

"Well, I'll be darned!"

"And Jonah was living in New Orleans the last I heard."

Jessamine set the coffee to brewing, and laid out their meal while Gabe brought her up-to-date. He placed a roll of money on the table. "I figure it's safe to give you this now," he said.

"I was just glad to be able to help those two angels, monsieur," she assured him. "They needed protection and love." Solemnly she filled his plate with chicken and sweet potatoes. "Sure as God makes little green apples, it's getting ready to happen again," she declared with an unhappy sigh. "Carter Bascombe was here last week, and I know that soon—perhaps in a day or two—he'll be delivering another unsuspecting girl to Monsieur Savanti." She closed her eyes as if fighting off a wave of pain. "I—I just don't know if I can go through it again."

"You don't have to." Gabe met her gaze with frank concern. "Leave with me," he urged. "Get out of this hellhole. Delphine asked me to bring you to New Orleans."

"You mean that, don't you, monsieur?" Jessamine looked into his blue eyes and saw the depth of his sincerity. And she reflected on coincidence and fate, for she had drawn all her money out of the bank just three days ago with that self-same purpose in mind. New Orleans, she had decided, couldn't be any worse than Charleston.

"Can you leave tonight?" he asked, and she chuckled.

"I've already got one valise packed. It won't take me long to fill the other."

"Then you'll come with me?

"Yes," she replied simply. "It's time for me to go."

Gabe gulped the last of his coffee. "Pack, then," he said. "I have to go back to the big house, and then we'll leave."

"What are you going to do?" she demanded, eyes wide and troubled. "You tell Jessamine."

"I've a score to settle before I leave Charleston," he explained, and she frowned. She cocked her head to one side as she prodded him. "Are you saying what I think you are saying, Monsieur Gabe?"

"I probably am, Jessamine."

"Then you are asking for big, big trouble. Monte can kill you with his hands — and wouldn't hesitate to do so. He moves like a cat — quiet, curious, and stealthy. He prowls, and you never know when he's going to be sneaking up behind you."

But, seeing that Gabe was adamant and determined for vengeance, she outlined Savanti's evening routine when he was without a female companion. "He goes to bed early," she said. "Right after dinner. When he goes upstairs, Monte takes up his post downstairs in the front hall. That means you can use the back stairs to reach his bedroom, which is at the far end of the south hallway." Gabe stroked his chin, trying to envision the layout. "But, monsieur," Jessamine warned, "don't let him pull the cord by his bed or you'll have Monte upon you like a raging bull."

She glanced at the clock on the wall. "The kitchen should be deserted now," she observed. "It will be uncommonly quiet, and Monte will respond to the slightest sound."

"And Savanti usually retires early if he doesn't have a pretty girl to torment?" Gabe repeated, beginning to flush out the plan in his head.

"Anytime now, I'd say," she confirmed, "but don't count on anything. You be on your toes every minute, you hear me?"

"Jessamine," he teased, "You are as bossy as that sister of mine."

"That doesn't make us bad," she retorted instantly. "That just makes us caring people."

A few minutes later, she peered out her window, but she could not see Gabe inching out from the stairs. Dressed in black twill pants and a black shirt, he melted into the blackness of the night.

When he neared the big house, he scanned the scene. The lavish velvet drapes in the elegant parlor had not yet been drawn, and he had a perfect view

249

of Monte poised in the chair in the front hallway. He sighted the opened archway and slipped around to the back of the house. The kitchen was dark as Jessamine had predicted and he moved slowly and soundlessly to avoid detection.

Gabe had not brought his pistol with him on this mission. The only weapon he expected to need was the surgically sharp knife he used to scale fish.

Warily, Gabe mounted the back stairs, relying on Jessamine's directions to lead him down the long dark hallway to the carved oak door that opened in Antoine Savanti's bedroom.

His nimble fingers unhurriedly twisted the knob of the door so quietly that Savanti heard no sound although he was still awake, propped up on satin pillows. Perhaps the cognac he'd imbibed after putting on his silk nightshirt had dulled his senses.

For a brief moment Gabe studied the despicable man who had become his enemy. He appeared dazed, staring at the ceiling. Was he devising some new cruel trick to play on his next victim.

Gabe's agile body and long legs had him at Antoine's side long before the forty-five-year-old man could react to the intruder in his room. Antoine's black eyes stared at this stranger who had invaded his privacy. Arrogant despite his vulnerability, he puffed himself up. "Who are you?" he demanded. "What are you doing here?"

Gabe had already slammed him across the bed so that he could not reach the cord that would summon Monte. His fiery blue eyes froze in icy hatred as he scrutinized the hawk-featured gent who had abused his sister and planned the same fate for

Chantel. Gabe felt no mercy.

"I'm here to seek revenge, Antoine Savanti," he intoned. His strong hands seized his antagonist's throat. He did not want Savanti's death to be fast; the swiftness of his blade would have dispatched him with no time for comprehension or reflection. He choked the life out of Savanti slowly and savored the strange sounds he made as he struggled against Gabe's strong hands.

"This is in repayment for what you did to my sister Delphine!" he said distinctly before Savanti's eyes lost all focus. "My name is Gabe O'Roarke."

Gabe's hands loosened their viselike grip only when he was sure there was no breath left in Antoine Savanti. He left the room secure in the knowledge that no other girl would be sullied by this villain. His mission was accomplished.

Gabe was not a vicious man. It wasn't in him to be cruel, but he truly believed that Antoine Savanti deserved to die. He had no qualm of conscience about the act he'd just committed. He felt exactly as his father had told him he felt about killing François La Tour.

Jessamine paced the floor anxiously as she waited for Gabe to return. The entire time he'd been gone she'd prayed that he would come to no harm. But there was no time for relief or prayers of thanksgiving when he rushed through her door, his bright eyes sparkling. "Have you got that valise packed, Jessamine?" he asked. "Are you ready to head for New Orleans?"

"Yes, sir, I'm ready," she declared, a broad smile coming to her face.

The hefty black woman and Gabe raced from the Savanti estate to the Charleston docks. Neither of them looked back at the grey-stoned mansion, and Jessamine knew without asking that the monster was dead.

And as the *Louisiana Lady* pulled out of the harbor, Jessamine whispered her relief to God and to Gabe. "Bless you," she murmured as they contemplated the illumination of the moon on the water. "You've saved many young ladies a lot of suffering."

Twenty-eight

By the time the sun came up the next morning, the *Louisiana Lady* was many miles away from Charleston, South Carolina and making fine time. Over the course of the night, Gabe and Jessamine had learned a lot about each other. "I never went back to New Orleans after I married Sam," she said ruefully. "We went to live in his part of the country—Georgia. But I was born and raised in New Orleans. I did leave my oldest brother there. He'd be about sixty-five now, I guess, and his name was Jonah."

Gabe said nothing, but he could not help thinking about old Jonah at *La Maison*.

Jessamine liked Gabe O'Roarke and she was overcome with emotion when he eased her concerns about finding work and a place to stay once they arrived in New Orleans.

"You're not to fret about that," he insisted. "You are to stay with us until you get yourself settled. I go into the city every day but Sundays and you can go with me to look for work." She had protested, but he had turned a deaf ear on her fear of imposing. "We're beholden to you," he explained. "You saved my sister. Chantel and Delphine will be excited to see you again, and I consider that issue settled, Jessamine." He grinned at her.

How wonderful life had suddenly become for her! Jessamine felt newly enriched.

Her life had changed in just a few short days and she owed it all to Monsieur Gabe. She breathed more easily now that she was away from the forbidding stone house and its dreadful secrets. But she had to confess that she was curious about what had happened the morning after their abrupt departure. And she prayed that Antoine Savanti's demise was never traced to Gabe O'Roarke!

The next morning Monte was not summoned by Savanti and he went immediately to the kitchen to see if Jessamine had sent up a tray. But Selma had taken charge. "Jessamine must be sick this morning," she told Monte. "And Monsieur Savanti's still sleeping."

Monte frowned. He could not recall a morning when Jessamine had not arrived at the big house and Antoine had not summoned him to his room.

The uppity Jessamine's absence irked him. She needed a dressing-down, and Monte was the man for the job. How dare she shirk her duties? Filled with self-righteous venom, he marched across the back gardens to the carriage house. He tried the unlocked door and made no effort to knock. The apartment was dark and quiet when he entered, and the curtains were closed as if unready for day-break.

"Jessamine." He called sternly but received no answer. He searched the kitchen and then the bedroom, and he noted that the drawers of the massive oak chest were empty.

She had left.

He turned and bolted out the door, stumbling down the steps in his eagerness to report the defection to Monsieur Savanti. He'd have old Jessamine's hide for leaving without notice. She wouldn't be so bossy after he got through with her, Monte thought, pleased.

He rushed into the kitchen and out the door to the hallway when an auburn-haired girl sat on the velvet bench. Carter Bascombe had arrived

"Good morning, mademoiselle," he greeted the girl. "May I be of service to you?"

"No, thank you. I'm just waiting here for Carter to return to take me to see his Uncle Antoine," she told him.

Monte bowed and excused himself. He never liked it when Carter let himself in and went directly to Antoine's bedroom. Monte preferred the protocol of personally escorting visitors upstairs.

He stood outside Antoine's door, struck by the odd quiet that had descended on the corridor. He should have heard voices — Antoine's imperious tones and Carter's obsequious flattery.

For a huge giant of a man he could move noise-lessly, and Monte joined Carter beside the bed before the purveyor was even aware that the black man had come into the room. When he did turn around to see the awesome hulk glaring at him, Carter's ashen face showed fear. "He's dead," he mumbled. "Antoine is dead."

Monte fixed on the stonelike stare on his employer's face. "I didn't do anything to him," Carter stammered nervously. Monte's hands closed on Carter's shoulder like the jaws of a steel trap. Carter flinched.

"Where are you goin', monsieur?" Monte's deep bass voice demanded fiercely.

"I — I'm leaving. There's no reason for me to stay now." Carter wriggled in Monte's dispassionate grasp.

"There's every reason for you to stay until the authorities get here."

"Let me go, Monte," Carter insisted, panicking at the intense, determined expression he saw on Monte's face.

"You will not leave, monsieur," Monte muttered and locked his suspect in the cramped confines of the linen closet.

Swiftly Monte descended the back stairs and sprinted to the carriage house to prepare the buggy for a trip into the city. When he had guided it to the front entrance, he announced to the auburn-haired young lady that he'd been instructed to take her back to Charleston.

"Monsieur Savanti is too ill for a visit and Monsieur Bascombe wishes to remain with his uncle until the doctor arrives," Monte told her.

"Oh, I'm sorry to hear that, but I will certainly accept your offer to get back to Charleston for I have a ship to catch," she told him, rising from the bench.

Within half-an-hour the loyal Monte had deposited Bascombe's young lady at the wharf and informed the authorities of Savanti's death. To the end Monte was determined to protect his master's name, and the girl never knew how fate had smiled on her.

Later in the day, the police escorted Carter Bascombe into Charleston for further questioning. He was jittery and nervous and obviously hiding something, they concluded. He gave too many conflicting answers and, before the afternoon was over, Carter found himself placed in a jail cell.

If, aboard the *Louisiana Lady*, Gabe could have known of the events unfolding in Charleston, he would have felt satisfied and avenged. It was fitting that Carter Bascombe be charged with the murder of Antoine Savanti. It was poetic justice.

Back in the bayou, Gabe was very much on the minds and thoughts of everyone at the O'Roarke's cottage. It was lonely for Chantel without Gabe, and time hung heavily on her, especially in the late afternoons. Delphine sensed her loneliness and knew that Gabe was not the only one in love; Chantel returned his affection.

But Delphine was troubled by Chantel's attitude toward her mother. She wished she could do something to mellow her bitterness for Chantel would never be happy until she resolved her differences with Lily.

Delphine also spent quiet moments thinking about Gabe and the mission he'd set for himself. She knew he'd not leave until he accomplished his objective.

But unlike Chantel, she was enjoying the days and nights back in her bayou. The time flew by and she found it strange that she'd never noticed before how good-looking Terry Monroe was. They'd known one other all their lives, but now, when he dropped by the cottage and they talked or walked together, she saw him in a different light.

She liked the warmth of his tanned, weathered hand when he held her arm on their walks. She also liked his gentleness whether it was directed toward her or a fallen sparrow they'd found in the woods one day.

She'd always suspected that Terry had been attracted to her but until lately she'd not felt anything more toward him than the warm friendly affection she had for many of the young men of the bayou. She didn't know when or how it had happened, but she felt differently about him now.

No one could have been happier than Terry, who noticed immediately the change in Delphine's attitude when they were together. The last time they had been together he'd almost given way to the temptation to pull her into his arms and kiss her luscious lips.

He had found it sweet and thoughtful when Delphine had taken a basket of food to his mother while he was on the fishing boat with her father. He was away a lot longer since Gabe had been gone. He was curious about Gabe's absence, but no one offered an explanation and he did not prod. Still, it wasn't like Gabe to leave the bayou, and Terry could not recall a time when Gabe had been away this long.

When Gabe had been gone six days, Terry picked up his wages from Scott and was pleased by the extra income the extra hours had brought him. Impulsively he bought a gold locket for his sister, a trinket he knew she'd yearned to have for a long time. She'd been having to work harder, too, with him away from the house more. For his mother he purchased a light wool shawl she could drape around her shoulders when she sat in her rocking chair out on the porch.

He'd had a chance to make his purchases when Scott had offered to make the delivery to *La Maison*. Both men were in high spirits when the *Bayou Queen* left the wharf to travel homeward. They had had a good week.

Scott had not expected to meet Lily Lemogne when he'd delivered the fish to *La Maison*. But Lily had made a point of being in the kitchen, expecting to talk with Gabe. But it was the young man's father she encountered and she immediately saw the resemblance.

Scott was still a fine figure of a man, even in his working garb. He had the same brilliant glint in his blue eyes, and Lily appreciated the warmth and understanding that spurred him to accept her offer of coffee so he could tell her about her daughter.

"We think most highly of Chantel," he assured her. "Come out to the bayou and see us. My wife would love to meet you."

"I would love to meet your family and see your bayou," Lily responded eagerly. "Chantel makes it sound like a most enchanting place."

"It is a very enchanting place. You'd like it, I think," Scott told her. He, like his son, saw the warmth and caring that made Lily unique.

"I'm very glad my daughter is staying with such nice people," she said as he was leaving. Scott saw the reflection of her inner sadness and wished there were something he could do to ease her pain and improve her relations with her daughter.

But all he could say was, "We'll take good care of her."

Twenty-nine

It wasn't until Scott and his wife had retired to their bedroom that night that he had the opportunity to tell her about his meeting with Madame Lemogne.

"She seems very nice, Angelique," he mused. "I think it disturbs her very much that Chantel doesn't wish to live under her roof."

"As a mother I can understand her feelings," she agreed.

"Perhaps you could pay her a visit," he suggested. "I invited her to our bayou sometime."

Angelique laughed, "I doubt that any other lady could say that her husband took her to *La Maison*."

Scott gathered her up in his arms. "Ah, but I know that you're my lady and only my lady."

"Still that conceited Irishman, aren't you, Scott O'Roarke?" Angelique taunted.

"No," he replied seriously, "but I am as sure of our love for one another as I was the day we got married." He continued to hold her close to him.

Twenty-six years of marriage had not diminished

the flame of passion. but Scott had to admit the next morning that he wasn't quite as ready to leave his bed to meet the new day as when he was younger. Angelique was still sleeping when he slipped out of bed to brew himself a pot of coffee.

"Well, sleepyhead, you almost didn't get your goodbye kiss this morning," he teased her when she came up behind him on the back stoop.

She grinned sheepishly. "You kept me up too late last night."

"I'll be in early today since it's Saturday," he reminded her. Then, with a hasty kiss, he ambled down to the boat.

Angelique let her coffee grow cold as she recalled last night's conversation. "Yes," she said at last. "Yes, I will definitely call on Lily Lemogne." She was curious to meet Chantel's mother after what her husband had told her last night.

Chantel had been in a quiet, thoughtful mood for the last day or two, and that was the reason Delphine had suggested that the two of them take a stroll through the woods before she had to change since Terry was coming over to see her this evening.

But Delphine was caught off guard when Chantel abruptly announced, "I'm going into New Orleans with your father Monday morning. I want to spend some time with my mother."

"I'm glad," Delphine said. "I think that would make her very happy."

"You told me in the beginning I'd find some answers out on the bayou." Chantel smiled. "Maybe

I've been too harsh on her."

Delphine gave her hand an affectionate pat. "Don't judge her," she suggested cautiously. "You don't know what happened in her life."

"That's what I've been thinking. Maybe I have been unfair."

Delphine didn't doubt that Lily Lemogne had been very protective of her only daughter. She herself was eager to meet the lady and hoped it would be one day soon.

Angelique, after a private moment with Delphine, realized that she no longer had a reason to visit *La Maison*. She was anxious to share the news with her husband and so was pleased at first when Scott arrived home early. But her delight was short-lived for he bore sad tidings.

"Terry won't be coming over tonight," he advised his family. "His mother's taken a turn for the worse." To Angelique he confided his misgivings about Maude Monroe. "I don't think she's going to be around here much longer," he said somberly. "I had that same feeling about my dad just before he died."

"I hope you're wrong, Scott," Angelique sighed.

"So do I, love. So do I."

After dinner, Delphine and Angelique sat outside on the steps.

"I'm going up with Momma to the Monroes tomorrow," Delphine said. "I want to help, and it will also give me a chance to see Terry before the week starts. Do you want to come?"

"I'd like to help, too," Chantel said politely, "but I've got to pack if I'm going to go in with your dad

Monday morning."

The next day, as soon as the O'Roarkes had had their lunch, Delphine and her mother loaded two baskets of food into the canoe and nosed up the bayou. Chantel puttered around the bedroom gathering up the belongings she wanted to take with her, and Scott O'Roarke checked the lines on the *Bayou Queen*.

It was almost three hours later before Angelique and her daughter got back to the cottage for they had found Maude in a very weak state and Terry quite distraught. "I don't think Maude has the strength to pull out of this," Angelique noted sadly.

"I'll take a run up there tonight then," Scott decided. "I want Terry to know I can manage by myself tomorrow. He should stay home with his ma." He wished Gabe would come breezing through the door. He'd been too many days away, and Scott missed his company as well as his help.

Gabe, wary of the weather, put in at Mobile overnight, hoping to avoid the storm that threatened.

By morning, the clouds had rolled by and the waters had calmed. With clear sailing the rest of the way, the *Louisiana Lady* reached New Orleans' wharves late Monday. Gabe released his crew with a generous reimbursement for their time and moral support and then turned his attention to Jessamine.

The black woman stood on the deck taking in the harbor and the city she'd left so many years ago. It was different, yet the same. She could see the hodgepodge of people milling about the levee. Vendors, tired from a day on the street, closed up their carts for the evening. Flatbedded wagons loaded with baskets of fresh fruits and vegetables rolled back to the farmlands till morning. Black women, turbaned in brightly colored kerchiefs, balanced baskets of flowers atop their heads.

She supposed that New Orleans would forever remain a fascinating city like none she'd ever lived in before. Was Jonah still here? she wondered. Or was he dead? She realized that she might never know.

A beautiful rosy-purple sunset filled the western sky when the *Louisiana Lady* pulled away from the dock to head for the bayou. Gabe called out to her. "We're here, Jessamine! We're home."

A broad smile lit up her black face. "Yes, Monsieur Gabe," she declared, "we are home." She had not felt that anywhere was home since Sam had died and with him all sense of home.

Although Jessamine had lived much of her life in New Orleans, she had never been into the deep bayou country. She reveled first in the quiet and then in the night sounds of the marshes. She stared in fascination at the grotesque trunks of giant cypress trees jutting out of the waters and marveled at the long cascading drapes of Spanish moss.

Jessamine might have been leery traveling through those murky black waters where she'd heard that snakes and alligators lurked had she not been with Monsieur Gabe. Somehow, he gave her a feeling of security and she found herself enjoying the night sounds of the bayou as they rounded each new bend in the stream. She strained to see the gleamings of lights as they began to pass by the cottages on the banks of the bayou.

She was amazed at how many people lived on the bayou. She had expected isolation, but she noticed that each small plot of property and cottage had its own dock and at least one canoe.

"One more turn and we're going to be home, Jessamine," Gabe told her, and she could see the excitement churning within him. It was contagious, for she felt an eagerness and anticipation mounting in her as well.

They made the final turn and Gabe focused on his father's dock just ahead of him. His long mission was now behind him, and he was elated that he'd accomplished what he'd set out to do and more. He'd rescued Jessamine from that horrible place and he'd come away unscarred.

He looked forward to a jubilant homecoming and a quiet walk with Chantel.

He guided the *Louisiana Lady,* homing in on the beacon of lamplight his mother had set in the front windows. He scrambled up on the dock and reached down to assist Jessamine.

In one hand he carried the two valises. His other hand kept a firm grip on the hefty black lady's arm so she'd not stumble and fall on the pathway that led to the front steps of the cottage.

Jessamine was at a loss to express her gratitude to this young man, so she simply told him, "Monsieur Gabe, you are something. Did you know that? You are really something else."

Gabe chuckled. "Funny you should say that, Jessamine," he confided. "My dear mother is always saying that, but I'm not sure she means the same thing you do. She's known me longer than you have."

"I'll bet she means exactly the same thing I mean, Monsieur Gabe," Jessamine declared.

Thirty

Scott O'Roarke's blue eyes could not have viewed a nicer sight than that of his tall handsome son coming through the front door, and no one had to tell him who the hefty black woman trailing slightly behind him was. That had to be dear Jessamine, the angel who'd helped his daughter.

"Dear God Almighty! Gabe, you're home, safe and sound!" He rushed to embrace his son, unashamed that tears of joy flowed down his face. In an instant the entire family was shrieking and crying, hugging and kissing, and engulfing Jessamine as one of its own. It was wonderful to be consumed by such warmth and love, Jessamine averred. She immediately felt welcomed into this little cottage.

It took a few minutes for all the jubilation to calm down and Gabe got the chance to ask where Chantel was.

"I took her into New Orleans this morning," Scott said. "She wanted to spend some time with her mother."

Both father and mother could tell that their son

was crestfallen that Chantel was not there to greet him, too. Gabe had never been one to mask his feelings. But he tried to put forth a carefree, light-hearted air as the five of them dined that evening. While the women cleaned up the kitchen before they retired to the front room, Scott and his son took a stroll outside the cottage for a smoke and a talk.

Gabe told him everything that had happened from the time he arrived in Charleston. Scott listened as Gabe related how he'd slipped back into the mansion and with his two bare hands choked the life out of Antoine Savanti.

"I'm proud of you, Gabe. God knows, I am!" Scott declared.

Inside the house, Delphine laughed as she brought Jessamine to her room to retire. "I shared your bed for over a week, and now you will share mine." She joked.

"Oh, Delphine, your room's much prettier than mine was," Jessamine exclaimed. "And you've got the nicest family in the world."

"I'll agree with you on that," Delphine concurred. But, before they drifted off to sleep, she pressed her for details on Gabe's Charleston escapade.

"It's all behind us now, Jessamine," Delphine sighed when the woman finished her story. "We can get on with our lives." Her hand reached out for Jessamine's hand and a reassuring squeeze.

"I'm going to find a job in New Orleans," Jessamine vowed, "and I'm gong to be much happier than I was in Charleston."

"And I'm going to enjoy my life here in the bayou and never seek to roam again," Delphine pledged.

Jessamine chuckled. "Those pastures aren't always greener on the other side, are they Delphine?" she asked.

"I guess I had to find it out the hard way," Delphine admitted as a sweet sleep overtook her.

Jessamine learned almost immediately that the people of the bayou took care of their own.

Tragedy struck, though not unexpectedly, when Maude Monroe died. For two days neither Gabe nor his father went out on their fishing boats, and Angelique paddled back and forth between the two houses, helping with funeral arrangements and consoling Terry and his sister.

On the third day, Jessamine noted that everyone's lives seemed to fall back into a normal routine. Gabe and his father left bright and early in their fishing boats to work the lakes. Grief was put aside, and life went forward.

It was also time, she decided, that she got on with her own life.

So Jessamine went into the city with Gabe and searched for a housekeeping position. At the end of the long day, she returned to the wharf dejected but not defeated.

The next day she decided to look up Mademoiselle Chantel at *La Maison*. She walked in the direction that Delphine had told her to take when she'd told her of her plans last night.

"Good, Jessamine," Delphine had encouraged.

"You can bring us some news of her. I know Gabe is a little down because she hasn't responded to his message that he's back. I'm sure he expected her to come down to the wharf to greet him."

Gabe had been disappointed, and the last few days had been especially long since he'd felt the need to make up to his dad for his long absence. He hadn't allowed himself to give in to the urge gnawing at him to take time off to go to *La Maison* to see Chantel.

Out on the bayou, his mother and sister were also putting in extra hours at the Monroe cottage so that Terry could go back to work. So he had to sacrifice his own personal desires right now. That's the way it was with the O'Roarke family.

Despite her slow pace, Jessamine arrived at *La Maison* long before the house was stirring. No one answered her knock, and Jessamine—her feet tired from the long walk from the dock—sought out the shady area she'd noticed at the back of the building.

She spied a bench under the spreading branches of an oak tree and made directly for it, slipping out of her leather slippers and massaging her instep.

She had been resting for several minutes before she realized that she was not the only one who had found comfort in this back garden. Belatedly she noticed the white-haired black man sitting on one of the other benches beneath a tall pecan tree.

He was whittling and Jessamine recalled how her older bother would sculpt toys for her out of wood

271

when they were kids. Their parents couldn't afford store-bought toys, but she had never wanted for playthings.

Suddenly an eerie feeling came over her. She slipped her shoes back on and moved with trepidation to the bench where the old man bent over his block of wood.

Her dark eyes scrutinized his profile but he seemed unaware of her presence. "Good morning," she said softly and Jonah turned suddenly to stare up at her. Jessamine felt she could surely faint for the many, many years had not changed his face that much. His hair had turned white and his skin was weathered, but he was clearly recognizable as her brother.

Jonah couldn't find his tongue. The face he was staring upon was that of his sister Jessamine. She was his little sister, only her figure had grown plumper.

"It is you, isn't it Jonah?" she asked, her voice quavering as she sank down on the bench beside him.

Overcome by emotion, he fought his way through a mist of tears. His voice cracked when he finally attempted to speak. "Jessamine," he breathed. "Is it possible?"

"It is, Jonah," she stammered, and her arms wrapped around his shoulders. They sat locked in an embrace, engulfed by tears of joy. They had no need to speak right then.

"It's a miracle, Jonah," Jessamine said at last. "A miracle that both of us would chance to be in this garden at the same time."

"The miracle is your coming here, Jessamine," he corrected, "for you see, I sit here daily. I work at *La Maison,* and I live at the carriage house."

"You work here?" she quizzed. "What do you do?"

"I drive the buggy and do odd jobs for Madame Lemogne," he told her.

"Then you must know Mademoiselle Chantel," Jessamine deduced. "I was coming to see her this morning."

He took her hand and directed her across the gardens.

"Come on, Jessamine," he urged, "we've got a lot of talking to do. We might just talk the whole day away."

She smiled as they walked to his quarters. What a coincidence, she thought, that they had both lived in carriage-house apartments these last few years.

She was startled by the quality of his furnishings, but he shrugged it off. "Madame Lemogne is always giving me something to bring up here," he explained. "And I get so many good meals from the kitchen at *La Maison* that I don't have much cooking to do."

With coffee brewing they tried to catch up on the lost years and current history.

"I always liked young Gabe," Jonah said approvingly when he learned the circumstances of her return. "But now that you're here, you can stay with me. And if I know Madame Lily, she'll give you a job."

"Oh, Jonah, I hadn't thought about asking Chantel's mother for work," Jessamine objected.

273

"But it would be nice to work here and be close to you."

"It's settled then," he said, grinning. "Now we have the whole day for talking. Later we'll go down to the wharf to tell Mister Gabe that you've found your brother and you're staying with him."

She learned from Jonah why Gabe had not heard from Chantel. "She and Madame Lily have been gone since Sunday," he said. "Madame Lily's gentleman friend took them to his sister's country estate for a holiday."

"That should make Monsieur Gabe feel better," she sighed. She had been worried that perhaps Chantel did not want to see him.

If Jessamine hadn't realized before how happy Jonah was to have her with him, he gave himself away when he asked, "Will you fry me some chicken tonight, Jessamine?"

"You bet I will," she promised.

A short time later they arrived at the dock. When Gabe looked up to see old Jonah bringing Jessamine back to his boat, he was glad that she'd not had the long walk. He was stunned by their revelation and delighted for them.

"You just bring my little sister's belongings in the morning, and I'll be here to pick them up," Jonah said to Gabe, chuckling. "Ain't going to let her out of my sight now that I got her back."

Gabe traveled the bayou that night in higher spirits. Chantel had not received his message. She was not ignoring him, and she would be back soon.

On their way back to *La Maison*, Jonah went back to the marketplace and bought a fine fryer for

Jessamine to fix for them and a generous supply of fresh vegetables and fruits.

Walking back to the buggy where Jessamine waited for him, his arms were filled with his purchases. One wrinkled hand carried a beautiful basket of colorful flowers which he handed to Jessamine. "Here, little sister," he told her, "these are for you."

Jessamine's dark eyes misted with tears. "Oh, Jonah," she cried, "it is so good to be home at last."

Thirty-one

That evening, Jonah and his sister sat down to a huge platter of crispy, golden-fried chicken with gravy, biscuits and okra fixed just the way Jonah liked it. He had not enjoyed a meal so much in a long time. It was not to say that Raul wasn't a good cook, but Jessamine's fried chicken was better than anything Raul could ever prepare.

Jessamine witnessed the consideration her brother received at *La Maison* when a knock sounded on his door and a serving girl from the kitchen arrived with a basket of food. "Raul feared you were ill since he'd not seen you this afternoon," she said with a slight curtsey. "He sent me over here with an apple pie and slices of roast. There's a loaf of bread, too."

"You thank Raul for me, Tessie, but I'm well." Jonah assured her. "My sister cooked supper for me tonight."

When Tessie was gone, he glanced at Jessamine with a hearty laugh. "Guess you won't have to cook tomorrow night," he twitted.

"It looks to me like you're a little pampered," Jessamine teased back.

"We're sort of like a family here at *La Maison*," he said thoughtfully. "Everyone takes care of everyone else."

"Jonah, I'm feeling the need to lay this tired body down. Where am I to sleep?" Jessamine asked, weary at last.

"Right in there, little sister," he told her, pointing to his bedroom.

"Now if I sleep there just where are you going to sleep?" she demanded, arms akimbo. "On a pallet?"

"I ain't sleeping on no pallet," he assured her. "See that daybed by the windows? I take myself many a fine afternoon nap over there, so that's where I'm going to sleep and that's that."

Jessamine's last thoughts before she closed her eyes were that all her prayers had now surely been answered and she'd never have need to ask for more. She was a contented woman.

Since Maude's death, Delphine had spent most of her free time at the Monroe cottage, helping Terry and Mary Jane adjust.

"I'm not a baby, Delphine," Mary Jane confronted her one afternoon. "I've been cleaning this cottage for months now, and I can have Terry's supper ready when he gets in."

Delphine noted the indignant tone in her voice and realized how threatening her presence might seem to the younger girl who only wanted to hold on to all that was left of her family. So she gave Mary Jane a warm smile. "I guess I just forgot

277

how much you have been doing already, Mary Jane," she apologized. "I have to admit I didn't have the responsibility you've taken on when I was your age."

Delphine's words soothed her and Mary Jane sat down beside her. "I felt like I was here by myself most of the time," she admitted. "With Terry away so much and mom in bed, I got used to my own company."

"I understand," Delphine allowed, "but that's not to say you couldn't come visit me once in awhile. Maybe you could go into New Orleans with me and we could spend a whole day there. Would you like that?"

Mary Jane's eyes sparkled with new life. "Yes," she exclaimed. "Yes, I would."

Later as Terry walked her to her canoe, he held her hand tightly. "That was awfully sweet of you to offer to take Mary Jane with you into the city. Poor little thing," he sighed. "She's not gotten out for a long, long time."

"I'll take her with me soon," Delphine promised.

"Well," Terry paused. "I want to thank you and your family for being so kind and considerate." He faced her awkwardly and then gave way to impulse. He swung her toward him and clasped her waist with his tanned hand. Bending down, he kissed her. He had wanted to claim her lips for weeks.

Delphine responded to his tender kiss, pressing closer to him. Releasing her, he murmured into the hollow of her neck. "I've loved you since you were no older than Mary Jane."

Delphine would have spoken, but Terry feared that she would tell him she liked but didn't love him. He placed his finger on her lips. "Sssh," he whispered. "You don't have to say anything. I just wanted you to know how I feel about you."

Delphine whirled and lifted her skirt as she stepped into the canoe. "You should have let me speak," she taunted him, a twinkle in her eye and in her voice. "Now, you'll never know what I would have said." With a giggle, she pushed against the dock with her paddle, and the canoe glided through the water.

Terry roared with laughter and waved to her. It was the first time he'd laughed in days.

Delighted to have her daughter home with her, Lily found herself receptive to Andre's suggestion that she and Chantel accept his sister's invitation to spend a few days at her country estate.

So she had left Adrienne in charge and finally gone to meet Andre's sister, Jacqueline Basheron.

It had been a long time since any world existed for Lily other than *La Maison,* but she found Jacqueline not only gracious but compatible. It took only one evening for the two of them to feel that they had become dear friends, just as Andre had predicted.

They shared similar likes and dislikes, and Lily wondered how Chantel and Nannette got on for they were so different in temperament.

One evening as Lily and Jacqueline sat together in the parlor sipping champagne, Jacqueline leaned back and announced dramatically, "Ah, Lily, you and I should go to Paris together. What a time we could have for ourselves!"

"We might have such a good time that we'd never want to come back to New Orleans," Lily agreed.

"Then I'd have Andre to reckon with. He'd never forgive me. But you would love Paris and Paris would love you," Jacqueline declared.

Reminiscing, Jacqueline told naughty stories of her adventures in Paris before she got married. It was not until she was in her room that Lily realized how easy it had been for her to talk to this earthy, worldly sister of Andre's.

Nannette had purposely plotted for the two of them to go upstairs early this evening for she wanted to talk to Chantel. Nannette had delayed the moment as long as she possibly could, but Chantel and her mother would be leaving soon to go back into the city.

She had overheard her uncle telling her mother about Chantel's ordeal, so Nannette did not feel restrained in addressing her own dilemma.

They had stretched out across Nannette's bed in their nightgowns, and the conversation was lighthearted girl-talk until Nannette abruptly asked Chantel, "Have you ever made love with a man?"

"What brought that on, Nannette?" Chantel

raised up on one elbow. "Have you?"

"Yes," she answered truthfully. "and now I'm scared I might be pregnant." Nannette studied her. "You never answered me," she prodded.

Chantel saw no reason to deny anything to Nannette after what she'd just told her. "Yes," she confessed. "I have made love with a man."

"Weren't you scared about getting pregnant?"

"I didn't think about it, I guess, Chantel admitted. "If I were pregnant, I suppose I would immediately go to Ga—the man."

"That's what has me so scared. He's left for Europe, and I can't tell him anything." Nannette sighed dejectedly.

"Oh, Nannette, honey! You're talking about Paul, aren't you?" Chantel recalled their summer picnic and how much Paul had impressed Nannette. Chantel tried to remember what she'd felt about Paul and his twin brother Peter, but the summer and their innocence seemed so long ago.

"I wish it were Paul." Nannette's words interrupted her train of thought and for a moment she had difficulty understanding what her friend had said. "It was Peter. Paul's still here."

"Peter? Dear God, Nannette!"

"Don't ask me how it happened. I can't say, because I actually detest him. But that afternoon, I was out riding and I met him in the woods. We dismounted and sat down to talk. I don't know why, but I let him kiss me. It got out of control. He was like a wild stallion, and I couldn't stop him. It wasn't making love." Nannette lifted a tear-stained face. "It was rape."

"What about Paul?" Chantel questioned.

"Oh, he's been over, but I feel ashamed and guilty when I'm around him."

"You're not guilty, Nannette." Chantel spoke firmly. "Peter took you by force. You've got to tell your mother. She'll understand."

"She won't," Nannette sniffed. "Not if I'm pregnant. And definitely not if I refuse to marry Peter just to save myself from shame."

"Perhaps you're not pregnant," Chantel suggested.

"I ride daily in hopes that if I am I'll have a miscarriage and lose Peter's bastard," she hissed venomously.

Thirty-two

Andre Deverone had shared dinner with them only on Lily's first night at the Basherone estate, and then he had returned to the city. He wanted them to get acquainted on their own. By the time he returned three days later, the vivacious ladies already considered themselves old friends.

The atmosphere was so relaxed between them that Jacqueline felt free to tease Lily. *"Mon Dieu,"* she pleaded, "marry this man and put him out of his misery."

When they bid farewell and Andre was handing Lily up into his carriage, Jacqueline gave them each an affectionate hug. "Hurry up and marry Lily," she charged her brother, "or I shall whisk her off to Paris with me."

They traveled back to the city in high spirits. Andre studied Lily and her daughter covertly and decided the visit with Jacqueline had been time well spent. He himself found his sister stimulating, an attribute shared by both Lily and Chantel—though not, alas, Nannette.

When they arrived back at *La Maison,* Chantel surprised Andre with a warm embrace. Then she dashed upstairs so that Andre and her mother could have a private moment to themselves before they said goodbye this early evening.

He did not stay long, for he knew Lily was curious to see how things had gone with Adrienne in charge.

But he held her briefly in his arms and gave her a kiss. "I'll see you tomorrow night, *chèrie,*" he promised.

"Thank you, Andre. Thank you for everything. I enjoyed every minute at your sister's. I think Chantel did, too," she told him as she lingered in the cozy warmth of his arms. "It was good for both of us."

Andre smiled down at her. "I see changes in Chantel, do you?"

"I know what you mean," she said, reluctantly withdrawing from his embrace. "Everything is going to be just fine between us; I feel sure of it now." They allowed themselves one more light kiss, then parted quickly before they could give in to the temptation to have him stay.

"Gabe is back, Mother," Chantel declared happily, "Oh, thank God!" she sighed. Waving the finally delivered message as Lily entered the upstairs parlor. Chantel flopped into a chair, an inane grin on her lovely face.

"So that's why his father delivered my fish

last Friday," Lily observed. "He's a very nice man, Chantel," she added as she removed her bonnet. But then she saw that Chantel was off in a world of her own, so she turned her attention back to the world of *La Maison*. The order of the afternoon was bath and business.

She had a light dinner brought to her room on a tray and was still eating when Adrienne arrived.

Adrienne accepted a glass of wine and expertly filled Lily in on the activity at *La Maison* in her absence. "Everything ran smoothly," Adrienne concluded. "You can go away as often as you want. I didn't have any trouble at all."

"Did you like playing hostess?" Lily asked, curious.

"The truth, Lily?"

Lily laughed. "Nothing but the truth, Adrienne."

"I loved it. And if I do say so myself, I did a damned good job," she declared candidly.

"I knew you would," Lily said. "You've got spunk and spirit, and that's why I left you in charge." She regarded Adrienne seriously. "Give me a couple of days," she went on, "and then I've something to talk over with you that could be to both our advantage."

Adrienne looked up sharply, then nodded. "I'm ready to talk about anything that would be to my advantage, Lily." Lily smiled reflectively as Adrienne took her leave. She reminded her a lot of herself.

Chantel, chafing at the hours yet to go until she could see Gabe, had an unexpected surprise the next day. "There's someone here who's most anxious to see you, Miss Chantel," Jonah said with rare ambiguity. He said no more, but led her to the carriage house.

The sight of Jessamine in old Jonah's quarters took her breath away. She gasped and rushed to embrace the old black lady. "Jessamine," she murmured over and over, "you got away! But how?"

"I was rescued by a gallant young man," Jessamine replied mysteriously and let her tale unfold.

"So that's where he went," Chantel mumbled, sinking to the daybed.

"Yes, ma'am. He set out to do two things—repay me and even the score with Antoine Savanti."

Chantel shook her head in disbelief. "I would have been worried if I'd known that."

"That's probably why he didn't tell you," Jessamine said sensibly. "But he did what he had to do and we got out of there—fast."

"Oh, Jessamine, this couldn't be more wonderful," Chantel cried. "Wait until I tell my mother you're here. She's anxious to meet the woman who saved me from a fate worse than death." Chantel reached out for Jessamine, and they hugged again, not wanting to stop, and traded stories of all that had transpired since they'd last seen each other in Charleston.

Chantel heard the chiming of Jonah's clock, and she couldn't believe how long they'd been talking. With girlish excitement, she urged Jessamine to come meet her mother.

"Oh, Miss Chantel, are you sure?" Jessamine asked reluctantly.

"Trust me, Jessamine. Come on." Determined, Chantel persuaded Jessamine to accompany her to *La Maison*.

Jessamine had never seen such opulence. The grandeur of the foyer alone outshone the lavish decor of Antoine Savanti's Charleston estate.

Her dark eyes darted in every direction as Chantel led her down the hallway. Openmouthed, she surveyed the elegant front parlor and the private dining alcoves with their brocade and velvet drapes. She hardly dared to step on the plush carpeted stairway.

Chantel did not bother to knock on her mother's door but marched right in with Jessamine trailing behind her. Lily lounged in her parlor in her satin dressing gown. She looked absolutely stunning with her thick dark hair cascading over her shoulders. The full, flowing dressing gown did not conceal her voluptuous figure, and Jessamine was struck by the lady's beauty. It was no wonder Chantel was so breathtakingly beautiful, she thought, even though the two were as different as day and night.

Lily saw the excitement on Chantel's face the minute she entered the room and in a few brief moments she understood why and made Jessamine welcome. The black woman never forgot how she graciously rose to greet her, firmly clasping her hand. "I'm forever beholden to you, Jessamine, for what you did for my daughter," she said.

"Madame Lily, I could do no less for Miss Chantel and Miss Delphine and live with myself," Jessamine told her. "My heart went out to them."

When she left Lily's boudoir, she had shared brunch with mother and daughter and secured a job at *La Maison*. She was to oversee the housekeepers, which meant she had no actual labor. Lily was being overly generous and kind to her, and Jessamine was grateful and content.

Chantel, meanwhile, quickly changed her clothes so she could go down to the wharf and wait for the *Louisiana Lady*.

She announced her intentions to no one, but secreted herself in her room, slipping out of her muslin gown and into the divided skirt and tunic Nannette had given her. She put on soft brown-leather boots—also courtesy of Nannette—for she planned to walk to the wharf.

She made her way down the back stairs and out through the back gardens. An eager sprite, she strode at a feisty pace down the dirt road. At the quay, her green eyes searched for only one fishing boat among the many gathered there—the *Louisiana Lady*.

Chantel's heart started pounding wildly when she saw Gabe O'Roarke standing bare-chested on the deck of his fishing boat. His tousled black hair fell over his forehead, and his faded pants were molded to the muscles of his body. He made a handsome figure, and she could not take her eyes from him.

Gabe O'Roarke would have sworn that it was instinct that directed his gaze to Chantel. Her golden hair flowed over the bottle-green vest she wore, accenting an ecru blouse. How striking she was, he thought, in her matching skirt and fancy leather boots.

Giving himself freely to the excitement that churned within him, Gabe leaped to the wharf and captured her in his arms. Hungrily he claimed a kiss.

In a husky, eager voice he whispered, "You're coming with me to the bayou tonight. I'll bring you back in the morning, but I've so much to tell you and I've missed you so much."

She offered no protest, and he called out to a small black boy, "Henry," he shouted, "come here." Hastily he scribbled a message on a piece of brown wrapping paper he found in his pocket, "Take this to Madame Lily," he instructed and gave him a coin for his efforts.

"I'll take it straightaway," Henry assured him, dropping the money into a pouch that hung at his side on a leather strap. "I promise." True to his word, Henry vanished instantly.

289

Gabe took Chantel's arm. "Poor little devil," he murmured. "I feel like gathering that little monkey up some afternoon and taking him to the bayou with me. He doesn't have much of a home."

Chantel had never known such a gentle-hearted man as Gabe O'Roarke. She could not have been happier than she was to be with him.

They stood for awhile on the deck, entranced by a sunset that surely had been created for them alone as the *Louisiana Lady* veered to enter the bayou. Content just to be close to one another again, they didn't speak at first, letting skin brush against skin as they leaned against the railing, side by side.

A quietness settled over the bay and the lake as the sun set on the western horizon. Fishermen were going home after a long day on the lakes.

But Gabe was neither tired nor weary from his day's work. He was pulsating with elation, for Chantel was with him.

His arms were eager to hold her for more than a few brief moments, so he turned the wheel over to Deke and he and Chantel sought the privacy of his cabin. Gabe sensed that she shared his desire to steal a few precious moments for themselves before they reached the O'Roarke cottage.

That was part of the magic and why he was convinced that destiny deemed that they were meant to be together. They had no need to

290

speak, for each one understood what the other was thinking.

There was no question in Gabe's mind that Chantel Lemogne could tame his reckless, restless heart.

Thirty-three

He led her through the door and closed it. Neither of them said a word for Gabe's arms eagerly enclosed her and Chantel found herself being carried over to his bunk. His searing lips ignited a passion that threatened to consume her.

Fired by her willing response and the warm tempting heat of her supple body pressing against him, Gabe fumbled with the buttons at her bodice.

Her green eyes gazed up at him with an emerald flame. He knew that her desire for him was as great as his own for her.

He brushed her full, firm breasts with the tips of his fingers, tantalizing them both before removing the rest of her clothes. He ridded himself of his faded pants and in a deep mellow voice, he cast an enchantment. "Come to me," he urged. "Let me love you as I've wanted to love you for so many nights."

Chantel did come to him — swiftly — joining with him because she, too, had ached for this moment of togetherness. His lips bewitched her and she was completely and willingly under his spell.

Gabe had never felt such soft satin flesh as Chantel's, and his tanned hands sought to caress every lush mountain and valley. But his passion mounted unchecked until he was an inferno ready to erupt, titillated by the frenzied undulation of the beautiful girl beneath him.

Not wishing to deny either of them any longer, he gave a mighty thrust and heard her gasp of pleasure. They soared so high that it took a few moments to descend back down into the real world.

But that didn't mean that Gabe was ready to let her out of his encircling arms or that Chantel was ready to move out of that circle.

When he felt her stir slightly in his arms, he whispered in her ear, "I love you, Chantel. I'll never love another. You've spoiled me for any other woman."

She giggled with pleasure and delight. "I've certainly tried to do just that." Playfully, she pulled away from him, declaring, "I don't intend to arrive at your folks' cottage naked as the day I was born."

"You look good to me," Gabe teased as she scrambled into her clothes.

"Gabe O'Roarke," she accused, "you're an evil man."

"You wound me," he replied with mock dismay. "I'm just a hot-blooded Irishman admiring your beautiful feminine curves." But he, too, had his pants back on and was reaching for his cotton shirt.

"What are you looking for, Chantel?" he asked, noticing her confused search of the cabin's counterspace.

"A hair brush," she wailed. "My hair is as wild as a certain Irishman I know."

He opened a drawer in a small chest and tossed her his brush. "You make yourself pretty," he told her, "while I go up top and see where we are."

Chantel had only to look out the window to see that it was dark outside. They couldn't be too far away from the O'Roarke cottage.

By now Chantel was familiar with the banks of the bayou and she recognized Deke's dock when they dropped him off. She calculated that just a short distance down the stream on the opposite bank was the Monroes' cottage. And around the next bend the O'Roarkes'. Tonight she was going to enjoy the bayou and Gabe's loving family.

They had no time to talk, for the bright lamplight beckoned to them through the grove of trees.

"We're home," he cried joyously, "and you're

going to be a pleasant surprise when you walk through that door with me."

A few minutes later the two young lovers jauntily went up the pathway. Delphine gave out a shriek of delight when she saw Chantel, and Scott got up out of his chair to greet her with a warm embrace.

"Chantel, what a wonderful sight you are," breathed Angelique, abandoning her kitchen. "We have missed you."

The evening went by too fast. For Chantel, this little cottage in the bayou was what a home should be and when she was around them she truly felt like she was with family. Nowhere that she had ever lived equaled the homeyness of this cottage.

She couldn't feel it at *La Maison* even though she knew Lily loved her and Andre was fond of her. She couldn't ask anyone to be nicer to her than Andre Deverone had been.

Her aunt's house had been her home for many years, but she had not had a feeling of family living with her old-maid aunt. In fact, she realized just how dull it had been now that she'd come to know a different way of life. She'd known more happy times at the boarding school with girls her own age then in her aunt's immaculate house.

Her Aunt Laurie was sweet, but she lived a celibate life, teaching and attending church every Sunday. She existed from one dull day to the next puttering in the garden of her cozy stone house. In the evening she worked her needlepoint or read a book. She would die never knowing the ecstasy of loving a man or being loved by him. Chantel suddenly realized that she would prefer to be like her mother rather than her poor Aunt Laurie.

Late that night, Chantel and Delphine finally had a chance to talk. "Terry asked me to marry him," Delphine confessed, her face suffused with a happy glow. "You're the first to know." Chantel stifled an excited whoop.

"Can I tell Jessamine?" she asked as she gave her friend a congratulatory hug. "I promise I won't say a thing to Gabe until you've told your family."

"You can tell Jessamine, Chantel," Delphine conceded. "Everyone will know soon anyway. My roaming days are over. I want to stay here forever with this sweet, gentle man who loves me dearly." She hesitated, instinctively lowering her voice. "My past doesn't bother him at all. I can't tell you how much that means to me. Terry's loved me forever." She frowned, happy but mystified. "I must have been blind not to have realized what a wonderful man he is before I took off on my wild adventure with a man that didn't begin to compare to Terry."

"Let me know if there's to be a wedding,

for I'll surely be here," Chantel assured her.

"I want you standing by my side," Delphine informed her, beaming.

Sluggishly, Chantel crawled out of bed the next morning so she could leave with Gabe. She was careful not to awaken Delphine when she left the bedroom to join the rest of the O'Roarkes at the breakfast table.

She nursed a cup of Angelique's strong coffee, feeling no need for food after the last night's feast.

Scott gave Angelique a quick kiss. "Got to pick up Terry," he explained, but paused for a moment beside Chantel. "Now don't you stay away too long, young lady," he commanded.

"I won't, Mr. O'Roarke," she promised. "I'd miss you all too much."

"Besides, I won't let her," Gabe interjected. "We've got to go, sweetheart," he added, turning to Chantel. She took a last sip of coffee and was on her feet following him instantly.

Angelique watched them walking down the pathway together. Gabe's hand held hers and he looked down at her with unmistakable adoration. Chantel's head barely came to the top of his broad shoulders. She was such a petite little thing!

"There's going to be a wedding in the bayou soon," Angelique thought as she stared at the empty dock long after both boats had pulled out into the marshland. "As sure as I'm standing here, there's going to be a wedding."

An hour later, Chantel found herself traveling back to *La Maison* in a buggy Gabe had hired. She had protested, but he had remained firm. "No, Chantel," he'd insisted, "I don't want you walking all that way."

So she had boarded the buggy after he'd given her a farewell kiss, and as the buggy rolled down the street, she peered behind her on the quay until Gabe was nothing more than a speck making his way back down to the dock to board the *Louisiana Lady*.

She'd been back for over five hours before Lily was aware that her daughter had returned. As soon as she'd changed clothes she went downstairs to search for Jessamine so she could tell her the news from the bayou.

It didn't take her long to spot the hefty black figure with a white kerchief tied around her head. Jessamine was in the front parlor with the cleaning women. In response to the inner glow that emanated from Chantel, a broad grin came to the housekeeper's ebony face. "I don't have to have anyone tell me that you had yourself a nice time," she observed.

"So you knew that I'd gone to the O'Roarkes?" Chantel asked.

"I was with your ma when Henry brought the message," Jessamine told her.

"Was she angry?"

"Angry? No. She was sort of quiet and thoughtful. Then she told me she guessed she didn't have herself no baby anymore, that you were a grown-up young lady."

Chantel was glad she'd had the chance to talk with Jessamine before she'd gone to see her mother.

Thirty-four

Chantel made no effort to see her mother until the time they usually shared brunch together. Mimi ushered her into the parlor. "You should wear that color more often, mademoiselle," the little maid told her. "That lavender gown gives you a kind of glow."

"I shall remember that when I purchase my next gown," Chantel declared, sitting on the settee. "Is mother up yet?"

"Yes. She'll be right in. May I get you anything, mademoiselle?"

"No, thank you, Mimi."

Chantel, engrossed with thoughts of Gabe and the O'Roarkes, barely noticed the minutes before Lily made her appearance. "Well, *chèrie*, you got back from the bayou. I'm sure you had a nice time with your dear friends," Lily remarked, picking up her silver cigarette case.

"I always have a good time with the O'Roarkes," Chantel responded. "I'd like you

300

to come with me sometime and meet them."

"Would you really like that?" Lily quizzed.

"Of course I would or I wouldn't have said so," Chantel replied — reassuring, not testy.

Chantel's declaration meant more to Lily than her young daughter could have possibly known. Lily had worried that Chantel was ashamed of her because of *La Maison*.

"Then I will go with you," she said, pleasing them both.

As they waited for brunch, Lily lit another cigarette. "Mother, could I try one?" Chantel asked suddenly, reaching for the silver case.

For a minute Lily was taken aback by the request. "Help yourself," she said, covering her discomfiture. "I didn't know you smoked."

"I don't," Chantel admitted. "But I'm curious to see what it's like."

Lily helped her light the cigarette, calling to mind the wonderful time in her own life when she, too, had been curious about everything. Chantel was no different. She expected Chantel to choke and gasp when she took her first puff, but to her surprise, she didn't and sat experimenting, quietly puffing on the cigarette until Mimi brought their trays.

They enjoyed a pleasant brunch and chattered well into the afternoon. For the first time, Lily allowed herself the hope that she and Chantel could become close. Andre had said that it would happen, but their start had been so stormy she just hadn't had the faith.

But Lily had yet to realize just how unpredictable her daughter could be.

Early in the evening Chantel presented herself to Lily in one of her most exquisite gowns. She had piled her hair atop her head in a hairstyle similar to Lily's and her radiance astounded Lily. "I want to go downstairs with you tonight," Chantel announced. Although Lily tried to dissuade her, she refused to change her mind. "What could happen to me with you there?" she asked. "I can sing with Brandy. I did it before. I was good and your patrons loved me. I want to share a night with you as Delphine shares nights with her mother."

Lily was deeply moved, and Chantel's logic was irrefutable. Nothing could happen to her. Lily wouldn't allow it.

"It will be a thrill to me to walk down those stairs with my beautiful daughter by my side," Lily asserted and was rewarded by the excitement reflected on Chantel's face. "This one night we shall do it, Chantel," she agreed, embracing her. Stepping back, she studied her at arm's length for a moment and then rummaged in the safe—hidden in the wall behind a painting—where she kept her most prized jewels.

"Put these on your dainty ears and you will be sheer perfection," she told her daughter as she laid a pair of emerald earrings in the palm of Chantel's hand. "They are yours now to wear and enjoy as I have over these last prosperous years. They are the first extravagant gift I bought for myself after I took over *La Maison*."

Chantel had never seen such exquisite gems. "Oh, Mother," she gasped. "They are beautiful! I'd just die if I lost them."

"They're yours, honey, so if you lose them that's your problem," Lily teased. "I want you to have them and this seems like the right night to give them to you. They match your eyes as well as your gown."

Chantel was so excited that her hands trembled as she tried to put the emerald earrings on her ears. Lily, checking the posts, felt a surge of elation. She had at last given her daughter something that had truly impressed her.

When they left Lily's quarters to go downstairs, they were two ladies in the highest of spirits, vivacious and alluring.

The gentlemen who observed their descent

that evening would remember it for many nights to come. The sight of Chantel in her emerald-green gown with the emeralds dangling from her ears and her golden hair piled high on her head and her mother, dressed in scarlet, ruby jewelry at her throat and ears, was enough to mesmerize any man.

At least two gentlemen—recently returned to New Orleans from France—were definitely entranced. It had been many years since Lucien Benoit had been in New Orleans, but he'd always remembered that *La Maison* was an exciting place and he'd wanted to show his son the best of New Orleans on their first evening back.

The beautiful Adrienne dressed in a deep-purple gown shared their table, but she was very much aware that both of the gentlemen's eyes were focused on Lily and her daughter as they made their grand entrance. Chantel's presence took Adrienne by surprise. Lily had been so determined to isolate Chantel from the downstairs activities that she had to wonder what had brought about the change.

However Brandy, unquestioningly, was happy to see Chantel, anticipating that she would join him at the piano as she had before. He gave her a nod and a big smile,

304

and Chantel left Lily to stand beside the piano. "Well, Mademoiselle Chantel," he grinned, "it's been awhile. Are you going to sing real pretty for me tonight?"

"If you'd like me to, Brandy," she acquiesced as his fingers caressed the keys.

"How about a ballad to start things off?" he suggested, playing a few bars of a familiar melody.

She faced the room and began to sing along. She had everyone's immediate attention, and all conversation ceased. A couple of new arrivals coming through the front entrance stopped just to gaze at the golden-haired goddess beside the piano. Lily greeted them and responded to their inquiry with pride. "She's my daughter," she informed them. "My daughter Chantel."

"Your—your daughter, Lily?" one man stammered.

"That's right, Phillipe," she replied brightly. "My daughter."

"She's beautiful, Lily!"

Lily shone as she led them to a table. As yet, she had not noticed Lucien Benoit and his son Lance in the secluded alcove nearby.

For a brief moment, she sat down at the table with Phillipe Moreau and his companion. Andre would soon be joining her, so she took this moment to have a chat with her old friend. She'd known Phillipe for years and he felt free to ask her, "Where's she been, Lily?"

"Back East at boarding school and with my sister in Boston. She's only been back in New Orleans for about three months," Lily told him.

"I had no idea you had a daughter, Lily."

"That's the way I wanted it, Phillipe." She smiled.

Brandy and Chantel followed the ballad with the lively tune she'd done before. As then, she created a stir in the parlor.

Lucien, seeing that Lance was entranced, excused himself to enjoy the pleasures of the gorgeous Adrienne. Lance hardly noticed that he was left alone at the table.

Once Andre appeared at the door, Lily rushed to greet him and they disappeared into one of the private dining areas enclosed with velvet drapes. She had so much to tell him.

So she was not aware that Chantel stopped singing and Lance Benoit raced to the piano with compliments for Chantel and Brandy. "Will you share a glass of my champagne, mademoiselle?" he asked, and he was so utterly gallant and charming that Chantel did not want to refuse him. She glanced at Brandy for approval. "Go ahead," he encour-

306

aged. "Enjoy yourself before I have you singing again."

Chantel accompanied Lance Benoit to his
table, and Brandy kept an eagle eye on
them.

The young Frenchman intrigued Chantel as
he generously praised her talent as a chan-
teuse. "Paris would fall at your feet, mademoiselle," he swore. "You sing like a bird
and you are so very beautiful, too. Ah, I am
très heureux my father brought me here tonight."

"Did you say your father brought you
here?" she asked, in surprise.

"Yes, my father. He used to live here, but
I was raised in France. We just arrived here
recently."

Chantel found it strange that a father
would bring his son to *La Maison* and no
one had to tell her where his father had disappeared to, for she'd seen him depart with
Adrienne.

In the course of their conversation Chantel
told him that she was the daughter of Lily
Lemogne, the owner of *La Maison*, and that
she, too, had not been back in New Orleans
too many months. It was a simple, innocent
conversation, and when Chantel finished her
champagne, she thanked him and rejoined
Brandy, oblivious to her effect on Lance Be-

noit.

Smitten, he was determined to see this gorgeous young lady again. In fact, he was planning already to court her, for she was the most breathtaking creature he'd ever met.

Chantel sang two more songs, and Lance's father returned to the room. Lucien was stunned to hear Lance flatly refuse to take his pleasure with any of the beauties featured at *La Maison*.

Shortly afterward, Lily and Andre emerged from their secluded alcove. "It's time I took Chantel back upstairs," she remarked. "She's stretched her wings long enough."

Her gay laugh was cut short when she spotted the aristocratic gentleman and his young counterpart eyeing Chantel — one with paternal speculation, the other with unquestionable devotion.

A chill washed over the lovely Lily. She'd not seen Lucien Benoit for years, and the young man sitting with him reminded her of the handsome, debonair devil Lucien had once been. Her past was rushing back to haunt her tonight and mar her happiness. She didn't want Andre to know how upset she was, but he sensed immediately the stiffening of her voluptuous body, although he couldn't determine the cause.

He took full charge. "Sit down, *chèrie*," he

urged. "I shall summon Chantel."

From her vantage point in the darkened shadows of the room, Lily confirmed that it was indeed Lucien at the secluded table in direct view of the piano. She watched Andre walk over to Chantel and bend his head down to whisper in her ear. She saw Chantel smile up at him and take his arm after she'd bid Brandy good night. Lily watched the two of them come across the room to join her. Andre was such a dignified gentleman with that thick mass of grey wavy hair and fine-featured face. She would be a fool not to marry him.

Suddenly she didn't care that she should be downstairs working the floor for many more hours. Leaving Adrienne in charge, she had a bottle of champagne sent to her quarters. She just wanted to be with her daughter and Andre for the rest of the night.

Chantel was very gay as the three of them talked and sampled the champagne. In fact, she proved to be quite a chatterbox as she felt the effects of the wine, and Lily and Andre exchanged amused glances. When she announced that she thought she should call it a night, Andre winked at Lily. "I think I should escort mademoiselle to her chamber," he declared gallantly.

Chantel giggled. "I think maybe mademoiselle might need escorting."

After he returned to Lily's parlor and they were alone, he asked her what had upset her so much.

"I should have known that I couldn't fool you, Andre Deverone," she yielded.

"Not easily. I know you too well by now, my Lily, but then that's the way it is when a man loves a lady as I love you."

Lily sighed. "Oh, Andre, why could we not have met years ago?"

"It obviously wasn't meant to be, *chèrie*, but all that matters is now and the future. We have the rest of our lives to enjoy one another." He pressed her hand against his lips. "But I am also a selfish man, Lily," he confessed. "I want to share everything with you. So tell me what was troubling you tonight?"

"A face from the past I never expected to see again," Lily told him readily. "He was sitting in a parlor alcove staring at Chantel."

"I'm listening, Lily."

"His name is Lucien Benoit, and his family is one of the wealthiest in the city. At least, they used to be. I've not seen Lucien since the night I announced to him that I was pregnant. He quickly left New Orleans and I've not seen or heard from him since."

"Lucien Benoit is Chantel's father?"

"Yes, and the young man who was with him tonight must be his son. He looks exactly like my Lucien of eighteen years ago."

"Will you tell Chantel this?" Andre asked her.

"Only if I have to." She considered. "I see no reason why I should."

"That's your decision, Lily, but there's another decision that I'm going to press you to make soon."

"The wedding," she said, and he nodded.

"I'm not only a selfish man, I am also an impatient one."

She threw back her head and laughed. "You're the most unselfish man I've ever known, Andre. Give me three weeks, and then I promise you a simple and speedy wedding."

Andre pulled her closer to him. "I want to make you my wife," he whispered, "so the two of us can live together the rest of our lives."

Lily snuggled against him and the smoldering heat of her voluptuous body pressing against him fired Andre with desire. He lifted her up in his arms and carried her to the boudoir.

With the fury of two young lovers, they gave way to the passion blazing within them, and Andre remained with her for a few more

311

hours before he sought to leave.

He could not wait for the day to come when he would not be slipping out of *La Maison* to go to his home after a night of fierce lovemaking with the sensuous Lily.

Andre, knowing in his heart that Lily was truly ready to marry him now, was content.

Thirty-five

Lucien Benoit could not ignore the evening's surprising turn of events. Had he known Lily Lemogne owned *La Maison*, he would never have dared take Lance there. But he'd had no inkling.

After they'd arrived back at his house in the city, Lance had gone immediately upstairs to his room and Lucien had retired to his study behind closed doors. Pouring himself a cognac, he'd sat down at his desk to think.

Perhaps, he mused, Lily Lemogne had not been lying all those years ago when she'd come to him in a panic to announce that she was pregnant. He'd assumed she was merely trying to press him into matrimony. After all, he was the son of wealthy Hubert Benoit and she was just another pretty girl living with her aunt in New Orleans.

He wanted neither to be married nor to be a father at that time. He was getting ready to go to France on a grand tour, and did not change his plans and never had one qualm of conscience about Lily Lemogne. During his sojourn in France, he met and married the daughter of a French nobleman and had no reason to return to New Orleans.

His wife Charlotte had died two years ago, and now — after almost seventeen years — he found it easy to return to his native country.

It had pleased him that his young son had chosen to accompany him instead of remaining in France with Charlotte's vast extended family of grandparents, aunts, uncles, and cousins.

Charlotte had been forbidden by the doctors to have any more children after Lance's birth. The pain and complications of that pregnancy had almost killed her, and they complied without question. Lucien had consoled himself with a series of mistresses over the last fifteen years, disillusioned that he and Charlotte had not found lasting happiness in their marriage.

A treasured only child, Lance was pampered by his doting mother and constantly at odds with his father. So it had surprised Lucien that Lance had opted to leave France and his mother's people.

But during the crossing, he and Lance had forged a deeper bond, and Lucien prayed it was not too late for them to achieve the closeness he believed a father and his only son should have. He had high hopes for New Orleans.

But their night at *La Maison* had not turned out as he'd expected. Lance was immediately lovestruck by the beautiful singer Chantel and he was so preoccupied with his dreams of her that he sat quietly in the carriage throughout the long ride home and refused Lucien's offer of a cognac in his study.

Once again Lucien was reminded that the two of them seemed to have little in common. Lance was his mother's son, not his.

He would have to put an end to Lance's determination to woo Chantel. If she were Lily's daughter, as she'd told Lance, then there was a distinct possibility that she could be his half-sister. And, he had noted, she had the same emerald-green eyes as he and Lance.

He downed a second cognac and knew that he would have to pay a visit to Lily Lemogne. He would demand the truth. He had a right to know.

The next afternoon Lily was stunned when Mimi ushered Lucien Benoit into her parlor. He stood before her as arrogant as ever and she was glad that when she and Chantel had finished brunch her daughter had gone in search of Jessamine. She didn't want Chantel near Lucien; she didn't trust him.

She made no effort to be gracious. "I've no time for a social chat," she told him bluntly. "I can't imagine anything you and I could possibly have to talk about. We said our farewells years ago."

Benoit heard the hatred in her voice, but he took a seat anyway. "I have one question to ask and then I'll take my leave," Lucien replied smoothly.

"Then ask it and leave," she snapped, inhaling on her cigarette.

"The beautiful young lady singing last night told my son that she is your daughter."

"I'm proud to say that she is," Lily confirmed.

"You have a right to be proud, Lily. She is stunning. My son thought so, too, so I must know if she is also *my* daughter."

It gave her a feeling of sweet revenge to reply to him, "No one could ever give you the answer to that but me, Lucien, and I'm going to let you wonder. Now, you can get out of here."

Lucien's green eyes sparked with fury. "You are a bitch, Lily Lemogne," he spat.

Lily threw back her dark head and showed him to the door. "You can thank yourself for that, Lucien Benoit."

Her laughter echoed in his ears as he

trudged down the long deserted hallway toward the stairway. His curiosity was whetted more than ever. He had to know if Chantel was his daughter.

This autumn was proving to be the season for weddings, Chantel thought. Usually, it was in the spring that romance led dewy-eyed couples to the altar. But Chantel knew the reasons behind the hastily planned wedding for Nannette. "Paul insisted that we get married," the bride had confided to her, "even though I confessed to him about Peter. I still can't believe that he can love me that much."

"Just be happy that he does, for it tells you what a fine, wonderful man Paul is," Chantel had said. "I know the two of you will be happy."

Nannette was as excited as any bride. "We're planning an early afternoon wedding," she'd explained, "so we can take the evening boat up to Natchez for a bridal trip. Paul has promised me that we'll have ourselves a grand honeymoon after the baby's born. He wants us to go to France this time next year."

Chantel was happy that everything had worked out for Nannette. It was good to see her excited about her marriage as well as the baby she was expecting.

At the end of the week, Andre, Lily, and Chantel traveled out to the Basherone estate. Jacqueline with her exquisite taste and flair had made it a grand—though intimate—affair.

Nannette was a radiant bride in a white satin gown lavishly trimmed in delicate French lace. She carried the traditional bouquet of snowy-white orange blossoms that the French considered a "must" for good luck. Paul looked dashing yet dignified as he stood by his bride to take their vows.

A delicious champagne brunch was served in the spacious dining room abounded with flowers in silver urns.

Nannette insisted that Chantel accompany her upstairs to help her into her traveling ensemble. The young bride bubbled with excitement as she dressed in the pale blue gown and matching jacket.

"It was a glorious wedding, wasn't it?" she exclaimed as Chantel tied the streamers of the pretty bonnet atop Nannette's head.

"It couldn't have been a more beautiful wedding."

"Well, you know who I'm going to throw my bridal bouquet to," Nannette asserted. "I want to come to your and Gabe's wedding."

"But he hasn't asked me to marry him yet," Chantel protested.

But a few minutes later, when Nannette's bouquet sailed through the air to the gathering below, Lily caught the spray of orange blossoms.

"I was trying to catch it," Jacqueline teased Lily. "It's time I got married again."

Chantel was a little crestfallen that she had not caught the bouquet. She wondered if it were a bad omen. Perhaps she'd been naive to think that just because a man told a woman he loved her it meant he wanted to marry her.

More than once she and Gabe had made fierce love, but he'd never told her afterward as she lay snuggled in his strong arms that he wanted her to be his wife.

Paul Chapelle had asked Nannette to marry him and the two of them had never made love. She *had* made love with his twin brother Peter, and *he'd* run off to Europe with no thought of her or the dilemma he'd left her in.

Nannette's wedding had posed a lot of disturbing questions for Chantel.

The next Saturday Chantel did not go down to the wharf to find Gabe on his fishing boat. If he wanted to see her, then he could come to *La Maison,* she reasoned.

Rains moved in over the Louisiana coast early Monday morning and lingered all day

319

and night. Tuesday morning they were still coming down steadily and Gabe could not get out on the lakes.

Scott, drenched by the rain on Monday, caught a miserable cold. Angelique noted that he was running a fever. "You're not going to make a run in the morning even if the sun is shining," she scolded, tucking him into bed early Monday night with a hot toddy.

It was Wednesday before Gabe and Terry were able to get the boats out again. Both the two young fishermen put in long, hard hours, pulling into the wharf at the end of the day before they prepared to head for their bayou homes.

Wednesday and Thursday Gabe searched the wharf for Chantel, but saw no golden-haired beauty in the midst of the parade of people.

He consoled himself with the reminder that he would see her on Friday when he took the order of fish to *La Maison,* but a week could be endless when a man was in love.

The constant rains had kept Chantel a prisoner inside the walls of *La Maison,* so the moment the sun came out on Wednesday she had Jonah take her out for a jaunt and a shopping spree. She resisted going down by the wharf. Why should she always be the one rushing to Gabe? she demanded in her inse-

320

curity. Let him come to her.

Nannette had encouraged her to ride her fine thoroughbred anytime she wished since he was going to remain at her mother's estate until she and Paul got settled in their new home. Chantel made plans to go out to the Basherones on Thursday.

She had Jonah take her to Simone's Boutique, one of her favorite emporiums.

He dozed in the buggy while he waited for her, but she made her purchases in less than a half hour and returned to the street in a new twill divided skirt and matching vest.

She was taken by surprise when the handsome young Frenchman Lance Benoit passed by the shop as she came out the door. He was thrilled.

"I've been exploring the city on my own this afternoon," he told her. "But you are the most exciting sight I've seen."

Jonah observed them from the buggy. He heard her decline an invitation and he was curious, but Chantel said nothing to enlighten him when she boarded the buggy. He fretted and wondered, all his protective instincts coming to the fore.

Lily and Andre were pleased that Chantel had taken an interest in the world outside *La Maison,* applauding her new riding ensemble and her plan to ride Baron in Nannette's absence.

"If Jonah can take you to Jacqueline's on Thursday," Andre suggested, "I'll pick you up late Friday afternoon. Jacqueline is a little lonely with Nannette away. She'll adore having you there over night."

When they were alone, Lily confessed to Andre that she was more than pleased with how everything was turning out between her and Chantel. "And I've got a surprise for you," she added, waiting for him to press her for details. "I've worked out a deal with Adrienne. It's the same opportunity I was given when I bought this place. We've set up a monthly payment schedule, but Adrienne is as greedy and selfish as I used to be. She plans to make double payments so it will all be hers that much sooner. Now I know why I like her so much."

"So there is nothing to delay our wedding, eh *chèrie?*" Andre asked, a pleased smile on his face.

"Nothing. We'll do it simply," Lily avowed. "The only person whose presence I'll insist on is Chantel."

"And I'd like Jacqueline, if that's all right with you."

"It sounds perfect to me, Andre."

Just before she went downstairs Andre slipped a magnificent diamond ring on her slender finger. The jewel was so perfect it sparked like fire and she couldn't resist glancing at it frequently all evening long. She could not wait to show it to Chantel tomorrow.

She was, however, disturbed to come upon young Lance Benoit in the downstairs parlor. He would be disappointed for although Brandy was playing the piano, Chantel would not be singing.

He was back again the next night after Jonah had taken Chantel out to Jacqueline's. Both evenings he had come alone. At least, she thought with relief, Lucien was not making an appearance.

He sought out none of her girls and Lily observed that as the night wore on he looked depressed. As much as Lily detested his father, she found herself feeling sorry for this young man who was Chantel's half-brother. He had to be almost a year younger than Chantel, but he didn't look it. His well-polished manners lent him an older appearance, for he'd lived in a far more sophisticated world than Chantel.

Despite his aristocratic air and expensive tailoring, Lily sensed that he was a lonely young man desperately seeking happiness. Perhaps that was why he'd looked upon her beautiful Chantel and was immediately lovestruck.

She ordered a glass of champagne sent to him and one for herself. Then she slowly ambled toward his table. Lily was a lady who could immediately draw a man's attention whether he was young or old. Lance was impressed by the alluring lady who joined him at his table and introduced herself.

He rose from his chair and gallantly took her hand to give it a light, gentle kiss. "Madame Lemogne," he enthused, "it is a pleasure to meet you. Please sit down. I—I am so honored to have you join me this evening."

Graciously he thanked her for the glass of champagne, and Lily found him charming. Nothing about him reminded her of Lucien. He had not inherited his father's annoying conceit.

Lily did not wish to tell him he was too young to come to her establishment and embarrass him. Nor did she wish to be so blunt as to tell him that if he were coming in hopes of courting Chantel that it was hopeless for she was his half-sister.

But when he began to praise her daughter, Lily found the opening she needed. "Chantel seems to cast a spell on most gentlemen," she agreed, "but her heart already belongs to a young man and they are to be married soon."

She saw by the crestfallen look on his fine-chiseled face that she had convinced him with her lie. "So she is already spoken for?" he asked.

"Yes, she is. The wedding is already planned," Lily told him.

A short time later he left *La Maison* and Lily felt confident that he would not return. She had tried to be gentle, for she had no desire to hurt Lance Benoit. He was a much nicer young man than his father had been.

Thirty-six

Gabe was in a gloomy, sullen mood as he went back to the *Louisiana Lady* after he'd delivered the fish to Raul's kitchen.

"Mademoiselle is not here," the cook had told him. "Jonah took her out to the Basherone country place yesterday."

Gabe kept up a casual air and gave a flippant shrug of his shoulders. "I just wanted to say hello," he remarked, but Raul was quick to notice that as soon as he was paid for his fish, Gabe didn't linger as he usually did for a little idle chatter.

As he left the kitchen Gabe saw Jonah in the back garden. "How's that Jessamine, Jonah?" he called out. "She treating you right?"

Jonah chuckled, "She's treating me just fine, Mister Gabe. She's fixin' me fine meals every night so how could I complain?"

Gabe laughed. "Want to come to my buggy and get some fresh-caught fish for your supper tonight?"

Jonah didn't waste any time jumping up from the bench and accepting Gabe's offer. The two of them walked to the buggy. "Heard you took Chantel out to the Basherones," Gabe commented.

"Yes, sir, I did. She's going to do herself some fancy riding on that friend of hers fine horse."

Gabe raised a questioning eyebrow. "Her friend's horse?" He felt a stab of jealousy in the pit of his stomach, but Jonah reassured him.

"Madame Basherone's daughter up and got married and left her thoroughbred for Miss Chantel to exercise."

But although his fears and jealousy were laid to rest, Gabe sailed for the bayou frustrated that he'd not seen Chantel as he'd planned. She had to know that he would have been bringing her mother's order of fish this late afternoon. Obviously she hadn't been as anxious to see him as he'd been to see her after all this time. She'd chosen to go out to the Basherones to ride a damned horse!

Delphine didn't know whether her parents noticed Gabe's bad mood, but she certainly did. She suspected that he and Chantel had had a lovers' quarrel.

"Want to take a walk with your sister, Gabe?" she asked as evening set in.

327

A weak smile came to his face as he replied, "Well, I guess so." He rose up from the chair and went over to the tin to get himself one of his cheroots before he joined her at the door. There was no doubt that he was not feeling as cheerful as he pretended to be.

At first they spoke of the weather, Dad's cold, and the week's poor catch. "Next week will be better, Gabe," she told him, trying to imply more than the yield of fish.

"Hope so, Delphine," he told her as he took a puff on his cheroot.

They walked a little farther and she asked him if he'd seen Chantel that afternoon. Gabe gave her a short, curt reply and tried to change the subject. "Nope," he said. "But I did see old Jonah and gave him some fish for his and Jessamine's supper tonight."

"How come you didn't see her, Gabe?" Delphine pressed.

"She wasn't there for me to see. She went *riding*." He spat the word out as if it were distasteful.

An amused smile came to Delphine's face and she was glad it was dark so Gabe couldn't see. Gabe had been spoiled by the young ladies in the bayou who'd fought over him since he was sixteen. They offered no challenge and Delphine thought that was why he'd never gotten serious about any of them.

Chantel had been so different and so much more beautiful that Gabe had lost his heart to her immediately.

Delphine was just as certain that Chantel adored her brother but that she was not one to sit around waiting for him to come to her when the notion struck him. Gabe still had a few things to learn about women and his sister hoped she could help open his eyes.

"What is so wrong with that, Gabe?" she asked innocently. "Chantel loves to ride."

"I suppose there's nothing wrong with it, Delphine, when you put it that way," he agreed, "but she knew I would be coming there this afternoon. I guess I'd hoped that she'd be wanting to see me, too."

"That doesn't mean that she wasn't wanting to see you, Gabe. It just means that she wanted to go out to the Basherones yesterday to ride that fine thoroughbred of Nannette's." Delphine paused, deliberated, and decided this was the perfect time for her to tell her brother of her own marriage plans. Maybe, it would give him some ideas.

"Gabe," she said, resting her hand on his arm. "There's going to be a wedding very soon here in the bayou. Terry and I are getting married."

Gabe took her in his arms and planted a brotherly kiss on her cheek. "Oh, honey, I'm happy for you. I think you've got yourself a good man and a good future here in the bayou."

"I know that now, Gabe." she avowed. "I know where I belong, believe me. What puzzles me is that I didn't take more notice of Terry before."

"Probably because he was always around," Gabe theorized, "so he didn't seem exciting compared to that smooth-talking dude who took advantage of the sweet, innocent girl you were."

Delphine squeezed his arm with warm affection. "Oh, Gabe, you understand me so well," she sighed. "But no one—not even you—can ever know the price I paid for my folly."

"No," he granted, his arms comforting her, "but you came home to the bayou a wiser young lady and I'm proud of you and so happy for you and Terry."

"We want you and Chantel to stand up for us," she advised him, "so be prepared." She shook her head. "Don't mention it at home. I haven't said anything to Momma and Dad yet."

"Don't you think you'd better," Gabe queried. "Especially if the wedding's to be soon."

She laughed a lighthearted laugh. "You know a bayou wedding doesn't take that

330

much preparation."

Gabe knew exactly what she meant. Any festive occasion could be planned hastily. As his father always said, there could be a party in the bayou at the drop of a hat.

Gabe cherished the time he spent with his sister that evening. Her company and talk had brightened his mood. Later when he lay on his bed, his thoughts drifted back to Chantel.

Delphine would have been pleased to know that she had spurred her brother to think more seriously about getting around to asking Chantel to marry him. Oh, there was no question in his mind that he was going to ask her! She was the only girl he'd ever considered marrying.

But Delphine's telling him about her plans to get married made him realize that, unlike Terry, he had no little cottage to which to take a bride. As close as he was to his family, he didn't want to bring Chantel to his childhood bedroom. He wanted his own home for their wedding night.

The next morning, saying nothing to his family, he took off in his canoe to go up and down the bayou checking out property. He wanted to see if there was anything for sale right now. It was late in the afternoon when he finally returned to his father's dock, and he'd made many stops along the way.

At his last stop he had been greeted at the door by an elderly grey-haired lady who introduced herself as Rosa Laveau. She instantly recognized his name, for she knew Angelique. "Now how did you know I was going to be putting my place up just next week, young man?" she asked with a friendly smile. She had a slight accent, which told Gabe that her heritage was French.

"I didn't," he confessed.

"So you wish to live here in the bayou like your folks?" she quizzed him. "Well, I find that very nice, monsieur. I've had the opportunity to meet your dear, kindhearted mother more than once over the last few years. She's brought me pots of soup and loaves of bread, as she has many ailing people. Your momma has majesty," Rosa Laveau declared.

Gabe knew the people up and down the stream called her the Queen of the Bayou and he swelled with pride at this stranger's praise of Angelique.

"Now you've come to see if I wish to sell my land and I do, for I'm forced to go to live with my children." She grew reflective, studying him. "My, how the years pass so swiftly! You are a grown man now, but I remember you as a little tadpole. You came here with your mother when she brought me

332

some stew."

She took him through her little cottage and it didn't matter to Gabe that it was small, for rooms could always be built on. It didn't matter—though it was nice—that all the furnishings were included in the price she was asking. Only the land on the bayou was important to him.

By the time he'd left Rosa Laveau, he had agreed to buy her place and Rosa was pleased to think of Angelique O'Roarke's son living in the home she loved. Gabe had confessed to her, "I'm planning to bring my bride here. This will be our honeymoon cottage, Madame Laveau."

A twinkle came to Rosa's eyes. "Ah, monsieur," she said with pride, "this cottage has known much love and great passions. My Jacques and I shared a long, happy life here, and so will you and your bride, I am sure."

That evening when the meal was over, Scott and Angelique not only learned that Delphine and Terry were going to be married but that Gabe was going to purchase the Laveau property.

Angelique glanced at her husband. "Can you believe these two?" she asked.

Scott grinned. "Looks like your mother and I are going to be back where we started before the two of you came to us. We're going to be here at this cottage all by ourselves."

"It's awfully nice to know that both our son and our daughter will be right here in the bayou with us," Angelique added. She also knew that there could only be one reason for Gabe to buy land for his own cottage.

She knew exactly what her only son was preparing to do. Gabe had asked Chantel to marry him or he was getting ready to propose to her.

Part Four
Bayou Magic

Thirty-seven

Delphine's arrival at *La Maison* was a delightful surprise to both Jessamine and Chantel. Having come to New Orleans on her father's fishing boat with him and Terry, she had arrived so early that she was able to have a nice visit with Jessamine before she went up to see Chantel.

"Delphine, come on in." A sleepy-eyed Chantel motioned her into her room. Delphine apologized for her early arrival, but Chantel was unconcerned. "I'm glad you're here now," she said. "We can have the entire day together until you have to get back to the dock to meet them."

"I had a special reason for coming to see you today," Delphine went on. "Terry and I have decided that there is no point in waiting any longer, especially since we both want a simple ceremony. So we're getting married next Saturday, and I want you to be my maid of honor."

Chantel gave her a warm embrace. "Nothing

337

would keep me from coming to your wedding, Delphine," she declared. "You know that. I'm surprised, though, I hadn't expected it this soon."

"It's hard to wait," Delphine blushed, "and we are both impatient. We'll honeymoon at Terry's cottage, and I'm ecstatic."

"This calls for a breakfast celebration," Chantel giggled. "And some coffee, though your announcement certainly woke me up."

"By all means get yourself wide-eyed, Chantel," Delphine urged. "I want you to go shopping with me to pick out my wedding gown."

"Madame Simone will have something that will be just right for you," Chantel assured Delphine as Jonah drove them to her favorite boutique.

"I can't afford something too expensive," Delphine reminded her. "Besides, we don't need silk or satin for a bayou wedding."

"Madame Simone has a variety of gowns to choose from, so don't worry we'll find something. And I shall buy myself something to wear to your wedding. It's a very special occasion for me, too, Delphine."

Simone Laroche was perceptive, and she had only to survey Chantel Lemogne's friend's simple frock to know that she could not afford the gowns Lily bought for herself and her daughter. But, she thought, the pretty black-haired girl with her dark complexion would certainly be fetching in the daffodil cotton gown with the lavish lace ruffle accenting the low-scooped neckline. Delphine loved it at once, for it was one of her favorite colors. Chantel found a similar gown in a soft shade of lavender. It had a squared neckline with a dainty lace edging.

While Delphine was occupied with purchasing herself some undergarments, Chantel bought a gift for her dear friend — a diaphanous pink nightgown that the clerk quickly wrapped for her.

They stopped at a tearoom for a light lunch, and all the time they were together Delphine was exploding to tell Chantel about Gabe's property. But that was not her news to tell.

Still, she could not resist letting Chantel know that Gabe had been disappointed not to have seen her Friday.

"I was ready to go out to the country by Thursday and get in some riding time," Chantel confessed. "The country is like the bayou. It's a breath of fresh air. It's dull and boring at *La Maison*. Life only begins at night."

Delphine knew what she meant, for it had been the same way at the Paradise Club. During the daytime hours, everyone slept to prepare themselves for the nightlife.

Back at *La Maison*, Delphine had her first

audience with Lily Lemogne. The lady intrigued Delphine. She had a dark complexion like Delphine, and Delphine saw no resemblance between Chantel and her mother except that each had a unique loveliness that was breathtaking. Lily Lemogne possessed a sultry, sensuousness that reflected in every move she made, whether it was sipping on her glass of wine or lighting her cigarette.

She recalled what Jessamine had told her earlier that morning. "Honey, these girls working for Madame Lily want to be here—she has to turn girls away. She don't tolerate any gent mistreating her girls either. They try, and they're refused entrance at *La Maison*."

Delphine was thinking that it wasn't that way at the Paradise Club.

Lily was as delighted to finally meet Delphine O'Roarke as Delphine was to meet Lily. She had wondered how Chantel would have gotten herself out of her dilemma in Charleston without Delphine and Jessamine.

As Delphine scrutinized her, Lily studied her daughter's friend. She had only to look into Delphine's dark eyes to know that she, too, had known hurt and pain.

Before leaving for the wharf, Delphine made an impulsive decision. "Would you come to my wedding, Madame Lily?" She asked. "I'd love for you to meet my family."

340

"I'd love to," Lily responded genuinely. "May I bring my Andre? I, too, am to be married soon."

Delphine's dark eyes darted from Lily to Chantel, for Chantel had mentioned nothing about this to her. "Of course, you can. We would be delighted to have both of you come." Her next words made an impact on Lily, revealing the depth of her feeling. There was an intensity in Delphine's eyes as she told Lily, "Chantel and I have a special bond of friendship."

Two pairs of dark eyes locked. "I understand," Lily murmured. "I'm very glad you were there with Chantel." Lily didn't need to say more. Delphine grasped the meaning beneath her words.

When Lily gave her an affectionate hug, Delphine was at first surprised and then realized that Lily Lemogne was a loving, warm lady like her own mother.

As the two girls descended the staircase, Delphine was as generous in her praise of Lily as Chantel was of Angelique O'Roarke.

"I like your mother," she concluded as they walked through the back gardens. "She's wonderful."

They left for the wharf, Jonah handling the buggy and Chantel's excitement mounted as she anticipated seeing Gabe. But it was her turn to be disappointed, for only the *Bayou Queen* was moored at the docks.

Terry greeted his pretty bride-to-be with a warm kiss, which brought a nostalgic smile to Scott's face. He well remembered the days of his youth and unbridled passion for Angelique. But, he chortled, the old wives' tales he'd heard were wrong. A man's ardor did not cease when he reached forty or fifty. His beautiful French Creole wife excited him still!

Delphine chattered happily, relating the events of her day.

Scott enjoyed seeing her elation. He wanted her to be happy. It was all he'd ever wanted for both his children. He wanted them to know the happiness and contentment that he and Angelique had shared all these years. He couldn't deny that he was delighted that Delphine would be living nearby. Now that Gabe had bought himself a piece of property and cottage about a mile away, he couldn't ask for more.

Delphine thought she might cheer Gabe up with an account of her day with Chantel and the news that she would be here for the wedding. But his fishing boat wasn't at their dock. "I expected to see Gabe's boat already home when we got here," she remarked to her father as they drew near.

"He did leave New Orleans ahead of us,"

342

Scott allowed, "but he was going to Mrs. Laveau's place."

"Anxious to get his deal settled." she smiled.

"One would get that impression." Scott laughed. "Gabe's excited about his new cottage, and Terry's flustered about becoming a bridegroom. I'm seriously thinking about declaring a three-day holiday for this grand occasion coming up Saturday."

As she was bringing her mother up-to-date, Delphine whirled around to see Gabe coming through the door. "Oh, Gabe" she repeated, "Chantel and her mother are coming Saturday."

"I heard, Delphine," he told her. "I'll pick them up at the wharf and bring them here for your wedding and then take them back to the city afterward."

"Madame Lily is going to bring her gentleman friend, too," she concluded excitedly.

"Sounds like you are going to have a grand wedding," Gabe observed. He was pleased to see his little sister so ecstatically happy, for she deserved a bounty of happiness after what she'd been through.

The O'Roarke family's future had never looked brighter.

Thirty-eight

"I bought it lock, stock, and barrel," Gabe announced in response to his family's inquiring looks. "After we get Delphine married, I'll take you down the bayou to see it," he told his parents.

"What about me? Don't I get to take a tour of it?" Delphine pouted.

"Of course you and Terry can have a tour. But I expect you'll be occupied in your own new cottage for the next week or so," her brother reminded her.

For the next three days, Angelique and Delphine spent hours in the kitchen cooking and baking. Angelique's neighbors were already bringing things to the house for the feast they knew would be served at the O'Roarkes after the ceremony. Baskets of fresh fruits and vegetables along with cured hams and sausage were stacked in preparation, and loaves of home-baked breads and pies lined an entire counter in the pantry.

As the wedding date drew closer, Scott did declare Friday a holiday. Gabe, mindful of his regular Friday delivery, stopped by *La Maison* on Thursday afternoon, and asked to speak with Madame Lily after he'd settled accounts with Raul.

Gabe had never been anywhere in *La Maison* but the spacious kitchen, and he was impressed. In the hallway, he saw old Jonah dozing in one of the velvet chairs.

He came alert when he saw Gabe. "Well, Mister Gabe, how are you doing?"

"I'm doing just fine. How about you?" Gabe asked him.

"Jessamine and I are just fine. We saw that little sis of yours a few days ago, and she invited us to her wedding.

"Then I will pick you and Jessamine up at the wharf along with Madame Lily and Chantel."

Jonah led him upstairs to Lily's door, then vanished. Chantel opened the door.

"Come in, Gabe. This is an unexpected surprise," she declared as she ushered him to the settee.

Lily was sitting on its mate. "Hello, Gabe."

"Afternoon, Madame Lily." He was very aware of Chantel, but he deliberately directed his remarks to her mother. "I wanted to let you know that I can pick you up at the wharf Saturday to take you to Delphine's wedding and, of course I'll return you to the city."

"That's very thoughtful of you," Lily said gratefully. "I shall tell Andre that he doesn't have to hire his friend's boat after all to get us there."

"Oh, no, ma'am, you don't need to go to that trouble. I'll meet you, Andre, Chantel, Jonah, and Jessamine at the dock Saturday afternoon," Gabe told her. "But I should be going." He rose from the settee. "Will you walk with me to my buggy, Chantel?"

As soon as the parlor door closed behind them, he reached out to take her hand. His blue eyes warmed at the sight and the feel of her. "Seems like ages since I've seen you," he murmured.

"You know where I've been, Gabe—right here," she retorted.

"I know, but it isn't easy after a long day out on the lakes for me to get over here."

He stopped suddenly and gently pulled her around to face him. His arms encircled her and he drew her so close to him that she could feel the heat of his hard, firm body. His dark head bent down until his lips captured hers. Chantel responded to the fire and passion of his lips pressing against hers.

When he released her, her green eyes stared

346

up at him, dark lashes fluttering, as she gasped, "You make me feel faint when you kiss me that way."

His laugh was deep and husky. "That's exactly what I hope to do, love. I want to do to you what you do to me."

He took hold of her hand once again and they seemed to glide down the stairway. Back in the darkened hallway in the other wing Adrienne had drawn back into the shadows to allow the young lovers their privacy.

She recognized the young man who held Chantel and kissed her with hot desire. She wondered if Lily knew, for it was readily apparent that they had shared moments like this before. This was no first-time kiss.

The tall, dark-haired Irishman was exciting and attractive, she concluded, but that was self-evident. What startled her was the magnetism that pulled Chantel's arms up to encircle his neck and caused her body to sway against him. Like her mother, Chantel was sensuous and utterly passionate.

Chantel and Lily went shopping the next day for a wedding gift for Delphine. Terry and Gabe took advantage of their day off, for Terry had confessed to Gabe, "I'm going to look like a clod beside Delphine in my old clothes."

Gabe had the obvious answer. "We'll go into the city and buy you a pair of pants and shirt." Terry invested in the most expensive trousers he'd ever owned and a white linen shirt, glad that Scott had paid him his wages the night before. Caught up in the excitement and extravagance, Gabe, too, purchased a white linen shirt. Their shopping spree quickly ended, Terry and Gabe headed back to the bayou about the same time Chantel and Lily returned to *La Maison*.

Chantel was amazed that her mother had bought Delphine such a luxurious wedding gift and she knew that her friend was going to be thrilled when she saw the pink satin coverlet Lily had purchased for their bed. Chantel had purchased the lovely gown for Delphine, and it seemed that everyone was busily shopping or working on something to make Delphine's wedding a happy occasion. Jonah and Jessamine had joined their skills to make her a wedding gift that they hoped she'd treasure. Jonah had been working into late night hours on a footstool and Jessamine had worked nightly on a piece of needlepoint to cover the top of it.

The only thing Angelique was fretting about was the weather. She had not worried about going into the city to buy herself a new gown. She had three or four gowns she could wear to her daughter's wedding, but she could only pray that it would be a fair, cloudless day and evening for Delphine had invited so many extra guests. There were only so many rooms in the O'Roarkes' cottage should a sudden downpour of rain overtake the bayou.

Otherwise, Angelique had everything perfectly planned for the grand occasion. Her cottage exuded a sweet fragrance from all the lovely autumn flowers she'd gathered from her garden. The white and yellow mums had never been more beautiful than they were this fall—an omen that boded well for their future, perhaps, since Delphine would be wearing a yellow gown.

She couldn't have been happier when she woke up the next morning to bright sunshine streaming through her bedroom window, and when she looked outside she saw a blue sky with no clouds.

She could have predicted Scott's reaction. With centuries of Irish superstition to draw on, Scott swore that the brightness of the sun augured a happy marriage.

"Remember our wedding day, Angelique?" he asked—as if she could forget! "That sun was out before the ceremony took place, but Ma was in a stew that morning when she got up to an overcast day."

Angelique remembered, "So we've got to figure that there is something to this Irish folklore of yours, for it has indeed been a wonderful marriage we've had. Now, I've got to get busy to see that everything goes just right for our daughter's wedding this evening."

Quickly, she got dressed and left the room to start a pot of coffee. But when Angelique entered her kitchen, Delphine was already there and Angelique could smell the coffee brewing. She teased her daughter, "You're suppose to be getting your beauty sleep since this is your last day on your own."

"I was too excited," Delphine admitted.

"That's the way a young lady is supposed to feel on her wedding day, I think. I felt exactly the same way," Angelique confessed to her daughter.

Only the very last-minute chores required Angelique's attention that morning. She had even laid out her clothes to wear this evening yesterday.

There were no more loaves of bread, cakes, or pies to be baked. Gabe and his father were taking charge of the side of beef that they were going to prepare in a pit out in the yard. At midday, a neighbor dropped by with two smoked turkeys.

Two huge pots of beans simmered slowly

on the old cookstove, and dozens of ears of corn were ready to be immersed in steaming pots of water.

Terry came over about noon, but Scott flatly refused to let him see Delphine. "It's bad luck, Terry my boy," he admonished. "But Gabe and I will let you help us set up these makeshift benches for our guests to sit on. And we have to put up a table for the wedding supper."

Delphine saw Terry in the yard, but she would not have dared stick her head out the door to say hello to her soon-to-be husband. She would not have dared chance anything that might have brought bad luck to her and Terry on this glorious day.

There was excitement at *La Maison* on Delphine's wedding day as well. Chantel was dressed in her lavender gown two hours before they were due to meet Gabe at the dock. Andre's carriage hadn't even arrived yet to take them to the wharf.

Jessamine had sent old Jonah up to Chantel's room with some lovely clusters of lavender asters she'd picked for her in the back gardens that morning. "Jessamine thought you might like to wear them in your pretty hair, Mademoiselle Chantel," Jonah suggested as he handed her the flowers.

"Thank Jessamine for me, Jonah. They match my dress perfectly," she told him.

Before she went across the hallway to her mother's rooms, she pinned asters to the side of her hair by her ear and was pleased with the effect. When she walked into Lily's parlor, Lily's first thought was that it could have been Chantel who was to be the beautiful bride today. She looked so enchanting in her simple little cotton dress trimmed in the dainty white lace with the flowers tucked at the side of her head.

"You look lovely," Lily assured her. As Lily appraised her loveliness, Chantel admired her. Lily projected a different image today to Chantel, but she was just as striking in her grey gown with its high-necked bodice and long, fitted sleeves. She wore none of her extravagant gems but had chosen a single strand of pearls and small pearl studs on her ears.

This Lily was vastly different from the lady of the evening Chantel usually saw garbed in fabulous silk and satin gowns of vivid colors, her ears adorned with flashing rubies or diamonds.

Chantel noticed that she had laid out on the settee a short cape of matching pearl-grey along with her reticule, but she was obviously not going to wear a bonnet.

A short time later Andre arrived, and the entourage boarded his carriage. Jonah carried the little footstool, and Andre took charge of the large package which contained Lily's coverlet. Chantel placed the gift-wrapped nightgown on her lap. Andre's wedding gift to the young couple was an envelope containing money, which he had secreted in his pocket. He knew neither of them yet, but he knew that newlyweds could always use extra funds.

Thirty-nine

Chantel didn't get the chance to tell Gabe how handsome he looked in his fawn-colored pants and new linen shirt, but she was affected by this new image of him. Andre took an immediate liking to Gabe and struck up a conversation the minute they boarded the *Louisiana Lady*.

"And they call us chatterboxes," Lily jested.

Chantel was pleased that the men got on so well. Lily, reading her thoughts, remarked, "Andre and Gabe are a lot alike as unlikely as it might seem." But there was no time to discuss it further, and she turned to Jessamine and Jonah with infectious goodwill and well-placed compliments.

Chantel noticed that Jessamine and Jonah were in an exceptionally jubilant mood, but she didn't know that Lily had just informed them that when she and Andre got married they were to come with her to Andre's home.

354

It meant everything to them to know that Lily was not going to leave them behind at *La Maison*. They had been pondering what the future held for them.

Andre was intrigued by this trip. As many years as he'd lived in New Orleans, he'd never been into bayou country and he questioned Gabe about everything.

The bayou was foreign to Lily, too. She was entranced by the strange new sounds and sights. Chantel and Jessamine exchanged glances when Lily became suddenly quiet, absorbing the surroundings around her.

There were several canoes at the O'Roarkes' dock when Gabe's *Louisiana Lady* tied up. Chantel spotted Terry's canoe bedecked with garlands of flowers; later that night he would be taking his new bride home with him. His sister was going to be spending the next few days with the O'Roarkes so Delphine and Terry could have the cottage all to themselves.

Torches were already lit along the pathway even though it wasn't dark yet. As they left Gabe's fishing boat, Chantel contemplated the mix of people who would be at Delphine and Terry's wedding.

There would be the O'Roarkes' bayou neighbors along with the two black people, Jessamine and Jonah. Then there was her

355

own mother Lily, who owned an infamous high-class house of pleasure, and her fiancé, the distinguished lawyer Andre Deverone. It could prove to be a most interesting evening, Chantel thought as they made their way across the dock. Gabe finally managed to join her as the group reached the pathway. He took her hand.

Several guests had already gathered and were seated on the makeshift benches that Gabe and his father had set up earlier. Now that the best man had brought the maid of honor, the ceremony would soon begin.

Chantel went immediately to Delphine's room and when Delphine saw that she had lavender asters pinned in her hair like the yellow ones Delphine had pinned to the side of her hair, she laughed. "Why, Chantel, you look like a bayou bride, too."

Angelique and Scott were reunited with Jessamine, someone—they professed—they would love forever. They were delighted to meet her older brother Jonah.

And finally, Angelique met Chantel's mother. Scott knew how much she had looked forward to their meeting, and as he had expected there was no formality between them from the minute they were introduced. They immediately addressed one another as Lily and Angelique.

Scott watched his beautiful wife embrace Lily. Everyone warmed to Angelique, he reflected. She might have been the daughter of one of the wealthiest gentlemen in New Orleans, but there was no hint of conceit or snobbery about her.

Like Scott, Andre was also observing the two ladies, and he was impressed by Angelique's grace and charm, and her exquisite French-Creole loveliness.

"We shall talk later, Lily." Angelique whispered. "I think, there's a wedding about to take place."

Angelique's garden was abloom with lovely autumn flowers, and the ceremony took place in front of a white trellis with ivy entwined around it. The setting grew serene as twilight descended.

In only a few short minutes Delphine and Terry were pronounced husband and wife, and Terry kissed his bride.

Chantel wondered if Gabe and Terry were feeling the same jitters as she and Delphine had had when they left her room moments earlier. She glanced in Gabe's direction and he seemed impossibly calm. But after Terry kissed Delphine, he whispered "My stomach is churning like crazy! This is the one and only time I'm getting married!"

Delphine giggled. "I'm going to hold you

to that, Terry Monroe."

By then the guests were coming forward to congratulate the young couple. Angelique slipped away to her kitchen to bring out the wedding feast. Jessamine left Jonah with Gabe's father so she could give Angelique a helping hand. A few minutes later she emerged with a huge bowl of fruit punch despite Angelique's insistence that she wanted her to enjoy herself.

Adamant Jessamine declared, "Ah, honey, I am enjoying myself, and so is Jonah. But I feel like family and want to help you just a little.

Angelique turned from her stove to give Jessamine a warm smile. "We shall always want you to feel that way, Jessamine, for that's the way we feel about you."

Several neighbors offered assistance carrying the platters of food to the long table in the garden. Lily helped out in the dessert line, serving the berry cobbler and chocolate cake. Chantel was delighted to see Andre and Lily enjoying themselves as they laughed and chatted with the other wedding guests.

"Your mother is absolutely charming," Angelique enthused. "You must bring her back so we can have a nice, relaxed visit."

"I will. I promise." Chantel told her.

Gabe, returning to Chantel's side with two

more glasses of fruit punch, made a point of reminding his mother while he had the chance, "The second dance is mine, Momma."

Angelique was in a lighthearted mood. With a devilish gleam in her dark eyes, she retorted, "I can't imagine who will have that first dance with you." Then she whirled around and disappeared into the milling throng.

Chantel had always thought that Gabe was more like his father, but tonight she could see the vivaciousness that Angelique O'Roarke displayed when she wished to.

After the guests had eaten, Delphine and Terry opened their wedding gifts. Chantel had convinced Delphine to leave her gift in the bedroom, "It's better you open it in private," she'd warned her.

Delphine especially treasured Jessamine and Jonah's footstool, knowing how much work and love they had to have put into it. "This goes in our front room," she declared, "and I dare Terry to put his dirty shoe on it."

This elicited a roar of laughter.

There was no question about the gift that was the most luxurious. It was Lily's pink satin coverlet. Andre waited until they'd opened all their gifts to hand Terry the envelope he'd placed in his coat pocket to present to the newlyweds.

The presents opened, the dancing began. Delphine and Chantel slipped away to her room to refresh themselves. It also gave them a private moment for Delphine to open Chantel's gift.

Delphine gasped when she saw the beautiful pink nightgown. "It's luxurious!" she exclaimed. "Seductive," she added with a timorous giggle. "I'll wear it tonight."

She reached out to embrace Chantel. "I didn't ever expect to be this happy," she said, tears of happiness streaming down her face. "I've had a perfect wedding, and all the bad things that happened to me have begun to fade away. I thought they never would."

"I'm so glad, Delphine." Chantel gave her a squeeze and dried her eyes with the corner of her lace handkerchief. "It has been a most wonderful night."

"You might not believe it," Delphine said quietly, "but tonight will be the first time for me and Terry. I think that's the way Terry wanted it because of all the things that happened to me in Charleston."

But what she'd not yet been able to confess to Chantel about the time she spent in Savannah at the Paradise Club she had not been able to bring herself to confess to Terry either.

"You've got yourself a fine husband and I know the two of you are going to be happy," Chantel predicted. "Now I suppose this is our last moment of privacy for the rest of the evening, since the crowd will be clamoring for the bride and groom to dance together in the garden."

But their conversation had confused Chantel. She tried to brush aside all her disturbing thoughts about Gabe for this night at least. In the garden, the band was playing and the atmosphere was festive. Tonight was not the time to ponder the questions that troubled her. Besides, she suddenly found herself enfolded in Gabe's strong arms. He led her to the plank floor and they whirled to the strains of the music.

"This is our first dance together," Gabe whispered. "It's the first time my arms have held you as we've danced, but it isn't going to be the last. We're going to do this many, many times." His gaze caught hers with an intimate promise. Chantel found it impossible to resist his Irish charm.

Gabe was a grand dancer, a talent she assumed he'd inherited from his graceful parents who glided effortlessly over the plank dance floor. Terry and Delphine also made a charming couple, her head resting on his shoulder while they danced, but what thrilled

Chantel most was the sight of her mother in Andre's arms as they danced. They were a striking couple. It was the first time she'd ever seen her mother dance, and she seemed to be having a wonderful time. Gabe, of course, had seen his parents dancing many times, for the bayou people loved a party and gathered together at the slightest excuse.

Chantel was slowly realizing that her disillusionment with her mother was misplaced. In spite of herself she was starting to admire Lily more and more.

Andre took Chantel for the second dance as Gabe claimed Angelique and Scott whirled Lily onto the floor. On the third dance, Scott persuaded a shy Jessamine to dance with him.

Andre saw that Mary Jane, Terry's sister, was on the sidelines of the celebration. "Please dance with me," he urged her, not wanting her to feel left out at her brother's wedding.

"I don't know how," she stammered, but she let him lead her in a nice slow ballad. She relaxed in his expert arms and even let herself smile when she found she could follow him without having to worry and concentrate.

Andre was such a gregarious gentleman that he danced with most of the ladies before the evening was over. The hour was late when the last guests departed from the O'Roarkes and Terry paddled his bride upstream in the flower-bedecked canoe.

As the last canoe left the dock, Angelique declared to her husband, "Gabe better get married soon, for I'm not going to be able to put together one of these gatherings too much longer. Age is catching up with me, Scott."

Scott shared her weariness, and his arm went around her waist. "I don't think you'll have to wait long," he said thoughtfully. "Then we'll be through with getting our children married, and we'll be here all alone."

Angelique found that comforting as they walked back to the cottage, for she was ready to collapse in their bed and sleep very late in the morning.

Forty

It was a night old Jonah and Jessamine would remember for the rest of their lives. He'd not danced but he'd sure clapped his hands and tapped his feet to the lively music of the guitars and banjo. That fellow playing the fiddle had really made that instrument talk tonight.

Jessamine would never have imagined herself dancing, but she had—not only with Mister O'Roarke, but with Gabe and Monsieur Deverone as well. She could see why Madame Lily found him so exciting. She'd never seen the side of him that she had seen tonight before. He was a fun-loving man.

And the nicest revelation was that the bayou people didn't look down their noses at her and Jonah because they were black.

It was late—past midnight—when the *Louisiana Lady* returned to the wharf, and its passengers were quiet and pensive. Gabe took advantage of a brief moment to give Chantel one quick kiss in the shadow of the boat before she joined the rest of the party.

Like everyone else, Chantel had fallen silent as they'd traveled back to the city, but he'd concluded that she was pleasantly exhausted. They hadn't had any real time alone for him to tell her about the small piece of property he'd bought. But then, this was not their night. They were celebrating with Terry and Delphine, and his sister could always look back on her wedding night as a most wonderful affair.

One of the most satisfying things for him had been how Lily Lemogne and Andre Deverone had blended into the bayou atmosphere so easily. It had not gone unnoticed by Gabe how Andre had graciously asked Terry's sister to dance with him, and what he had seen tonight was enough to earn Andre his highest esteem.

When they arrived at *La Maison,* Lily and Chantel went through the kitchen so they could go up the back stairs, without running into anyone.

"Bayou parties are exhausting," Lily breathed, and they went quickly to their rooms and collapsed, prepared to sleep late in the morning.

Andre had his first coffee of the day served out on the terrace and enjoyed the tranquility of his garden. It was a place where he'd often sat to mull over the events of his life. He'd made many decisions in this peaceful setting, and this morning he pondered how nice it would be for him and Lily to have a cottage on the bayou where they could take refuge when they wanted to get away from the city for a few days. Perhaps, he determined, he'd just have to have a talk with Gabe or his father one day soon to see if they knew of any property for sale.

The more he thought about it as the afternoon went on, the more excited he became. Later at Jacqueline's, he outlined his plan to her.

But Jacqueline was skeptical. "Do you really think Lily would like spending time out there, Andre?" she asked.

He did.

"She sure had herself a good time last night," he noted. "It's a refreshing change from life in the city; it's like your place out here."

Conceding, Jacqueline pressed him to stay for dinner with her. "Paul and Nannette will be here," she coaxed, but he was expected at Lily's.

Sundays around *La Maison* were quiet, lazy days for everyone but Raul. He did his extra baking then and prepared Madame Lily's evening meal as well as supper for the girls in the west wing. He swore that because they didn't work on Sunday nights they sat in their rooms eating all afternoon and evening. Girls were constantly bouncing into his kitchen to fix themselves a tray to take back to their rooms.

Chantel felt no great rush to get dressed when she got out of bed and she nibbled at a light breakfast of coffee and a jelly roll.

Her thoughts were on Delphine and her wedding night. Delphine's confession had astonished her. Terry had known that Delphine had run away with a young man, so obviously he also knew she was no longer a virgin. On top of that, there were the many months she'd been enslaved to Antoine Savanti. Yet, he was willing to deny himself until he made Delphine his bride! Chantel was touched that he should love her so much.

She wondered what Gabe's reaction would be if she were to deny him the next time he sought to make love. How would he react if she refused him until the day they were to be married? Perhaps she should challenge Gabe to see once and for all the depth of his feelings for her.

Gabe would have been stunned to have learned of her confusion. He assumed it was understood that when he'd gone to Charleston to seek his revenge against Antoine Savanti, it had been for Chantel as much as Delphine.

He had repeatedly told her that she was the woman he loved and adored, so it had never dawned on Gabe that Chantel was yearning for his proposal of marriage to erase the doubts and fears that had begun to plague her.

That evening after she shared the evening meal with her mother and Andre, she excused herself to go back across the hallway to her own room. She was certain they would prefer to be alone and at the moment she wasn't very good company. She wasn't in a happy mood and it wasn't easy for Chantel to pretend. Besides, she didn't want to dampen their high spirits.

But once in her room, she found herself pacing like a cat. She was hardly ready to go to bed after sleeping until noon, so she went down the back stairs and into the garden for a stroll. It was as beautiful a moonlit splendor outside tonight as it had been on the bayou the previous evening. She sat down on one of the little benches, observing that the night birds didn't sing as sweet or as often in the city as they did in the quiet of the marshland. Was it just her imagination that the night-blooming flowers did not give off a fragrance as sweet as the blossoms in the O'Roarkes' garden?

Someone else was roaming the back gardens, and a dark figure suddenly stopped behind the huge oleander bush, peering at the cluster of benches. A sudden glow of moonlight shone through the branches of the tall trees, illuminating a mass of golden hair. Relieved, Jessamine made her way to Chantel.

"Miss Chantel," she called, "it's me, Jessamine. Lord Almighty, you gave me a fright until I recognized those pretty yellow curls."

"Can't you sleep either?" Chantel asked.

"No, ma'am. I'm wide-eyed and bushytailed, but that Jonah's been asleep for over an hour." she heaved a sigh as she eased herself down on the bench with Chantel.

"We're not used to such exciting nightlife," she chuckled.

"I think everyone there had a glorious time," Chantel remarked.

"I know we did. Jonah talked all day about last night. I guess Madame Lily's going to be the next bride, and I'm just as happy for her as I was for Miss Delphine. I truly love her, too, Miss Chantel. And," her dark face flushed with excitement, "she's going to

369

take us with her to Monsieur Deverone's big house."

Lily's plans were news to Chantel and made her realize how imminent her mother's marriage to Andre truly was. She gave a forced, weak laugh. "I guess everyone is going to be marrying but me."

The tone of her voice immediately alerted Jessamine to her depressed mood, but she gave a cheery laugh. "You, Miss Chantel— you'll not have any trouble getting married. Mercy me, no! That Mister Gabe has his eyes on you, sure as I'm sitting beside you."

Chantel's voice was caustic. "Well, Mister Gabe hasn't asked me to marry him yet," she said morosely.

"Oh, Miss Chantel," Jessamine protested, he loves you, but he just hasn't gotten around to asking you to marry him yet."

"And what am I suppose to do, Jessamine?" Am I suppose to just sit and wait?"

Jessamine chortled. "That would go against your nature, Miss Chantel, so you're going to have to prod him like I did with my Sam."

"I prod him?"

"This old black lady is going to tell you what prod means when you're dealing with a man." Jessamine leaned back relishing the explanation. "You do a little pushing, a little shoving. There's another trick that always works: You make him jealous. He won't be able to stand the thought of some other man having his lady. With Sam, I just gave him a hard push and it worked. I just let him know his time was running out, and he got busy and asked me to marry him."

Chantel broke into laughter. "Oh, Jessamine I should have had this talk with you weeks ago. But it's not too late. I can start prodding Gabe now."

"I don't think you'll have to do too much prodding, Miss Chantel," Jessamine reassured her. "I've seen that young man when he's around you, and unless I'm very mistaken, that's a look of love I see on his face when he's with you.

To her surprise, Chantel found that her spirits had lifted.

Forty-one

After Chantel had left them Sunday evening, Andre and Lily had a serious talk about their own marriage. "Let's not wait any longer," he pleaded. "I've got a lovely home waiting for you across town. Adrienne is capable of taking over *La Maison,* and you can always come back over here during the day while I'm at my office to tie up any loose ends."

Lily let him ramble on, but it was hard for her to keep an amused smile from coming to her face. He told her that Jacqueline had suggested Chantel come to her place while he and Lily honeymooned.

Lily wanted no more delays either, now that she'd been to Delphine's wedding. He almost fell off the settee when she replied, "How about this Sunday?" When Andre finally found his tongue, he bit it in his enthusiasm. "You'd better be serious," he warned, his thick brow raised as he scrutinized her face.

"I'm very serious, Andre. As you said,

372

there's no reason to wait any longer." She would have followed up the comment with supporting statements, but she found herself in Andre's strong arms, his lips cutting off further conversation.

He didn't even give her any fuss when she requested that he go home early. "I've got a busy day to put in tomorrow if I'm going to be your bride a week from today," she explained. He nodded in agreement.

"Truth is, Lily," he said, I may not be over tomorrow night. I've got a lot of work, to do. I'll need to go over my cases.

He encountered Chantel in the hallway. It surprised her to see him leaving so early, but there was such a happy expression on his face she knew it wasn't because they'd quarreled. He mentioned that both he and Lily had a busy day tomorrow. "I didn't get any work done Saturday what with the wedding," he explained.

Chantel didn't linger long in her mother's quarters since she found her at her desk going over some papers. It was apparent that her mother was preoccupied and not in her usual talkative mood.

The next morning Chantel was not the only one surprised by Lily's early rising. Perplexed, Mimi slipped down to the kitchen to tell Raul to prepare a breakfast tray. "At this hour?" he questioned. "For *Madame?*"

As soon as she'd finished her food, Lily dressed and had Mimi fix her hair. When each tress was in place, she instructed Mimi to have Jonah ready for errands. The sun not yet high, Lily left the house looking very elegant in her tailored ensemble with its fitted jacket.

"I wondered at first if she were sick when I saw her up so early, but she is fine," Mimi assured a worried Chantel as the hours went by.

Chantel had her carafe of coffee in her mother's quarters. She expected her to come through the door any minute. But she didn't return by the time Chantel had finished two cups of coffee, so Chantel returned to her own room to get dressed. A half-hour later Chantel went back across the hall, feeling sure that her mother would be home, but she wasn't and Chantel was utterly confused. "What is going on here today, Mimi?" she asked. "I have no idea, mademoiselle," the little maid admitted sinking in the chair next to Chantel. "Everything about Madame Lily has been different today."

The words were scarcely out of her mouth when Lily breezed into the small parlor, packages and reticule in hand. She looked radiant.

"Well, Mother, you've been a busy lady today, it seems," Chantel declared as Lily removed her rich, blue-velvet bonnet. Lily knew that both of them were as curious as cats, but she preferred to keep them in suspense for awhile. "I *have* been a busy lady. I could use a glass of wine, Mimi—the vintage white. And, Chantel, would you like to go shopping with me tomorrow?"

"You know I always love to go shopping, Mother," Chantel acknowledged agreeably. "But what are we going to shop for? I've got an armoire full of gowns."

Lily paused dramatically and invited Mimi to take a seat with them. Then, glowing, she made her announcement. "We're going shopping for your mother's wedding dress and, of course, a gown for you, too, Chantel. Andre and I are getting married next Sunday."

"Oh, madame!" Mimi shrieked excitedly. "Madame, I am so very happy for you."

Lily looked at her daughter. "Chantel, honey," she questioned, "are you happy for Andre and me?"

Chantel embraced her. "You know I adore Andre, and I have no doubt that he loves you. Why shouldn't I be happy?"

"Just wanted to be sure. Now, Mimi, get a glass of wine for Chantel—and one for yourself as well. We have to celebrate!"

Giggling, Mimi brought the wine and glasses and they toasted future happiness.

"And you're to come with me to Andre's after I'm married," Lily said to Mimi as she unfolded some of her plans. "You'll be my maid, just like here." Lily touched her glass to Chantel's. "Now we'll have that real home you've always wanted. I'm just sorry you had to wait so long for it."

"Oh Mother, I wouldn't want to think that you're marrying Andre just for us to have a fine home," Chantel objected.

"I'm marrying Andre Deverone because I love him with all my heart and soul," her mother affirmed. "If I'd wanted to marry some gentleman just to get us a home, I could have done that years ago. Until Andre came into my life, I loved only you and *La Maison*. You were with Laurie from the time you were eleven, so I devoted myself to *La Maison* and made it special. I look at it as a safe haven for girls who have nowhere else to turn."

"I understand things now that I didn't when I first got here, Mother. Really I do," Chantel said with conviction.

"A woman is sometimes forced to do a lot of things to keep from starving. I thank God you were spared Savanti's cruel treatment. But you now know how easily a young woman can find herself in a trap before she even realizes what's happened." Lily pointed out.

"I can certainly attest to that," Chantel sighed.

Their talk finally came to an end when Lily

376

noted that it was past time for her to meet with Adrienne, but she told Chantel as they parted, "Life doesn't always work out as we expect it to."

Chantel lingered in the hall before she entered her room and watched her mother hurry into the west wing to find Adrienne. Never had she felt so close to her mother as she did this evening, and she vowed that she was going to make up for her actions of the past in the days to come.

Chantel had no time to mope in the days that followed even though the wedding was going to be small and private with just Jacqueline and Chantel in attendance in Andre's parlor.

By Thursday, Lily and Chantel had purchased their new gowns and accessories. Lily had picked out a creme-colored dress of satin and lace, and Chantel had chosen a gown of blue-green silk. Lily told her that her eyes turned the same color as the gown.

Andre was in a state of elation. He had a boyish-like enthusiasm when he came over one evening for dinner, and the next afternoon he'd taken them to his home and urged Chantel to choose a bedroom and Lily to select one for Mimi.

Chantel quickly made her choice when she

stepped out onto a railed balcony outside one room. "We should have known this was the one Chantel would like," Andre commented agreeably.

As the trio walked back downstairs, his two strong arms wound around each. "It will be wonderful to have those rooms filled with people I love so much," he declared. "And it still leaves three bedrooms, for our grandchildren when they come to pay us a visit."

Lily laughed gaily. She'd never known a time in her life that she'd been so absolutely and completely happy.

Andre left no details undone. He had furnished his cook with the exact menu he wanted for their wedding dinner along with the champagne and wine list. He left orders with his housekeeper for specific flowers and their placement along with a lighting plot for candlelight in the parlor and the dining room.

Andre was used to dinner parties, but for Sunday evening everything had to be perfect.

At first Chantel refused to tell Andre about Lily's wedding dress, but Andre finally persuaded her to reveal just the color. She had, however, no reservations about describing in detail her gown.

That was all Andre needed to know when he went to his jeweler. He purchased Lily earrings with canary diamonds to match her engagement ring. For Chantel, he bought a delicate aquamarine necklace and earrings.

By Friday, Andre was nervous, a situation he had not anticipated. He kept going over everything in his mind, afraid he'd forgotten something important.

Friday was a very busy day for both Chantel and Lily, for this was the day that Jonah was going to transport some of their clothing and belongings to Andre's home.

But everything was going just as Lily and Andre had planned, and tonight she promised herself she wouldn't even get out of her dressing gown. She was ready to totally relax in her suite.

Tomorrow night she would put on a fancy gown and mingle with the patrons. It would be her last night to be Lily Lemogne, proprietress of *La Maison*.

Sunday evening she would become the wife of Andre Deverone and a whole new life was going to begin for her.

Forty-two

It had been a busy but exciting week for Gabe O'Roarke, because after he put in a full day of fishing on the *Louisiana Lady* he went down the bayou after supper to the little cottage he'd bought from Rosa Laveau.

She had moved out over the weekend, and Gabe was free to make changes. Some of the furnishings he would keep, but other pieces had lived a long lifetime and were due to be tossed out.

Gabe ridded the front room of two old rockers that she'd probably kept for sentimental reasons. There was a nice sofa which she'd recently recovered paired with an overstuffed chair.

She'd left behind two lovely lamps, but one of the tables in the front room was beyond repair and he tossed it on the bonfire with the rockers.

Gabe was pleased that the cookstove was in fine shape as well as the table and chairs.

Rosa had left her lifetime accumulation of pots and pans along with her dishes and silverware. She would have no further need of these utensils living with her children

The nicer furnished bedroom could remain as it was, but the other bedroom—the one he planned for himself and Chantel—would have all new furnishings. His bonfire grew higher and hotter in the clearing at the back of the cottage.

So one bedroom was bare of any furnishings. Gabe wanted the little cottage to look as nice as he could possibly make it when he brought Chantel here to see it. He wanted to invite her to come out to the bayou on Sunday to spend the day and paddle down the bayou to see his newly acquired property.

Scott and Angelique realized how excited their son was about his new venture. With Gabe working at his cottage after dinner and Delphine no longer at home, the O'Roarkes found they had time to talk privately as they'd not done since Angelique was expecting Gabe. They laughed about it, and Scott declared, "We didn't realize what a difference a baby was going to make in our lives, did we, honey?" He reminded her of the times when they would be in the most amorous, intimate situations only to be interrupted by the loud wailing of Gabe in his crib near their bed.

Angelique laughed. "Well, Gabe will know those same nights, Scott."

Knowing how energetically and vigorously Gabe had worked in the last two evenings, Angelique suggested to Scott that they might go with him this evening to give him a helping hand.

"Sure, honey. He'd probably welcome two more hands to get his place in order. I think I've got it figured what our Gabe's got in mind. Once he gets that place looking just like he wants it, then he's going to ask that pretty Chantel to marry him," Scott told his wife as if he were revealing a hidden secret.

Angelique smiled. "I would say that you are exactly right, dear."

But Gabe did not come directly home on Wednesday afternoon. He wanted some daylight hours to take a careful survey of the grounds and Rosa Laveau's flower garden. For more than an hour he ridded the garden of weeds which the elderly lady had not been able to pull. He trimmed back the shrubs, which were sorely in need of pruning.

So Gabe was leaving his cottage at twilight to go back up the bayou to his father's house. He knew he was running later than usual but knew they'd understand.

His mother had kept his dinner warm for

him, and he ate heartily.

"Your dad and I will go to the cottage with you tomorrow night if you'd like some help," Angelique suggested as she kept him company at the table.

"I got the yard in order tonight, and I've finished stripping the house of what I didn't want," he told her proudly. "Now I need to buy some furnishings. Then I'll invite Chantel out to the bayou when I take the fish order in on Friday. Maybe the four of us could go to my cottage on Sunday afternoon while Chantel is out here," he said decisively.

"That would be wonderful, Gabe," Angelique approved. "Chantel could have dinner with us before you take her back to the city."

So Gabe as well as his parents anticipated the nice Sunday afternoon they would have on the weekend. But his plans were shattered when Gabe arrived at *La Maison*. Raul went on and on about the madness of the week in preparation for the wedding Sunday evening. When Gabe left the kitchen, he didn't go out to the back garden. Instead, he mounted the stairs to Lily's rooms.

Gabe had a few moments of conversation with Lily before Chantel stepped into her mother's parlor. Seeing Gabe was a delightful surprise, for she'd forgotten that this was his delivery day. She'd been so busy she hadn't had time to think about Gabe.

There was a perky smile on her pretty face as she remarked, "Well, I guess you must know by now there's to be another wedding this weekend."

She looked refreshingly lovely in her simple muslin frock, her hair glowing from the brushing she'd given it after her bath. When she sat down by Gabe, he smelled the sweet fragrance she'd dabbed behind her ears and throat.

"I just heard and I couldn't be happier," he smiled at her. But he also knew that this was not the right time to speak to Chantel about the little cottage he was so excited about and had worked so laboriously on this week. That was going to have to wait. He reconciled himself to the knowledge that he was not going to be taking Chantel to the bayou this Sunday.

"I confess that Delphine's wedding spurred us on," Lily admitted.

"That will please Delphine, and I don't have to tell you that you have my best wishes. I know I speak for my parents as well," he said as he rose up to depart.

Chantel walked with him downstairs and out through the back gardens toward his buggy. Gabe was very disappointed that the exciting news he was so eager to tell Chantel was going to have to wait another long week.

The only soothing balm that late Friday afternoon was the one sweet kiss Chantel gave him before he leaped into the buggy. "See you next Friday, Chantel. I've got a big surprise for you," he called to her as he put the buggy into motion.

She yelled after him. "Gabe O'Roarke, you know what a curious creature I am! Now I'll be fretting all week wondering what your surprise is going to be." She shook her finger at him, admonishing him for taunting her so. Gabe's deep laughter echoed in the air as he drove away, leaving her standing in the middle of the dirt road.

It dawned on her as she returned to the house that she'd not asked him about Delphine or his family. Delphine had been married almost a week now, and in two more days her mother would become Andre's wife.

She seemed to be the only one not marching to the altar this golden autumn.

It was not Lily's usual lively Friday evening. She and Chantel shared a quiet dinner together and both of them felt weary and retired early. Little Mimi was glad for she too was exhausted from the day's activities and followed her mistress' example.

Saturday was a bittersweet day for Lily

even though she was anxiously anticipating the new life and world she was about to enter as Andre's wife.

It was her last day and night at *La Maison*. It was consoling to her to be taking some of her "little family"—Mimi, Jessamine, and Jonah—with her to Andre's home. But this place was a part of her and had been for many years. Tonight when she descended the stairs she would be consumed by a certain sadness.

Being the level-headed, practical lady that she was, she anticipated a period of adjustment, but her dear Andre was such an understanding man that she knew he'd be patient with her.

One thing which Lily had been concerned about was the housekeeper who'd been with Andre so long. She wondered if the two of them would get along, for Lily would have to be the mistress if this were going to be her home. She'd settle for nothing less.

Andre, able as always to read her thoughts, confirmed that he expected her to take full charge of their home. "It's your home, too, Lily. Anything you wish to change to make it to your liking, go ahead and do."

"Be prepared for some special touches of Lily Lemogne," she teased him.

"Lily Lemogne Deverone," he corrected.

* * *

Delphine shared Lily's feeling about her new home reflecting her personality. The first week of their marriage, while Terry was away on the fishing boat, Delphine began to change the dull, colorless kitchen into a bright, cheery room.

She put a coat of paint on the little oak table and four chairs. One day she and Mary Jane went into the city with Terry and her father and roamed the stores and shops. She treated Mary Jane to lunch in a tearoom and bought enough yellow chintz to make new curtains for her kitchen and cushion pads for each of the chairs. She would have liked to have paid a visit to Chantel but she felt she should devote this day to Mary Jane.

Mary Jane liked Delphine, but Delphine realistically accepted that there was some resentment within her as well, for Delphine was, in a sense, an intruder in their cottage. There were times during the last week that Mary Jane had gotten too bossy and Delphine had had to sweetly but firmly let Mary Jane know that she, Delphine, was now the mistress of the cottage. As her mother was always saying, "You nip something in the bud before it gets started, or it just grows."

It was always when Terry was away that Mary Jane exerted herself, never when he was home. Delphine was aware of the girl's ploy and didn't hesitate to tell Terry about the incidents and how she handled them. "Let me take care of it, Terry," she said. "That way she won't resent me for telling you. I think she'll accept me; it's just going to take a little while."

On their shopping expedition, Delphine spent some of the wedding money Andre had given them to let Mary Jane purchase a store-bought dress, for she'd never had one. Mary Jane was thrilled, and Delphine dared to hope that she'd sown a seed of friendship. She was all the more encouraged because Mary Jane's surly moods lifted for a day or two and she chattered nonstop about the sights of the city.

By the end of the week when Terry left the *Bayou Queen* to go up to the cottage, Delphine had finished hanging her new yellow ruffled curtains in the kitchen and the yellow cushions were already placed on the chairs.

She stood back, feeling pleased with her handiwork, and when Terry ambled in, he gasped with astonishment. "It's so darn pretty I don't have the words to tell you," he lauded her.

She smiled and flung her arms around his neck. Her eyes twinkled brightly as she grinned at him. "I've only just started. Our

388

cottage is going to be the prettiest place on this bayou."

Terry lifted her up in his arms until her feet no longer touched the floor, and he whirled her around. "You just do whatever makes you happy, honey, 'cause you sure are making me happier than I've ever been in my life."

Delphine swore that it was the most pleasant evening meal they'd had in Terry's kitchen, and she believed it was primarily due to the cheery atmosphere she'd created.

The three of them were just finishing up the fried fish which Terry had brought home from his catch when Gabe came through the front door. "I had to get away from the folks for awhile," he told them, sharing his dejection that Chantel would not be spending Sunday on the bayou.

When he finally did tell his parents about Lily's wedding, they were pleased. "How wonderful," Angelique remarked. "Chantel will finally have herself a home like she's always wanted." But the minute she said it, she noticed the strange fleeting look that crossed Gabe's face. She wished she'd not spoken so quickly, for she realized that he had surely been thinking that she was to share his place once they were married.

His mother's words pricked him, for it was

389

his little cottage he desired for Chantel to want for her home, not Andre's grand estate.

Now that Chantel was going to be living in Andre's palatial mansion, Gabe wondered if she would want to marry him and live in the bayou. Perhaps Andre, who'd traveled to Europe, would take Chantel and Lily to exotic, faraway places. With Lily's marriage to Andre Deverone, Chantel would no longer need the O'Roarkes or their bayou for her haven, for she would no longer be living at *La Maison*.

But Delphine and Angelique both believed that Chantel truly loved Gabe and that Lily's marriage would not change a thing.

Delphine had never seen her older brother when she'd sensed that he was scared or unsure of himself, but tonight she felt his insecurity. Bayou girls fawned over him, but Chantel Lemogne challenged him. The handsome Gabe O'Roarke had surely lost his heart.

Like Delphine, Angelique saw that Gabe was troubled. But Scott had a simple answer for her. His arms held her close to him as he told her, "He'll just have to count on Chantel's love for him as I did with you." Angelique knew he was absolutely right.

390

Forty-three

Chantel would never forget her mother's wedding as long as she lived for it was performed with such simple elegance. Now she knew why Andre had been so insistent when he'd questioned her about the color of their gowns. He'd wanted to buy them jewelry to match.

She had never seen anything as exquisite as the canary diamond earrings he'd bought for her mother, and she loved the necklace and earrings he'd chosen for her with the aquamarine gems and small diamonds.

All she could think was that her mother was to have a paragon as her husband, and she could not have been happier.

When the ceremony was over, the four of them had remained in the parlor to have a glass of champagne before they went into the candlelit dining room to feast upon a delectable dinner.

But when it was time for Jacqueline and

Chantel to leave the newlyweds, the light shower of rain outside had become a torrent. Andre would not hear of their starting out in the downpour so they stayed for another glass of champagne. The rain kept falling, but Andre's supply of champagne was limitless and the impromptu party in the parlor grew more and more convivial. They tittered and guffawed at Jacqueline's risque stories of her youth in Paris. The four of them enjoyed themselves as much as if forty guests had mingled and joked in the parlor.

The thunderstorms continued long past midnight, and Andre insisted they spend the night.

When Chantel and Jacqueline stole away the next morning, they left a note. As they boarded Andre's carriage, Jacqueline giggled like a teenager. "I don't think they'd wish to be disturbed."

Chantel was in awe of her dramatic animation. Jacqueline always seemed so happy. "I'm so thrilled by this marriage," she confided to Chantel. "I utterly adore your mother." Chantel was convinced that Nannette was solely her father's daughter, for she was nothing like Jacqueline Basherone.

As the carriage rolled along the dirt road toward the country estate, Jacqueline had an idea.

"What is it, Madame Basherone?" Chantel asked, her curiosity piqued. This vivacious lady had a great sense of humor and really knew how to live.

"Well, we've got Nannette, your mother, and Andre married, *oui?* I think you and I should take off and have ourselves a Paris holiday. I could show you a world like none you've ever known — one you'd never forget. Everyone should go to Paris at least once."

"You make it sound exciting," Chantel told her.

"It would be exciting, *ma petite*. Think about it. Right now, you've got a new home to get settled in, but later we'll speak again. Winter is not when I'd want to go to Paris; spring is the perfect time."

Chantel found Jacqueline wonderful company and the rest of the day went by. Tuesday morning they went for a ride and had their lunch on the veranda.

She didn't get to see Nannette before she had to return to New Orleans for Nannette had accompanied her husband Paul up to Baton Rouge.

It was late afternoon when Chantel arrived back at Andre's house. Andre had returned to work that morning. As capable as the young Cecil Bertrand was in the office, upcoming lawsuits demanded Andre's attention.

Lily's sleeping habits had not yet changed, and it was past noon when she woke up. Andre had told her she could rely on his man Todd to take her anywhere she wished to go. He had driven to the office himself in his gig.

About three that afternoon after she was dressed and had had her light lunch, she summoned Todd to take her to *La Maison* so she could tie up all the loose ends and get Jessamine and Jonah situated in their new quarters. She also planned a careful survey of her suite to determine what else she would move to her new home.

So neither Lily nor Andre were there when Chantel arrived home. The only familiar face was Mimi's, and the little maid seemed overwhelmed.

"Ah, mademoiselle this is a very big house," Mimi breathed. "I think I shall be getting lost for a while. I turned the wrong way twice just going down to get your mother's brunch tray."

"I'm sure the same thing will be happening to me, too. But a week from now we'll know all the corners and hallways."

"Of course we will, Mademoiselle Chantel," Mimi agreed with a sudden display of confidence. "It is beautiful here, and all the servants I've met have been very friendly and nice."

Chantel suspected that Andre had issued precise orders that all courtesies were to be extended to his new wife, her daughter, and her personal maid.

Like Lily, Chantel wondered how Andre's housekeeper Milly was going to take it when her mother started making changes. Certainly she was so accustomed to running the household that she had come to feel as if it were her own after so many years. Chantel also wanted to know what position Lily was going to assign Jessamine.

When she went downstairs about six-thirty she found a relaxed Andre sipping a glass of wine. He gave her a warm greeting, "I was told you had returned," he said. "Now you can keep me company until your mother arrives." Chantel accepted the glass of wine he poured for her.

"She had some final business to discuss with Adrienne," he remarked, very much at ease. "So Lily will get here when she finishes everything she set out to do. You see, I know your mother very well, Chantel. She could never conform to convention, but that was what made her so intriguing to me. She is a rare gem!"

The clock on the Italian marble mantel was chiming seven when Lily came breathlessly into the parlor and rushed into Andre's arms, planting a kiss on his lips. Chantel observed their loving embrace, noting that Andre was completely content now that she was in his arms. If he had been a little impatient, that was swept away now by her kiss.

When they broke their embrace, Lily gave Chantel an affectionate hug. "When shall I tell Milly to have dinner on the table?" Andre asked.

"I'll be ready in a half-hour, Andre," she declared as she dashed upstairs.

But this evening set the routine Milly would have to adjust to. Dinner would no longer be served promptly at seven every evening. The changes were subtle, but already beginning. For instance, Monsieur Andre had never requested trays sent to his room except on the rare occasions when he was ill.

Monsieur Deverone always had a light morning meal before he went to his office. This routine continued, but everything else was subject to change. The new Madame Deverone had to have a brunch tray; she was obviously not the kind of wife that got up early to join her husband at breakfast.

That afternoon Milly looked up from the pots on her stove to find the fair-haired daughter of Madame Deverone intruding upon her kitchen. She was prepared to dislike her, but courteously told her to help herself to one of the apple fritters she'd just placed on a platter on her worktable, when Chantel confessed that she'd like something to nibble on.

Chantel took a couple of bites of the fritter and sighed with pleased delight, "That's the best apple fritter I've *ever* eaten," she declared.

Do you think so, miss?" Milly turned to face her and found it impossible to dislike Chantel.

"I know so, Milly," Chantel avowed. "Could—could I have just one more to take with me?"

"Why of course, you can." Milly was so flattered that Chantel could have had the entire platter. That brief exchange made Milly much more understanding a few hours later when Andre arrived home with Cecil Bertrand and informed her that dinner was going to have to be delayed until eight.

The men were sequestered in the study for almost two hours, and then Andre insisted that his assistant stay for dinner. Cecil was a young bachelor, and Andre suspected he might enjoy one of Milly's good home-cooked meals.

Cecil was honored by the invitation and accepted without hesitation. He held Andre in high esteem and tried to absorb everything he could in his close association with the senior barrister.

When they emerged from Andre's study, Andre gave him a comradely pat on the shoulder, declaring they deserved a glass of wine before dinner. He guided Cecil across the hall.

Cecil was unprepared to come upon the most beautiful girl Cecil had ever seen, in Monsieur Deverone's parlor. She sat in the chair in a coral gown, her thick golden hair flowing around her shoulders. He found her smile ethereal. Cecil was so affected by her radiant beauty that he could hardly breathe.

Andre introduced them and Cecil managed to hold onto his dignity and keep his voice from cracking.

After Andre had served the young man and himself a glass of wine, Chantel told him, "Mother will be joining us shortly, Andre. She got in just a few minutes ago."

"Ah, wonderful! If you two will excuse me, I shall tell Milly that we will be ready to dine shortly," Andre said as he left them alone in the parlor.

Chantel had already concluded that Cecil Bertrand was a serious young man. He was about Gabe's age but certainly nothing like him. There was nothing carefree about Cecil.

She sensed that Cecil was ill-at-ease with her and she broke the silence in an attempt to make him more comfortable. "You and Andre have put in a very long day, Cecil," she observed. "It must be challenging to be a lawyer."

"Working with Andre Deverone is a daily challenge to me. I admire him so much," he replied.

"Well, Andre just became my stepfather, but I share your feelings for different reasons. I admire him tremendously," Chantel informed him honestly. Cecil found her a pleasant change from so many of the young ladies he'd met. All they could do was twitter and giggle, which made him uncomfortable.

He could tell that Chantel was much younger than he was. But as they talked, Cecil realized that she was not only breathtakingly beautiful, but she had grace and charm as well.

It amazed Cecil that he found himself becoming relaxed in Chantel's presence. Andre swelled with pride when he returned to the parlor and overheard the young couple speaking about him in such admiring terms. His beautiful Lily joined them shortly, and by the time Cecil Bertrand left the two-story mansion he was a young man in a trance, believing he had dined with two of the most beautiful ladies in New Orleans. His head was actually whirling by the time he returned to his one-bedroom apartment on the other side of the city.

After spending four hours at Andre Deverone's luxurious home, his meager place seemed dull. But he saw it as an incentive. One day he wanted to have exactly what Andre Deverone had, and he was willing to work his guts out to attain it. He wanted a fine home and a beautiful wife.

That night before he went to bed he set himself a goal. He was still young — not yet thirty — and Cecil was sure that he could attain his dreams.

Forty-four

Whatever disappointment Gabe had felt about Chantel's not coming to the bayou over the weekend, he didn't let that stop him from putting in extra time at his cottage.

Instead of showing off his new house to Chantel as he'd anticipated, he invited his sister and Terry to come down the bayou Sunday afternoon.

Not having seen the grounds of the cottage before Gabe weeded out the flowerbeds and cleared the flagstone pathway of grass, they couldn't appreciate the many hours he'd put in getting the yard in perfect shape.

He'd given the shed in the backyard a fresh coat of paint as well as all the shutters.

Inside, Delphine was immediately alerted to the amount of cleaning her brother had done, for the smells of beeswax told her he'd recently mopped and polished.

"Very nice, Gabe," Delphine commented as she surveyed the fruit of his labor of love.

401

With a woman's touch it would make a cozy, comfortable home. She decided to make him some pillows for his sofa. And, she thought, a couple of vases filled with the colorful flowers that bloomed so profusely in the garden would add wonders to the front room.

When they had seen all the rooms of the house, Gabe took them out to the backyard. By the back steps, Delphine spied what had to be Mrs. Laveau's herb garden. The aromas that came to her nose were a sheer delight. She turned to Terry. "Come next springtime," she vowed, "I'm going to have myself an herb garden like this one."

Hearing her, Gabe dashed to the porch to get one of the many wicker baskets Rosa Laveau had left behind.

"Here, little sister, you just pick yourself some of my fresh herbs to take home with you. I guess I ought to cut Momma some. I wouldn't have even thought about it if it weren't for you," he grinned.

"Momma would love that," Delphine agreed. "If you get me another basket, I'll gather her some while I'm getting mine."

"You've got yourself a real nice place here, Gabe," Terry praised.

"It's an enchanting cottage, Gabe," enthused Delphine. "I love that little picket fence around the front yard and the lattice above the gate.

Did you know you've got wild jasmine twining around that trellis, Gabe?"

"Jasmine—of course!" cried Gabe. "That's what's responsible for that wonderful sweet smell? Delphine, you have to come back again and point things out to me that I've missed in my hurry to get everything ready," Gabe told her.

Delphine gave her brother an affectionate kiss on the cheek. "We'll be back. Now, what color are you going to have in that main bedroom? I might just get busy sewing up something for you."

"It's going to be green," he told her without any hesitation.

Gabe walked them down to the small wharf to their canoe. "I just spotted another repair job," he said. "I've got a cracked plank here."

"You're going to find there's always something to be done when you own a place," Terry told him as he crawled into the canoe. "You might as well expect it."

Gabe worked several more hours before he locked up and returned to his folks' place. But he'd set the basket of herbs Delphine had cut for Angelique by the front door so he'd be sure not to forget them.

When he arrived home with the basket filled with the pungent green plants, his mother was overjoyed. "You have your own herb garden?"

He laughed. "I didn't know it until Delphine pointed it out to me."

"Well, I've got to get down to see this cottage of yours now that you've done so much work," she told him, taking her basket of fresh-plucked herbs into the kitchen.

Gabe, weary from the long day he'd put in, was ready to seek the comfort of his bed. But just before he went to sleep he thought that by now Lily Lemogne was the wife of Andre Deverone. Come next Friday, after he'd made his usual delivery to *La Maison*, he would head for Andre's house to invite Chantel to the bayou.

The *Bayou Queen* and *Louisiana Lady* worked from sunrise to sundown all that week, for the fish were abundant and they were making tremendous catches each day. So Scott, Terry and Gabe were in the highest of spirits by the time Friday rolled around.

Another streak of luck had come Gabe's way thanks to Terry. Terry learned that some neighbors upstream were leaving the bayou. "I don't think the wife ever got to like the bayou," he mentioned to Gabe. "They're putting their place up for sale and selling all their furniture. She's just inherited a house in New Orleans."

Gabe wasted no time buying a high-poster

cherrywood bed and dressing table. With Terry's help, he loaded it onto the *Louisiana Lady* to take it down the bayou to the cottage.

Things were going well for the O'Roarke family. They had already made up the time the boats had stood idle for Delphine and Terry's wedding.

Gabe had always been frugal with his money, and buying the cottage and land made a big dent in his savings. But he promised himself that he'd build that back up in the next several months. The cottage and land was important to him.

That night he entertained sentimental, romantic dreams about himself and Chantel. Spring was the time for weddings, he told himself, but he wasn't sure he could wait out the winter to marry Chantel.

Six or seven months was an eternity.

Besides, he reasoned, he didn't have to wait that long now, for he had a home to take her to when she became his bride. And with the furnishings in place, there was nothing to delay him any longer in asking her to be his wife.

He knew just when he was going to do it. He wanted that special moment to happen when he showed her his cottage. Assured and optimistic, he was certain that nothing was going to keep him from bringing her out here this Sunday afternoon.

The next morning, Gabe woke at dawn, ready to start out his day. He and his father pulled away from the wharf at the same time, one boat following the other. Gabe was slightly ahead of the *Bayou Queen,* for Scott had to stop at Terry's wharf for him to get aboard.

They worked throughout the morning hours and then pulled in to the marketplace in New Orleans.

It was a glorious autumn day and so mild and warm that both Terry and Gabe shed their shirts, their firm bronzed bodies gleaming in the sun.

For the next three hours they sold their fish to the eager customers, and Gabe chose his finest to take to *La Maison*. He also picked some extras to take to Andre's.

By four-thirty he had nothing left in his bins to sell, the fish replaced by a hefty sum in the box where he tossed the money he took in from sales.

He took time to go to his cabin to pour some water in the basin and wash his face and neck and put on a clean shirt. In hurried strokes, he ran his hairbrush through his thick, dark hair.

With the two wrapped bundles in his arms, he left the *Louisiana Lady* to board the buggy to go to *La Maison* as he always did on late Friday afternoons.

"How's it going Raul?" he asked the cook as he laid the bundle of fish on the worktable.

"Very well, Gabe. I guess you could say it is going pretty well considering Madame Lily isn't here. But there's no denying that something is missing with her not around. Lily Lemogne is—or I should say was—the magic that made *La Maison* work," Raul told him.

When Gabe prepared to go, it suddenly dawned on him that he didn't know where Andre lived or how to get there. So Raul told him the streets to take.

"The property is surrounded by a stone wall and sets back away from the street." A teasing twinkle came to Raul's eyes as he asked Gabe, "Going to call on Mademoiselle Chantel?"

Gabe grinned but didn't answer him as he went out the back door. "See you next Friday, Raul."

He made a mad dash to his buggy to get over to Andre's house and see the beautiful Chantel. It seemed forever since they had truly spent any time together. He was anxious to see how she liked her new home now that she'd been living there almost a week.

When he came to the estate that he was sure had to be the Deverone property, he was reminded of another fine mansion just as grand and of the late afternoon when he'd ap-

407

proached the stone-walled grounds of Antoine Savanti.

But certainly different emotions stirred within him as he went under the impressive archway and up the long winding drive edged by boxwoods. A young black lad took charge of Gabe's buggy when, at the front entrance, he leaped down with the bundle of fish in his arms.

"I wish to see Mademoiselle Chantel," he told the young girl who answered his bold knock on the carved oak door. She must have smelled the odor of the fish, for he noticed her staring at the bundle in his arms as she invited him to have a seat.

Lily, told that a young man was asking for Chantel, directed the girl to show Gabe out to the terrace where Chantel was sitting with Andre and Cecil. Lily herself had just left them, coming inside to find her gold cigarette case. The four of them had been enjoying a glass of minted tea. Andre had brought Cecil with him to pick up some documents that required his attention over the weekend.

But when Gabe was ushered outside, he felt uncomfortable. Chantel looked very much at home in this elegant setting, head bent in conversation with Lily, Andre, and a handsomely attired young man.

It should have eased any apprehension Gabe

might have harbored when Chantel leaped up from the chair to rush up to him. "Oh, Gabe, it's so good to see you."

Had they been alone, he might have thrown aside the fish he was holding and taken her in his arms. But he could hardly do what he yearned to do with an audience so he told her, "Good to see you, too, Chantel." He sounded very cool and casual even to his own ears.

Gabe didn't feel like he fit into this setting when he compared how he looked with the other young man who seemed scrutinize him.

Lily sensed the awkwardness of the situation which she felt Chantel did not recognize. "Gabe, is that some of your fabulous fish that you've brought?" she asked and rose from her chair to relieve him of his bundle.

"Yes, ma'am. I took the usual order to *La Maison*," he replied, realizing belatedly that he should not have mentioned *La Maison* since he didn't know who their guest was. He was feeling like the worst kind of idiot.

By now, Chantel had begun to question Gabe's stiffness and cool manner. It never dawned on her for a minute that her happy-go-lucky Gabe O'Roarke could feel insecure since she herself had made no comparisons between Gabe in his old workclothes and Cecil Bertrand dressed for business.

Andre made the introductions and called for

a glass of mint tea for Gabe. One sip and Gabe knew this was not a refreshment he would relish drinking often. The ever-genial host, Andre sought news of the bayou folk he'd enjoyed so much.

Although to Gabe Cecil appeared dignified and unruffled, Cecil found the fisherman's presence disquieting. Gabe's firm, muscled body and handsome bronzed face made the young lawyer look like a pale weakling in comparison. Gathering up his papers, Cecil bade his farewells.

Lily and Andre escorted Cecil to the front door. Finding himself at last alone with Chantel, he wasted no time leaning over to plant a kiss on her lips. He was pleased about her eager, warm response. Greedily, he sought her lips for a second kiss before Andre and Lily returned to the terrace. But they drew back at the doorway, observing the romantic scene. "I don't think our company will be missed, *chèrie,*" Andre whispered.

Lily hugged him. "I think maybe there could be another wedding very soon."

Gabe welcomed the privacy. When his lips finally released hers, he sighed, "Oh, Chantel, the week is long for me when I don't see you."

"I miss you too. I got used to having you

come in every night when I stayed with you on the bayou," she admitted.

"Come back to the bayou with me," he pleaded. "Come on Sunday. I've a wonderful surprise to show you. Please let me come get you this Sunday."

"Of course, I will come," she agreed quickly. "But do I have to wait till Sunday for you to tell me about your surprise?"

A mischievous twinkle filled his blue eyes. "I'm afraid that that's the way it is. It's something I have to show you, not something I can tell you about. You've just got to see it."

"Oh, Gabe!" she snapped. "I think you like to drive me to distraction sometimes! Your sister warned me about you."

Gabe laughed for she excited him when her emerald-green eyes were flashing with either impatience or ecstasy. He's seen her in the heights of anxiety and joy.

He knew how passionate she could be. That was one of the reasons he was also convinced that she was the only woman in the world for him. She was the only woman he wanted to share his cottage with. No one else would do.

Forty-five

Lily noticed her daughter's radiant face at dinner that evening and she knew that Gabe's visit had to be the reason for her exuberance.

Andre shared Lily's speculation. Living under the same roof with these two ladies for the last week, Andre had come to the conclusion that whether they realized it or not they were very much alike. Seeing Chantel this afternoon so willingly surrendering to Gabe's kiss, he knew that she was as passionate as her mother. He well knew they both could be volatile, but he was used to his younger sister Jacqueline, who had the same temperament.

Andre and Lily understood Chantel's glow when she announced that she was going to the bayou with Gabe on Sunday.

"Ah, that bayou! I loved it out there," Andre declared.

Chantel was utterly astonished when Andre told her, "You tell Gabe and the O'Roarke family if they ever hear of any of those little cottages

412

for sale that I would be interested in buying one of them."

"Are you serious, Andre?" she gasped.

"Very serious, *ma petite*. Your mother and I have already talked about it. It would be a marvelous place to have a little retreat, and we both loved the people and atmosphere at Delphine's wedding."

"I will tell them when I'm out there Sunday," she promised solemnly, feeling a rush of pleasure at the thought of such a retreat.

A different Gabe returned to the bayou late Friday afternoon, and it was apparent to Angelique why her son was so happy when he announced that Chantel was going to be coming out to spend the day on Sunday.

Her Gabe was hopelessly in love with Chantel Lemogne. She could not deny that she was more than pleased with the young lady he wanted for his wife. She adored Chantel.

The next morning she sent Gabe out to get her the bucket of crawfish she would need to fix her *étouffée* that she knew Chantel liked so much.

As Gabe was leaving she called out to him, "Stop by your sister's and invite them to come for Sunday dinner, too. I know she'll be happy to see Chantel while she's out here."

413

Gabe gave her a nod of his head and went out the door. It was obvious that his mother was delighted about Chantel's visit on Sunday. There was no doubt in his mind that both of his parents would be very pleased to hear that she was the lady he wished to marry. They loved Chantel already!

Gabe got the crawfish and he stopped by Delphine's with the dinner invitation.

He didn't know it, but his younger sister was depressed and worrying that her sins might be catching up with her. She had hoped by now to be expecting a baby, but she wasn't.

Now that she was back in the bayou living the life she should never have left, she was beginning to wonder if she were barren. She had been reliving her past from the time she had run away with her riverboat swain through the months at the Paradise Club. For almost a year, she had been degraded by Antoine Savanti, but she'd never become pregnant.

Terry was a virile man with a healthy sexual appetite, but she was still not expecting. She needed a woman to talk to and decided that Lily Lemogne was the only person that would understand her feelings and apprehensions.

Like the rest of her family, Delphine eagerly anticipated Chantel's visit, but Terry could not share their enthusiasm. His attention was focused instead on his sister, who was proving to be a problem. She was annoying and obnoxious, flaring up at Delphine's changes in the household.

With the exception of Mary Jane's room, the entire cottage had a different look about it. Delphine's labor had made it a cheery, inviting place, and he looked forward to coming home at night. Delphine had added a bright and colorful touch to all the rooms except Mary Jane's. She had not dared to intrude there.

It was nice to Terry to come in after his long day out on the *Bayou Queen* to a good meal waiting for him and a pretty wife to warm his bed. All they needed now was a baby to make their life complete.

It never occurred to Terry that Delphine might never have his son or daughter. But Delphine could think of nothing else.

It was a golden autumn day. The temperature was mild and the breeze was calm as Gabe left the wharf to go up the bayou into New Orleans to pick up Chantel. He already arranged for a buggy.

Gabe had put on his fawn-colored pants and his best white-linen shirt. He'd brushed his thick black hair much longer than he usually did, but he could still not conquer that one unruly wave that wanted to fall over the left side of his forehead.

When he arrived at Andre's home, he got to have a brief talk with him while he waited for Chantel. Andre took the opportunity to ask Gabe to be on the lookout for property for him.

"You're interested in buying in the bayou?" Gabe asked, raising his eyebrow. When Andre assured him that he was, Gabe told him of the Beauchamp cottage, where he had found his four-poster, and promised to arrange an appointment for Andre.

At that minute Chantel entered the room, breathtakingly lovely in her white gown splattered with a yellow buttercup design. Her golden hair flowed loose and free over her shoulders, swaying to and fro with each step she took toward him. To Gabe, she was even prettier than the last time he'd seen her.

"I'm ready, Gabe," she announced.

"One would think that she's anxious to be on her way to the bayou," Andre teased.

"What this pretty lady wants is my command, so we'll be leaving now," Gabe quipped, taking Chantel's arm.

Andre watched the attractive young couple leave the house. The wise, experienced Andre was thinking to himself that if these two weren't lovers already then they would be very soon. The look in their eyes had convinced him.

Gabe had his lady love in the buggy, and they were rolling down the road at a fast pace to go to the wharf to board the *Louisiana Lady*. His arm reached around her, urging her closer to him on the buggy seat. "You're too far away from me," he complained.

She smiled complacently, enjoying the heat of his firm, muscled body.

As they walked toward the fishing boat, his hand held hers, and Gabe thought to himself that Chantel was like the golden autumn, which he considered the most beautiful season of the year. Helping her onto the deck of his boat, he declared, "Chantel, it's a sin for a woman to be as beautiful as you are. You can drive a man crazy."

Chantel laughed. "Oh Gabe, you and your Irish blarney!" She had decided that she was going to take a cue from her two good friends, Delphine and Nannette. Neither Paul nor Terry had had love with their brides before they were married. Chantel could not undo what had already been done, for she had surrendered to Gabe more than once. But she had sworn last night that she would not submit to his sweet persuasive charm today when she accompanied him to the bayou.

Oh, she had no doubt that she would be tested to the limit, but then she would be testing Gabe as well. She knew that the two of them would be alone on the trips to and from the bayou.

417

The minute they were aboard the *Louisiana Lady,* Gabe put the boat into motion and they began to plow through the waters. Chantel stood beside him, watching the sights in the bay. Seagulls were following the shrimp boats into the dock. The shrimpers could not afford to give themselves a day off like Gabe and his father did on Sundays.

Chantel had made this trip so many times now that she recognized the cove up ahead that Gabe would veer into. That would take them into the bayou stream.

Once in the bayou stream, the open sky disappeared for the banks were lined with tall trees. Their long branches stretched out to meet the branches of the trees on the other side of the stream, forming an arbor for the boat to pass beneath. Long garlands of Spanish moss cascaded down from the trees.

Chantel was familiar now with the different bends and turns in the streams, but the sights on the banks were constantly changing. The alligators sliding into the waters or crawling up on the bank still repelled her. She always flinched when she happened to spot one of them, fearful at the prospect of being in the water at their mercy. She marveled at how easily Angelique and Delphine got into a canoe and traversed the streams of the bayou.

She could never be so fearless.

As they traveled down the stream Gabe told her how much Delphine was looking forward to seeing her. "She and Terry will be over to Momma's for dinner tonight. My mother's making your favorite, her crawfish *étouffée*."

"She didn't have to go to all that trouble," Chantel protested, "but I've got to confess I loved it."

He filled her in on the happenings in the bayou. With a brother's pride, he described the transformation Delphine had made in Terry's cottage.

"I'm so happy Delphine found the contentment back here in her bayou," Chantel said, a wistfulness underlying her words.

"Terry worships her, but then he always has," Gabe commented, noticing that they were now passing by the Monroe cottage.

Soon they would make that last turn in the stream that would bring the O'Roarkes' wharf into view. Gabe was already wondering how she was going to react when he sailed past the dock. Slowly the *Louisiana Lady* moved on through the waters.

"What's the matter? You went past the house." Her green eyes questioned him, a small frown pursed her lips.

"I know that, Chantel."

"What are you up to, Gabe O'Roarke?" She was confused and almost in a temper. Gabe found her disorientation most appealing.

"To another bayou cottage I want you to see," he answered without giving her details.

She was so befuddled that she said nothing more. She wasn't interested in going to any other cottage but the O'Roarkes' and fell into a deep silence as they traveled the short distance from the O'Roarke wharf to Gabe's. It was difficult for Gabe to hide his amusement for he knew he had put her into a quandary.

When they arrived at his dock and he helped her from the *Louisiana Lady,* her eyes flashed with irritation. "I swear you are puzzling me today. I wish you'd tell me what this is all about."

He led her up the path where wild ferns grew profusely among the boulders and rocks. He led her up the two front steps and to the front door. He took out the key, and she gasped, "Gabe O'Roarke, what on earth are you doing?"

Gabe unlocked the door and gently urged her over the threshold. He could not restrain his laughter any longer. "I'm showing you my cottage, love. It is my own front door I'm unlocking."

Wide-eyed, she stared up at him for a few seconds before she, too, began to laugh. "Oh, Gabe, this was the surprise you told me about."

"Yes," he acknowledged and guided her into the home he hoped they would share.

Forty-six

As Chantel roamed from room to room, Gabe found to his surprise that he was apprehensive and nervous. Now he was the one in a quandary.

Chantel was rather hoping to keep him off balance by remaining silent. She could feel his tension as she examined the front room, bedrooms, and kitchen. She inspected the pantry and each individual cupboard.

Gabe trailed behind her as she made her tour of the house. Of all the rooms in the cottage. Chantel found the kitchen the most inviting with its many windows lined with plants.

Her silence was killing him. He was going to be shattered if she didn't like it. His impatient nature could not be restrained any longer as he demanded. "Well, do you like it or not?"

She was the one now with an amused look on her face as she whirled around to announce, "Oh, Gabe it's an enchanting little cottage!"

"So you do like it?" he stammered, a slow, pleased grin coming to his face.

"It's beautiful and I love it. I *am* surprised," she confessed.

"I thought it might startle you, and I've been so damned impatient to show it to you." He led her to the settee and urged her to sit down beside him for he had a more serious look on his face now. His blue eyes probed deep into hers as he told her, "I didn't buy this cottage just for myself. I bought it for us to share, with you as my wife. I fell in love with you the first afternoon I saw you at *La Maison,* Chantel Lemogne."

"Oh, Gabe," she sighed. That was all she had time to say, for Gabe's arms were around her and he was kissing her passionately. When she was finally released slightly, she gave a breathless gasp. She knew if she allowed him to keep kissing her that way all her great intentions of not surrendering to him would be forgotten.

"You asked me to marry you, Gabe. Don't you want to hear my answer? What if I should say no?" she teased him. After all, she'd waited far too long for him to ask her to be his wife.

"Then I'd just have to convince you to change your mind," he grinned, pulling her close to him again and silencing further remarks with another kiss.

But when his lips were almost ready to meet with hers, Chantel stiffened and leaned back from him. "Gabe, you should never take anyone or anything for granted."

He was startled. He couldn't believe that she wasn't going to say yes to his proposal. The conceited young Irishman was shaken enough that he released his hold on her so he could look into her eyes. Chantel detected a hurt look on his handsome face as he asked her, "Don't you want to be my wife, Chantel?"

"I want to be your wife, Gabe, but I just wanted you to give me a chance to tell you," she said coyly. His body sagged in relief. Turnabout was fair play. She had gone to sleep at nights wondering if Gabe were ever going to get around to asking her to marry him. In the last few months, she'd been to Nannette's wedding and Delphine's. Her own mother had married Andre, as she had still waited for Gabe to ask her to be his bride. She had been afraid that he only wanted to make love to her, not to marry her.

He interrupted her sober reflection. "Now, may I kiss my bride-to-be?" he inquired.

Her green eyes glinted as she replied, "You may." What she didn't tell him was that his kiss was not going to lead them to the bedroom as it had in the past. He could wait until they were married, just like Terry and Paul had waited for their brides.

His sensuous lips captured hers, and Chantel found it difficult to resist the churning desires that stirred within her. She found it hard to deny Gabe, for it meant also denying herself the pleasure she enjoyed when their bodies were close—as they were now—and his hands were caressing and touching her.

She felt a liquid fire flowing through her that was like a wildfire out of control. She knew that if she did not stop him right then and there, she'd never be able to.

"No, Gabe, no, not this time," she protested. "We're going to wait until our wedding night. That's the way I want it."

Gabe had always considered himself a strong-willed man, but he was certainly being tested this Sunday afternoon. He would never have forced himself on Chantel, for he loved her far too much. Nevertheless, he was a hot-blooded Irishman who found it almost impossible to draw himself away from her warm tempting body. Flippant, he replied, "Your wish is my command, my lady."

Chantel had no inkling that she had put him in a state of utter confusion and dented his cocky male ego. But she had accepted his proposal of marriage, and that was what really mattered to Gabe. If it meant that much to her

424

that they not make love again until their wedding night, then he would abide by her wishes.

He thought he understood why she felt as she did, and his wounded ego began to heal by the time they left his cottage and boarded the *Louisiana Lady* to go back down the bayou to the O'Roarkes. As they traveled down the stream, Gabe asked if she wanted to tell his family.

"I don't see why not. We can't set a date yet until I've had a chance to talk with my mother and Andre, but it will be soon," she promised.

That was enough to make Gabe happy, for he had wanted to be able to make the grand announcement this evening when the family was gathered there together.

They walked up the pathway holding hands. Angelique, glancing out the window, smiled approvingly. Chantel would make a beautiful bride for her son, she thought, and she and Scott could look forward to equally beautiful grandchildren to spoil and coddle.

Delphine, hearing their laughter from the front room, ran to greet them. The two girls embraced with excited shrieks of delight, and even Terry hugged her warmly. Chantel loved the way the O'Roarkes always made her feel welcome.

Once everything settled down, the topic of conversation was Gabe's cottage and Chantel's opinion of it.

"I think it is a beautiful cottage and so are the yards," Chantel told them. Gabe could have made his announcement then, but he did not wish to do so yet.

Angelique's crawfish *étouffée* was delicious as always, and for the special occasion that it was, Scott had cooled a bottle of his white wine in the creek that ran behind the cottage. It was as if they sensed that this was a very special evening.

He waited impatiently until dinner was over before making his announcement and throwing the group gathered around the table into a state of pandemonium. "When?" Delphine demanded. "When's the wedding going to be?"

Shaking her head, Chantel confessed, "I can't tell you that until my own family has heard the news."

It was a glorious evening, and Delphine's only regret was that she never had an opportunity to talk to Chantel in private. But she did get to ask the one question that was most important to her. How could she get in touch with Lily Lemogne Deverone?

She learned that the best place and time to catch Lily alone was at *La Maison* around three in the afternoon.

When Delphine and Terry left in their canoe to go to their cottage, Gabe and Chantel also left to go back to New Orleans. Chantel would never forget Angelique's departing remarks to her as she warmly embraced her. "I could not have picked the more perfect bride for my only son, *ma petite*," she told her. "I could not be happier. I shall think of you as my daughter and not my daughter-in-law."

Gabe was a man of his word so he curbed his amorous desires as they traveled up the stream into the bay and returned to the city. Both of them were heady from the excitement of the afternoon and evening. When he had seen her to her door, he kissed her chastely good night. "I'll see you next Friday," he told her, "and I'll be anxious to know when we can have our wedding. I'm afraid I'm an impatient man."

She gave him a tender kiss as she softly murmured in his ear, "Oh, Gabe, you won't have to wait that long, I promise you. I'm just as anxious as you."

That was enough to soothe him a little and he went back to the buggy in high spirits, for the beautiful Chantel Lemogne had promised to be his wife.

On his way back to the bayou, Gabe kept thinking about what Chantel had said on the way in. "I wish we could have a bayou wedding like Delphine's," she'd sighed, "I can't insult Mother and Andre. I'm sure they'll insist that I be married in New Orleans. And I couldn't hurt their feelings." She'd added wistfully, "Delphine's wedding was so gay. Everyone had such a good time."

"Don't you fret your pretty head about that," Gabe had chided. "After we're married we'll have ourselves a shindig any time the notion strikes us."

But neither of them knew what a decisive man of action Andre Deverone could be when he set his mind to something. Gabe's mere mention that there was a piece of property on the bayou for sale made house-hunting a priority for Andre on Monday morning.

At midday Andre hired a boat to take him out to the bayou, where he made Beauchamp an offer he could not possibly refuse. By evening, Andre had acquired the bayou retreat he wanted for him and Lily. Since Chantel had announced to them that she had accepted Gabe's proposal of marriage, Andre wanted her to have a bayou wedding like Delphine's.

He knew instinctively that this would be Chantel's preference. Gabe's people were bayou people. Andre wanted Chantel to have the perfect wedding, and he was determined to make it all happen. But he said nothing to either of them about his intentions.

Andre had learned a long time ago that if he had money he could buy anything. In the last three days, he had bought not only the bayou property he wanted for himself and Lily but the ideal setting for Chantel's wedding to Gabe.

Within the week a crew of men invaded the old Beauchamp property. The yard was manicured and a gazebo constructed at the side of the house closest to the flowerbeds. They even laid a temporary plank floor for dancing at the wedding. Fresh paint and French country furniture gave the cottage a quaint look and a complete transformation. Pleased with the results, Andre was eager to take Lily and Chantel to see his own enchanted cottage.

Andre was a perfectionist and he'd left no detail unattended once he was ready to take his wife to the bayou. Huge colorful pottery planted with greenery sat on either side of the steps. The front room of the cottage was enhanced by a tall palm plant, and the mantel of the stone fireplace displayed matching pots of Holland Ivy.

Andre wanted Lily to find their retreat inviting and warm the minute she stepped through the front door. She could add her own personal touches to the place as they came out for visits, but right now his desire was to have it ready for the wedding.

He assumed that Gabe's friends would feel far more relaxed coming to this cottage than

429

they would to his home in the city. And the Deverone retreat would be convenient later on, because Chantel and Gabe would be living in the bayou after they were married.

The O'Roarkes saw the miracle Andre had performed before Lily and Chantel. All week they'd heard about the work going on at the Beauchamp place, so they had boarded their canoe late Thursday afternoon to see for themselves. By chance they encountered Andre, who was inspecting the progress of his workmen.

He was delighted to welcome the O'Roarkes. Angelique had only to walk through the front door to be captivated by the atmosphere he'd created. She loved the colorful cheeriness, the ruffled floral curtains at the windows, and the floral covered sofa and overstuffed chairs on either side of the fireplace. The fabric matched the cushion on a white-wicker rocker.

"It's eye-catching, Andre," Angelique declared. "And cozy."

"Well, then I am truly pleased, Angelique. Come, let me show you the rest of the house," he proffered, eager to show off the converted cottage. "At heart I'm romantic and sentimental," he confessed. "I've tried to recreate a lovely little French country cottage I was in years ago. It was so inviting."

"I think you've succeeded." Angelique shook

430

her head in amazement. But she and Scott were to be treated to another entrancing sight as he took them out to the gazebo.

"Is it not the perfect spot for a wedding?" he asked with a wink.

Scott's blue eyes twinkled with pleased delight. He liked Andre Deverone. "You'll come to love our bayou with its peace and serenity," he prophesied.

"I already do, Scott," Andre said quietly.

Forty-seven

Never had Lily loved Andre more than she did right now. All week he had been like a young boy, excited and alive about the purchase of the cottage in the bayou.

His dark eyes were sparkling with excitement every evening when he finally arrived home from his office and his trips out to the bayou. What truly endeared him to her was his affection for her daughter.

Lily had quickly found that she was not missing *La Maison* as much as she'd anticipated, for Andre filled her days and nights. Never had she felt such complete happiness as she had since she'd married him. "I can't imagine why I didn't marry you months ago," she confessed.

"You should have listened to me, *chèrie,*" he teased her. "But at least, you finally came to your senses."

* * *

Chantel was thrilled by the undertaking. She could not have loved Andre more if he had truly been her father, and she wished that he could have been.

When Gabe came on Friday she was going to have a wedding date to give him, and she knew that he was going to be pleased. The fourteenth of October was only a week-and-a-day away.

Lily and Chantel left the house together on Friday. Jonah took Chantel to the dress shop to look for her wedding gown, and then he took Lily to *La Maison*. Lily knew that Adrienne was working as hard as she could, but profits had been going down since she'd left. Lily's charisma had been a part of the magic that had made the place so successful.

Lily had enough conceit not to deny that. But Adrienne had spunk and Lily had approved of her plan to hire two new girls. "I figured it would add a little spice and new life to the place, Lily. You're missed, you know?" Adrienne told her.

Lily was more than pleased to hear that the new girls had worked out. "It's been a better week," Adrienne sighed with relief.

"You'll make it," Lily said encouragingly. "You try one approach, and if that doesn't work, then you try something else. Believe me, I know. I'll never press you to make your payments as long as I know you're trying."

"I'm trying hard," Adrienne assured her. "One day I want the name Adrienne to mean as much as the name Lily Lemogne meant to this place.

"If you feel that way," Lily said with conviction, "then you'll make it happen."

She left the office where they had been sequestered for the last half-hour and roamed the familiar surroundings. She slipped into the kitchen for a chat with Raul, who was experimenting with a new dish to tantalize the patrons. He poured her a glass of her favorite white wine as she sampled on the delectable catfish. "It's delicious. I like it," Lily told him. In response to her praise, he included the entrée on the week's specialty menu.

So it was in the kitchen that Delphine found Madame Lily, taking her by surprise.

"Delphine, how nice to see you," Lily greeted her.

Delphine moved slowly to the table and accepted a glass of wine but politely refused the fish. "Would it be possible for me to speak to you privately, madame?" she asked tentatively.

Lily immediately led her to one of the secluded dining alcoves. When they were seated within the draped enclosure, Delphine spoke quickly. "I knew of no one to go to but you, madame. It was something I could not speak

434

about with my own mother, but I'm so scared that I felt the need to seek to talk to you."

"Let's you and me have a talk, then," Lily encouraged, studying the girl's pretty face. Delphine with her black eyes and hair could have been her daughter more than Chantel with her golden hair and green eyes.

"No one knows about this part of my life, madame, and I have never been able to bring myself to tell even Chantel about this as close as we've been. I—I just felt the need to talk to you, to ask you what you thought. When I was desperate and alone in Savannah, I went to work at a place called the Paradise Club. I did exactly what your girls do here, but it was hardly the place *La Maison* is." Despite her embarrassment, Delphine told Lily the whole, sordid story of her life at the Paradise Club and with Antoine Savanti. "But through all of this I never once got pregnant," she concluded.

"Thank the good lord for that, Delphine," Lily declared.

"Yes, but that is what is bothering me now that I'm married to Terry. I love him very much and we want to have children."

"So you are afraid that what Savanti subjected you to might have left you barren, Delphine? Is that your fear, honey?"

"Yes," Delphine confessed.

Lily walked over to her and hugged her.

435

"Don't worry," she said. "It isn't anything you've done. Give yourself some time, and relax. You're young. You and Terry have your life ahead of you." She felt the tension slowly begin to leave Delphine's shoulders. "Besides," she added, "it takes two to make a baby. It isn't your fault—or Terry's."

Delphine gave her a grateful look. "I'm glad I came here to see you, Madame Lily. I'm going back to the bayou feeling much better thanks to you."

"I'm glad." Lily squeezed her affectionately. "You just enjoy this happiness you have with Terry, and if it's meant to happen then it will."

When Delphine left *La Maison*, she didn't take the main road for she didn't want to chance meeting Gabe. Instead, she walked down the side streets that brought her out by the wharf.

When she boarded the *Bayou Queen*, she got a big hug and kiss from Terry, and he declared, "Gosh, you didn't buy much, honey."

"I did a lot of looking though," she laughed.

"Why don't you go down to your pa's cabin and relax while we're traveling home?" he suggested with concern. "You look tired. Those legs of yours must have done a lot of walking,"

She reached up to give her husband a kiss.

436

"I think I'll do just that. Come to think of it, my feet are tired."

Lily left shortly after Delphine. She was in high spirits as Jonah drove her home, confident that Adrienne had the drive and determination to make it work.

It had done Lily's heart good to know that she'd eased Delphine's troubled mind. She was such a sweet little thing and Lily could never forget that she'd been there for Chantel when she'd sorely needed a friend.

This late Friday afternoon Lily had arrived home ahead of Andre, not surprising what with Andre's current involvement on the bayou. She didn't resent his lateness—how could she when she knew why he was working so industriously?

Lily went directly to her room and Chantel, just missing her mother's arrival, waited on the terrace for Gabe.

She, too, had had a wonderful afternoon and she had been ready for Jonah to pick her up long before he was due. She'd found and purchased her wedding gown and coordinated slippers. For her bayou wedding she didn't want satin and lace as Lily had had. Yet, she wanted to be the most beautiful bride she could be for Gabe.

She'd found the perfect dress—a white silk with a demure sweetheart neckline. Tiny pearl buttons fastened the cuffs of the long, fitted sleeves and the back of the gown. Instead of satin slippers she chose white leather with bows of grosgrain ribbon. She selected a head-band of white silk lined with delicate silk orange blossoms and baby's breath in place of the traditional veil.

"Gabe—over here!" she called when his buggy rolled up the drive right on schedule. Her heart pounded faster as he cut across the lawn and ran up to the terrace.

He caught her up in his one free arm, for the other one was holding a bundle of fish for Andre and Lily. He planted a kiss on her honey-eyed lips. "Am I to assume you are happy to see your husband-to-be?" he teased with a joyful grin.

Her green eyes twinkled brightly as she looked up. "I bought my wedding gown today," she bubbled, finding it hard to contain her excitement and happiness. She wanted to tell him about every minute of her day and listen to the details of his.

"Does this mean we're getting married soon?" he demanded eagerly. "Tell me yes, Chantel. It's taxing me to the limit, each hour that we have to wait."

She grinned impishly. "Would it be too taxing on you, Gabe O'Roarke, if you had to wait until next Saturday?" she asked.

Gabe was overwhelmed with surprise that it was going to be that soon. His elation matched her own. He was so thrilled that his deep voice hushed to a whisper. "I can make it that long," he declared. "My consolation is that these arms are going to be holding you for the rest of my life."

"We were meant to be together," she agreed, clinging to his arm.

"My folks will be so delighted," he said calmly. Then he whirled her around the terrace and shouted to the sky, "There's going to be a wedding in the bayou next Saturday night and it's going to be ours!"

Twilight had spread over the bayou when Gabe approached the O'Roarke wharf. It had been a most wonderful day. The extra hours he'd put in on the *Louisiana Lady* had paid off, for he had a pouch filled with money. He was especially pleased since he'd almost wiped out five years of savings to buy the Laveau property and purchase Chantel a ring. He'd wanted her ring to be special, more than a simple gold band to slip on her finger.

He'd spotted it in the jewelry shop window as he strolled down the street toward the emporium to purchase himself a new pair of pants. One look was all it took for Gabe to know that this was the ring he should buy for his bride-to-be. The gold circlet with the brilliant emerald stone in the center of the band surrounded by small diamonds reminded him of Chantel's beautiful eyes.

He had her wedding ring, and she had her wedding gown. They were ready for the wedding.

As he left the dock that evening to go up the pathway, his pace was spritely. He was eager to share his happy news.

As usual his mother's lamp glowed brightly in the front windows. He reminded himself to tell Chantel that he'd like to have that same warm beacon in the windows of their own cottage.

It had always been a welcoming sight for Gabe to come home to.

Forty-eight

Gabe was not the only one with exciting news. He'd never seen his mother's black eyes sparkle so brightly as they did tonight. "Your Aunt Gabriella is coming to see your pretty bride," she told him. "You know how she's always adored you. She and Kirby will be arriving from Natchez next week, so this is perfect!"

Gabe had always known that he had been named to honor his mother's half-sister. He was also familiar with the events of their younger years that had formed a bond of endearment not unlike the attachment between Chantel and Delphine.

Gabe was glad that Gabriella and Kirby were coming to the bayou, but he also recognized the awkwardness of the situation, for Gabriella was an octoroon. Her mother had been a quadroon, her father a white man—the same white man who'd sired Angelique, the only daughter he'd ever claimed.

Fate had brought the young women together when François La Tour abducted Angelique and locked her in his fortress hideaway in Pointe à la Hache. Gabrielle helped Angelique escape with Scott O'Roarke, so Angelique had named her firstborn Gabriel in tribute to her half-sister.

Gabe had always been proud of his name and his heritage. He found his Tante Gabriella most exotic with the turban that she always wore to match the color of her gown. He also admired Gabriella's bravery.

There had certainly not been anything dull about the courtship of his father and mother, which like any good love story had had a happy ending. And Gabriella had found happiness with Scott O'Roarke's best friend, Kirby, who loved her for the woman she was. For the last twenty-five years they'd shared a beautiful life together.

Angelique was pleased that her son's wedding date coincided with Gabriella and Kirby's visit. They'd not only get to meet the beautiful Chantel but share the celebration of their marriage.

Andre turned his vigorous attention to making Chantel's wedding an evening she'd remember forever. At midweek he took Jonah and

Jessamine to the cottage to begin the preparations.

Jessamine quickly determined that he was planning on inviting every family on the bayou when she inventoried the food they'd brought with them. It was enough to feed an army.

Lily had not been idle either for she found herself caught up in Andre's frenzy. She bought Delphine a pretty frock to wear to the wedding, a delicate pink gown from Simone's that she personally delivered to Terry on the wharf.

Terry was overwhelmed by her generous act. "That's mighty sweet of you, Madame Lily," he thanked her. "Delphine will be thrilled. I think she's as excited about Chantel's wedding as she was about ours."

That evening when Terry brought Lily's gift to her and she took it out to gaze at it, Delphine reflected that she had never worn so expensive a gown except in Antoine Savanti's lavish jail. Wisely, she kept her thoughts to herself.

But she had only to feel the exquisite softness of the silk and the fine cut of the material to know the tremendous cost of such a garment. It was a simple gown with no frills, but it had the touch of elegance. She surmised that Chantel's wedding dress would be in a similar style.

Meanwhile Jessamine and Jonah had put in their first busy day at the cottage and could already discern that it was not going to be an overwhelming chore to carry out Andre's instructions. Jessamine discovered she could mark off many items on her baking list because the ladies of the bayou had begun to come by the cottage to drop off cakes and pies for the feast. With more than enough loaves of bread lining the pantry, Jessamine could see no reason to bake more.

"Can you believe these people out here, Jonah? I've never seen such goodhearted people in all my life," she told her brother, awed by the strong sense of community.

Jonah had had his own experiences with bayou camaraderie. Scott O'Roarke's husky friends had assisted him in anchoring all the torches in the ground, setting up the makeshift tables. They only needed a tablecloth draped over them to be ready for the wedding supper.

"I'm going to be lazy on Friday," he chortled.

The next morning Delphine came by with two chocolate cakes. "You don't know how that brother of mine loves chocolate cake," she warned Jessamine. "Mother's making them a special wedding cake."

Come Friday morning, Jessamine and Jonah had accomplished all their chores almost effortlessly. Their clothes were pressed and ready for the big day on Saturday, and there was nothing left to fuss over.

Jonah chuckled. "Know what this old man's going to do, Jessamine?" He flopped his straw hat onto his head as he started toward the back door.

"What are you up to, Jonah?" Jessamine asked, wiping her damp hands on the bottom of her apron.

"I'm going to enjoy the afternoon fishing off the wharf. Gonna' catch me a catfish or two once I cut myself a pole from one of the saplings."

"Well, you just cut two while you're about it," she responded. "I might just catch me a catfish too."

As the two of them enjoyed the serenity of the October day, Jessamine recalled a time long ago when a young girl sat with her thirteen-year-old brother trying to catch a fish on the banks of a river. Now here they were together again in the golden autumn of their lives, and she had Gabe O'Roarke to thank for that wonderful blessing. And Miss Chantel, too. No one wished them more happiness than Jessamine.

By the time the sun was sinking, they had four nice catfish to fry for their supper.

"I'll make a pan of cornbread and a skillet

445

of fried potatoes to go with the fish," Jessamine thought aloud as they trudged back to
the cottage.

A big broad smile came to Jonah's face.
"We're living pretty good, ain't we, Jessamine?" he observed.

"Mighty good, Jonah. Mighty good." she
agreed.

It was not the usual Friday for Gabe as he
moored the *Louisiana Lady* near his father's
boat to sell their fish. He could think of nothing but Chantel and the wedding tomorrow,
and he was oblivious to the snickers of his
crew.

By the time he gathered up the order to take
to *La Maison*, Gabe's addle-brained preoccupation was the joke of the day.

"I did pay you guys your wages, didn't I?"
he jested with the crew. "I'll be better come
Monday."

Most of his men would be coming to the
wedding, for he and his father hired their
neighbors.

Raul also had his fun with Gabe when he
started to leave without taking his pay for the
fish or the gift Raul had just presented to him.
"You don't wish the bottle of wine I gave you
for you and your bride at the midnight hour

after all the festivities are over?" he asked, affecting an innocent air. "And you're also leaving my special pate."

Sheepishly Gabe picked up the money, the wine, and the pate. "A fellow doesn't get married every day, Raul. It's a good thing, I'd never do anything right."

Raul had never expected the happy-go-lucky Gabe O'Roarke to be a nervous bridegroom.

Late Friday, Jacqueline's carriage arrived at the front entrance of Andre's home. Nannette and Paul accompanied her. By now Nannette's pregnancy was obvious and just the trip in from her mother's home was enough for her to ask her uncle if she might go to her room to rest. She was weary for she and Paul had also traveled from their home to her mother's that morning.

Once Paul had seen to his wife's comfort, he and Andre unloaded the carriage, consigning luggage and wedding gifts to an upstairs room.

Jacqueline smiled at Lily. "Nannette thinks she's the only one who has ever been pregnant, and dear Paul mother-hens her as if he's fearful she's going to explode at any minute."

"She must be carrying a large baby to be no further along than she is right now. But then Nannette is such a tiny little thing," Lily re-

447

marked as she invited Jacqueline to have a seat.

"She is too large, but then she is doing it to herself. She lies around all the time, and Paul pampers her too much," Jacqueline confided, breaking off when Chantel came breezing through the parlor, her arms loaded with boxes and packages. She flung the packages on a nearby chair to give Jacqueline a warm embrace.

"Was Nannette able to come?" she asked solicitously.

"She did and she's upstairs resting, dear. She told me to tell you that she'd see you at dinner," Jacqueline replied. She held Chantel out at arm's length. "I'd say you are a radiant bride, Chantel. I brought you something both old and blue. I brought you my blue garter."

Chantel chuckled softly. "Well, my wedding gown will be something new." She looked at Lily. "Mother, have you something I can borrow?"

"You bet I have, sweetie. I'll give it to you this evening," Lily declared, knowing exactly what she planned to let Chantel wear with the pretty white gown she was to be married in. But she could only let her daughter borrow the lovely pearl earrings, for they had been the first piece of jewelry Andre had given her.

Chantel turned to gather up her packages

again before she excused herself. "I'll see you all later. I've got to get this upstairs and I've still got some packing to do," she told her mother and Jacqueline as she dashed from the room.

Jacqueline turned to look at Lily as she remarked, "I can see that all's worked out well between you and your daughter and I'm so very happy for you. I know the fears you had, but they no longer exist."

"No, Chantel and I have a wonderful relationship now. As you say, I couldn't be a happier lady, Jacqueline. I just wish I'd married that brother of yours sooner," Lily affirmed.

Jacqueline laughed with gusto. Andre had heard his wife's comments, and he stood back feeling smug and proud, delaying his appearance in the parlor a few seconds so neither one would suspect that he'd overheard their conversation.

The evening was gay with a spectacular menu and the finest of wines.

Chantel was not prepared for the changes in Nannette since the last time she'd seen her. She was huge, and her movements were gawky and clumsy. Paul was sweet and attentive to her, but Chantel had reservations about having her own body transformed like that. Nannette told her how difficult her pregnancy had been already. "I'll never allow this to happen to me again," she vowed. "I am absolutely bored to tears. I can't do what I love more than anything in the world—ride my thoroughbreds."

"But Paul's so completely devoted to you, Nannette," Chantel pointed out to her.

"It's not enough," Nannette confessed. "I don't want to have Paul's baby—or any man's baby—after I get through this miserable ordeal."

Her comments saddened Chantel, and she feared that Paul's and Nannette's marriage was doomed.

The longer she was around Nannette, the more depressed she grew, but Chantel was determined that nothing was going to spoil her happiness tonight. She made a gracious exit but happened to notice the look on Jacqueline's face. She sensed she was out of patience with her pregnant daughter. But Chantel's sympathy went out to poor, despondent Paul.

She left everyone else's problems behind her and immediately felt her own spirits lift as she climbed the stairway and walked down the hall to her room.

This time tomorrow night she would be out on the bayou and she would also be Gabe's wife. That was all her heart desired!

Forty-nine

It amazed her that she slept late the next morning, but when she saw the beautiful, bright sunshine gleaming through her window she was delighted. She wanted no cloudy, overcast skies for her wedding day.

Chantel had expected the day to go by slowly, but there were so many last minute things she found she had to do that — before she knew it — the time had come for her to have Mimi prepare her bath.

Her pretty white gown was laid out across the bed along with her slippers and lacy undergarments. One her dressing table lay the exquisite pearl earrings Lily had lent her and beside them was Jacqueline's blue, satin garter.

At five o'clock, the entourage left Andre's house to go to the wharf. Andre had hired Captain Fred Driscol to take them to the bayou.

Once his five passengers were aboard and Chantel's belongings and the wedding gifts were loaded on the deck of the *Sea Gull*, Captain Driscol's boat plowed through the bay to the bayou.

A gentle breeze blew across the waters, and it was a mild autumn day. Everyone aboard the *Sea Gull* was in a most jovial mood, and the vivacious Jacqueline repeatedly told Chantel how gorgeous she looked.

"Thank you, Madame Basherone. I'm so very happy that you are going to be at my wedding. I just wish poor Nannette could enjoy it more. She seems so miserable," Chantel told her.

"Ah, *ma petite,* you must not concern yourself with Nannette. She is indulging herself with self-pity. This is your day. Enjoy it. I intend to have myself a wonderful time out on your bayou," Jacqueline told her.

"Oh, I hope you do," Chantel told her.

"I will, *chèrie!* My daughter can act as sullen as she wishes, but she'll not dampen my good time."

Chantel recognized the bends in the stream. Andre's entourage was to arrive at his wharf only a half-hour before their first guests, but Jessamine and Jonah were there to attend to every detail.

Jacqueline was enthralled by the beauty Andre had created at the cottage, and the small party made themselves comfortable in the

452

front room. Chantel retreated to the back bedroom to put some order to her windblown hair.

Nannette asked if she might go to the other bedroom to rest until the ceremony began. Andre, vexed by her behavior, spoke sharply to her. "You rest all you wish," he told her. "Meanwhile, your husband and I are going to join Lily and your mother with a glass of wine. I hope Paul can at least enjoy himself." Andre shepherded Paul into the kitchen so he might pour the four of them a glass of wine before the guests began to arrive.

As Andre poured the wine, he told Paul in a fatherly manner, "Young man, I'm impressed that you are so devoted to my niece, but women have babies every day and Nannette is a healthy young lady. She doesn't require a slave."

"I never seem able to do enough to please her. She seems so miserable all the time," Paul admitted.

"Then quit trying to please her, Paul! Quit coddling her! She's disgruntled that she can't ride her stallion, but that's not your fault and she's going to have to accept reality."

The heady wine and the lively conversation proved to be a good tonic for Paul Chapelle. It had been a long time since he'd enjoyed himself, and he took Andre's advice for the sagest of wisdom.

The O'Roarkes' cottage had already had a night of gaiety with the arrival of Gabriella and Kirby from Natchez. Delphine and Terry had joined them all for dinner.

Delphine was always thrilled to be around her exotic aunt with the beautiful almond-shaped eyes. Her loveliness had certainly not faded with the years.

"So my little Gabe is taking himself a bride?" Gabriella teased. "I can't wait to see this beauty."

"Prettiest thing you've ever seen, Tante Gabriella," he boasted. "You'll see for yourself."

Saturday afternoon Gabe swelled with pride as he viewed all the dark-haired lovely ladies of his family gathered in the front room. Gabriella wore an enchanting gold frock with a matching gold turban wrapped around her head. His mother looked stunning in her purple gown, and she wore the amethyst earrings her mother Simone had left her. Delphine was lovely in the pink gown Lily had selected for her. "What a fine-looking family," Gabe applauded as they boarded his fishing boat to go to Andre's cottage.

It was twilight by the time they approached Andre's wharf, and Jonah already had the torches lit. Lily saw the boat docking and urged Chantel to go to her bedroom. "I'll send

Delphine in," she promised, "but Gabe can't see you till you meet him in the gazebo to take your vows. It would be bad luck!"

Chantel laughed. "Are you sure you're not Irish, too, mother?" she asked.

Delphine gave a gasp of admiration when she saw how beautiful Chantel looked in her wedding gown. "You are a vision," she declared. "No man's ever had a more beautiful bride. Gabe probably won't even be able to utter a word." She giggled.

Chantel broke into a laugh. "As long as he can say two words—I do—nothing else matters."

It grew very quiet as everyone left the house for the gazebo, and then Andre was leading her into the garden. All eyes were on Chantel—especially Gabe's. Chantel's green eyes saw no one but Gabe inside the gazebo, and she'd never seen him look so handsome.

Gabriella could see why her Gabe had lost his heart to this golden-haired enchantress. She was a petite little thing, just like Angelique. The simple lines of the soft silk wedding gown displayed to perfection the curves of Chantel's diminutive body.

She leaned over to Angelique to whisper, "She's so lovely that she takes your breath away!"

Angelique smiled and whispered back to her,

"She has the same effect on Gabe."

Gabe was incredibly nervous, and when he finally heard them proclaimed husband and wife, they were the grandest words he could have heard. Eagerly he embraced his bride and kissed her.

Chantel had realized just how tense Gabe was when he tried to slip the ring on her finger. But once he was kissing her, she could feel his firm, hard body relaxing.

For the next several minutes they accepted the congratulations of their guests. When Gabe was finally able to lead her over to meet his aunt. Gabriella and Kirby had already started to move through the crowd gathered around them. Gabe urged her to come with him as he took her hand, "I've someone I want you to meet."

Standing next to Gabriella and Kirby, Chantel had to look up to both of them. Gabe's aunt's jet-black eyes were warmly looking down at her nephew's bride as Chantel heard Gabe telling her that this was his Tante Gabriella and her husband from Natchez. Gabriella's hand reached out to her, followed by an affectionate embrace.

"I've never seen a more beautiful bride, Chantel, with one exception and that was Gabe's mother."

"That's awfully sweet of you, Gabriella,"

Chantel smiled up at her.

"Gabriella always speaks the truth," the husky Kirby chimed in seriously and they all began to laugh.

Lily and Andre had slipped away from the crowd, for it was time for the wedding feast. Scott and Angelique had also slipped away to lend a helping hand.

Delphine noticed that there was only one couple who didn't seem to be joining into the gaiety of the occasion, and that was Jacqueline Basherone's daughter and her husband. So Delphine and Terry went over to give them a friendly bayou welcome.

"It was a beautiful wedding, wasn't it?" Delphine said to break the ice. "The gazebo your uncle had built was the perfect setting."

"Uncle Andre always thinks of everything," Nannette replied shortly. Terry found Paul more talkative.

When Delphine remarked on Nannette's pregnancy, however, she was quick to learn that Nannette was not happy about her condition. With a weak smile, Delphine took Terry's arm as an indication that it was time to move on.

No one was enjoying herself more than Jacqueline until her brother summoned her away from the crowd. "Paul was wondering if I could have them taken back to New Orleans so he could get Nannette home," he told her. "But why don't you stay here and enjoy yourself tonight, and we'll get you home tomorrow. I'll just have Captain Driscol take them back to the city. I think home is where they should be. Poor Paul can hardly enjoy himself with Nannette in the mood she's in." Jacqueline sensed that Andre's patience with Nannette had worn as thin as her own.

"I think that is a grand idea," she concurred.

As soon as Paul assisted his wife out of the chair, Andre escorted the two of them to the wharf and aboard the *Sea Gull*. As soon as Driscol had his orders from Andre, he immediately prepared to leave the wharf and Andre hastily made his way up the pathway to join Lily.

During his absence, Delphine and Lily had had a chance to enjoy a chat. When he joined the two of them, he brought Lily up-to-date "so Jacqueline will stay with us tonight," he concluded.

"Where is she to sleep?" asked the practical Lily. "Have you forgotten that Jessamine and Jonah are occupying the other bedroom?" Andre sighed. He had.

But Delphine quickly solved that dilemma. "We've got a spare room that Jacqueline can have tonight because Mary Jane is in the city with her aunt," she told them.

458

"We accept your gracious offer," Lily said promptly, and the matter was settled.

It was past ten before everyone, pleasantly sated, was ready for the dancing to begin. This was one night that Gabe had no intention of picking up his guitar to play with the band.

At the first strain of music, Gabe led his beautiful bride to the plank floor for the first dance of the evening.

Terry wasted no time getting his pretty wife up to dance, and age had never discouraged Scott O'Roarke from swinging his favorite girl around a dance floor. Andre was delighted that the guests were in such a festive mood.

Friends and neighbors shared in the happiness of the newlyweds. Most of them remembered Gabe as a young lad accompanying his mother as she took her pots of stew and fresh-baked bread to shut-ins up and down the stream. The bride was delicate and dainty like Angelique, but the bayou folk knew that Angelique was not a fragile flower. She was a spunky, spirited lady, and they presumed that Chantel would be the same.

The guests began to leave about midnight. Delphine remembered how exhausted she was the night of her wedding, so she whispered to Terry that they should seek out Jacqueline and start for home.

Scott and Angelique had the same idea.

Jacqueline was her most vivacious self as she bid everyone good night. "I haven't had so much fun since my husband and I stopped at a gypsy camp in Spain during our travels and I danced the night away," she declared.

Andre roared with laughter, for he knew Jacqueline was tipsy "We'll get you back to the city tomorrow, dear," he told her as the three of them started for the wharf.

Finally Gabe and Chantel were free to go to their honeymoon cottage. He was more than ready to be alone with his beautiful bride.

Fifty

As soon as they arrived at the wharf, Gabe swung her up in his arms to carry her up the pathway to his front door. That white gown was too beautiful to get snagged or soiled, and she had to be feeling weary after the long night of festivities.

Chantel welcomed Gabe's strong arms lifting her up so that she didn't have to walk up the incline from the wharf. She did feel tired, but it had been a glorious night that she would remember forever.

She shared Gabe's yearning for them to finally be by themselves.

He lowered her onto the porch so he could unlock the front door. "Stay right there until I get the lamp lit," he commanded. As soon as lamplight glowed in the front room, Chantel felt serene. This was her home. This was actually her and Gabe's home! Instantly, she truly felt she was home. It was obvious that her darling Gabe had gathered every flower in the gar-

461

den for everywhere she looked were colorful bouquets.

Gabe lit the kitchen and bedroom lamps. He had a grin on his handsome face as he came back into the front room to admit to her, "I forgot your valise. I'll be back in a minute." He dashed out the door and down the incline to retrieve the suitcase he'd absentmindedly left on the dock. Getting married had surely unnerved him, he had to admit to himself.

By the time he returned to the cottage, Chantel had removed her new slippers. It felt good to just rub her bare feet against the floor.

"I'll be in better form tomorrow," he promised and went back to their bedroom with the valise.

Chantel followed him. "You could have fooled me, Gabe O'Roarke," she challenged. "I thought you were in fine form tonight."

"Let's put it this way," he replied. "I'm just glad we're finally here in our cottage, just you and me. Now you do what you need to do about unpacking and I'm going to pour us a glass of Raul's fine wine." He left her in the bedroom to get her nightgown and wrapper out of the small valise she'd brought with her from Andre's cottage.

Lily had bought her a coral peignoir set lavishly trimmed in white French lace. It had been her intentions to slip out of her wedding

462

dress and into her nightgown and then join Gabe in the front room, but she struggled in vain to unfasten the back of the gown.

With a look of frustration and her green eyes sparkling, she marched back into the front room. "Can you unfasten this," she asked.

"Now that I *can* do," he attested. "Turn around." In a matter of seconds, he had unhooked the long row of buttons.

"That didn't take you long," she commented as she started to move away.

"I've had practice," he teased.

She stepped out of the gown and stood before him in her lacy undergarments. "Yes," she allowed, "I imagine you have at that."

"I meant *your* gowns," he protested.

She turned to walk back to the bedroom with her gown flung over her arms. She made a most tantalizing sight for Gabe's eyes to behold as she moved across the room. He sipped his wine in anticipation, and soon she returned, a vision of loveliness in her coral gown.

He went to her, drawn by a force he could not control. His hands took hers and he led her back to the settee. She saw the intensity in his blue eyes as they danced over her. "I never had any desire to take off any other woman's gown once I took yours off that first time," he said seriously.

She grinned. "And you managed to do it before I knew what was going on."

A glint of Irish devilment sparkled in his eyes and he taunted her. "Now be honest with your husband tonight. You didn't really mind, did you? You wanted me to make love to you."

"I desperately wanted you to make love to me," she confessed.

Right now Gabe desperately wanted to make love to her. The excellent wine there in his glass was not as tempting as her lips that were sweeter than any wine he'd ever tasted.

He took the wine glass from her hand, his head bending so his lips could caress the side of her face as he murmured in her ear, "And I want you desperately right now, love."

His lips moved across her face to meet her lips and his arms pulled her to him. As always happened when their bodies touched, a blazing flame ignited within them.

But he did not want to make love to his bride on the small sofa, so he swept her up in his arms and carried her to their bedroom.

When he had laid her down on their bed, he hastily removed his new clothes and flung them carelessly on the floor, then ridded her of the gorgeous gown she was wearing. It wasn't the sheer material of the gown he wanted to feel or touch. It was her silken flesh his hands

464

longed to caress.

Just feeling the mounting passion churning in Gabe's firm muscled body heightened her own desire. Gabe felt her supple body pulse against him, exciting him, and he could no longer deny her or himself.

He gave a mighty thrust, fusing himself to her, and he heard her sweet moans of delight. They clung together as though they were rushing along with the surging currents of a river. Faster and faster they were carried until Gabe's firm body quaked in fierce spasms.

His little bride did not speak another word to him for the rest of the night, because she fell into an exhausted sleep in his arms.

The rest of the night he continued to hold her close to him. He, too, fell into an exhausted sleep. But Gabe woke up before Chantel the next day and had a pot of coffee brewing by the time she stumbled into the kitchen.

"Well, Mrs. O'Roarke, you finally decided to get up?" Gabe greeted her. She made her way to the table and sank down on one of the wooden chairs. Gabe got up to pour her a cup of coffee and as he set it in front of her he planted a kiss on her cheek. She smiled up at him as she sighed, "Oh, Gabe, I'll never forget last night as long as I live. We shall never know another night like that."

"Oh, but we will," he contradicted. "We'll have many wonderful nights, but I'll grant you that will always be special. But we'll have many exceptional times to share as husband and wife."

He allowed her to have two cups of coffee to get her green eyes wide-eyed and alert before he reminded her that they had to go to Andre's cottage to gather their wedding gifts and the rest of her belongings."

"He and Madame Lily will be returning to New Orleans this afternoon," Gabe reminded her.

"Give me an hour and I think I can have myself put together, Gabe," she said as she rose from the chair.

An hour later she was not only dressed in the only frock she'd put in the valise, but she was ready to go down the path with Gabe to board the *Louisiana Lady*.

"You look like a bayou girl," Gabe said, giving a nod of approval to her simple lavender cotton.

By the time the sun was setting low that Sunday evening, Gabe and Chantel were heading back to their cottage and Andre and Lily were preparing to head back to New Orleans after they stopped by Delphine's to pick up Jacqueline.

As they departed from Andre's wharf, Lily

466

was feeling sentimental. "My daughter is starting a new life, and we are going back to our own life now," she said, her eyes misting. "I have to wonder what a year from now will bring in all our lives, Andre."

He gave her an affectionate hug as he assured her, "I am going to believe that it will be a wonderful year for all of us, *chèrie*."

As they were traveling back down the bayou toward their own cottage that Sunday afternoon, Gabe told her, "My dad always told me he'd pondered why he'd named his fishing boat *Bayou Queen*. He told me he knew why after he married my mother, for she was and has always been his queen. I share his sentiments now that you and I are married. I know why I named my fishing boat *Louisiana Lady*."

"Are you saying because of me, Gabe?"

"That's exactly what I'm saying. You are my *Louisiana Lady*!" Gabe declared, all the love he felt for her gleaming in his eyes.

"I never knew I could be as happy as I am right now," she confided to her new husband.

"You just keep telling me that, Chantel, and I'll be the happiest man in the world," he replied.

Chantel found happiness and fulfillment in their bayou cottage. Life was never dull or boring. She was delighted to hear that Delphine was expecting a baby for Chantel knew how much she wanted Terry's child.

That midsummer Delphine gave birth to a son whom she named Scott. "I know he was conceived on your wedding night," Delphine told her privately. "I'd swear to it!"

Nannette's baby was born stillborn, and—ironically—Paul and her marriage improved. They were much happier, Jacqueline reported when she came to the bayou for a visit.

Chantel could always count on getting to see her mother and Andre at least once a month when they came out to the cottage. Often they brought Jessamine and Jonah with them.

The O'Roarkes had quite a gathering for the holiday season. Scott and Angelique added a new grandson to their family circle. Gabriella and Kirby came from Natchez. On Christmas Eve, Andre and Lily joined them.

In a moment of privacy that Chantel and Gabriella happened to share that Christmas Eve, Chantel told her that she thought she was pregnant. She'd not even said anything to Gabe yet.

Gabriella was willing to confirm Chantel's suspicion on the basis of the radiant glow that emanated from her nephew's young wife. Her gift to Chantel that night was an exquisite cross, one of the many pieces of jewelry she'd

468

acquired when she'd been the mistress of François La Tour. She had never had any qualms of conscience about keeping them for she had earned them.

"So your baby would be coming in September, eh *ma petite?*"

"I guess so, Gabriella."

Chantel had no inkling of what was going through Gabriella's mind. When you lived in the bayou, there wasn't time for a doctor to come to deliver your baby. She had been with Angelique when Gabe made his arrival and Gabriella wanted to be with Chantel when Gabe's baby arrived. But babies were so unpredictable!

Spring arrived, and there was no question about it that Chantel was expecting. Summer for Chantel was miserable. She was heavy with Gabe's child, and she saw the concerned look on his face every morning when he left her to go out on the lakes. She couldn't deny that it did frighten her that she was at the cottage all day by herself while Gabe was out on his fishing boat. But the O'Roarke family were constantly looking in on her.

The second week of September Gabriella arrived unexpectedly, and Angelique could not have been more pleased. But what amazed Angelique was Gabriella's reason for visiting her.

"I want to be here when Gabe's child arrives, and I think it will be any day now," Gabriella told Angelique. For the next three days, Gabriella took the canoe down the stream to check on Chantel.

Chantel had refused Andre's and Lily's offers that she come to New Orleans to wait out the last month of her pregnancy. She would not leave Gabe, and Lily and Andre admired her for that.

"She's gutsy," Andre commented to his wife. He could not help but compare her to his whining niece.

When Gabe was reluctant to leave her, Chantel calmed his fears. "There's Delphine, your mother, and now your Tante Gabriella to look after me," she assured him.

No one was more excited about Chantel's baby than Andre. He was already referring to himself as "grandfather" with a smug look on his face. He'd brought the most beautiful cradle to her for her baby, along with enough blankets and baby clothing for twins if she should have them.

Chantel loved Andre devotedly for he'd been the father she had never known. She was truly convinced that no father could have loved her more than her stepfather did. She had said nothing to Gabe yet, but if she should have a daughter she wished to name her Andrea after

Andre Deverone, who'd never been a father and never would be. Chantel hoped to make it up to him.

But this early September when Gabe looked out the window he saw angry skies and he left for the wharf with grave misgivings. Being an expectant father was proving to be nerve-racking.

Gabe as well as his father and Terry were glad when the threatening clouds moved on. It was going to be a nice day after all, and his concern for Chantel's safety diminished.

Back in the bayou Angelique was preparing to go to her daughter's cottage because Scott had told her last night that the baby was sick. Gabriella joined her in the canoe, planning to stop in on Chantel while Angelique went on to Delphine's.

She came through the cottage door to find the golden-haired Chantel writhing in agony. "Am I glad you're here!" she moaned.

"And so am I, *ma petite!* Your baby's getting ready to come, so we must get you to your bed." Gabriella immediately took charge, assisting Chantel to her feet.

"I — I was feeling just fine when Gabe left," she stammered. "Suddenly I started having these sharp pains, and I've been scared to death."

"You had a right to be, honey. Being all

471

alone would be enough to scare any woman," Gabriella told her as she helped her get into a gown. "We'll see this through together."

She got her into bed and set some water heating in the kettle. Gabriella laid out some clean towels and sheets on a chair. She took Chantel's hand and saw her through a contraction and into a brief moment of peace.

"You've obviously done something like this before, Gabriella." Chantel observed.

"Several times," Gabe's aunt replied. "In fact, I helped bring that husband of yours into the world."

Chantel didn't have a chance to respond, for a new series of pains struck. For the next two hours Gabriella stayed on the bed with her and washed off Chantel's face with a cool cloth as she went through each new onslaught of pain.

She knew the young lady was fighting back the moans so she told her not to worry about being brave. "You scream and yell all you want. You're doing fine."

This baby would come quickly, Gabriella judged. It would not take as long as Delphine's son. When Chantel had her next pain-free moment, Gabriella hastily went to the kitchen to pour herself a cup of coffee. She wanted to be alert for what she would soon be facing.

She noticed that the kitchen clock read one-

472

thirty and estimated that Gabe might be a father by the time he arrived home at five-thirty.

By four o'clock both Gabriella and Chantel were very busy. Chantel was sweating profusely as she followed Gabriella's instructions to bear down with all the strength she had.

"This baby's coming for sure, honey! Another hard push or two, and we're going to have that little imp out of there," Gabriella encouraged her.

By now she didn't try to restrain the screams as the pains became excruciating.

Chantel's baby daughter was born, and Gabriella held her in her arms, tears flowing down her cheeks. It was a living little doll she held in her arms, Gabriella thought. The ordeal of the last five hours came crashing down on her, and she couldn't stop the tears of joy.

Her voice cracked with emotion. "Let me get this little doll cleaned up and wrapped in a blanket so you can see your darling little daughter," she told Chantel.

Gabriella doubted that the wee one weighed even six pounds. Her delicate features were Chantel's, but that mass of black ringlets was reminiscent of Gabe when he was born, Gabriella recalled.

She handed the little bundle to Chantel, and Chantel had only to gaze upon her beautiful little daughter to have tears of joy mist her eyes. "She is beautiful, isn't she Gabriella?"

"Oh, yes. I told you we'd pull this thing off, didn't I?" Chantel managed a weak smile and nodded.

When Angelique came to pick up her half-sister, she was hardly prepared for Gabriella's greeting. With a glowing smile, Gabriella said, "Hello, Grandmother. Chantel and I just had ourselves a beautiful baby girl this afternoon."

"Dear God!" she gasped. She rushed into the bedroom to see Chantel and her new granddaughter. But she did not linger too long for Chantel was very weary. She told Chantel, "You rest, dear, for there'll be no way I'll be stopping Scott from coming over here this evening to see his granddaughter."

Chantel's eyes were already closing by the time Angelique left the bedroom. Gabriella urged her to go home and tell Scott the wonderful news. "I'll stay here with them tonight. I think they'll be glad to have my services for the rest of this evening. You can take over tomorrow."

By the time Gabe strode up the pathway to his front steps, Gabriella had a pot of potato soup simmering on the stove and a fresh pot of coffee brewing. Chantel and her baby had been sleeping peacefully for almost an hour.

Gabriella saw him coming and she was already anticipating the startled look he was going to have on his face when she told him the grand news.

But she never got to make her announcement to Gabe, for his daughter made her own announcement by giving out a wail.

Gabe's blue eyes went wild with excitement, and he was so dumbfounded he didn't say a word. He made a mad dash to the bedroom, and Gabriella went back to the kitchen. Her presence was not needed right now.

Chantel was so deep in sleep that she didn't know that her husband stood by her bed smoothing the damp golden hair that fanned out on her pillow. At her side lay the baby snugly wrapped in her blanket. Fatherly pride swelled up in him as he gazed down at his daughter and saw the black ringlets covering her head. "She has my hair," he whispered in awe. "My hair and her mother's face."

Instinctively, Gabe knew he had a daughter. She was too beautiful to be a boy!

Carefully he picked the blanket-swaddled baby up in his arms and gave his daughter a kiss. At his gentle touch she stopped crying. Gabe carried her into the kitchen cradled in his arms. Gabriella noticed instantly that he didn't seem at all awkward or ill-at-ease holding a baby. Being a father seemed natural for Gabe.

The long nap Chantel took had refreshed

her and she ate ravenously when Gabe brought her a tray. Gabe was delighted to see her eating so heartily. "You must let Mother and Andre know about their granddaughter the first thing in the morning," she reminded him.

"Andre made me promise that I'd let him know the minute the baby was born so he could get Jessamine out here to stay with you until you were able to be up on your feet."

Scott had no sooner finished his dinner than he was impatient to see his new granddaughter, but Angelique told him he could just go smoke one of his cheroots because she was going to do her dishes and put her kitchen to rights.

While Gabe's parents and Gabriella were there that evening, Chantel decided it was the perfect time to announce what she and Gabe had decided to name their baby daughter. He could not have been happier about the choice of the two names she'd picked for their little daughter, for it told him the depth of emotion she felt.

There was not a dry eye in the bedroom when the O'Roarke family arrived to see their granddaughter. Gabe knew what an ordeal his beautiful wife must have gone through today and she did look pale, but she'd never looked more beautiful to him than when she sat propped up in the bed with her hair loosely flowing around her dainty shoulders.

Her green eyes darted over to Gabe before she began to speak. There was almost an impish look on her face as she asked them if they would like to know what this new O'Roarke was going to be named.

All of them immediately responded that they were most eagerly wondering about that. Chantel held up her daughter. "Meet Andrea Gabriella O'Roarke," she said.

Once more today tears were flowing down Gabriella's cheek as she embraced Chantel and acknowledged the great honor she felt that the baby should carry her name. Angelique was also emotional. Her son had surely picked himself a rare jewel of a wife!

Chantel realized what a sentimental breed of men the Irish were when she saw the mist in both Gabe and his father's eyes.

As Gabe had promised Chantel, he left early the next morning not to go fishing as he would normally have done but to go into the city to proudly announce to Andre and Lily that they were grandparents.

As Angelique and Gabriella had planned, Angelique arrived at Gabe's cottage to take charge and Gabriella left to go back to the O'Roarke cottage to gather up her belongings and get packed for her trip back to Natchez

477

and Kirby. She had, however, assured Chantel
that she'd be coming back to the bayou often.

Once the Deverones were told the exciting
news, Gabe went to the lakes to put in the rest
of the day. But Andre closed his office and by
late afternoon he, Lily, Jessamine, and Jonah
were heading for the bayou. He loaded Captain Driscol's boat with baskets of food and
dropped Jonah at Andre's cottage to prepare
for their overnight stay.

Gabe stayed out on the lakes longer than
usual, confident that his wife was in good
hands. He had no doubt that Andre and Lily
were already in the bayou.

Lily, like Gabe, had only to look on her
beautiful granddaughter and feel smug about
the black hair curls atop the baby's head.
Black, like mine, she thought proudly.

As Chantel had done the evening before she
asked them if they'd like to know what she'd
named her daughter.

"What's her name, Chantel?" Lily asked.

"Andrea Gabriella O'Roarke," Chantel replied.

Lily was sitting at her bedside. "What a
beautiful name!" She reached over to kiss
Chantel, and then her dark eyes gazed up at
Andre. She knew how deeply affected he was
by the tribute Chantel was paying to him.

That very dignified gentleman stood for a

moment before he bent down to kiss Chantel, unashamed of the tears that rolled down his cheeks. "I never knew the joy of having a child of my own, but it couldn't be grander than having a little granddaughter named for me!"

In the months to follow Andrea Gabriella's birth, the people of the bayou came to love Gabe's young bride just as they had come to love his mother, Scott O'Roarke's young bride but a stranger to them.

But no one adored her as much as Gabe, and Gabe was still the handsome Irish fisherman who'd come into her life to steal her heart away. Her little cottage there in the bayou was her home and her castle where she lived with her handsome Prince Charming.

There in their bayou paradise they lived and loved one another forever and a day.